A REBELLION IN ANTORIA

Swords of Faith, Book Two

Revised Edition

Written by Jeremiah D. MacRoberts

ISBN: 978-1310918971

Table of Contents

Dedication

This work is dedicated to the Lovers of Liberty.

Who lend their great courage when others know
only the fear that forfeits all.

Prologue

"Alright, my braggart-prince, so fine at fighting, how is your Elvish?"

"When you are away, Mother only speaks to me in Elvish — I am really quite good," the strangely handsome boy told his father, the king, in a voice that tried not to brag too much.

"Oh?" the boy's father replied, "She tried to do the same with me, yet I remain rather terrible."

The boy quirked his lips, giving his father a playful glare and an accepting smile.

The king gave a light chuckle, continuing, "Go to the Master Archivist and tell him I want a document entitled 'On the Hero-Saints, Who Were Called Gods, and the Rise of Vandorish Monotheism.' Tell him you don't want him to translate it or to make a copy. I want you to bring me the only copy from our archives and you will read it to me in Elvish, tonight."

"It is rather late, father," the boy commented.

"Am I not lord in this hall? Am I not the Overlord of Kings and Thanes from all the Races of Uhratt? Wake the Master Archivist and issue him the King's Decree!" the boy's father's voice rose, playfully thunderous, as he stood from his chair, and with a grand, sweeping motion, turned, pointing to the door.

His son, grinning from ear to ear, offered a deep and flourished bow, replying, "Yes, at once, Your Majesty."

"Go!" the king's voice boomed again, stretching the word out, though ending in gentle laughter as the boy fled the room.

Skilled at running, the boy's long, elegant strides, even from limbs not fully grown, almost disguised the mighty thews that powered him forward. He ran through the royal rooms, lightly rebounding from the wall where the stairs down began. He slowed as he dropped and turned, foot after foot, descending the long spiral stair unto where it opened into a grand throne room.

Without pause, passing at the back of the empty hall, he ran behind the thrones, to the doorway on the opposing wall. Where turning right would have taken him toward the front of the palace, to parlors and foyers and, ultimately, the courtyard, near the smithy. The young prince turned left instead. He went

1

deeper into the compound, where elegant palace gave way to strong castle. After a few twists and turns, he arrived at a grand library.

Passing through shelves, he carried himself with the confidence of familiarity, no stranger to the stacks. The boy went straight away to a door in back and thrice rapped upon its surface. Nothing happened.

He waited a minute longer and nothing happened. The prince balled his fist and held it above his head. Pounding thrice more, he took up his father's theatrical tone, shouting.

"The Prince, the Prince! Your liege lord summons you, archivist!"

The door opened almost immediately, an ancient looking man with a bewildered look upon his face answered, pulling his blankets around him.

"Is this how you greet your prince?" the boy growled.

"Your Grace, unless you would like your ears boxed, you will explain yourself at once!"

"Father is home," the boy's voice became casual, continuing, "He has asked me to retrieve 'On the Hero-Saints, Who Were Called Gods, and the Rise of Vandorish Monotheism.' He neither wants it translated nor copied–"

"I would think not!" the ancient archivist interjected.

"I am to bring the document to him and read it aloud tonoght," the boy finished.

"Strange," mused the archivist, again pulling up his blankets, "Tis in the secure stacks. If Your Grace would allow his humble servant to dress, I would be glad to retrieve it for you."

The prince smiled and nodded. The under-clothed Master Archivist returned the nod, closing his door. As it clacked shut, the prince went to the nearest shelf and perused the titles. He found many copies of 'Nehul's Fundamental Alchemy' and 'First Principles of the Mind, its Will, and the Subjugation of Forces' and single copies of similar books: 'Conjuration, Summoning, and Binding: The Essential Guide' and 'Dresden's Primer on Evocation Magic.'

"Away from there, Your Grace," the then-clothed Master Archivist ordered from his doorway, though in a voice that sounded more like an invitation.

"Is magic so different?" The boy asked, "I mean, is it so different from what the Church teaches the priests and paladins?"

"Not really," the Master Archivist said simply, motioning the boy to follow, and continuing, "It is different in practice, but not in principle or effect. I mean, iron is iron. If a soldier runs a man through with a pike, or a knight side-steps and decapitates a man with a sword, the man is just as dead, and it is iron that killed him. Perhaps the pike gave the soldier distance to make up for his lack of defenses. Perhaps better alloys and training gave the knight confidence to wade in and kill more swiftly. Their enemies are just as dead, and it was iron that killed them. In this metaphor, iron is magic, the soldiers represent the paladins and priests, and the knights are equivalent to classically trained sorcerers and wizards."

They completed their walk, across half of the ancient library, to the locked door, in silence.

"I can hear your wheels turning," the archivist said, touching his pointer finger to the prince's brow.

"What?" the prince said, confused.

"In your mind, the cogs and the little mouse that drives them," the archivist chuckled.

"It makes a lot of sense, the iron example," the prince admitted his musings.

"I thought it would," the archivist offered, drawing a key from within his robe, "I came up with it years ago when you first asked. Been waiting for you to ask again. You are always in and out so quickly with your studies, we never talk like this any more."

"I didn't think–" the prince began to say.

"Ah, you are a busy young man, with far more to learn than I can teach you. A prince need not justify his actions to the like of me. I serve at your pleasure, and I understand. Just know that teaching a prince is a great privilege. You especially. If you ever want to come by and pick my brain or learn something new, I serve at Your Grace's pleasure," the Master Archivist finished with a bow, inserting his large iron key into the door, and turning it.

He stepped into the room, snapped his fingers, uttering a syllable, "lum," and a small orb of light appeared above his hand, moving with him. He waved his hand about, directing the light as he walked among the shelves of books, making his way to a cabinet in back. There, he opened one of a dozen drawers and eventually pulled out a thin, well-preserved scroll.

3

The Master Archivist handed it to the young prince.
"Run along now, Your Grace."

The boy returned to his father as quickly as he had gone, scroll in hand.

The king still stood, examining a particularly fine suit of golden armor, with many unique, uncustomary features, such as shield-like oval disks built into its gauntlets, chainmail at the flanks attached to hinged abdominal plates, and every inch of it inlaid with runes. It had been mounted to a stand, assembled and placed as though to guard the room.

His son returned. The king sat. The boy pretended to notice neither his father's lingering gaze, nor the protracted affect of nostalgia that played about his father's face.

"You are being polite, and I appreciate it, but we will be talking about it soon enough," the king said, taking and unrolling the scroll; glancing at it, he sighed, handed it back to his son, and sighed again, saying, "That is the right one, please, read it aloud."

The boy began reading. The soft cadence and enunciation proper to the elvish language fell naturally from the lips of a child. The prince spoke it well:

On the Hero-Saints, Who Were Called Gods, and the Rise of Vandorish Monotheism.

A "god," as once defined, was any being whose powers and knowledge were beyond the scope of mortal understanding and who wielded those powers over mortals, for good or for ill.

With the rise of the Holy Family, we saw the belief in, if not the nature of, "gods" evolve to exclude the "for ill" and include that such a being be worthy of worship. For this reason, there were a number of entities that, in a variety of ways, fell somewhat in between the status of "god" and cultural "hero."

These entities became known as the Hero-Saints. The veneration of which was not heretical and the worship of whom was permitted within the culture of origin, provided that any such cult neither denied the existence of the Holy Family nor proselytize other peoples.

The Mother, Ellenofae First-Born, Singer of Truth, has further revealed to us of the mystical union of Father and Son, Vandor and Dinnothyl, into the final and supreme expression of true divinity. This, in truth, happened long ago, outside of time and understanding, but has only been revealed to us now, so that we

4

might better accept and understand. For our Great Mother could have been part of this mystical union, the completion of the Oneness she birthed, yet she felt her role was to remain one with the elven people and fae courts, that we might believe, through love, word, and deed in this greater truth of Our Holy Family.

For as surely as She is our Mother-Progenitor, then also is Holy Din yet our Brother in blood, and we elves, therefore, Siblings of God. For the Holy Family served as the chosen instrument of spiritual incubation for the manifestation of The One True God.

The veneration of Hero-Saints remains orthodox, holy, and true. Thus, with Wisdom's Song, we lift up, rightly, our Holy Mother as chief among them. She remains, as She ever shall, the Mother of the Holy Family: Van, Din, and Len.

Of this term "God." It must now exclusively refer only to The One True God, who was born from our own Mother and her love for One so great and good and holy.

The historical persons of Vandor and Dinnothyl shall remain referenced as separate entities, but in the understanding that they now exist, beyond life and death, time and space, a singular entity, called God. God, who is the ultimate expression of the Divine Creative Force and Its Divine Love for all of the cosmos thus created.

The Mother calls for the continued denouncement of all past heresies along with any that would deny the claims contained herein. Moreover, She also calls for your continued love and fidelity to Her and the One True God, whom you have already served all these long and arduous centuries.

Written in the hand of Aelriss Songleaf,
a monk of Lensgrace, verbatim the decree of
Haertlan III, High-Priestess of Ellenofae,
Servant of the Holy Family,
She Who Listens to the Mother's Songs.

"Is Mother really so old? So ancient?" the young prince asked.

"Indeed she is," the king answered.

"Then why does she suffer now? After all she has known and been."

"I shall tell you, but there are other things you must know first."

Chapter 1
Returning Thanes

The Paladin-Prince Bengallen Hastenfarish and his standard-bearer, Sira Roselle Taversdotter, came out from the open gates of Woodhaven to greet their travel weary allies and welcome them to their sojourn destination. The southwest gate opened onto less than half a mile of land between it and the river. A mile or so south from the gate was the Lake with Twelve Names.

The river, called the Umber, flowed south by southwest from those northern Umberlands. It had a stone bridge, barely wide enough for a wagon, as well as a much larger wooden bridge, upon which two wagons could go side-by-side with room to spare.

Arriving at that moment, having crossed the stone bridge, were Prince Bengallen's mighty thanes: The half-orc squire, Malcolm Ironclaw, Hero of the Rogueswood and wielder of the ancient greatsword, Dawnsong. Alpona the Athgonian, a warrior of great ability, trained in the precise and versatile ways of the Zil-jahi Warriors of distant lands and wielder of the ancient greatsword, Flammerung. Shomotta al'Hazar, an accomplished wizard from the western deserts and warrior-priest of Saint Amar. Ruffis, a dark elf with dark talents as shrouded in mystery as his own past, but a deadly man and useful ally without a doubt.

"Hail, my thanes, hail!" Prince Bengallen called to them.

"Hail to Your Majesty!" Malcolm called back.

"You kiss a lot of ass for an orc," Ruffis commented in hushed tones.

"Not to worry," Alpona chimed in, "I doubt he'll be bending down to kiss yours anytime soon."

"Not that he could bend so low, shorty," Shomotta could not resist but add.

"You know what?" Ruffis asked rhetorically, "Rork you guys. Rork all three of you all rorking day."

"You're not man enough," Shomotta jabbed again, raising an eyebrow, "but I'd be a good sport and let you try."

Ruffis peeled away from the group in response, without further comment, taking a course away from the city gates, south, toward the Lake.

"There he goes. For how long will he disappear this time?" asked no one in particular Malcolm, speculatively.

To which Shomotta eagerly replied, "If you are taking bets, put me down for three days. I've developed an arithmetic to his pouting absence."

"He has to learn," Alpona said, calmly, "that if he intends to dish it out, he'll be taking it as well. Caanaflit and I agree on that and I thank you for helping with the lesson, but you could enjoy it a little less."

As Prince Bengallen watched the three continue forward and Ruffis split away, he commented to Roselle, "Would you look at this? This is still a thing. For shame. Are we not men?"

"Apologies, Your Majesty," the lady-knight began, "But you are boys. Big, violent, scary boys. Boys I'd storm the Gates of Hell with, but boys all the same."

"The mouth on you," the Paladin-Prince playfully scolded.

"Again, begging your pardon, but you asked."

"The mouth on you but speaks your mind ... a task I have set it to," Bengallen relented, turning to face her, "but does even the man who would be your king yet also seem so a boy to you?"

"Less so than the others, but all nobles are boys from the view of the common folk," Sira Roselle explained.

"Well," Bengallen laughed, continuing, "I less a boy and you less common. I dare then to ask, after all I have done, what must I yet do to be seen as a man?"

She meant to answer quickly. She had an answer. Yet as his head jostled with laughter, the light caught, reflecting oddly upon, the Prince's metallic green irises. It always unsettled her, every time, reminding her that something mysterious, something neither man, nor boy, nor human at all within her Prince. Doubtless for the good, but inhuman power was not something a woman raised simply upon the Frontier could take lightly.

Thus she stammered, "Your Mah– my Prih– I, uh..."

"I asked for it, go on and speak it, before they get here."

"Even boys can rescue maidens and go on adventures. Men toil. They won't see the work you do as 'man's work' as they understand it. Yet there is one thing. Even as a boy, they respect you. Were you to put the crown upon your head and take the title of a man—" Roselle was cut short.

"Enough!" Prince Bengallen interrupted sourly, "You all know my mind in this. I will sit in my father's hall, upon my father's throne, his lands secure and free, before I would dare claim to call myself his successor. I am not yet a king."

"And so, in this one way, you uniquely remain a boy."

"Thank you for the insight," Bengallen offered, voice flat, tone uncertain.

"With apologies, you are welcome, Your Majesty," Sira Roselle accepted with a marked humility and sincerity.

Finally, Malcolm, Alpona, and Shomotta drew to within speaking distance and dropped to one knee before their lord and leader. Bengallen smiled to hide his surprise and bade them rise, asking, "Tell me, my thanes, of your adventures and what of Caanaflit?"

"So long away, Your Majesty, Caanaflit diverted to Spearpointe to attend his interests there," Shomotta answered.

"And mine too, we shall dare hope," Prince Bengallen added, turning to Malcolm, continuing, "And how was the family reunion?"

"No union to speak of, Your Majesty—" Malcolm began.

"But more than a few dismemberments!" Alpona interjected with a smile that barely withheld his laughter.

"Indeed," Malcolm agreed, grinning, "They were less than happy to see me, Your Majesty—"

"Must we be so formal?" Prince Bengallen interrupted Malcolm this time, continuing, "Have we not bled and slain together? Are we not brothers?"

"Of course," Alpona replied, "Yet we've been away now for nearly so long as

8

the time we were then together. I thought it best not to make too many presumptions."

"Gratitude," Prince Bengallen said, "Sincerely. In such private company, however, such is not necessary."

The thanes nodded.

Roselle spoke, "Alpona, Shomotta, I would show you to your lodgings. Malcolm, will you take the standard and attend His Majesty for me?"

"Honored, indeed I would."

Both stood tall. With two hands, one high on the shaft, one low, Sira Roselle handed the bright blue banner, with sigil of white griffin ascendant, to Thane Malcolm. He took it from her in like manner, two hands, one high, one low. So relieved, the lady-knight led the other thanes into the city walls, as Bengallen and Malcolm lingered at the gate.

Chapter 2
Visiting Orcs

"So," Bengallen began, "Your family reunion turned into a family dismemberment? It would be dishonest for me to claim that such a bloody possibility was unforeseen."

Malcolm grinned, knowingly.

"And so you sent a Zil-jahi Warrior with me; one might think that blood was certainty."

"Orcs are of a notorious temperament," Bengallen admitted, "Though I had every confidence in the two of you, the task before you was important and worth the risk, was it not?"

Malcolm's grin flattened and, his affect serious, nodded.

"What of it then?" The Prince asked.

"My father," Malcolm began, "Knows that I am no longer his. That I am no mere runaway, but emancipated. I think he likes it even less, but Your Majesty is correct, tis an important distinction — for me, even if not for him."

"How was this distinction made?"

"I will tell you of it:"

> Alpona sat at the left hand of the Orc Chieftain, Blagrogk, being plied with wine. Careful, with great difficulty, he consumed with exacting moderation.
>
> The orcs below the platform – *the whole of the clan by the look of them* – had formed a great circle in their midst. Malcolm had demanded that before his father pass judgment upon him, he should be at least allowed the rites of manhood, so that he would face his punishment as a man.
>
> The Chieftain laughed, clearly amused at the prospect, but why he ultimately agreed, no one will ever know. Malcolm expected only to declare his intent to be a man in regards to his clan and father. For his own purposes, the declaration alone would serve. It came, therefore, as great surprise to both Malcolm and Alpona that the Chieftain honored the attempt, granting the rites.

When at last they had come upon the third day, Malcolm had passed both the Nine Feats of Pain from the first day and, with but one concession, the Nine Feats of Pleasure upon the second day. The concession being that the eighth feat, which required the young orc to take and rape an older woman, had been replaced so that he merely had to lay with a volunteer.

Requested by Malcolm, formally out of affection for his own mother who had been so ill-handled, though only one of a thousand reasons in his heart, the clan elders granted the concession on the grounds that no woman should be forced to mother any weak 'part-human child' alone. Since, they presumed, following the rites, Malcolm would be executed for his past treason.

If a volunteer stepped forward, however, she would be agreeing to take on the inferior offspring. Even more surprisingly, not merely one but two volunteers offered themselves. This so amused the Chieftain that he hastily decreed that Malcolm should have to lay with both of them.

In truth, Malcolm did not succumb to temptation, mating with neither of the orc women. They were of their own temptations. Although he took them to tent and slept there with them, the pair took their pleasure in each other's company, leaving Malcolm's chastity intact.

Thus, on the next day, when all three were brought before Chief Blagrogk and the women were asked if they had been sufficiently pleasured, they honestly answered yes, they had been. After being examined by the clan's oracle, she did concur that they both appeared to have been vigorously used.

Alpona laughed to himself about these things as he witnessed the fights on the third day.

After being beaten for a day and indulged for another, the orc clan required any boy, who would become man, to spend the third day fighting the Nine Battles. These Nine Battles were a kind of remnant, representing some aspect of orcish mythology long forgotten by the oracles. Yet they remained as part of their living tradition only in these rites of manhood. Typically, the fights were largely ritualistic, but the orcs that Malcolm faced were seasoned warriors all and appeared to be out for real blood beyond mere spectacle.

Malcolm had become a fine warrior even while still under his father's rule. He trained hard when afforded the opportunity and had trained himself further in secret. Since his escape, the world had only seasoned him all the more. Time and again, Malcolm proved himself in real battles for just causes. Moreover, he had returned home with aid of magic arms and armor: A mysterious helm of some consequence and a storied blade, the Dawnsong, that stood elite among the finest weapons ever forged by gods or men.

So able and aided, he rained ruin and destruction upon the day's opponents. The Dawnsong was a blade of truth, justice, and beauty. While it would never prevent its wielder from defending himself, it sought only to bring light into the dark world and justice to those that deserved it. There before it had been spread a feast undreamed of. A banquet of marauders and rapists beyond the reach of laws and courts.

No darkness escapes the light forever. As the opponents turned from sport, to do true harm to Malcolm, he but brought himself into harmony with Dawnsong to resolve these discordant echos, unleashing its thirst for justice upon them, quenching it with their blood.

Closing in on the final contest, Alpona had begun to keep the degree of his entertainment to himself. Noticing the anger swell within Chief Blagrogk, with each of his warriors smote or sundered, by his half-blood son. Feigning drunkenness, Alpona offered no response when the Orc Chief halted the last bout in its first moments, replacing the final opponent with Malcolm's own brother, the half-ogre Dorthglax.

So that was his game, Alpona realized, *not to deny his son the rites of manhood or to kill him thereafter, but he did not believe Malcolm could survive them at all. What a surprise this must be, here at the last challenge.*

The fighter substitution came as a surprise to all, including Dorthglax, who initially failed to hide his fear before pride took hold, urging him forward, brave faced. Malcolm wore his brave face as well, even as his body ached from the Feats of Pain and his wits were dulled by the Feats of Pleasure. Even as his early opponents had left him wounded and exhausted, Malcolm wanted this fight and would meet it with certitude, if not clarity.

These orcs were a terrible lot, disgusting, base, and villains all, with Dorthglax possibly the worst among their horde. Chief Blagrogk at least did what he thought he must. Often brutal, enjoy it though he did, he acted as a leader. In everything, he felt that he had to establish, to a people composed almost solely of marauders and monsters, that he remained the strongest.

Dorthglax, on the other hand, was merely his father's instrument. Terrible and perverse, twisted and violent, more for his sick pleasure, maintaining his vile state of being, than any goal. Yet the Iron Claw Orcs claimed him as the pinnacle of their culture. What does that say of the culture, so broken it takes a half-ogre to ascend its heights? Malcolm could not decide which was worse, *the monster or the father who would shape his son so*.

It did not matter. They both needed to die. Here, Malcolm had his chance, but if the others had merely been playing at killing him, Dorthglax would stake nothing less than the purpose of his existence upon it.

Malcolm stepped forward, flinging from his blade the blood and gore of his previous opponent, a foe made armless yet clinging to life. Taking another step, he brought the sword before him in a low, defensive stance; a new one, some small piece of a Zil-jahi kata, yet unseen by the orc of this region. The stance low, with the sword high, Malcolm's legs were wide, knees bent, feet at right angles. In this, he could bring the right leg forward and sword down to attack or he could bring the left leg backward and sword across to fend off even the mightiest of blows.

Dorthglax stood a third again taller than Malcolm, himself as large as the largest of humans. He took four steps for Malcolm's two. Strides really, chest exposed, a large, spiked club in each hand. He lumbered in recklessly, glaring down at the smaller half-human.

Pointing both massive cudgels at Malcolm, he taunted with words as simple and clunky as his posture, "Little brother, you want to be a man? You gonna die a man, maybe. Maybe you run away again. Maybe I let you."

Malcolm simply growled, long and low. Hardly audible, but somehow they heard it. They all did. Whether by the primitive intuition of the orcish mind or by some sonic resonance with the Dawnsong, a hush fell and Malcolm's growl rolled in their ears and through their ranks like the sound of approaching thunder.

Charging, Dorthglax heaved both massive clubs over his head. Malcolm, right foot forward. The obvious move would have been to prepare for the massive blow and try to move out of the way. Yet there were two clubs to dodge and Malcolm did not want to take a hit from either one of them, even deflected.

Instead, in the long moment Dorthglax took to set his attack, Malcolm stepped in, right foot forward. Swinging, he sliced off the top of his opponent's right thigh, hip to kneecap. As the blade tripped over the bone in the knee, Malcolm thought of his fight with the troll in the wilderness, nostalgically.

Clubs landed to the left and right of Malcolm, some of their umpf lost, only Dorthglax's wrist struck Malcolm upon the shoulder and with negligible effect. Nearly instantaneous, Malcolm's follow-up strike raised the tip of his blade from the ground, quick and wild, in a reverse of his previous strike. This time, rather than position the sword to reset, Malcolm leaned forward, mid-swing. In this way, the blade both lacerated Dorthglax across the ribs and, once passed them, the Dawnsong plunged deep into the monster's chest.

Dorthglax stumbled backwards. Dropping his clubs, he removed himself from the greatsword that impaled him. Powerful pulses of blood torrents shot from his chest, one, then another, then another.

The first sprayed Malcolm full in the face. The next about his neck and chest. The third did not make it so far and Malcolm knew: His brother was dead.

Chief Blagrogk shot to his feet immediately as all the orcs around Malcolm drew their weapons in response. Blagrogk reached to draw his own sword, however, Alpona flicked the ancient Flammerung from its scabbard with more grace and speed than any of them could anticipate. Slicing keenly, it severed the Orc Chief's sword arm, removing hand and wrist, in one swift motion.

Only as Alpona jumped from the platform, escaping Blagrogk's guards and joining Malcolm, had his magical greatsword time enough to spill forth its arcane fire. Side-by-side, Malcolm and Alpona cleaved a path through the orcish horde and broke stride to see them clear.

"Huzzah!" Prince Bengallen roared to Malcolm's telling.

"After all that had happened," Malcolm added, "the enemy pursuit was but halfhearted. Not at all like the first time I left. They pursued the slaves and I for weeks."

Bengallen smiled.

"They let you go. I mean, you definitely fought your way clear and instilled the proper motivation for them to let you go, but in the end, they chose to not run you down as mere errant slave."

"Aaaaand that was the point. I admit that I did not see the value when you sent me, but I was content to defer to your command. Yet, with the proper counsel to frame the experience and the event itself, I do confess to now glimpse the wisdom that moved you to send me back there, my Prince."

"My father," Prince Bengallen replied, "Trained me in leadership. He taught me that a good leader does not merely force and coerce others into doing his will, but he encourages, inspires, and empowers his men, so that they want to follow."

"Count me among those so motivated, Your Majesty."

"I am sorry that your father did not honor you so," Bengallen lamented, placing his hand upon Malcolm's shoulder, "but the spirit of my father is grand enough to share, and as my friend and comrade I will be glad to let his spirit breathe, from time to time, and impart his wisdom upon you."

"Tis a tragedy that mine yet lives while yours has been taken from us."

Bengallen replied, "A tragedy, yes. Understood, no. Yet tis the reality and so move we forward in our own lives and make the most of them."

"Wisdom, again. Alpona, though he oft seems the madman or plays the fool, is also yet wise," Malcolm offered.

Bengallen concurred, "I benefited from his counsel before sending you on your quest. T'was he that suggested that he might go with you. I am indeed glad that he was of benefit."

"Indeed," Malcolm agreed.

Chapter 3
Discussing Matters

Alpona the Athgonian, Zil-jahi Warrior, his arms, legs, and chest thick with muscles, his jaw square, usually clean-shaven – as was his custom – presented a match in size and strength to any frontiersman. Hung across his back, the ancient greatsword, Flammerung, flirted with the mane of black hair that spilled from beneath his leather cap to his shoulders. He also possessed a proper helm and light armor that he wore into battle, but he did not prefer them. Thus they had remained with Prince Bengallen's supply caravan.

Although no one could deny that he was a well-built human, he had done an inordinate amount of travel in recent years and much of his bulk, fat and muscle, had leaned away. For this reason, he had taken to wearing a red cloak with black sleeves. He was self-conscious as he and his companions made their way through the streets of Woodhaven, a very different feeling from the reckless glee he had felt upon his previous visit. At last, what remained of his belly growled, pleading for dinner.

"If we have much further to go," Alpona the Athgonian began, "might we first stop for a meal, sira?"

"Tis not much further, my thane," Roselle replied.

"Why do we call you that?" Shomotta asked.

Roselle looked to Alpona. He looked back to her. They both looked to Shomotta for elaboration.

"Athgonian," Shomotta elaborated as Roselle looked back to Alpona.

"Oh!" Alpona laughed and waited to hear if Shomotta would say more.

Shomotta, perennially deep of tan, appeared much more dark complected than anyone around him. More so than any human in more than a thousand miles – if it mattered – but certainly not the darkest even among his own people. Shomotta al-Hazar, Novice Priest of the Marzi, an ancient order of St. Amar, and a former peace officer of the Free City-State of Amar'tip, hailed from that grand beacon of civilization, called the Diamond in the Dust. It lay on the other side of the continent, beyond the Dreadwood and the Plains of the West, and far across the Hazar Desert from which his family name was taken. Not so tall as most of his companions – although he had an inch on Ruffis and at least two on Roselle – he maintained a bodily strength, but again not fully comparable to Bengallen, Malcolm, or Alpona.

Shomotta's strength came from his mind. One filled with the secrets and skills that formed an art, which allowed him to perceive the fabric of the cosmos and directly work his will upon the world around him. While not the most widely accepted description of magic, it fairly described Shomotta's use of it. He could hold his own in most fights, but his magic could make the difference, not only for himself, but for his allies as well. Wizard, warrior, priest, Shomotta was a good man to have at your side in any situation.

"I have traveled much and learned of many lands," Shomotta continued, "You have come from the Far Continent, from over the Sea of Memory, but you were born here, in these lands. Your stories are of a place called Zillis. There they called you Athgonian. I know of no such place in this part of the world."

Alpona tried to listen well and take the question seriously, but he chuckled despite himself.

Pausing until Shomotta clearly finished, Alpona replied, "It actually doesn't make much sense, not now that I am returned to the lands of my birth — hadn't thought about it. People been calling me an Athgonian for so long."

After another pause, Alpona's thoughts drifted, until Sira Roselle spoke up.

"Okay, so now I'm curious."

"I made it up!" Alpona blurted out, laughing anew before continuing, "It sounded like some place from over here. Some half remembered version of Antoria, Alcyone, Avigueux, or some other place. They all sort of look like me. I supposed I could be from one of them. I don't think I ever really knew where I was from, but Athgonia sounded right. You call the many lands across the sea the Far Continent and, when I was there, I called all of this over here Athgonia. In a sense, you're both Athgonians too."

"We call this continent Uhratt," Shomotta stated, attempting to playfully hide his amusement, as though that was the game.

"I know," Alpona replied, "but I didn't know that when I was a kid, who needed somewhere to be from. Besides, everyone all over the world calls the whole world Uhratt. Sort of arrogant that this land has the same name as the whole world. To their ear, I'd have been running around calling myself Alpona of the Whole Darn World."

Roselle, also amused, added, "Yes, so now you're just Alpona of the Whole Darn Continent."

"I always was, I suppose," Alpona agreed with mock subtlety.

They all laughed together. Alpona liked it when they all laughed together. So many years alone on an island were not that far from him. His life before that had not been so great either. Conflict awaited him around every turn, before and since. Yet there were times, beautiful, precious moments – sometimes lasting for days and days – that he was with people who could simply enjoy each other's company. All the strength and wisdom of the world could not compare to these moments or so it felt while he was in them.

He could forget about many things. It was nice to forget. A little bit of that first trip to Woodhaven came back to him. For a moment, he felt young.

"A good point though," Shomotta offered as the laughing faded, "That we Athgonians equate our lands with the Whole Darn World, even knowing that there is more out there. Athgonia is as good a name as any. I say we start calling this Near Continent, Athgonia. I'll label my maps this way and discuss it with others. Perhaps we make a thing of it. What do the people from it call their land that we call the Far Continent?"

Alpona, only having recently ceased to laugh, immediately began anew, but managed to get out, "People – the same – everywhere – all over – world."

Alpona kept laughing, wiping a tear from an eye.

"What?" Shomotta asked uncertainly.

With a wide smile, Roselle explained, "They must call their lands Uhratt too."

Alpona nodded in confirmation and his laughter increased. Shomotta shrugged his shoulders and chuckled too. With little more conversation and much more laughter, they finally arrived at Bavin Hall. The place had been set aside for Prince Bengallen and his companions during this official stay as a royal guest of Woodhaven.

Chapter 4
Staking Claims

Places, like people, have their secrets. Emblematic of his many contradictions, Ruffis guarded his secrets as diligently as he sought out the secrets of others. On his first trip to Woodhaven, the dark elf had made contact with the criminal underground, to pointedly glean some vision of Woodhaven's mysteries.

Elves passing through the towns and villages of the Frontier, every once and awhile, was not completely unheard of, though in fact it happened more often than most people knew. They even slipped in and out of Woodhaven and Spearpointe from time to time. A simple hood hid the difference between an elf and human at a glance, with a little added work on language and dialect, any elf could pass for a cloaked human woman in a pinch.

Ruffis, of course, native to distant lands, knew none of this. So when he sought them out, men of ill repute were all too eager to oblige the first elf – at least to public knowledge and common memory – to visit this bastion of human civilization upon the Frontier. After being forwarded through a few echelons of hoodlumry, he eventually found himself the guest of a pimp named Slabisck.

One step further an oddity than any other elf, Ruffis was black. There were men of all colors across the lands between the twelve great city-states. Few nearly so milky white as Bengallen and yet many of far darker shades than Shomotta's desert brown, but even the darkest man was not truly black, not in the manner of Ruffis' inky flesh.

Among the elves, an even greater variety of color appeared. On the same scale of pale to dark tone as humans, their flesh went beyond red-brown hues and flirted with gold, orange, yellow, and green. Yet Ruffis was black like the moonless night sky, like the center of a young man's eye, like coal, like blindness, like death. No one in this part of the world had heard of – let alone seen – any creature, man, elf, or monster, black like the dark elf Ruffis. No one who cared to speak of it, anyway.

Yet so Ruffis was and, to him, his beautiful black skin was the most normal thing in the world. It was his own flesh, from the day he was born. It looked like that of the father who raised him. The people of his distant, native continent knew of the dark elves and knew to avoid them. Some people here had similar superstitions regarding elves in general, but others regarded even the whisper of the word "elf" with intense curiosity.

Neither superstition nor curiosity shaped the opinions of elves in Ruffis' native lands. The orcs there desired elf flesh for their totems and fetishes and, wherever an elf was seen in the lands of men, it was considered an ill omen, harbinger of destruction. Given that packs of murderous orcs were likely not so far behind, the superstition could only barely be considered such.

In Woodhaven, this pimp, Slabisck, was of the curious sort. He had met an elf once before. Kidnapped him by accident while scouting for new talent to fill a brothel. Slabisck had bartered a magical trinket in exchange for the elf's release — which is to say that he robbed the elf and cut his losses. Yet Slabisck had often wondered, in the time since, what might have come from handling the situation differently. So he had befriended Ruffis and shared with him many of Woodhaven's secrets.

There was a bluff out from the city-state's southern wall that dropped down some twenty or more feet to the Lake. When Ruffis split from the other thanes, he went down to the Lake rather than follow the rise up to the bluff. There, knee high in water, about two feet above his eye level, directly below the tallest point, Ruffis found the storm drain with the rusted latch and let himself in the back door.

After a few twists and turns, a couple of miles, and about an hour, Ruffis found himself sitting across a table from the pimp named Slabisck. In the past, Slabisck had amused Ruffis, but things had changed. Ruffis had become accustomed to better company. More to the point, Slabisck possessed a similar look and build to Caanaflit, the companion that Ruffis disliked most.

Ruffis and Slabisck were counterpoints. Ruffis dark. Slabisck pallid. Ruffis with long white hair and Slabisck bald. Ruffis short, Slabisck tall, Ruffis marked, face and body, with white tattoos, and Slabisck relatively nondescript, no distinguishing marks of any kind.

Ruffis had seen it many times in his life, watching as Slabisck's eyes traced along the vine-like and spiral patterns of the dark elf's white tattoos. They appeared to have a mildly mesmerizing effect on dull people. Ruffis nibbled at his food until at last they made proper eye contact.

"What brings you back to Woodhaven?" the pimp asked.

Ruffis drank the glass of wine in a single gulp, answering simply, "Work."

"If you need work, Slabisck can provide," the pimp offered, continuing, "If you need help, distraction, or vice, Slabisck provides that too."

"I don't need anything from you," Ruffis explained, "I'm merely politely informing you that I'm on your turf."

" 'Polite,' he says, but makes no offer to cut Slabisck in."

"Not that sort of work."

"Slabisck does all kinds of work."

Did he always say his own name like that, Ruffis wondered. *It was very annoying*. With his peeved thought, he paused, holding out his glass. Promptly refilled by a porter and promptly re-drained by Ruffis. *It tasted more expensive than good.*

Only once finished did Ruffis speak again.

"I'm not generally polite and the fact that you're throwing it back in my face right now makes me want to rorking spit."

"Ruffis, you offend while in your attempt to be polite. Slabisck thinks you must not be very good at this."

Ruffis thought of Caanaflit again. He remembered the way Bengallen's pet rapscallion always talked down to him. Already in an ill mood, whatever Ruffis had thought to find here – and he had himself become unsure – here it clearly was not. So he murdered the pimp.

As quickly as he thought to do it, it was done. Ruffis pulled the dagger from his boot, with a flick of the wrist, flinging it underhanded across the table, and impaling Slabisck's brain through the left eye. One of the pimp's bodyguards swung a sword at Ruffis's chair, but the dark elf was already out of it, standing on the table, plucking his dagger from Slabisck's skull, and picking the pimp's pocket.

A hefty purse next to his light one, that explained a few things.

Ruffis swung around Slabisck's body, using it as a shield against the other bodyguard's attack. In the next instant, he rolled forward and under a second chop from the first bodyguard. Pocketing the coin purse, he popped up in time to slice the man's throat wide open.

Ducking as he turned, Ruffis dodged another swing from the remaining bodyguard and, snatching up the dead one's sword, put it to the throat of his assailant.

He stopped a hair shy of shedding the man's life-blood.

"Drop the sword."

The thug did so without a word.

The blade clanged to the ground before Ruffis.

"Why are you still alive?"

"I don't know," the man almost cried.

"Better come up with a reason before I kill you."

"I know stuff," the thug offered quickly.

"Liiiiiike?" Ruffis drew out the word making a hurried gesture with his off-hand.

"I know which watchmen are— ah – were – ah – in Slabisck's pocket."

Ruffis accepted with a wicked grin, releasing the man.

"That seems worth knowing."

His foul mood was much improved.

Chapter 5
Holding Court

The next day, the Thanes of Prince Bengallen gathered in the parlor of Bavin Hall for a lunch. There among them was a dwarf-lord, Traldor Drumhammer, who entered last.

"Haird yoo lads were finally aboot," Lord Traldor shouted into the room as he entered.

Ruffis had been sitting alone. He used the interruption to pick-up his plate and move next to Shomotta, sitting with the others. He replied as he moved.

"And you are?"

"I am Lord Traldor Drumhammer, Lord of the West-Most Keep, a son of King Odemkin of Dwarvehame."

"Fancy," Ruffis replied, "aren't you supposed to have an army or something?"

"My retinue," Lord Traldor scowled, explaining, "haz returned to Dwarvehame to summon a mighty force to ally with His Highness, Prince Bengallen."

"Lord Traldor, I am called Alpona, my vocal friend is Ruffis, this is Malcolm and Shomotta," the Zil-jahi Warrior interrupted into the conversation, motioning to and introducing himself and the recently arrived companions.

"Thanes," Traldor addressed them, stepping forward, "I greet you as brothers."

"Please, Lord Traldor, join us," Alpona accepted, "This has been your table for months now. We are but a day here. Please, consider us as your guests and we will behave as such."

"Gratitude," the dwarf acknowledged, declining, "This is your master's table, let us fellowship as equals."

Malcolm cut a slice of meat from the boar at the table, placed it on an empty plate, and handed it over to the empty place across from him, gesturing with invitation. Traldor took the plate, scooped up some potatoes and gravy, and took his seat in time for the serving girl to bring him his drink.

"Thankee, lass," Traldor looked up, smiling at the server, before shifting to Malcolm, "and thank yah, thane. Suspicion of dwarves from an elf, political flattery from the human, both to be expected, but hospitality from an orc? Bless ya. Yoo are the first orc that I'll considered callin' friend."

"I have no hate for dwarves," Malcolm shared, "and if you call an army, for true, I can imagine there is a place for your people in my heart."

"Sentiment?" the dwarf-lord questioned, amused, "Yoo're somethin' special."

Ruffis reasserted himself in that moment.

"He is the most precious snowflake to survive all the hells of his kind."

Everyone groaned. Someone was about to apologize for Ruffis, another was to chastise him, and everyone else was intent to ignore him.

Before the moment proceeded into true awkwardness, however, Sira Roselle burst into the room and called:

"His Majesty, Prince Bengallen Hastenfarish!"

Bengallen entered the room in the same moment and everyone there seated stood to, although Ruffis with decidedly less snap. The Prince removed his gloves and took his place at the head of the table. A plate was served to him by a waiting attendant and everyone took their seats once more.

"Lord Traldor, you've met my thanes," Prince Bengallen began, "Apologies for the absence of Caanaflit, his responsibilities detain him in Spearpointe."

Prince Bengallen took a long drink from his mug and the guests at his table took the opportunity to do likewise. Sira Roselle came to the table, grabbed a plate, but before she could cut her own slice of meat, Malcolm had already done so, serving it to her.

"Sira," he offered.

"My Thane," she accepted, a surprise blush in her cheeks.

"My Thanes," Prince Bengallen addressed them, "I need to explain to you the situation here in Woodhaven. It has all played out about as far as it shall. Something is about to happen, one way or the other, and soon. I need your best. Anything we can do for these people, I beseech thee, do it."

Everyone began or continued their meal for a time. Bengallen, after he had finished eating, called for their cups to be topped off. Thereafter, settling himself comfortably in his chair, reflected aloud for the benefit of his thanes.

"As Caanaflit, Malcolm, and Alpona attended to other matters, Shomotta and I traveled from Spearpointe to Woodhaven with a few knights to respond to our dwarven allies. By the time we had arrived, the dwarves had, unfortunately, come and gone. Lord Traldor, here remained, however, to greet me and alert his people should I return. So I had. So he did. Lord Traldor's retainers were dispatched to Dwarvehame and, as he is a noble lord, unattended on our behalf, we will extend him every courtesy."

"Thankee kindly, Yer Highness!" shouted Traldor raising his cup.

The others raised their own with him.

"Then I was again torn, between the immediate needs of the people of Morralish, if there be people there at all, and my commitments away from them, made on their behalf," Prince Bengallen continued, "I still have no word from the Expeditionary Forces abroad. The Spearpointe Company and Knights of the Spear, impressive as they are, are not nearly enough in number, not by a decimal, for the task of the north, for the threat that awaits there. I need all my allies, so my people and my land yet wait, as I wait, now for dwarves, still for word from my own soldiers afar."

"Any word from your priestess, the Sister Bethany?" Malcolm asked.

"You've seen Caanaflit since I have. If there was word, he would be the one to deliver it," Bengallen answered with heavy sigh, continuing, "With little more to do but wait, and considering my need for allies, I decided to take a cue from my political successes in Spearpointe. I thought to create a Frontier alliance, to resist any threats that may yet come from the north, by uniting Woodhaven with Spearpointe under my banner. Ambitious, yes, but tis for the good of all."

As Prince Bengallen paused to drink, Sira Roselle noted the faces, possibly of disapproval, that Alpona and Ruffis wore, before speaking to the group to remind them, "I testified. Of the goblin raid. Of the Beast. Of the capabilities and strength His Majesty has given to Spearpointe in training her sons and daughters in the ways of war."

"Tis not so simple as that, however," Prince Bengallen resumed his account, "The Lord-Mayor of Spearpointe was obstinate, yet he was but one man. The Frontier City-State of Woodhaven is ruled by a two-tiered elder council. All governance is decided by a two-thirds majority of the Council of Elder-Lords and ratified or vetoed by a simple majority of the General Council of Elders."

Ruffis leaned back, yawning dramatically. Alpona rapped him across the chest, theatrically. Ruffis nearly fell from the back of his chair, secured his footing, and returned to his meal, although glaring at Alpona from the corner of his eyes.

25

"Moreover," Bengallen proceeded, "the relationship between Woodhaven and Spearpointe tis not as it might seem. Woodhaven considers itself rather superior to Spearpointe. Many council elders were interested in union with the Kingdom of Morralish. We have enjoyed many economic and cultural relationships and Woodhaven has suffered the decrease in trade and concern for distant relatives therein. So there is an extant investment in Morralish. Yet also a reluctance to 'sign on' second to something their 'bumpkin' neighbors in Spearpointe were first to. They consider it a slight and are uncertain they want to be equal with Spearpointe in the eyes of their would-be Prince."

Alpona cleared his throat, asking Shomotta and Roselle as much as Bengallen, "Surely their rivalry and bigotry might not have been enough to override their other interests?"

Shomotta rolled his eyes and Roselle flattened her mouth and shook her head in the negative.

"Restoring the north and uniting the Frontier against that same threat do weigh more greatly in our favor," Bengallen explained, "Except. Except that there is a third opinion, potentially valid, that joining with me, the occupied north, and their smaller, supposedly weaker southern neighbors might be the wrong move. Such alliance might bring a suddenly struggling, but surviving, Woodhaven further down."

"Potentially valid?" Alpona questioned, "You don't really believe that, Your Majesty?"

Prince Bengallen took a long drink before replying, "You've seen much, with me and from before, I'm sure. Yet the wave of skeletal soldiers, the undead legions, that poured upon my homeland are something else. I shan't lie to myself, you, or anyone else. It may be that they cannot be defeated."

Alpona took a drink as well, agreeing, "We did see them, actually. At the first port, when we arrived in these lands. A horror beyond nightmare. The captain didn't even consider a fight. We sailed south without a thought. We tried to forget, in fact. I concede the point, Your Majesty."

"So now I am embroiled in council debates," the Prince continued, "concerning what they have decided to call 'annexation.' News of our valor, heroism, and victory over the Beast has won the hearts of the people and the polling indicates that we are all but guaranteed ratification by the General Council of Elders, but we lack the two-thirds favor needed from the Council of Elder-Lords. They vacillate at around an even split. Short either way."

"We'll do what we can, Your Majesty," Alpona spoke for all of them.

26

"Gratitude," Prince Bengallen accepted, "I feel certain that if the dwarves would return in force, confirming confidence in my alliance building, many votes from the peerage would swing in our favor, with the commercial benefits likely to further solidify popular opinion. Yet, the formal vote is in a week and tis unlikely they'll arrive by then."

"Nay, Yer Highness," Lord Traldor groaned, continuing, disappointment clear in his voice, "Heralds would arrive days ahead and a wizard would send magical word besides. We've neither at present. So nay."

Bengallen smirked, finished the small puddle of ale in the bottom of his cup, redirecting his account.

"Today's shenanigans: The Elder-Lord leading the opposition of annexation, has challenged me to a personal combat to prove my worth."

Ruffis laughed.

"Are you worried?"

"He is an old man," Prince Bengallen replied, maintaining his serious tone, "There is no honor in it. Refusing him loses favor. Beating him? Sure, I can. To what end? What will beating an old man in front of his neighbors gain me? Yet I cannot risk the certain loss of refusing him. So, do come on the morrow to bear witness to this latest indignity."

Alpona shook his head, disagreeing, "Respectfully, Your Majesty, how you accord yourself will determine the indignity."

"Agreed," called Malcolm, "You have taught us to fight with honor. Show the man and these people respect in how you meet the challenge. Everyone will know it was his choice to get beaten by a younger, stronger man. There are other factors you can control."

"Has Caanaflit died?" Shomotta joked, "The voice of his ghost in this room."

Sharing a laugh with them, Prince Bengallen smiled, accepting, "My thanes, I thank thee. You ever prove yourselves my friends."

"Me," Ruffis mused aloud to ruin the mood, "I just want to see you beat up an old man."

It worked.

Chapter 6
Contesting Visions

"This is a contest of arms," the announcer – a baker on any other day – began, "agreed upon by two men of station. The Elder-Lord Hrodknoff, Third of the Nine, has challenged Prince Bengallen, Throne-Lord of Morralish, to prove that Woodhaven would benefit from annexation by the Kingdom of Morralish. The proof to be measured by the outcome here achieved."

The Elder-Lord Hrodknoff, a prune-faced Northman, white of beard, likely descended from mountain folk, claimed a smallish battle axe, bladed on one side with a ball mace on the other, and a wooden shield. The boy beside him, likely a grandson or nephew, carried an additional shield.

Hrodknoff looked to the leading elders of his alliance, reminding them, "Whatever happens here, your votes are yours. Your hearts are yours. If you are swayed, be swayed. If you stand resolute, be resolute. As for me, that man will fight for my vote. Earn it. Ever I fight for Woodhaven, come what may."

Prince Bengallen could hear him. *How can I hear him?* He looked to Malcolm who handed over the short sword. *Malcolm appears unable to hear them.* Bengallen looked around to Alpona, Caanaflit, Shomotta, and many others. None of them noticed the Elder-Lord going back on his earlier decree.

Bengallen remembered the Elder-Lord's words from yesterday clearly:

> "I must relent to Prince Bengallen's valor and reputation, but
> I cannot in good conscience surrender Woodhaven's
> independence. If Prince Bengallen is worthy, then he can take
> it. Those elders who support me, if I am defeated, then His
> Highness has won, move your votes to support unification
> with the Kingdom of Morralish under Prince Bengallen."

If Bengallen was the victor, they were to vote in his favor. *Why had he told them to vote as they will?* Prince Bengallen needed the Frontier unified as part of Morralish and he was, with reservation, willing to send an old man to his grave to see it done. He was not so keen, however, on the idea of killing an old man merely because he was a stubborn old bloke who yet refuse to kneel. Prince Bengallen admired Hrodknoff's resolve, even his respect for the autonomy of his peers, but that he would go back on his own word, to his own people, was unsettling.

Assessing his opponent, morally and physically, Bengallen forgot about his odd moment of over-overhearing. The Paladin-Prince took one of two shields from Malcolm and made his way to the fight. If the shield of either man was broken, the battle would be paused. They could forfeit or claim their second shield. If they claimed the second shield, they retained the right to yield and surrender at any time. Doing so ensured the safety of the surrendering fighter. Second shield shattered, however, only victory or death resolved the contest.

This was the customary form of ritual combat of the Skyalds, islanders off the eastern coast in northern Morralish. How the custom had made its way down here presented something of a mystery. Yet the Frontier was full of such oddities. Individuals from every Antori province and region of Morralish had settled in Woodhaven and Spearpointe. So done, many of the old traditions changed or faded, but some things, especially the functional and sensible things, were assimilated or became the new traditions. Skyaldish ritual combat was an honest, fair, and relatively safe way of fighting over differences: Both sides had control over how far they wanted to take it and yet it was still a brutal fight, which neither should agree to lightly.

The two men faced each other, just out of reach. Not about to take the first strike against the old man, Prince Bengallen also hesitated. Again, Bengallen heard what ought be out of his earshot.

Hrodknoff told the boy, "Step back a ways, lad. See how the Prince of Morralish accords himself against an old man."

Another wave of guilt took the Prince. He sincerely did not want to fight, beat, or possibly kill this respected elder. Furthermore, it appeared, mayhap, the old man intended to sacrifice himself to see the people of Woodhaven harden their hearts against him. Yet it was too late. They had both committed to this battle, to call it off would be a true shame, one beyond the mere embarrassment of surrender.

The Elder-Lord's attendant backed off. So did Malcolm. The two combatants continued to face each other. This was the moment when lesser fighters would begin to circle one another, trying to press the other for a weakness or misstep. Yet here, each stood resolute, still as stone.

Taller than Prince Bengallen remembered him to be, the Elder-Lord, his arms and hands larger, held the axe with an unexpected, confident proficiency. Rather than taunt each other, each appeared to be offering the other the courtesy of making the first attack.

For a long moment, neither took it. Eventually, Prince Bengallen decided that as the guest – not his city, not yet, and the battle not his choice – to accept the hospitality of his host. Bengallen struck first.

The old man caught the blow at the edge of his shield, a clear notch and split could already be seen. The Elder-Lord swung back at near the same time, but Bengallen stepped through with his own swing, which dodged the attack of his opponent completely.

Bengallen made a quarter turn, speaking to Hrodknoff, "Doubtless you were once a warrior. From Morralish mayhap. Though a warrior's heart still beats, his arms and eyes grow slow. No shame in it. We need go no further."

"Awful young to shy from a fight," Hrodknoff replied, "You talking or fighting?"

Bengallen narrowed his eyes, charging forward. Hrodknoff dropped a fearsome blow with his axe, though it landed center to Bengallen's shield, which itself slammed center to Hrodknoff's chest. At the moment of impact, the opposing ball mace end of his axe struck the old man's sternum and the weapon came out of his hand. Bengallen pushed out and to the left with the shield, flinging Hrodknoff, unarmed, to the ground. The old man braced against his fall, but the impact caused the split, already rent in his shield, to fail completely.

"Stay down!" Prince Bengallen called out.

Hrodknoff stood and called out as well: "Shield!"

The boy brought him another shield and Bengallen called again.

"Beg off, old man!"

"Old man?" The Elder-Lord returned in a questioning tone, "Alright, lad, time to learn some respect."

Bengallen spared half a moment to regret his hasty chastisement, but spared a full moment to remind himself that he had *tried to respect this man at every moment leading up to this*.

Prince Bengallen pulled the Elder-Lord's axe from his shield, tossing it to him. The old man held his hand against his sternum as he bent over to get it. The ball of that axe's mace-side had clearly done some damage.

Without standing completely, Hrodknoff charged forward, using Bengallen's own move and catching the Paladin-Prince off-guard, partially. Bengallen took a half step and braced for impact. The old man's shield pushed the Prince's sword arm away as it struck the side of the younger man's shield. Swung, the axe came down on the other side of it. With force from both sides, Prince Bengallen's shield – already damaged – split in two, down the middle.

Both men fell to the ground, collapsed in a heap, Hrodknoff atop Bengallen. The Prince laid his sword aside and, with both hands, grasped the elder's shield, tearing it off of his arm as he came to his feet. Hrodknoff stood as well, grabbing up Bengallen's sword. Looking to his younger opponent, he witnessed the Prince break the old man's second shield over his knee.

It hurt more than he expected, wrists and knee. For an instant, Bengallen was certain that the shield would not break, but he had put just enough power into it, and the shield folded as his foot returned to the ground.

Hrodknoff, refusing to stare befuddled for too long, hurled the axe at Prince Bengallen. He batted it away with half of the broken shield, throwing the other half back at Hrodknoff in retaliation. The throw was sloppy, no genuine attack. Hrodknoff easily stepped aside.

"Stand down!" Prince Bengallen yelled at the Elder-Lord as Malcolm handed him the remaining shield.

"Stand down!" Someone shouted from the crowd.

"Stand down!" A pair of Hrodknoff's own allied elders called to him.

Hrodknoff ignored them all and, sword in hand, charged at Prince Bengallen. The Prince brought up his fresh shield, holding it square in front of him, a wall parallel between them.

At the last moment, he raised the shield, swinging it upward. This deflected the chop from the sword in a way that left Hrodknoff's body wide open. Right hand empty, Prince Bengallen clenched a fist, punching Hrodknoff center mass, in his wounded sternum.

The old man gasped for air and released the sword. The weapon clattered upon and slid across the surface of Bengallen's upraised shield, as he lowered it. The Paladin-Prince snatched the sword hilt with his hand as it returned from landing the punch. Then Bengallen walked around the staggering old man, grabbing him from behind, around the waist.

Sword to his throat, he whispered in the Elder-Lord's ear, "I could kill you now. Before you catch your breath. Even if you begged me not to, by the rules of your own contest, I can open your throat and piss on your corpse. But I'm not going to do that. Oh, you pain in the arse, I'd like to and I think that you'd like me to as well — an ugly show. There is, however, one thing you did not consider—"

"What?" Hrodknoffed wheezed, finding his breath.

"I am a good man. I am a Paladin. By the grace of Vandor and for the sake of His people," Bengallen answered, "I am the hero of this saga."

"You say it?"

"I say it."

"We say it," the Elder-Lord Hrodknoff took Prince Bengallen's words for prayer and oath in whisper, but then cried out so that all could hear, "I do not yield! I spit on your mercy!"

At last, Prince Bengallen understood. Hrodknoff did not want Prince Bengallen to kill Woodhaven's beloved elder to sour the people against him. Past dealing with the Lord-Mayor of Spearpointe had tainted his own assessment. This was different.

This old man wanted to test Prince Bengallen's quality of character. He intended to see, for himself, whether the title Paladin-Prince meant anything and to expose the truth of the man who would be Woodhaven's king.

Bengallen knew what he had to do. He dropped the sword and the shield as well. He walked in front of Hrodknoff – standing under his own power – and turned his back to the old man.

He called to the crowd, "Then I shall yield! I cannot kill you. You are not my enemy. So I can only ask for your mercy. Mercy!"

"Then you shall have it," a familiar voice answered.

32

Chapter 7
Taking Heart

Prince Bengallen awoke. His mind felt slow, yet it grasped at the images sleep left him. *Was it a vision? A sign. Some esoteric hope for the future.* His thoughts moved from the dream toward the past and a life denied to him.

He lay there, bewildered, until one foot found its way out of bed. A small light came into the room from his window and served as a touchstone. The light grounded him to reality, as he forced the rest of himself from the quilts.

Dragging himself out of the door to his rooms, Bengallen entered directly into the parlor of the home Woodhaven had provided him. There, he found Sira Roselle. Many of his company were residing elsewhere, within Bavin Hall, but Roselle alone had taken to the parlor so early this day. Sitting, she was startled by the Prince's entrance and stood to.

Sira Roselle was neither a young nor traditionally beautiful woman. Not that there was anything wrong with her, necessarily, but she did not curve in all the ways that men liked their women to curve. Even less so after her rigorous physical training and combat experience that had culminated in her knighthood. She was strong and lean, her body considered, by many, as masculine as feminine.

Yet her face appeared soft and plain. Her brown eyes were level on a face as symmetrical as anyone's. Despite her thick neck that indicated countless hours of strength training, her jaw, her lips, her cheeks, her brow all remained decidedly feminine. No, she was not a traditional beauty, but she was healthy and easy enough to look at. She had been loved once, and more than one man had come to desire her since.

Rosey was mayhap the sort of woman who came along and redefined what it meant to be beautiful. She possessed all the sweetness and charm of a lady. Yet she could be stern and assertive, as needed, with confidence enough to inspire it in others. Still, a maidenly gentleness resided within, native to her, a sincerity, innocence, and hope that were almost contagious. As much as some might criticize Roselle for becoming like a man, most men would do good to become more like her. Prince Bengallen believed this. She reminded him of the better parts of himself, too easily lost in these dark days. Thus, he made her his standard-bearer and kept her close when he could.

Bengallen groaned some inaudible command and unceremoniously waved the lady-knight back to her seat. She sat slowly, gazing at her Prince with an uncertain countenance as he slugged toward her table, barely taking notice of the beginnings of a cook fire burning in its place across the room.

"Your Majesty?" Roselle asked.

Bengallen groaned and mumbled once again before taking a seat beside her. He placed his bare hands at his temples, leaning forward, resting on his elbows. Turning his wrists slightly, he placed his forehead in his palms and stretched out his fingers into his golden hair. He sat there for some stretch of moments, listless.

Unsure, Roselle had returned to her studies, when Bengallen spoke at last.

"Tis early yet."

"Indeed, Your Majesty," Sira Roselle replied, "I've found a particularly interesting book of lore from the Church stacks loaned to us. It details several races of demons, what goals, motivations, and foils are unique between them, and speculates as to what they might look like in their natural forms."

She had more to say, but Bengallen groaned yet again before briefly mimicking the sounds of someone speaking a sentence that goes on and on.

Looking up, he repeated, "Tis early yet."

Roselle smiled, closing her book.

"Too early for demons, I suppose. Why do you yet stir, my Prince?"

"Terrible nightmares."

"We've seen – you've seen – terrible things."

"Tis the things unseen that haunt me."

"The woman?"

"Di'Andria."

"Tell me of her, the Lady Di'Andria."

"Can you not hear?" Bengallen asked in reply, pausing, a brief hesitation before adding, "Her mere name trembles upon my lips?"

"Then try, my Prince," she implored him, "I will listen."

"She is beautiful," Ben began, "There are lots of beautiful women in the world. I suppose tisn't so remarkable a thing. I feel like I should be more quick to say something else about her. I feel like I should tell you of her gentle ways or her kindly intent. Yet tis her beauty that transfixes me. Of all the many noble girls – princesses – trotted out before me, it has ever been her that

34

enchants me so. They all do and say what they think will impress others and tis all so false, so fake, so farcical. On the surface, she is not so much different than the rest, but there is an honesty, an earnestness, a genuine believability in all the things she does and says. She does not talk with me about the people because I am a prince, but because she cares about the people. She does not carry herself with poise and elegance because princesses are supposed to, but because she is composed – in the very fabric of her being – of confidence and worth. Her physical beauty is the raw expression of all these things. The summary, the completion, and the symbol of all the goodness and value of which she is possessed. Yes, there are many beautiful women in the world, but I can think of none more deserving of the beauty that she radiates — and blinds me with. Tis her beauty that always comes to mind. It is the quality that speaks to all that she is: Beautiful."

The silence stretched between them. Sira Roselle could feel the sacredness in the room. No mere romance, but a fragment of Divine Love, spoken into existence by the Prince in the Light. It lived and breathed in this space they had created for it.

She felt the force of it. It laid upon her chest. It made her want to love and be loved so. The Holy Family had given this gift to Prince Bengallen. Yet the forces of darkness had divided him from the one he loved and yet, the greater testament, the love itself remained, as real and unblemished as it ever must have been.

"Those were not all the right words," Ben broke the silence.

"Begging your pardon," Roselle, still stunned, could barely whisper in reply.

"When I say it out loud," he explained, "it never seems enough. I need better words. Say some things in a different order. Say more things. Better things. In my mind, she and my love for her are so clear, but spilled out into the world, like this — I cannot quite get it right."

"It was right, my Prince," Sira Roselle replied, her full voice returned, "I've never heard any man say such things about a woman. Never heard anyone say as much about any other. There is no woman in all the world who does not desire someone to speak of her with such passionate sincerity. If you insist your words were not perfect, so be it, but the love you hold for her is unquestionably so. I am honored to be its witness."

"You do me the honor," Bengallen accepted the praise, returned in kind, continuing, "I worry for her. I think of our plans and dreams. I fear for them. I grieve for them. For myself, in a fashion, as I need her. Yet beyond myself, I am concerned for her. Where is she? How is she? What is being done to her?

What should I be doing for her? We make plans, here. I secure allies and await reinforcement, and I do it for all my people because alone, even with my mighty band, I cannot save them. She is one of them. Yet when I think of her alone, even as one man, I am compelled to act. To seek her out. So much has happened because I was discontent to rally forces over a year — been more than a year now. T'was not enough to be a leader who moved when the time was right. I left this place, twice, to find her. Jeopardized the line of my father, the leadership of my people, because every day, when all else is said and done – or else silent and unfinished – I am naught but a man separated from the woman who needs him. Every day, that part of me does nothing and it consumes me with worry — and shame."

"What you hold for her in your heart," Sira Roselle dared explain, "is holy. I felt it, in this room, as you spoke it. Your love for her is a part of the Divine Love. She is a boon bestowed upon you by the Holy Family. Let your drive to save her stand beside your drive to save your people. Draw strength from it. Trust that Vandor does not cast his blessings about carelessly. You have her in your heart, bonded so strongly, for a reason."

"I know," Ben said, "Most often they do work in concert. Bless you for seeing it — for saying it and for reminding me. You ever prove a good choice to be made a paladin. Rest assured, I have the faith and know your words are true. And yet there are moments, when I am but a man, and all my faith provides neither recourse nor consolation for the longing and obligation I feel for her."

Bengallen went over to the cook fire, retrieving two bowls of porridge. It smelled plain, but whole and wholesome, as it also grounded him. How many of us can say a prince served us breakfast?

The small act spoke volumes about what the exchange had meant to Prince Bengallen. They shared their breakfast with no more weighty words between them. They spoke of simple things and compared accounts of the exploits of the thanes so recently returned to their company.

Afterward, Sira Roselle returned to her studies and Prince Bengallen called for a bath. Alone once again, something in her broke. The spell of the holy moment. Her awareness of her own needs. Both? More? Who can know?

She wept.

Roselle wiped a tear away and another replaced it. She closed her book, remembered to breathe, and began to sob. She clutched at her heavy heart, beat her chest, and cried the tears of the woman she used to be and apparently yet remained. The lady-knight grabbed the table with both hands, calmed herself through an act of sheer will and dignity, and made a choice.

Chapter 8
Fading Life

Alpona pulled himself before the tarnished silver-steel mirror.

"Tarnished as we both are."

He twisted his thumbs where the reflections of his bloodshot eyes stared back at him.

"I've got to stop drinking."

Clearing some few flecks of crud from the surface, he traced two lines up to the reflection of his hairline.

"Thinner and thinner, I won't be hiding this for much longer. What would they make of me, if they knew?"

Alpona washed his face and hair in the water basin that had been provided for him and picked up the leather cap that he had taken to wearing since Spearpointe. Only when removed was it evident that Alpona's thick, black mane was no longer his own, but was someone else's woven into the cap.

Anointing himself with costly olive oil, Alpona fitted the tight cap onto his head, mashing it a bit to ensure contact between the two surfaces and a proper fit. Afterward, he took what remained of his own long hair and combed it so that it blended with the horsehair spilling from the cap. Pulling the hair from over his ears, he joined the blended locks from either side. Fixing them together with a small strand of leather in the back, he wrapped the cord several times, around the tail laid over the loose hair in back, tying it off.

With the tedium of the task, Alpona became lost in his thoughts, speaking them into the mirror:

"Like a woman, playing at my hair each morning. Then again, they've all got pretty hair, even Malcolm, as far as orcs go. Now I sound even more like a woman. Need to just shave it off. If only I hadn't told them it was a mark of shame among the Zil-jahi. I need to quit drinking. These hangovers are getting worse and worse, harder and harder to recover from. My own father, he was about as old as I am now when this sickness took him. That I've made it this long and am still this healthy, that counts for something. Alright, hangover or no, there is much afoot. I don't guess it takes a clear head to watch a young warrior kill an old man. Ugh, I need to quit drinking."

Splashing and toweling his face one last time, the Zil-jahi warrior pushed his shoulders back, stood tall, and strode out to meet the day.

37

Chapter 9
Fighting Champion

The Elder-Lord who led the opposition to annexation and the lordship of Prince Bengallen, actually called Hroddan, in every other way looked and acted like the man Prince Bengallen had fought in his dream.

Hroddan spoke with confidence.

"Let His Highness, Prince Bengallen, prove that he can lead the people of Woodhaven. Let him show us, in contest of arms, that he is mighty enough to stand against the emerging threats of this world. He has fought for Spearpointe. Now let him fight for us. If he would win the votes he needs from the strongest among us, let him win them in a contest of strength."

"To which I have already agreed, esteemed elder," Bengallen reminded all who would hear as he stepped forth.

"Many have gathered this day, Your Highness," Hroddan continued in his announcer's voice, "who are uncertain of what is transpiring. I merely summarize our stance for their benefit."

Politicians. Everywhere they claim to speak for the people. Everywhere they shade the truth of a thing in colors that favor their own appearance. *Of all the things my father taught me,* Prince Bengallen thought to himself, *how to beat them at their own games, no matter how much I loathe them, has been surprisingly paramount in these times. Everyone wants everyone else's power though. I merely would have these Frontier people united. I'm content to let these elders and their council reign in Woodhaven. Yet if this is what it takes – whatever it takes – I shall see it done.*

"The Elder-Lord's concern for his people is noted," Bengallen shared again, "Come I, not to conquer Woodhaven, but to unite it. Frontiersman and Northmen united against the threats that beset us all. Yet, if thy need is for me to win a battle for thee, even to bleed for thee, Woodhaven, I doth accept."

"So Your Highness does not intend to name a champion to fight in his stead, despite so many warriors at your disposal?" Hroddan asked.

The question surprised Prince Bengallen, even as he laughed it off, replying, "No. Anyone of my companions would gladly fight for me and do well on my behalf. Yet they have nothing to prove to anyone. We mountain folk take to fighting our own battles, prince to pauper, tis our way."

"I am not so young as yourself, Your Highness," the Elder-Lord Hroddan countered, "With only small injury to my pride, I do request that I may name another to fight on my behalf, as a man of noble birth, as custom entitles me."

Even more surprising, Bengallen expected the dream to be more literal. Mayhap it pointed him only to humility.

Prince Bengallen accepted to fight Hroddan's champion instead, "Agreed."

The Elder-Lord cried but a single word, "Brunsis!"

Bengallen recalled the unusual name from his last days in Morralish. He nearly made a joke about the similarity to his companions, only to stumble upon a lonely and somber awareness: *None of them were with me in those days*. With heavy heart, a memory of the Paladin Di'Gilcrest began to take shape in the Prince's mind, but he shrugged it off, instead musing aloud.

"It seems I am fated to fight a man named Brunsis."

"Oh!" Elder-Lord Hroddan spat with glee, "Fighting you is the only things he has talked about since we found him over a year ago."

Brunsis stepped forth, no man at all. In fact, how no one noticed him in the crowd came as yet another surprising. Then again, no one had been looking for a minotaur amongst Woodhaven's elders.

The minotaur, as tall as Malcolm, his head and neck barely larger, the pair of massive bull horns jutting from the sides of his forehead gave him a much larger appearance. Prince Bengallen looked at those horns with more than a little trepidation.

Those were things to die upon. This would not be an easy fight.

He longed for Flammerung or Dawnsong or even The Laughing Axe, if it would have him. To face a legendary creature, it only made sense to have a legendary blade. That Axe was in Spearpointe with another of his knights, however, and to use a greatsword, Bengallen would have to forfeit his shields. He had a feeling that he might need them.

Brunsis, the minotaur, moved nimbly forward and struck a pose that, to the untrained eye, would not look unlike something Alpona might do. Covered in ruddy-brown fur, Brunsis appeared to be under remarkable control by his masters. *That or he was fairly intelligent in his own right*. The creature clearly had hands, like men, and the laced up boots implied feet rather than hooves.

After Hroddan handed him his first shield, Brunsis wiped his snout with the flick of his thumb, waving his fingers into his open palm as though to say "give me." Uncertainly, Hroddan gave the minotaur his second shield as well.

Brunsis settled low in his stance, a shield on either arm. Bengallen knocked his sword and shield together, signaling that he was ready. Brunsis echoed, knocking his shields, but did not move.

When Prince Bengallen took his first step, Brunsis hurled one of his shields at him. The creature spun his whole body, with a lithe grace, stunning for his build, and the shield sailed through the air like some sort of disk weapon. Too surprised to dodge, Bengallen barely pulled his own shield up in time to block the strike.

The shields clashed hard. Bengallen staggered back and as he lowered the one he held, mere inches, to see the minotaur charging at him full tilt. Again, with no time to dodge, all the Paladin-Prince could do was move the shield. It shattered between himself and the oncoming strike.

Amid the blow, Brunsis grabbed Bengallen's sword arm with his free hand, prying the Prince's hand open in such a way that caused the sword to fall free. Bengallen and Brunsis both pulled away from each other, re positioning themselves, almost at a reset. The Paladin-Prince, unsure the minotaur understood the rules, darted for his sword on the ground rather than his shield.

Rather than charge, Brunsis again hurled his second shield in the air. This time, it struck Bengallen as he bent over to retrieve the sword, toppling the Prince over. As he righted himself, he saw Brunsis, both of his own shields broken, holding Bengallen's second shield. Brunsis made a gesture at tossing it to him, a mocking gesture. As Prince Bengallen took up the sword and gestured that he would receive the shield, the minotaur threw it, as he had the others, as Bengallen knew that he would. He dodged the last shield as it slammed harmlessly into the wall behind the Prince. Shattering, however, its destruction signaled the dire turn in this combat.

Brunsis charged Bengallen again. With no shield this time, the Paladin-Prince dove at the minotaur's knees, at the last instant, and used the creature's own momentum against it, toppling it. Brunsis tried to grapple Bengallen's legs as their bodies spilled about, passing one another, but there was too much speed and chaos in the collision. Bengallen slipped loose.

Brunsis lifted himself from the mud and turned about to face the Paladin-Prince, already on his feet and at the ready. The minotaur spoke to him, "Your boldness may have once been posturing, but now you surely own it."

"Seems I've misjudged you," Bengallen admitted, "You speak well."

"I am wise beyond your ken, boy."

"Good," Prince Bengallen, wiped the dirt from his face with a smile, before continuing, "Then you know we don't actually have to fight to the death."

"I never planned on murdering you, Princess. Yet, as you said: We were fated to fight," Brunsis explained, "I've never missed a fight. I thank the gods that they've kept you alive all this long while and deliver you to me now. I wouldn't dare disrespect them by killing you on purpose. Fighting is dangerous sport though. No promises."

"I hope you caught some breaths with all that stalling," Prince Bengallen taunted, "Tis time for round two."

The minotaur snorted as a wicked grin curled at the sides of his own face. He liked this Prince Bengallen and hoped he would not maim him too severely.

They were already standing nearly within arm's reach of one another. Brunsis leaped into the air, grabbing Bengallen at the wrist and kicking him in the chest. A strange and unexpected attack. The minotaur stripped the Prince of his sword, again, and rolled away, tossing the sword behind him.

Bengallen realized that his opponent assumed the sword to be more important than it was. The Paladin-Prince did not want to kill the minotaur either. Moreover, the creature once traveled with the mysterious Baron Tolthar who may have some connection to the tragedy in Morralish.

If he thinks I need the sword, however, that could be useful.

Bengallen tried to walk left around the minotaur to get to his sword. Brunsis shifted right to block him. Bengallen wheeled on his heels, turning right, but Brunsis effortlessly put himself between him and the sword once more.

The Paladin-Prince dove, anticipating a blow from Brunsis as he fell forward. He thought his opponent would attack from above and his falling would take some of the force from the blow. It was short sighted.

Brunsis had demonstrated himself a highly competent martial artist. The minotaur kicked upwards into the Prince's breastplate, the shock transferring throughout Bengallen's torso. The Prince lost his breath and found some small bit of breakfast returned to his mouth. He knew not to panic, however, instead controlling his breathing so that his breath could more easily return.

Bengallen rolled away, chest to back, at least four times as the crushing steps of Brunsis dropped behind him, missing again and again. All the while, the Prince took small, intentional breaths until Brunsis reached down to grab him.

In the same moment, Bengallen sprang forward, dodging the minotaur, and taking a deep breath as he came to his feet. Running around to the back of his opponent, the Prince, at the other side, collected the sword. He held it up, playing the fool, like acquiring the sword attained the victory.

Brunsis leaped left and caught Prince Bengallen around the torso with both arms. The minotaur tackled him to the ground, taking Bengallen by the wrist and slamming his hand repeatedly to the ground. The sword dropped again.

Yet Bengallen mostly ignored this. He head-butted the minotaur, his broad forehead to the creature's snout. Brunsis reeled back and Bengallen flipped them over, so that he was atop. The Paladin-Prince stepped on the minotaur's thighs with his shins, forcing the creature's legs apart as he leveraged himself against the ground, and pried himself from his opponent's grip.

Bengallen stood. Brunsis, flexible, brought his legs together, standing up right after, no worse for wear. Prince Bengallen had required, however, only that instant of lead time. As his opponent's face presented, before his feet were firmly planted, the Paladin-Prince delivered a devastating, steel armor-clad uppercut to the minotaur with his right hand. With his left, Bengallen grasped the off-balanced creature's snout from the top, flinging it downward. Sufficient force applied, the dazed minotaur fell, slightly sideways. Off balance, Brunsis dropped to a knee.

As the minotaur fell, Bengallen stepped opposite to the turn in his opponent's fall and, as they say, grabbed the bull by the horns. Hoisting himself up, he grappled his legs around the minotaur's waist. Twisting himself full to the creature's back, the Paladin-Prince began pulling the minotaur's horns apart as they toppled over into the mud.

Brunsis gathered himself quickly, but everything had happened that much more quickly. As the creature began to rise up, he could feel the pressure building within his head.

Bengallen, feeling the tension as well, whispered, "Yield or we see which gives first, your horn or your skull. So much as flinch and tis done."

Everything in the minotaur told him to attempt to fling or crush the Paladin-Prince, to make a last effort. Everything except the building pressure between his ears and his will to survive. Any move he made might have gotten the best of Bengallen, but not before Brunsis brains were in the mud.

"You tricked me," grunted the minotaur.

"Yield."

"Well played."

"Yield," Prince Bengallen growled sternly.

Abruptly, a crisp and unexpected POP sounded to their mutual dismay.

"Yield!" yelled Brunsis the minotaur, again and again, "I yield. I'm done. You win. I yield!"

Prince Bengallen released him, worried that it might have been too late.

Brunsis placed an open hand to either side of his head, pushing inward. Nothing happened. He opened his mouth and wiggled his jaw in about every direction possible, all while blinking. Nothing happened.

The minotaur sighed in relief.

Prince Bengallen, having stood his ground, allowed the minotaur a moment before extending a hand in respect.

Brunsis noticed, eventually. The two clasped at the wrist, a firm shake.

Still ahold of one another, Bengallen stated plainly, "You don't get to call me boy or princess anymore."

"Granted," Brunsis agreed, letting go of the Prince's arm, flexing his jaw again as he chuckled.

Prince Bengallen released the handshake at the same time and asked, "You said you've never missed a fight. How many have you lost?"

"Losing a fight is not so great a thing," Brunsis explained, "I learned how to win by remembering how I lost. When I was young I lost a lot. Now that I am older, I lose a lot less. Today is the first time I've lost in Woodhaven."

"Might we speak later?"

"Certainly."

Baron Tolthar Gerring, the noble visiting from Darrkeep, had once challenged Prince Bengallen to fight Brunsis. Yet events transpired that finally brought them together for their battle after all. Despite much the Prince wished to ask him, the matter of the elders and their votes remained.

"I assume you'll vote on the annexation proposal," Prince Bengallen asked the Elder-Lord Hroddan, "in a new light?"

"We shall," Hroddan answered directly, "in five days at our regular monthly voting session, Your Highness. I shall vote in favor of Woodhaven's annexation by Morralish. You have won my vote, and I am a man of my word. I doubt, however, wrestling in the mud with a monster has won you any votes beyond my own."

Politicians.

Chapter 10
Going Rogue

"Pah?"

"Yes, Vincent," Caanaflit replied, turning a page in one of the many books on his desk.

A young man – a boy in honesty – stood in the doorway and came through at the speaking of his name. Vincent's short stature, fuzzy black hair, and dark complexion were an interesting contradiction to the lanky, bald, and light skinned Caanaflit. As the boy drew closer, Caanaflit pointed to the seat across from him without looking up. Vincent sat there patiently.

A moment passed, Caanaflit closed his book, and addressed his young friend, "Okay, Vincent, what do you need?"

"Socynus is gone. That puts us down to eleven."

"Okay," Caanaflit acknowledged, "Are you sad? Can his duties be divided?"

"I'm worried, Pah," Vincent said, indignant, "More kids have come and gone than are here. They put us all at risk."

"So serious," Caanaflit laughed, "You are allowed to miss your brothers when they leave."

"Am I allowed to hate them when they turn us in for a hot meal or a quick escape from the stockade?"

"Children need parents until they don't, Vincent," Caanaflit explained to him, "They run away from home and return again. Eventually they grow up and leave home, but if things go badly, and they had a good home, they return. If they had a good home, they return from time to time, to visit. If they had a good home, they remain loyal to their family."

"So don't worry?"

"What will worrying accomplish?" Caanaflit asked, still amused, "Yet, you are certainly allowed to worry over your family. Tis normal, healthy, natural. We are building a family here. We will be here for your brothers and they will be out there for us."

"So they haven't really left?" Vincent asked, clearly unsatisfied and frustrated with Caanaflit's light-hearted approach, "They are still part of the family, just not living at home anymore."

"Fammilllee," Caanaflit leaned forward, his face sudden and serious as he drew out the word, "Family is forever."

Vincent smiled, a wicked smile for a child, but continued to sit patiently as Caanaflit stood, taking his cloak from a hook on the wall and flinging it about himself.

"Pah?" Vincent spoke to Caanaflit's back.

Pausing at the door, Caanaflit responded, "Yes, Vincent?"

"Are we working tonight?"

"I am."

"Then so am I."

"Good," Caanaflit affirmed, walking through his doorway and down the stairs, "Very good."

The Lord-Mayor's mansion in Spearpointe was as lavish as the hall of any noble south of Morralish Prime and east of Antoria Royal. It was, in short, fit for a king. As Caanaflit skulked its corridors in the midnight shadows and soft candlelight, he understood the Lord-Mayor all the better.

After living like this for nigh on three decades, how could a man live other? If he were of dubious merit, and admitted it to himself, of course he worried. Of course the man saw a threat to his way of life at every turn.

With the Beast of Spearpointe slain and the local goblins routed, many men of wealth had developed a taste for hunting. Necessary for survival to the common man, even in dire times, it had become a luxury sport with the surrounding woodlands made safe by the blood of heroes.

It was one of many things that Caanaflit bore disdain for. Having recently returned from Antoria, he was troubled by the ways that men of means did not live as though they were upon the Frontier, but as if they were amid civilization. Not so much on principle, but because he assessed these men.

Caanaflit discerned that they were not of a quality to live such luxurious lifestyles in the places conducive to them. These mediocre men with city ideals, came among superior – if not simpler – men and contorted the lives of the common folk, these otherwise freemen, to suit their otherwise unattainable wants and whims. *These tinpenny tigers deserved naught but contempt.*

Caanaflit had nothing against wealth, developing a right nice hoard of his own. Yet he would not amass a fortune on the backs of the less fortunate.

Moreover, he had made his money lifting people up and achieving suitable goals. It was Caanaflit who brought Bengallen to Spearpointe. It was Caanaflit who housed, fed, and clothed the orphans of these dark times: Boys who had gained skill and coin to call their own and pursue what life they would. Caanaflit lived a healthy life, eating well and worrying little over money, but neither did he flaunt or waste it. It was not jealousy that moved Caanaflit against the Lord-Mayor and his cronies, but disapproval.

Prominently displayed atop the Lord-Mayor's chest of drawers lay a smaller, ornate locked chest. Caanaflit approached it, the object of his current exploit, and examined its tiny, intricate locking mechanism. *Key driven*, to Caanaflit's relief, he pulled out a thin length of rigid wire. The rogue romanced the lock, a little to the left, right and up, until at last he had seduced the lid to spread open before him: The treasure he sought therein.

The long leather tube, commonly referred to as a map case, also served as the perfect receptacle for preserving parchment scrolls. Caanaflit pulled off the end cap and plucked out the various curled documents within. One was a deed to this property, which indicated that the Lord-Mayor had loaned the Free City-State of Spearpointe a large some of money and that, in lieu of two decades of interest payments, the city-state relinquished ownership of this mansion to the current Lord-Mayor and his heirs, regardless of their election.

Which was precisely to the point. Caanaflit rifled through the papers looking for a last will and testament. The Lord-Mayor had a wife, but no children of his own.

Who were his heirs?

Caanaflit knew that the Lord-Mayor's designated successor would have a strong claim to the office himself and sought to place someone favorable in that role. Forgery an art, Caanaflit possessed a master's stroke. It would be a small matter, if only he could find the will itself. Passing through another dozen or so equally disreputable documents, a veritable chronicle of the Lord-Mayor's abuse of office, the single sheet produced itself at last.

What did Caanaflit there find? He had to look twice to believe it himself. A happy accident? Mayhap the Lord-Mayor was turning a new leaf? He left little things to this friend or that relative, but it was his brother's son, Sir Jason, that he had named his principal heir and designated successor.

The very name that Caanaflit had thought to place there himself. Recalling the Lord-Mayor's approval of the young man when he returned to Spearpointe, knighted amongst the host of heroes. Despite the Lord-Mayor's suspicions of and misgivings toward Prince Bengallen, he had named his one relative, most loyally in the Prince's direct service, as his own heir.

It did not make much sense to Caanaflit. Unless... *unless the Lord-Mayor really did have a change of heart or had himself originally placed Sir Jason in Prince Bengallen's confidence for some nefarious purpose.*

Caanaflit pushed both thoughts from mind. Neither fit what he had seen. Caanaflit had come to know Sir Jason fairly well. The man, at that very moment, ranged west of the Lake with Twelve Names for no other purpose than to make contact with the local villages and do good deeds.

There was some chance that they might inherit Spearpointe's goblin problem. Accordingly, Sir Jason had made it his personal duty to protect them. He was clearly of like mind with the Prince.

Or was he? Caanaflit pushed the thought aside again. *Now who is being paranoid?* His task complete, Caanaflit returned the documents to their case, minus a bearer bond for a moderate sum, closed up the lock box, made sure it latched tight, and walked over to the window.

Two panes of glass, one opened left, the other right. He went out the window and hung there, from the top of the window, with the panes opened outward beside him. He shifted left, closing the right pane. He shifted right, closing the left pane.

With only a little lip to stand on, he bent his wire in an "L" and slipped it snugly between the panes. He could feel the wooden latch against the bent portion of the wire, rotating it until both were parallel to the ground.

Next, the tricky part, he lowered the wire, while holding the latch up with the point. As the wire moved down, the point scraped against the latch, moving closer and closer back to the pivot point.

Inching beyond that point, he pushed the wire back up. Point nearly perpendicular with the latch, he slid it upright. With enough force it would flip the rest of the way over and re-latch. So it did as Caanaflit dangled there, three stories above the ground in the middle of the night.

At that same moment, he felt something pulling at his cloak. He nearly lost his grip, if not for the small margin for error the tiny ledge at his feet provided. Righting himself, he felt it again. He looked down and around, seeing nothing but the black night all about him. Again, a third time, and he realized the jostling came from within one of the pockets sewn into the inside of his cloak.

Intriguing. Caanaflit thought as he began his descent.

He dared not linger near the mansion, so he made his way, quickly, to the nearest dark alley. There, he reached into the becalmed pocket and found the small, neglected thing, wondering if the black dragon brooch would try to call out to him again.

Chapter 11
Amassing Forces

Sir Jason and the companions with whom he had come to ride, called the Immortals, arrived at Woodhaven in the days following Prince Bengallen's martial contest. Worn and dirty, some were wounded, but their name had not yet been proven false. Sir Jason and his Immortals thundered through the city gates and rode straight to Bengallen's abode.

Jason whipped through the door and into the meeting room unceremoniously, speaking these words:

"Orcs! Lots of them. Your Majesty, they march and they come to here."

Prince Bengallen himself aided the exhausted Sir Jason in removing his breastplate and pauldrons, inviting, "Please, continue, sir."

"We were ranging on the wilder side of the Lake. We've taken several passes through the country there, further and further from the Lake each time; you wouldn't believe how far out we found farms, villages, isolated for generations. We've done more than a few good deeds out there, Your Majesty. Took down a troll, thanks to Thane Malcolm's tale, we knew to use fire."

Sir Jason paused only to nod a thanks to the half-orc compatriot seated near Prince Bengallen, before continuing.

"Cleaned out a few goblin hives, small, nothing like what had infested this side of the Lake. Anyway, on this pass, we came across utter desolation. Farms that looked to have been much like the others until recent times. Picked clean and burnt down, men, women, and children, defiled, murdered, and left to rot. We had heard of an orc tribe in the area, that they were unpleasant, but could be bribed off with supplies. At the first farm we assumed the negotiation had gone poorly, but as we traveled throughout the day, we found two farms likewise raided. That night we discussed the accounts of these orcs in light of these new attacks. They did not correlate well with our emerging map. So we rode out the next morning to find these orcs. When at last we found their camp, not so large, but all the men were gone."

"The attacks on those farms were the work of orcs," Malcolm interrupted with disgust in his voice, "I have seen this most of my life. The men leave the women behind when they go raid."

"And we thought the same," Sir Jason continued, "So we considered the farms and the order they appeared to have been hit. Like us, it seemed, the orcs were going roughly north. We eventually picked up a clear path, a lot of

50

moved earth for a single tribe. We came across other farms. Holy Family bless them, I say it. Found a man barely alive. He told us there were – and I did not believe him – 'hundreds beyond counting.' As terrible as this was, we're but a dozen men, so we decided to come here to request aid – except – They are coming here. We almost rode through them in the evening. We harried their flank as we rode around them. My men earned their name again that night, not a one of us fell. Though Bols took an arrow to the knee and I fear his adventuring days may be done. Another three days it has taken us to get here. So the horde, at their pace, is little more than a week out. And, Your Majesty, tis truly a horde. It must be every tribe east of Three God's Pass out there."

"There are dwarves ach'komen!" Traldor called out, "An army. I'll leave at once ta meet them. Mayhap they're yet close enough ta deliver aid."

Prince Bengallen went to the dwarf-lord, placing his hand on the other's shoulder with a doubtful look in his eye.

"How likely?"

"Yer Highness," Traldor began, "Not very, sorry ta say."

Malcolm was about to speak when Prince Bengallen looked up at him, shot him a glare and a turn of his head that said, "No." Malcolm remained silent.

"Lord Traldor, you may do as you think best. If the Dwarves lend aid in this too, I shall be thrice in their debt. Sir Jason, how many orcs?"

"Several thousand."

"Several thousand!" Ruffis shouted, amused, "Best shut the walls and reinforce them. I've taken the time to get to know the city watch here: A runt orc will take them down five at a time."

"So we need an army — again," Prince Bengallen said, continuing, "We'll have to call for aid from Spearpointe."

"By the time pigeons reach them and they can marshal what is left of the Company, this will have started. By the time they get here, it will be done," Sir Jason disagreed, "I think we need to evacuate the city."

"Abandon the greatest fortress in the Frontier!" a new voice challenged from outside this inner circle, "I will not abandon Woodhaven! Is this your idea of how to include us in your lordly protection? Abandon our city. Our walls have weathered orc raiders before. They will get hungry and they will go home."

Elder-Lord Hroddan, leader of the resistant faction of the Elder Council,

51

pushed his way into the conversation, planting his feet, arms crossed, intent to stand defiant.

Before he could settle, however, and the brazen smugness he intended to wear on his face had become too plain.

Malcolm strode over to him, delivering a warning, "This is no raid. A thousand orcs will knock every bowman from your walls. Two thousand orcs will tear down your walls with their bare hands. Several thousand orcs won't raid Woodhaven. They'll raze it. Annihilation, you have no defense against this. You are not prepared for this. There are at least four dozen clans, a dozen smaller tribes composing each, between here and Three God's Pass, that I know of. If they all have rallied, you won't be facing several thousand orcs, you'll be facing ten-thousand, more, even. They know that Antoria and Thalos are far to their backs. If they also know that Morralish will not ride out in retribution, there is nothing to stop them. They'll conquer the whole Frontier in a fortnight!"

Fear plain in Hroddan's eyes, he feigned bravery in his disbelief.

"Then why haven't they? This fear mongering won't earn you any new votes from the Elder Council! I— "

"'Tis beyond that now!" Prince Bengallen interjected, continuing, "Art thou blind? Hast thou eyes? No one here is playing politics. We men – and women – shall fight alongside your people, whatever choice may yet be made, whether to flee or stay, whether join my alliance, take up my banner, or fly your own alone forever. We believe in facing evil and protecting the innocent and not a soldier here would leave the good people of Woodhaven to face yon horde merely because our affairs of diplomacy have yet to conclude."

"I'm doing it too," the the Elder-Lord confessed.

Allowing himself to see the earnest countenance worn upon the Paladin-Prince's face in the impassioned plea, Hroddan took note of the solidarity in every face around them as he continued, "I kept telling myself that I wasn't like the Mayor of Spearpointe, that he was – that I was – Oh, my shame, I'm just like him. You, you all mean what you say. You want to strengthen and unify the Frontier. What more, you can actually do it. I eat my words. I can sway enough elders to follow me in changing our votes. Woodhaven is yours, Your Highn— Your Majesty. I cannot lead the people through this, but by the grace of the gods, mayhap you can. Let me hinder you no more."

"I was prepared to go on," Prince Bengallen admitted, "now you have caught me off-guard, good elder, and I can only thank his Lordship for the sensibility and courage to follow his change of heart. Lesser men would merely hold their position out of stubbornness, even unto the doom of us all."

"Your Majesty is too kind. I am quite stubborn."

"Would you please consult the city watch and the elders about what an evacuation would look like? Just so we are ready if it comes to that."

"You don't think it will?" the Elder-Lord asked, "Your Majesty did not seem so confident that the Dwarves were yet close enough."

"Dwarves, no, would we be so lucky," Prince Bengallen looked around, finding his wizard before continuing, "Shomotta, can we contact Caanaflit in Spearpointe?"

Shomotta looked uncertain at first, but realization soon washed across his face.

"If he's still there, yes. We still don't know if anyone else is listening, however."

"Then we don't say anything secret," Bengallen replied easily, "There are thousands of orcs marching on Woodhaven, not going to be a secret for too much longer. To face that, the city-state of Woodhaven, stalwart though it be, shall need all the help she can get. Nothing secret about that either."

"I'll use the device right away."

"What?" the Elder-Lord asked.

Prince Bengallen waved everyone away.

"We have many preparations to make. Whether or not any allies can get here, we've not a moment to waste."

Bengallen looked to the befuddled Elder-Lord, explaining as his thanes and soldiers went to work.

"We might have a magical means to get Spearpointe reinforcements en route a few days sooner than birds, but even if we do, that means withstanding a siege. Convene the elders and other leaders of the city. Find their thoughts on both siege and withdrawal. I shall join you shortly."

Chapter 12
Arriving Orcs

At midday, on the sixth day, they began to arrive. Far sooner than anyone expected. By nightfall, Woodhaven was besieged by orcs from more than two dozen clans! The best estimates counted seven thousand, the worst called it more than a full ten. In raw numbers, Woodhaven out numbered the orcs at least five to one, but not a tenth of those were fighters. *Hells, more than two-thirds of them were women or children, although plenty of them would be warriors before this was over.* Whether they would be enough to make the difference, was yet to be determined.

At final count, the city had less than a thousand stout bows, only half so many men properly skilled at using them. They had as many more of poor quality and assigned them to the boys old enough to fight, but too young to know how. Bows and bowmen aside, arrow supply remained the greater concern.

Aside from the archers, the city could field five thousand foot soldiers, less than a third with swords or respectable armor. Another five hundred properly outfitted cavaliers, with their total number rounded out to two thousand including the lesser men, horses, and equipment. Despite these deficiencies, the defense of Woodhaven would simply have to make do and would be glad to have all that it did.

Less than ten-thousand fighting men, more than half of them ill equipped and untrained. Upon the field of battle, a third of this force would not survive the initial contact. Yet this fight would not take place upon an open battlefield, where half as many orcs would kill twice as many poorly prepared men with little thought in the doing. Between them, not to be underestimated, the stalwart walls of Woodhaven stood. Moreover, there was magic in the city, alchemists, wizards, and a few priests with some knowledge of the higher mysteries of the Holy Family Church.

The orc were fierce, but the people of Woodhaven had the Heroes of Spearpointe on their side and, with their help, might yet survive to name heroes of their own.

For better or worse, 2,000 bowmen, 5,000 infantry, and 2,000 cavalry would face as many or more orc in the fight to come. The remaining few thousand men would travel with the southern evacuation, either because they refused to fight or there was nothing substantial with which to equip them. Public prayers were made to the Holy Family for their safe passage. In private, all – of those who did not curse them for cowards – prayed that the men among the evacuees might find the courage to stand to, should the women, children, wives, daughters, and young sons find some threat upon them. They would make for Burntleaf, traveling south upon the Frontier Road.

The Ironclaw Chieftain arrived on a mobile encampment surrounded by the largest army of orcs in living memory. The ger was pulled from the front by four dozen animals of mixed type. It was possible that they rounded up what animals they could and, eating the weak, had replaced them en route.

It rolled on four massive wheels, more than twenty feet apart, left to right, with nearly thirty feet front to back. Atop the wheels, a tent encampment was set up on a wooden disk, nearly forty feet in diameter. There was a clear main tent, center front, and half a dozen other tents, of various size, randomly arranged.

The Orc Chieftain's ger had traveled up what was called the Old King's Road. From a forgotten age, a road was built to connect the Antori Peninsula with the inhabited lands far to the north-east, what had become Morralish. It traced the massive forest, called the Dreadwood, from south, rounding east, to north. One might suppose that it had not always been called the Dreadwood, in past centuries, or else no one would have built a road along it in the first place.

In more recent times, the Dreadwood had come to earn its name. Though deep in its heart was the home of gentle creatures, such as elves and fairy-folk, its periphery was filled with monsters and mysteries. An alternate route was needed in this age, so a much longer route was found. It struck the middle distance, between the forest and the sea, including the great lake on its path. Many towns were founded along the way and, as it was solidified into the "Frontier Road," two fortified locations at either end of the lake, Spearpointe and Woodhaven, became free city-states of relative wealth and regional importance.

These orc, however, had taken the Old King's Road. It was laid with large stones, struck and placed when the world was young. Though some had been displaced or removed, this was rare. For those willing to brave such proximity to the Dreadwood, the way was easy and travel fast. For Blagrogk, the Orc Chieftain, many dangers of the Dreadwood, orc tribes, became allies and the other fell things cowed in the wake of his horde.

By the time they had traveled so far north as Woodhaven, the orc army rendezvoused with many others of their kind, already cutting a path across the countryside. That path brought them into the land beyond the lake, to the north, west of the river and near to Woodhaven. The army amassed there, cleverly beyond bow shot. Across the river, they waited until, late in the night, at last the gargantuan ger of the Orc Chieftain rolled into place.

Chapter 13
Making Love

Following the evening meal, many of the men not assigned to stand the watch, took to drinking. As the fight was imminent, this had been discouraged, but we all find our courage where we can. Thane Malcolm, as a leader, made a point to abstain, even as others of his elite cohort did not. Sira Roselle, having watched him leave, made a point to follow after him. She came up beside him, right outside the tavern.

"So you never told me about your adventure," Sira Roselle prompted him.

"Adventure, skha!" Malcolm attempted to dismiss in reply.

"...But an adventure, yes?"

"It was ugly and brutal, as are all things of the orc."

"Oh, come now," Roselle challenged him, "not all things. You are not so. You have always been quite gallant with me. Come. Walk with me. Tell me."

Malcolm gave Roselle his arm. She took it and he escorted her on a journey to nowhere in particular. He told her of his bravery and morality with as much humility as possible, but she made it very, obviously, clear that she was highly impressed.

Eventually they found themselves walking the fortified walls of Woodhaven. The escape of Malcolm's tale was not so far removed from their current plight and their subconscious minds ever drew them toward tomorrow's battle.

They approached a city watchman, who stood to with snap.

"We will take this watch until your relief comes," Roselle offered somewhere between a suggestion and an order, "Go check on one your compatriots, keep company, it is a terrible night to be alone."

"Aye, Sira," the watchman accepted.

Malcolm leaned a shoulder against the wall and the bulging relief of his muscles became outlined with shadow, bathed as he was in a soft moonlight, as he sighed, "So now we are on watch duty."

There they looked out over the mustering force of thousands of orcs. In the distance, he could see small torchlights, indicating that even more would be added to the enemy's number over the night.

"Look at them," Roselle said, gesturing out to the milling of the orcish horde,

"I don't think so lowly of your people as you do. They fail at morality – they've not been taught better – but their nature is one of strength and confidence, despite all else, can we not admire that?"

Malcolm rolled right, nearer to Roselle, placing his back flat to the wall and the orcs beyond it, speaking, "You'll not admire it so on the morrow."

She kissed him. Although he did not expecting it, the kiss had been her plan all along. With each word of his story, she only grew with desire. Finally, once they were at last alone, she kissed him.

He kissed her back. Malcolm hardly knew what he was doing, but he knew that she wanted it. He knew that he wanted it, mayhap to go on forever, so he did his best and kissed her back.

That is the secret about kisses: There is no secret. Some fools have opinions about what makes a good kiss or a bad kiss, but if you are kissing someone who wants you to, that you want to, it simply cannot be bad. Therefore, it was a good kiss. A long kiss, escalating into an escapade of good, long kisses.

Soon therein, hands began to explore each other's body. The thickly formed muscles of Malcolm's chest and stomach quivered like mere sacks of jam under the grasping of her solid embrace. His coarse hair clung to her hands and shot tingling needles through his skin, toward his heart. His rough hands played about all the soft and secret places of her body and she enjoyed the juxtaposition of their textures.

Some time passed, held in embrace, neither of them could be sure how much. It was an eternity of sensation in an instant of desire. Malcolm stopped, stopped them, holding her at slight distance.

"You are paladin."

"I am," she acknowledged.

"In all of magic, virginity is one of the most powerful forces. I would not rob you of it – on the eve of what is to come."

"You cannot rob something that is freely given."

"Still," Malcolm uttered.

"Be still," she replied, sweetness on her lips, "You have learned this from your books? All those legends of the nigh forgotten past."

"Indeed and, in the last year, I have seen so much of them, things once only dreamed of, proven as truth."

"There remains one power," she claimed, "that is yet greater."

"Love?" he whispered.

"True love, through what other force do the true gods act more truly?"

"I – ya-you love ... me?"

"I loved you from the moment you aided me in my first knightly contest. You, with no reluctance, treated me as what I had become, what I sought to be. Oh, Malcolm, how I have loved you for it," Roselle confessed, continuing with passion in her voice, "I have seen you, at my Prince's side, ascend in value and virtue and I could only love you all the more. You have faced the dark corners of your past and done nothing but shine light upon them. Now, as I worry over the onslaught of such darkness, you impart your company and courage upon me and, if that was not enough, where other men would take advantage, you still treat me with virtue and an earnest humility. Malcolm, how could I not love you?"

"I ..." there was a long pause as Malcolm cherished her words and struggled for his own, "I am but crudely formed in the likeness of men. I did not presume any woman could love me."

She wept. Not overly, but tears streamed from her face as she kissed him.

"Am I so beautiful? Beyond my marriageable years. Now thick with muscles and hands so full of scars. Yet, I have seen how you look at me. You are rugged, but so what, but so am I. You are strong, your body hard, your words clever, your heart noble. You are beautiful to me."

Malcolm took her fully then. They shared an embrace and he kissed the tears from her cheeks.

"You are beautiful, Sira. I never thought to tell you. I thought you knew. Never considered that you may not know. You are beautiful. I will show you," Malcolm told her, placing his hand around the back of her thigh, "With the moon as our lord and the stars as our witnesses, I make you mine and I become yours. Let us give to each other the only gifts we have to give and take our love with us into the morrow's battle."

Roselle could but swoon.

So Malcolm and Roselle were married that night, in the old way. They made love under the open sky. They literally made love. They brought all their emotion and innocence to bear in the crucible of their passion and, when the night was over, there was more love in the world than there had been the previous day.

58

Chapter 14
Besieging Woodhaven

The Siege of Woodhaven began less than an hour before noon. Blagrogk strode out from his mobile encampment, stepping down, out onto the battlefield. Climbing up the single siege tower possessed by his horde, at the top, fist in the air, he roared. In reply, the front line began its advance toward the river and the city walls beyond.

Blagrogk's fist was an interesting sight. In his off hand, he wielded a bizarre shield that looked like two axe heads on either end of a short iron club, itself locked into an over-sized gauntlet. Odd though it was, it was almost unnoticed compared to the prosthetic fist and forearm attached to Blagrogk, replacing what had been severed by Alpona.

It looked like a massive mace, like the head of a warhammer had replaced his hand. Except it was neither. The appendage appeared as the base of a tree, where trunk bulges and the roots begin. Wood twisted in a way that exaggeratedly mimicked muscles and entwined together at the terminus, a knot. There it formed into the dire cudgel that replaced the orc chieftain's hand.

Alpona distinctly remembered cutting fairly close to the wrist. This tree trunk prosthetic, however, went all the way up to Blagrogk's elbow, where it ended in a spike that extended and laid perfectly, almost hidden, against the back of his upper arm. It was a well-designed device and appeared beyond the ken of orcs.

Shomotta took the spyglass back from Alpona, saying, "Think this is when we signal the archers."

Alpona the Athgonian came out from under the canopied battlement and onto the rampart wall. For a long moment, the unusual visage of Alpona's best approximation of Zil-jahi armor, especially the almost triangular helm, was the only silhouette visible to the orc army. He raised the ancient Flammerung, its flames flicked dramatically, even in the full light of day, and a full two hundred archers rose up, bows drawn. Alpona chopped the greatsword through the air and the bowmen loosed their arrows at the oncoming enemy.

At the same moment, nearly two miles away, Ruffis heard Shomotta's voice communicating to him through a black dragon brooch, "The attack has begun. Arrows away."

Ruffis waved to Prince Bengallen and Malcolm from a rooftop and they opened the south-east gate to begin the evacuation. Ruffis thought about the orcs advancing across both bridges as he climbed down from the roof. They had intended to take out the larger wooden bridge, even possibly damage the stone one, but the army of orcs arrived so much more quickly than anticipated.

The dark elf retreated further into his mind as he went into the home and lowered himself into the secret door that passed through the floor. Ruffis had been this way before, recalling his last time coming this way:

"What do you wan' 'ere inny way, helf?" he remembered the way the hoodlum spoke down to him with disdain.

Ruffis held his contempt for once, he did want something after all, and replied, "There is a secret way in and out of the city, you know of it?"

"Fa course."

"If there is an evacuation, a large amount of loot could be removed from the city this way, you think?"

"Mayhap ya sho let us do da tinkin' round here, helf."

"I know about the plan. If you can get a crew to help me get something out sooner, I won't tell anyone."

"Soona?" the thug questioned, "You wanna move somethin' out thar, weres all the horks is, before they be inside?"

"Yes."

"You crazy!"

"Yes."

The hoodlum blinked at him.

Initially unsure how to reply, he ventured, "Well wadda ya wan' den?"

"Can you steal magic goods?"

The thug clearly did not want to unveil his master plan and said nothing.

"I know you intend to rob the apothecaries and the wizards," Ruffis relented, "Their shops are full of the lightest and most valuable goods. It's obvious. I just want to know how you are getting in and if you could loan me a dozen men. What I want to steal is not what you want to steal. You take what I want, then you take what you want. You store it down here until you're ready to leave the city."

"Money."

"How much? Aren't you already going to be weighted down with magic trinkets more valuable than gold?"

"Still. Rep'uah'ta'shun an all."

"Fine. There is twenty gold coins," Ruffis said, tossing a clangy sack to the ground. When the thug bent over to pick them up, the dark elf pulled a knife, from what the onlookers described as nowhere, and stabbed the man in the neck. Looking up, he called to the shadowy corridor, "You. You there. You want to help me or do I have to kill all of you tonight?"

A man, who Ruffis only ever described as "looking exactly like the one he just killed," came out from the shadows and agreed to help. Several hours into the night, Ruffis had six large sacks of the explosives the alchemists had been making. Prior to dawn, he had personally floated all six down the river and placed them precisely.

He knew Prince Bengallen kept him around because he was useful. He also knew that the Prince did not think terribly highly of him. Rather than try to sell his plan to the Prince, Ruffis went off on his own way and made himself useful.

More than two miles away and underground, Ruffis felt safe. He activated the black dragon brooch and called upon Shomotta, "Can you make a fire under the bridge?"

"No," Shomotta answered.

"What do you mean, 'no'?" Ruffis replied.

"I mean no. I cannot."

"Like not with magic or anything?"

"We are fighting a war out here," Shomotta continued, "I cannot get into the specifics of why not, but no."

"Flaming arrows!"

"We have some, but they won't burn the bridge down, they're pouring across it as we speak."

"Under the bridge!" Ruffis exclaimed.

"What?"

"Trust me. Fire – under the bridge – then take cover."

Immediately, Shomotta knew what had happened. He had personally overseen the movement of the ordnance to the west wall and thought some were missing. At the time he dismissed it as pessimism, *but that sneaky thief…*

"Alpona," Shomotta said, stopping his friend from reloading, "come with me!"

Most of the archers were arrayed along the balustrades to the south of their battlement, but Shomotta led him north. They moved from a place with a mostly straight-on view of the bridge, to one where they could see its side at more of an angle. Shomotta pulled an arrow from the quiver and, left hand, held it at the middle.

First, he focused, touching the fletching at the rear and whispering, "trooha."

Next, he touched the ancient greatsword, Flammerung, whispering "scanda" as he moved his right hand to the arrowhead.

Finally, Shomotta reverently handed the arrow to Alpona, who wore an impatient look on his face.

"Shoot this arrow beneath the bridge."

"What am I aiming for?"

"There should be something attached to the beams, but it won't matter. Just get it under the bridge."

Alpona nocked the arrow, pulled the bowstring, and loosed the missile. It soared straight and true and disappeared under the bridge. In the same instant, Alpona felt Flammerung grow cold against his back and a flame erupted underneath the bridge. It barely startled a few of the frenzied orcs. Yet, in the following moment, those same orcs were flying in a dozen directions along with the splinters of the bridge.

The explosion posed no threat to the men upon Woodhaven's wall, let alone Ruffis, two miles across the city and underground, but he did not know that. As for the orc's below, they bottle necked at the smaller stone bridge, which was also damaged and made narrower in the blast.

"What the hell!?" Alpona shouted, with some relief as the cold feeling to his back abated.

Shomotta touched the black dragon brooch and called to Ruffis, "Brilliant. You missed a spectacular show. Now we need your help patching the wall before the orcs find another way across."

Alpona looked to the wall again. *It was fine.*

"Ruffis planted some of the alchemist's explosives under the bridge last night without telling anyone," Shomotta explained, "He didn't know how big the boom would be. If he gets pissy about my exaggeration of the damage, tell him we lied because we didn't know who might be listening in on us."

Alpona laughed. He drew arrows and began firing at the larger clusters of orc storming toward the wall because he could not stop laughing long enough to make a proper aim.

Chapter 15
Defending Woodhaven

The first wave of the orc horde beat upon the walls of Woodhaven. Archers, the accuracy and lethality of many aided by the eldritch power of mages, rained down the city's limited supply of arrows to great effect. With the wider bridge blown and a bottleneck in place, for a brief time it seemed as if the orcs, all of them, might be slaughtered there, in what Shomotta dubbed, "the kill zone," between the walls and the river. While the orc were not generally known for their intellect, they did know how to fight, and with half the city's supply of proper arrows already exhausted, reality grounded hope. This enemy knew how to win and could be counted upon to change tactics any moment.

So they did, withdrawing to the river in a defensive posture, more than a thousand orc had been disastrously slaughtered. Yet more converged at the river with them, the number of their advancing horde swelling. Their chieftain had disappeared from atop the siege tower.

In hindsight, that should have been the first sign. It continued forward, unabated and turned about. The orc dropped the tower, back to front, across the river and, without pause, began to storm across its flat surface.

The makeshift bridge dropped into the Umber. North and above stream of the mostly intact stone bridge, which securely braced the new crossing, so it did not wash down into the Lake. Before it had even settled into place, a mixture of orc archers and torchbearers packed across the widened bridge.

Counter archers picked the brave Woodhavers from the city walls with lethal accuracy. As pitch and torch made their way to the city gate, the tide began to turn in favor of the orcish onslaught.

The Woodhaven bowmen began to hide more and shoot less as they ran out of proper arrows and began to take significant casualties. Hastily firing the poorly made arrows, with their off wood and sorry fletching, had little effect and, evidently, was not worth the losses the defenders were taking in the exchange with the orc's own archers. All in all, the bowmen had slew an orc for each man that had stood the wall, achieving a respectable casualty ratio of four to one when, at last, Alpona ordered them to withdraw from the battlements.

With the walls abandoned and the gate all but breached, Woodhaven did the unthinkable. Woodhaven was its walls. This was a dire day. Sacrifices had been made. Many more would yet would be. They sacrificed the western wall. Magical ordnance fell from the ramparts onto the sieging forces below.

The explosions reduced the walls to rubble, but they incinerated the orcs beyond, between the wall and the river, reducing them to nothing. Another thousand orcs had vanished in fire, smoke, and shrapnel. The evacuation continued unimpeded and the odds returned to stand in Woodhaven's favor.

With the western wall strewn about, a mounded debris field, a second wave of orc would have to dig through the mess or come around to the north of the city to the Northeast Gate and the Frontier Road. Unexpectedly, they did both. They had the numbers. Yes, the orc knew how to fight.

At first, as they began crossing at their new bridge, splitting off as they did, it seemed foolish to divide their forces. Soberingly, the Prince and his thanes realized that the evacuation, incomplete, continued. This meant that Woodhaven too would have to split her forces. To defend the battle line, in the west, as well as the evacuation, to the east.

"I'll take the Immortals and a hundred skilled riders," Sir Jason told Prince Bengallen, as the leadership reconvened at Bavin Hall, "The orc have no cavalry. They are running round the city like an undisciplined pack of dogs. A hundred riders will cut them to shreds."

"They'll form up as they get closer to the gate," Malcolm warned.

"All the more reason to strike fast and first," Sir Jason drove his point, "We have twice as far to go, across the city within and back around to meet them beyond. Every moment we plan, they send more troops and have more time to assemble."

"The evacuation will be complete," Prince Bengallen interjected, "We can move the whole of our force to the rear, to guard them, to prevent those orcs from pursing. Victory there, we can then re-take the city."

"That's not the plan –" Alpona began to explain, but was cut short by the impassioned knight.

"Your Majesty," Sir Jason pleaded, "Victory. Re-take the city. You lead bloodied survivors back into this city, with the orcs holding the high ground, we'll be killed to a man and can only hope to take them all with us."

Prince Bengallen began to disagree, but remembered a song of his ancestor, played for him on a lute by a girl he once saved. He saw the grim countenance shared by Alpona and Malcolm. These things moved him. He swallowed and altered his words, "You are right. There is no time to plan this fully. Your tactic will hold them, but they are many. Sir, you are a fine knight and have exceeded my expectations in all things. I will not order you to do this. Yet neither will I stop you."

Alpona's disapproval increased while Malcolm's lessened.

"I know my duty, Your Majesty," Sir Jason said, "and I have learned my trade well. We ride!"

"Make a path for them. Through the infantry. Have them to arms," Bengallen ordered, in the general direction of this thanes.

They did so as Jason rallied his Immortals and selected his other riders for his cavalry charge. The foot soldiers had assembled and made a way through their ranks, all holding weapons aloft in salute. At the last were Bengallen and his mighty thanes. The Dawnsong shining clear and the Flammerung burning bright flanked their exit like beacons.

Sir Jason put orders to his riders, then called to them.

"For justice. For Woodhaven. For our lord and king! We ride!"

No time for speeches. No time for a parade trot. That they pulled together a send off at all was luxury they could ill afford. So, with few words, the Immortals charged down through the way made for them and tore through the vacant city.

"To the line!" Bengallen ordered the infantry as the last horseman cleared.

"To the line!" echoed, time and again, throughout the rough columns of foot soldiers.

"You should have ordered him," Alpona told Bengallen as the city defenders reorganized themselves.

Prince Bengallen thought to rebuke Alpona, but his heart was not in it.

Instead, he replied with, "I know."

66

"You shouldn't let me talk to you like that either," Alpona pushed again.

"I know," insisted the Prince.

"These men need to see your confidence in them," Alpona pushed even further.

"They have. They will. Just," Bengallen fumbled with the thought before continuing, "Sir Jason just rode to his death and I couldn't do that to him."

"I know," Alpona relented, partially taking up the Prince's own tone and words, "But he was riding to his death either way. You could have at least given him your word and will to lean upon in doing."

"Easier said than done," Bengallen finally pushed back, "You are not the one who has to live with that order."

"I'm not the one trying to be a king," Alpona dared, "I only know that I too follow you and – and I hope that if I too must die for your cause one day, that you make me believe I can win, even if I know I cannot. I've asked you for nothing, but now I ask you for this, Your Majesty, that you have the courage to take the responsibility for my life and death."

Prince Bengallen walked away from their private aside. There were no words. He returned to Bavin Hall where the leadership convened once again.

"Your Majesty," Malcolm said, catching Prince Bengallen at the door, "You gave him the choice. You did him no wrong."

"Neither did I do right by him," Bengallen replied, "I was selfish in the face of Sir Jason's selflessness. May the Holy Family strengthen his resolve and forgive my weakness. Neither of us can afford any less in the trials we yet face this day."

Chapter 16
Charging Immortals

The Last Charge of Sir Jason & His Immortals

Half a league outward,
From city wall's safe abode.
Half a league onward,
As along the river flowed.
"Forward for hearth and home!"
"Forward, faith and fidelity!"
"For whatever love you've known!"
They charged in solidarity.
"Forward, fine companions!"
Ne'ery a cavalryman dismay-ed.
O soldiers through and through,
Theirs was not to make reply,
Theirs was not to reason why,
Theirs was but to do or die.
Rode the brave one-hundred.

They clashed upon the enemy swarm,
Each smote a spray of blood-red,
Did they true, their duty's due,
Through the foemen line they broke,
Possessed by all their hearts bespoke,
Villains felled by swords' swift stroke.
Rode the brave one-hundred.

Trampling their hooves a' thundred.
Enemy upon the river's bank,
Enemy on the western flank,
Enemy afore and aft,
For lo they were surrounded;
Assailed upon by claw and spear,
Rode, they bold, no heed of fear,
Into the maw of Death,
Into the jaws of Hell,
Rode the brave one-hundred.

The battle's tide yet turned.
They prayed their lives not squandred.
Gallant steeds lost their speed,
Riders falling through the air.
Horses charging, panicked, bare,
Men but tossed, here and there,
Shattered and sundered.
Only one who e'er rode back.
One of the one-hundred.

Victory achieved at dearest cost.
The river yet flowed pink and red.
One given word, heeded and heard,
As e'ry horse and hero fell,
Even those who rode so well,
Souls upon celestial ships did sail
But for one of the one-hundred.

Their glory it shall never fade,
Though loosed of mortal coils.
O wild the charge that they made,
The charge of Jason and his Immortals!
Save one so that the story spake,
The world not left to wondered.
To honor, then, his brothers' fate,
How rode the brave one-hundred!

Chapter 17
Going In

The orc were clearing rubble on the other side of the fallen walls, digging out the gate. The exhausted citizen-soldiers of Woodhaven could hear it more than see it. Occasionally, a man was sent up the debris heap to spy their progress. Less occasionally, he took a potshot with the few inferior arrows that remained. Even less occasionally, such a man would hit his mark. That was until the orc reinforced their diggers and began shooting back.

It was not too long before the tide began to turn once more. The height of the rubble began to tumble down. Dark heads and yellow eyes began to peer over the top and the 'occasionallies' began to belong to the enemy. Before long, the gate would be dug out and, so cleared, the orc would pour in the way made. Time was limited.

"I should go back. I need to go and look at his tent one more time," Shomotta said, his voice littered with doubt as he paced Bavin Hall.

"You've seen it a dozen times already," Ruffis challenged, "you've left to go back twice since we've got here."

"Three times, then," the wizard-priest declared, "Three is a number of power. Three for the Holy Family."

Alpona placed his hand on Shomotta's shoulder. With no excitement or nervousness, in a calm and confident voice, he told his friend, "You can do this."

Prince Bengallen and Sira Roselle entered the room.

"I wish I was going with you," the lady-knight entreated.

"Welllll..." Ruffis replied unhelpfully.

"Once again, I need you to lead the charge in my stead," Prince Bengallen told his faithful knight, "On our signal, bring down the wrath of God."

She nodded, taking a torch from Malcolm, who had two, handing it to Bengallen.

"Are you ready?" Bengallen asked the wizard, not without confidence, but in sincere uncertainty.

Shomotta swallowed, closed his eyes a moment, answering with a question, "Are you, Your Majesty?"

Bengallen replied quickly, "Nay do I like the sound of that."

"I can do it," Shomotta said plainly, sweat streaming down his face. "but if we end up wrong – I warned you."

"The Hells does he mean by 'wrong'?" Malcolm asked.

"There are so many things that can go wrong, that seemed the best way to generalize it," Shomotta explained.

"The word 'best' just became a lot more relative," Ruffis teased, laughing at his own joke or mayhap at the whole situation.

Everyone looked at him like he was crazy. Alpona tightened his hand on the wizard-priest's shoulder to lend him strength.

Shockingly, Bengallen also laughed, saying, "A lot of firsts today. So here is one more. I'm with Ruffis. Let us do this."

Shomotta walked up to the front door of Bavin Hall and stretched his arms out wide, an open palm pointed to either door side of the door frame. It had been covered with recent markings, runes, arithmetic, and intersecting geometric shapes. Placing each hand to the frame and grasping each side, Shomotta formed the picture of Blagrogk's tent in his mind.

It was hazy, so he sharpened it. He tried to think of every last detail. The clasps that held the flaps open. The ropes tied to the clasps. The angle at which they met the surface. The difference in shade from the brown of the outer hide and the tan of the inner flaps turned outward.

Shomotta breathed in and out. His gasps became whispers. His torrent expirations became prayers. He prayed to the Father to bless them. He prayed to the Mother to sing of this moment. He prayed to the Son to stir the magic in his blood. He prayed to Saint Amar to give him the clarity to fight in the moments that would come after. It was his only concession to a thought outside of the task at hand. Each time his focus threatened sway, his mind dared to stray, the wizard-priest's iron will grasped the pieces of the moment

71

in time and forced them together according to his resolve.

Where once there had been an opening to the street outside of Bavin Hall, a rectangle of roiling darkness snapped into existence, filling the doorway. Shomotta slowly backed away, careful to retain his hands and arms at their distance and position. Making enough room between himself and the doorway, the portal, for the others to pass, he simply stated, "Now."

Prince Bengallen leading the way, he and his mighty thanes stepped through the portal, weapon in one hand, torch in the other. They emerged atop the large ger, in the middle of the orc army, with the opening of Blagrogk's tent behind them, roiling the same strange inky void as the portal they had entered.

Ruffis held two torches. When Shomotta, himself the last to come through, the dark elf stuffed the burning torch into the wizard's right hand as Alpona placed the scimitar into his left. As anticipated, Shomotta was forced out from the tightened coils of his inner mind by the need to concern himself with handling flaming torch and sharpened sword. The conjured portal faded accordingly.

"Th-thank you," Shomotta said, remarkably clearly.

No one ended up wrong. Everyone was immediately relieved, but there was no time for congratulations. Besides, they were in the midst of an enemy army, surrounded on all sides by orc. Congratulations would have been drastically premature.

"Burn it. Everything," Prince Bengallen commanded them.

Malcolm walked around to the back of the tent. Alpona tossed his torch onto the roof, needing two hands to wield the mighty Flammerung, cleaving the first baffled orc sentry, shoulder to groin. Ruffis sat his torch next to some crates at the front of the tent and drew his twin blades. Shomotta, to his own amazement his mind rapidly became fully present, tossed his torch into the tent. Another orc sentry came out from within and Ruffis stabbed him in the throat and eye as Shomotta placed both hands to his scimitar.

It was Malcolm's turn to laugh. Behind the main tent, he came upon a mostly empty trough of what was certainly some sort of oil or grease. Malcolm, holding his torch at opposite length, grabbed up an end of it, spilling the contents and slinging some in a crude half circle as he tossed the troff aside. He dropped the torch and the viscous fluid blazed immediately. Holding the Dawnsong before himself, she catching the light, humming gently in the afternoon sun, Malcolm rejoined his embattled companions.

Prince Bengallen came off of the ger's platform and went beneath it. As the craftsmen of Woodhaven had speculated, the great wheels were greased, significantly. The wood all round was soaked with oil. The Paladin-Prince had only to hold his torch to it for a short moment before the wheel and its mounting were both aflame. As he went across the axle to the other side, he heard it.

"Help!" a boy called, not in Antori, but in the Morralish tongue. There were not only animals pulling the mobile encampment, there were people beneath it too.

Undaunted, Prince Bengallen went to the opposite wheel and set it aflame as well. There he found four men and an orc bound in place with an extension of the axle before them, to be pushed when ordered.

Bengallen freed the men, imploring them, "Free the others, at the back of this thing, then hide. Tis about to get violent and you should save what strength you have left."

They lurched off together.

"What for me?" The orc spoke in common Antori.

"I was getting to that."

"I no fight agint me kin," the orc continued, "and no fight wid dem eadder."

"You'll flee? You'll run away?" Bengallen asked.

"Yeah!"

"Then go!"

The Paladin-Prince, in his mercy, cut the binding and turned back to aid those he had left at the other fire. It had gotten out of control in a hurry.

Darting through the flames, Prince Bengallen arrived to find five men and – not a boy – an elf. At least one of the men was already being burned by the fire, so Bengallen freed them wordlessly.

Only once finished adding, "The others are hiding to the back!"

No time for guilt, no matter how badly they were burnt, they would heal.

Survive the battle. Wounds would heal.

Above, things continued to get interesting. The main tent had collapsed in on itself and, consumed in fire, was billowing black smoke. Orcs appeared to advance from nowhere, or everywhere, and set upon the thanes in ever increasing numbers. Undaunted, they handled themselves, and the orcs, with the astonishing proficiency for which Bengallen's thanes had become known.

An inner circle of orc heads and arms surrounded them. A circle of corpses had formed a couple feet out from that, along with the handful of wounded orcs attempting to crawl and roll away even as their own trampled them. It was at least three dozen enemy, defeated, when they stopped coming.

Alpona had suffered a cut of uncertain significance, near the shoulder on his left arm, right below his armored pauldrons, and Malcolm had been stabbed in the leg, but his armor limited the depth of the wound to superficial. Ruffis was nicked in the ribs and Shomotta's knuckles were busted, but everyone was, clearly, still fighting effectively.

Sira Roselle watched from a surviving battlement, to the south of Woodhaven's west wall. She saw some figures in the distance, some small smoke trickling up from the camp. Then, like the signal it in fact was, a column of smoke began to pour from the center of the orc army. It only continued to increase in size and thickness.

"Smoke!" Sira Roselle called as she came down from the balustrades, "Smoke!"

There, at their ramp, her noble steed, Thumu, stood at the front of nearly two thousand cavalry; her lance loosely lashed to his saddle. Most of their men were not expert riders. Most of their horses, not trained to charge. So they put the best out front, hoping the rest, man and beast alike, would follow in fashion.

"There is the signal!" Sira Roselle called as she seated herself upon her mount, "Over the wall!"

Everyone had readied for it, were as ready as they could be. It all happened so swiftly. She affixed the pole with the sky blue Hastenfarish banner, griffin ascendant, to the leather mounting built into Thumu's tack. Instead, Sira

Roselle took up her lance, leading the cavalry up one of the dozen ramps the citizen-soldiers dropped into place, over the remaining shrinking rubble mound.

"Charge!"

They fell upon the digging orcs, taking their bow-wielding skirmishers, who were only expecting another scout or two, completely by surprise. The cavalry charge trampled, cutting a swath through the orcs at the ruined wall and the infantry foot soldiers piled over behind them, pressing the advantage.

Bengallen ascended the stairs to the encampment about half way. Seeing the smoke – all fires combined, there was plenty of it – he paused, calling to his thanes.

"The whole thing's coming down. Get clear!"

Alpona and Ruffis did not wait. They both dropped off the side, turning about to catch it and dangled a moment, before dropping the rest of the way to the ground. Bengallen met them there as Shomotta and Malcolm descended the stairs right behind him. The three at the bottom were immediately set upon by orcs, returning from the forward lines, responding to the fire, and there were even more coming behind them.

Malcolm noticed the animals, leashed to the ger, were beginning to panic. He bumped Shomotta, pointed, and they both ran toward them. Leash after leash, Malcolm cut them free and Shomotta, right behind him, roared at them, waving his arms wide, and encouraging them to run forward, toward the oncoming enemies.

A few bolted wildly. Before they set the last one free, however, the random livestock had become a menagerie stampede, trampling at full hoof toward the front lines. A bloody mess ensued.

The heroes had reassembled, still fighting off the few orcs not tackled by the stampede, when the left ger wheel gave with a deafening CRACK! The disk dropped on its south-east corner and things began to slide off of it in that direction, raining down upon Bengallen and the others. As they moved away, a second CRACK heralded the collapse of the other forward wheel and everything, tents, furniture, orcs, flames, all of it, slid off the whole front as the ger touched the ground, bowing to the east.

Few of the stampeding animals made it through the orc lines, into the clear.

An odd sight indeed as stray cattle, of every sort, charged alone, advance of the enemy, toward the cavalry drawing ever closer to their orcish foes. Sira Roselle allowed her focus to drift. She laughed. Despite the distance between them, she felt like Malcolm and the others had found a way to tell her a joke, even amidst the battle.

Alpona and Shomotta found themselves buried under some debris. Ruffis and Malcolm, respectively, had aided them immediately. Bengallen decapitated one foe and tripped another, as he turned and saw it, calling to his thanes.

"Watch out! Beside you!"

The four turned about quickly, easily spotting the orcs, apparently still in tents when the ger collapsed, rising from all around them. Ruffis found one still tangled in a tent on the ground and stabbed him in the neck and back a few times. As Bengallen joined them, Malcolm and Alpona had already locked their swords with the axes of a pair of orcs and Shomotta was uttering a spell.

Shomotta hurled his scimitar at Bengallen's left, striking an orc square in the chest. The Paladin-Prince turned to see this and also saw many more orcs advancing on them. Some wounded by the stampede, others fresh, their attention only recently drawn to the center of their camp. Worse still, the orcs to the rear of the ger had surely been alerted as well.

"About to be surrounded!" Shomotta called, as Prince Bengallen and the wizard-priest's own scimitar, arrived at his side.

"You dropped this," Bengallen said nonchalantly, handing over the sword.

"You're welcome, Your Majesty," Shomotta accepted.

"We were already surrounded," Ruffis reminded them, "Went in knowing that, well, at least I did."

"Yes," Bengallen agreed, "but now tis imminent."

Chapter 18
Raging Orc

Alpona and Malcolm fell back to their allies. They formed a circle, backs to the center. The blood on Ruffis' twin blades began to sizzle, but smelled of old oak and new honey. Alpona's greatsword burned intensely with arcane fire. Shomotta whispered a secret to his scimitar and its edge was traced in a line of starlight. Prince Bengallen was surprised to see the borrowed broadsword he wielded aglow with the Light of Van. Malcolm's greatsword caught the reflection of it all and sang soprano as though a choir of angels. There was a dark sorcery in their midst.

A few dozen feet from them, a chest and a shelf flew apart, up and away from the ground to which they had fallen. The orcs digging about in their vicinity were staggered back as Chief Blagrogk himself burst free from under them. His strange twisted, tree-like mace-arm pointed skyward.

Blagrogk brought the warhammer down before him. A shockwave traveled outward, clearing a path between his ambushers and himself. Only then did he and Malcolm lock eyes and death became destiny. At least one of them would not leave this battlefield.

The Orc Chieftain and a ragged band of his elite guard charged forward. Alpona closed in first. Blagrogk swung his arm out wide, batting the Zil-jahi warrior aside. The uncanny reach of his weapon appeared to elongate even as it struck.

Recovering his balance quickly, Alpona spun on his heels to re-engage the foe, but another came at him from behind. He flipped his magical greatsword behind him, a blind rear block, only possible with so long a blade. The attack, only barely parried, distracted Alpona.

Ruffis pretended to let the Orc Chief pass him, as though focused on some other fighter. At the last moment, however, the dark elf lunged toward Blagrogk's left flank. Either by his own misjudged timing or his opponent's lightning reflexes, Ruffis' attack failed. The Orc Chief, pumping his arms as he ran, brought his bizarre shield-like weapon up to his side, pushing out and smashing the flat of it into Ruffis' face.

Alpona and Ruffis became engulfed in a rolling fight against many elite orcs.

At last, Malcolm squared off against his father, Blagrogk, Chieftain of the

Ironclaw Orc Clan and, here apparently, general to an orc alliance conjured from nightmare.

Malcolm felt responsible. *Was this vengeance? It certainly was not coincidence. Would every life lost in this battle be the price of Malcolm's ... what? Freedom? Self-worth? Vanity? Could a man be fairly blamed for the tantrums of his oppressor, when merely taking back what every man should have by right of existence?*

It was Blagrogk's sin. All of it. It was his sin to rape women. It was his sin to enslave others. It was his sin to treat his children like pawns and property. The Ironclaw Chieftain bore his son malice, but even that was a sin of his own making. Whatever transpired this day, the blood was firmly in the hands of its perpetrator.

Malcolm needed that peace of mind. The concern that this was all, somehow, his fault had lingered with him. Ever since Prince Bengallen had silenced him at the report of this advancing army, the doubt grew. Finally, he had exercised it like a demon, but mayhap too late.

Malcolm lashed out at his father as these thoughts came to the surface. His angst and concern weakened him, dividing his focus. His rage and doubt unbalanced him, robbing his clarity of spirit. Even his relief and revelation betrayed him, the euphoria blinding him to a thunderous blow.

The two traded a swift series of strikes, parries, and dodges. At last Chief Blagrogk connected, bashing Malcolm with an upward swing of his mallet fist, lifting his son from the ground, with a strike that sent him, through the air, several feet away.

Prince Bengallen upon him, strike already underway, Blagrogk turned and his strange fist unfolded. Six distinct tentacles unfurled and resisted the Paladin-Prince's attack. Two each wrapped around Bengallen's wrists and a third around his throat. Another pushed against his chest. A fifth reached to the back of the Prince's head, pushing it downward. While a sixth grasped the sword blade directly, absorbing the strike.

That one, burning in the Light of Van, withered, cut away, destroyed in the process. Blagrogk ignored this, dragging Bengallen down, off his feet. He slammed the Prince's face into the ground.

Pulling his right arm back sharply, the Orc Chieftain thrust his elbow spike into Shomotta's ribs. Nearly so, but the approaching wizard-priest's leather

78

armor slowed and deflected the blow. Landing thus, it pierced only his side, rather than completely gutting him.

In the same instant, Blagrogk dropped down on his left arm, attempting to decapitate Bengallen with the strange shield of axe heads, but the Paladin-Prince rolled away at last instant. The shield slammed to the ground and Shomotta took the chance to chop at the Orc Chieftain. Yet as the wizard's blade came down, Blagrogk's tentacles became rigid, taking the form of a clawed hand. Claw and scimitar met in a parried attack, as Blagrogk dislodged his other weapon from the ground and stood.

With a flick of his wrist and the skitter of claws, the Orc Chieftain disarmed the awed Shomotta and brought about his bladed shield, held parallel to the ground, to strike. It came right at Shomotta's neck, but at that moment, Alpona had returned to the fight. The ancient Flammerung struck the top of Blagrogk's razored disk. Trajectory deflected, the shield's razor edge but tore, harmlessly, at the chest of Shomotta's armor.

Blagrogk himself lurched forward, jarred by the awesome parry. Alpona reversed the strike, slashing upward, cutting the Orc Chieftain from jaw to ear and burning the hair from the left of his face.

"Feel familiar?" Alpona growled the taunt.

Blagrogk reeled backward. Bengallen, at a knee, about to stand, paused to slash across the Orc Chieftain's right shin, before himself getting stuck in the back by the axe of an interloping orc. The Paladin-Prince's armor took the cut, but the man felt the jolt of the blow, again returned face down into the muck for his trouble.

Shomotta lifted his scimitar, recovering from the exchange of blows. He stepped to put himself between Prince Bengallen and their rampaging foe but his legs slackened and his body became loose and weak. The wizard-priest's hands trembled as his sword fell from grasp once again and he too dropped to his knees. He had pushed himself too far.

He had bent space. For a moment, a long moment, through sheer force of will, Shomotta forced two points, otherwise unconnected, to exist beside one another, impossible angles on a dimension inconceivable to the untrained mind. By no means a novel idea, it was a significant benchmark nonetheless.

One that the wizard-priest was, and knew he was, unprepared for. He had hoped the focus on the attack would have allowed him to delay the repercussions, but apparently not for long. He had forced himself to consciousness, to fight alongside his friends, for as long as he could.

His face went cold and streamed with sweat. He was numb. His vision blurred. Shomotta had broken through a new barrier. His body paid the toll, sure; it was the receptacle. It was his mind and will that he had pushed too far. His soul.

His body would suffer. His mind would break. He would recover, but he would be changed. In the instant, he saw the cosmos whole. The longer he could force himself to stay conscious, the more frayed threads of existence he could grasp. His control over the coming change would be instinctual, elemental, and minimal in any case, but whatever sway he would have would be determined by what he saw in this instant.

His will unraveled, his body went limp, and the closer he and the ground came toward each other, the slower time moved around him. It was as though he would be trapped in the moment forever. The battle would never end.

Sira Roselle, mounted upon Thumu, her steed whose name meant strength, rode at the head of nearly two-thousand horsemen, minus a sorely missed one-hundred. She lost a few more, tripped up or landing too hard coming off the ruined wall. In retrospect, however, horses so lost were miraculously few.

They rode out, tearing through the forward orc scouts and skirmishers, bowling them over, trampling them down, as they thundered toward the enemy lines. Scant few of the horses were proper warhorses. Few of the riders had ever, even once, trained to ride into battle. Yet horses and men are both herd animals. Enough of them knew what they were doing, so that raw instinct drove the herd to do likewise.

It was glorious.

The orc line stood faced, braced against the charge, but they were not prepared for significant cavalry. They had few spears or pole weapons and even the strongest orc had less than half a chance standing his ground against a charging horse. Men and horse were injured, plenty of them died, but they would be mourned as "too many" at another time. The attack wave itself was a resounding success. More than a thousand orcs slain or maimed in a flash. Blink and you might have missed it. Beheld, it was glorious.

Sira Roselle and the more proficient riders steered the charge right, to the north, after wading through the first few ranks of the orc troops. There, they harried the flank before peeling away and doubling back.

The orcs of the right flank, those not cut off, those not embattled by continued mounted attacks, those not diverted toward the ambush at their center, moved forward. They staggered over ranks of their own dead to charge. For oncoming, a few hundred feet behind the initial cavalry charge, came five-thousand armed citizens of Woodhaven lead by the likes of the Elder-Lord Hroddan, the Dwarf-Lord Traldor, Brunsis the Minotaur, and over half of the city watch.

At last, all the city's fighters were on the battlefield. Half of the entire orcish horde had been slain already, the superior tactics and brave sacrifices of Woodhaven's defenders. Thus the two forces finally stood on equal footing, upon this field of battle.

For the first time this day, with everyone engaged, the fighters of Woodhaven had a slight numerical advantage. Yet also for the first time this day, they lacked the advantages of strategy and surprise. No one knew if the battle could yet be won, or who would win it. No matter its outcome, however, the Battle of Woodhaven had already earned whatever legends would undoubtedly be told.

The Dawnsong fell from Malcolm's hand as he flew through the air, following the massive blow. After thudding to the ground, he wasted no time standing to recover it. Immediately set upon by an axe wielding orc who wore the war-stripe of his father's elite guard, Malcolm instead grabbed the axe shaft as the elite orc swung the weapon. They began to struggle for control over the weapon.

They twisted left and right in what might have looked like an absurd dance, but neither could get the upper hand. Malcolm saw additional elite guard advancing on his allies to aid their chieftain. Abandoning control of the weapon, he pushed forward, driving his opponent backwards into another of the orc elite guard.

The tackled orc, surprised, let loose his grip and Malcolm pulled the axe free. Off balance, both opponents were easily dispatched. Malcolm saw Prince Bengallen in the mud and the orc behind him. Immediately, running four strides forward, he hurled the axe.

He missed. This elite orc, aware of the battlefield, saw Malcolm throw the axe. The elite simply dodged it, true to his appellation.

Malcolm continued forward to aid his prince, leaving his magical greatsword behind him. Yet another orc elite guard intervened, blindsiding Malcolm. Toppling them both, grappling, the tangled pair fell to the ground.

Prince Bengallen raised his head from the muck and saw Shomotta on his knees, eyes blank, and body listing. Eyes forward, the Paladin-Prince knew the orc stood behind him. He rolled to his back, left leg passing over right. Catching the assailant's ankle in between, the Prince tripped the orc.

Facing skyward, he grabbed his enemy's belt, using the other's falling momentum to counter lever himself up from the ground. Bengallen added forward momentum by chopping his sword forward. Landing the blow in the orc's ribs, he pushed off the pommel of the impaling sword, to lift himself the rest of the way to his feet.

Blagrogk had also recovered. Turning his fist back into a club, he slammed Alpona, the same instant as the warrior had turned to aid Bengallen and Shomotta. Blagrogk stepped on Alpona as he charged down the Prince, reforming his hammer-hand again into a terrible talon. Prince Bengallen faced him bravely, of course, but as he went to raise his sword in parry, he found it resistant, lodged too deeply in the ground beneath the stabbed opponent.

The sword moved, but it would have been too late. From seemingly out of nowhere, Ruffis jumped out from somewhere and landed on Blagrogk's back, stabbing him in the neck, repeatedly. One long knife went in the pocket of the right collarbone as the dark elf landed and wrapped his legs around the Orc Chieftain.

Inside, the dagger braced itself against the backside of the shoulder blade. Thus secure, Ruffis rained a flurry of stabs down upon the left side of Blagrogk's shoulder and neck. If he stabbed him once, lightning quick, it was a dozen times.

The Orc Chieftain's attack still followed through, but Ruffis gave Bengallen the instant he needed to parry and then some. Recoiling from the deflection, weakened by the assault, Blagrogk careened beyond Bengallen, twisting and falling onto his back. He landed on top of Ruffis and the dark elf knocked skulls with one of the many dead orcs that littered the battlefield. Ruffis' fingers released from his daggers.

Blagrogk, bent at the waist and, rocking back, sprang up onto his feet. At the same instant, Prince Bengallen and Alpona came at him from either side. Together, they swung their swords, chopping down upon him from both flanks.

Even as his feet landed, the Orc Chieftain blocked both attacks, stopping Alpona with his bladed shield and Bengallen with his claw. Each man pushed their attack forward, attempting to off balance their foe. In response, Blagrogk transformed his talon back into a club, locking Bengallen's sword within and, twisting, disarmed the Prince.

Chief Blagrogk pushed Alpona's strike aside and brought his hammer hand around to nail Prince Bengallen with the sword stripped from him an instant before. It did not happen. Raised to zenith, poised to strike, Blagrogk's onslaught relented.

The blow did not fall. For the Dawnsong rang bright and clear, as Malcolm, his legendary blade recovered, came to the end of his charge and impaled his vile father through the abdomen.

The Orc Chieftain's eyes went wide as his arm club slackened back into tentacle form. Raised above his head, the sword, fixed within, likewise fell free.

The Paladin-Prince caught it from the air as it tumbled down. Swinging, Prince Bengallen decapitated Blagrogk in a single, swift, and decisive motion.

Alpona came about, slicing off the tentacle arm, after the fact, stabbing it for good measure, and holding it at a distance. The mass of tentacles, skewered upon the ancient Flammerung, writhed and hissed as they burned in the inescapable arcane flames.

Chapter 19
Battling On

The orc warriors to the rear of the ger began moving forward, filling in behind the forward advance of the southern flank. Most pushed their way ever closer to the front lines of the battlefield. Many, however, noticed enemies within their midst, their slain master at the feet of these ambushers.

Not since before the Great Cataclysm and the Slumbering of the World had so many orc, of so many different tribes and clans, marshaled under a single leader, who was also one of their own kind. He was slain. Their hope was slain, but hatred aplenty bubbled up from within to replace it.

Ruffis regained consciousness to find himself surrounded, on all sides, by the backsides of his allies. They had formed a defensive ring around him and Shomotta, who still lay unconscious beside him. As he regained the ability to focus beyond his protective friends, Ruffis did not have to ask. He saw it. They were themselves surrounded by orcs, their leader chieftain slain, pissed off orcs.

Ruffis sprung to his feet. Taking up a spot between Prince Bengallen and Malcolm, he grinned at them, widely.

"Standing there," Malcolm said, "There is a good chance you'll be killed or saved by an orc today. You okay with that?"

"Not an orc out here got what it takes to slay me."

Malcolm grinned to one side, the side Ruffis could not see, and simply nodded in acceptance.

The circle of orcs around them hesitated to mutual benefit. Prince Bengallen and his thanes needed the moment, but the swelling number of opponents gave their enemies a growing advantage. None knew if they had another fight within them. Then again, no one ever does.

Even without clear leadership, one of the orcs rushed and the rest followed. They flooded in at once and many at the front were immediately skewered. It was difficult as more orc pushed forward before swords could be withdrawn from the ones slain. Bengallen and his thanes slammed into each other and each hoped that, whatever they were stepping on, was not Shomotta. They were all sure that it was.

The combat unfolded messily. Ally and enemy alike stumbled over one another. There was little room for weapons. Blades were ripped from bodies and found no room for swing. Punches and elbows were vital. The corpses of the slain were shields to absorb the slashes and deflect the stabs of the foe.

The Woodhaven horsemen had rode round and set-up to make another run at the enemy line, in conjunction with the foot soldiers. They needed the help. The citizen-soldiers of Woodhaven had a fine push following the mounted charge, but the orc, one-on-one, were vastly superior warriors. The four to one victory of the Woodhaven archers was quickly to be undone.

Even the combined forces of the infantry and cavalry, who held their own for a time, were not enough to push through to the center. They were of no aid to the Prince and his thanes. Moreover, as the tide turned against them, untrained horses began to throw their riders and flee.

It had been a desperate plan from the start. There never was any certainty that it would work, any of it, simply a plan to die well in the defiant hope for something more. That the battle plan had progressed so successfully, so far, was something of a victory in and of itself. Hope, though insufficient for the dead and dying, had won that much. But who would have the tenacity to dare to hope for more?

Without apparent cause, the southern flank of the orc horde broke. The ones swarming Bengallen and his companions ceased to be immediately replaced once slain. Rather, more and more of their would-be assailants turned about to face the calamity that had come upon them from behind.

Caanaflit, at the head of the Knights of the Spear, their Spearpointe Company, and reinforced with four-hundred riders from Spearpointe, had pushed hard, no rest, day or night, since receiving the call. This day, they rode as close as they dared with the morning light upon them.

Straight out from their concealment, completing the distance, they charged into the fight, only once the awaited signal, a column of smoke as Shomotta had described, rose high into the air. They drove their steeds into the heart of the battle, to their allies, surrounded and fighting for their lives within, at the center of this foul army.

At the same time, the mixed unit of Woodhaven's citizen-soldiers drove in against the isolated orcs of southern files and front ranks. Cut off from retreat and reinforcement by the arrival of the Spearpointe Company, the orc in the forward right quarter were quickly annihilated. The allied Frontier forces merged and took the center.

There was finally room to work, space enough for a proper fight, and Prince Bengallen and his mighty thanes pressed the unexpected advantage. Swords swung out in attacking arcs and fast fell as colossal cleaves. Three dozen orcs, in half as many heartbeats, their attentions divided, fore and aft, were thus dispatched, clearing the way to rendezvous with the commanders of their allied forces.

"Mine eyes!" Prince Bengallen shouted.

"Doth not deceive His Majesty!" Caanaflit returned.

"Sira! Caanaflit! Reform the line," Prince Bengallen gave the order, "We make our stand here!"

With the smoldering ruins of the wheeled encampment between them, the Frontiersmen formed their line to the south-east and the orc fell back, beginning to reform their own forces. The orc horde was less than half its original strength, but so too was Woodhaven's defense. Though their morale high, Prince Bengallen's forces remained outnumbered. The Woodhaven foot soldiers had taken the heaviest losses and, even with the aid from Spearpointe, that deficit was far from filled.

What Woodhaven's defenders had not seen were the reinforcements from the north. Already attacking the orc horde, from opposite their new line, before the orc could themselves properly adjust their ranks. As Prince Bengallen took up a stray horse and was about to assess the formation of his troops, he alone saw it. As he wheeled the horse about, he saw the clash to the north.

Without hesitation, or even proper assessment of his lines, still reforming, he charged and roared, "With me!"

The Frontier force charged unevenly. For a moment, Sira Roselle was frustrated, having led such a novice army to such great effect only to have it fall apart at another's lead. Yet when her own eyes turned from their own troops, toward the enemy, she too saw. Every horseman saw it, with the enemy beset from the north, to roll upon them from the south, would surely break their foe.

The surviving infantry foot soldiers followed behind the charge and the orcs stood their ground for but a shamefully short moment. Orc on both fronts, north and south, attempted to fall back, falling into each other. There was no call to retreat. In the confusion that followed, orcs died or orcs ran. In every direction they scattered. Broken. Defeated.

Prince Bengallen removed himself to the rear to check on Shomotta as the Frontiersmen soldiered on. Dismounting near the broken and smoldering ger, he was greeted by Lord Traldor, "Narry so great a victory in three generations, laddie … er, Yer Highness!"

"Not mine alone," the Prince accepted, "Were those dwarves I spied, joining us from the north?"

"I saw them as well," the Dwarf-Lord replied, "Though why they sent no word, I do not know."

"Worry not, with timing like that, they need make no excuses or apologies," Bengallen said, kneeling down next to Shomotta. Ruffis was there with the wizard-priest as well.

"He has mumbled much," Ruffis provided, "but nothing else. Now he is silent and still."

Bengallen put his hand to the wizard's mouth, adding, "but breathing. Tis a good sign."

"Can you do anything for him?" Ruffis asked.

"The High Priest in Woodhaven could, but we sent him with the evacuation," the Paladin-Prince explained as he put a hand to Shomotta's chest, "I know not what gods the dark elves observe, but the elves here are my brothers and sisters in faith. If you would pray to the Mother to give me strength, the Holy Family may answer our prayers to wake him."

With no reluctance, Ruffis placed his hand to Bengallen's shoulder, bowed his head, and whispered, "You say it."

The Prince likewise bowed, uniting the prayer, "We say it."

In the next moment, Shomotta coughed. Spittle rained back down on his face. Flem slung out around his lip and slapped to his chin, as he coughed and coughed again. Finally, he gasped and spoke, "I take it we won?"

"Hard fought," Bengallen began, "and with much sacrifice, we have—"

"You're resonating," Shomotta interrupted.

"What?" Ruffis asked.

"Something here is linked to the Prince. I can see it."

Prince Bengallen pulled his sword from the ground and stood to. Ruffis followed suit.

Shomotta rolled forward and, pushing himself up, rested on one knee.

"No, Your Majesty, there is no danger. Something positive. A sympathy. A synergy. Over in the collapsed encampment."

Ruffis helped the wizard to his feet and the three walked over to the ruined mobile encampment. Reuniting with Caanaflit, Alpona, Malcolm, and Roselle along the way, no one was sure what they would find, but find it they did.

Chapter 20
Weeping Mystery

"The wages of sin is death."

"Have I not confessed all? Have I not submitted myself and beseeched the gods' forgiveness?"

"Your error is great, but ignorance is not sin. You have absolution. And now … now that you know the truth?"

"Of course. In my ignorance, I submit myself to the wisdom of the Church. I will not return to him. Though it shall be hard to remain hidden from him."

"Indeed."

A long silence stretched between them. He, bald, clad in fine robes, trimmed in silver, the collar of his office bold about his neck. She, highlights in her red hair almost glowing in the dim room, pale form covered by a tunic of warn sackcloth, neck bare, vulnerable. The silence whispered many things. He had the position of power in the moment, but what she, and her presence here, meant was a power beyond his means.

At last his eyes yielded a softness, a sympathy, and her own reflected in kind, accepting. The man stood, walked to the door, and spoke again, "Bring her something to wear. Something fine. Something in white, no," he paused, "something in light blue."

"Does the forgiveness of the Holy Family not free me from the judgment of their priest?" she challenged.

The bald man rubbed his head as he paced back to their table. Seating himself again, he folded his arms stoically.

"You must understand, tis difficult for me. Knowing what you are, the whole truth of it, means knowing what might have been. There are so many worthy, young paladins to whom you could have been wed. To fight alongside him and the family line you could have produced."

Her eyes widened, their sparkling blue fading in the act, as her mouth gaped, silent for a moment.

"Is such a thing no longer possible?"

The bald man pursed his lips, ponderous, whispering, "As I have said, your error is great, but not technically sin, not one that we have words for. While certainly the forgiveness of our Holy Family is upon you, actions have consequences. Your error has consequences. Consequences that I, even as a D'Tor of the Van-god, cannot fully assess."

The young woman hung her head in shame. Red hair fell forward from her shoulders, hanging loose to the sides of her face, creating a thin wall between her and the world, behind which she shed a single tear. Wiping it away, she lifted her head and pulled her hair back, speaking, "I was his wife. I did not know what he was. I didn't even know what I am."

"And now that you know?"

The question had brought them in a circle, back to moments before. She inhaled and replied the same as she had earlier, as she always would, "I submit myself to the wisdom of the Church."

"Your soul is intact, but what corruption now lies upon your body, upon your womb... You gave yourself to him! Done in ignorance or not, in that act is the power of life, between beings such as yourselves there is no precedent. If my assessment feels like judgment, I can only apologize. It's too significant to take lightly. The possible implications, myself being one of the few living men that can address them, and yet I am woefully unprepared for the task ... tis all rather daunting."

That silence crept back into the room. These two were not enemies, yet they were poised as adversaries. She, wrong, but defensive. He, to address her wrong-doing, and overwhelmed at the prospect. Though she was derived from a higher order than himself, in this life, in this room, he was the holy man. He had not shown her nearly enough compassion. Mayhap this was his test. Mayhap, even, this was the first step.

He unfolded his arms and walked around the table to her. She began to stand, a defensive reflexive, but he gently flattened his palm which she took as an invitation to remain seated. The D'Tor of Vandor in Antoria, the second highest ranking clergyman within the Antori Imperium, knelt beside her.

Carefully tugging the bottom of her sackcloth tunic, he pulled it down so that it came all the way to her knee. Turning his head away from her, he laid it upon the top of her thigh.

This, of course, took her by surprise. Even in the following moments, realizing nothing untoward about to happen, it still felt rather odd.

The senior priest began to weep. He had seen so much, good and evil. Forgiven and condemned so much error and sin. Blessed so many by the power and mysteries of the Holy Family and bearing witness to the contesting powers of the Hells in the doing.

He had seen so much. Yet the plight of this young woman – for whatever else she was, she was also this, it was a young woman that he saw before him – was unprecedented. What ought to be so full of light, and life, and potential, come so near to ruin over an error, an unknowable error. The irony of her unfathomable intellect to still be subject to the price of ignorance, that too hurt his heart.

In point of fact, from his perspective, it was the most tragic thing he had ever seen. Far sadder than anything he could have imagined. All the more so with the young woman herself unable or unwilling to comprehend it.

So upon her leg he wept heavily. The back of his head would bump her abdomen as he coughed and convulsed. Clumsily, he hugged both her leg at the calf and the leg of the chair upon which she sat. She could feel him on her thigh, the swallowing, the gaging, the labored breathing through his nose, the opening and closing of his right eye, and the tears that began to soak her threadbare garment.

He wept far beyond what most men live and die without being seen to weep. He wept in pain. He wept in fury. He wept for her. He wept for us all.

She felt it. One of the highest holy men in all the world had lain his head upon her lap and was weeping like a baby. She had realized that what she had done was bad. Only then had she considered the extent.

Yet, to look upon this great man, so otherwise humbled before her, she felt that she could deal with her own pain and fear. A glimmer, a spark, of something she must have known in another life, shone forth from her heart and she laid her hand upon his bald pate.

She left her hand there, for a moment, as his weeping faintly increased. As if the contact of her presence began to strengthen him, she gently stroked the curve of his head.

She whispered, "There, there."

Repeating this several times before the high priest's clutching about her leg loosened and several more times before his breathing came under control. At last he looked up at her, face beet red and undignified snot in his mustache, both of which only served to highlight the dilated, watery eyes he cast up to her.

She too streamed tears from heavy eyes. Though she had maintained some composure, the reality of what had happened, finally, weighed upon her. Sliding her hand from his face, she extended it to him and leaning upon her and the table, the high priest pulled himself to his feet.

He walked over to his chair, dragged it around the table, where it had once been across from her, and placed it beside the young woman.

Sitting, he took her hands into his own, and said, "I will learn all that I can. I will help you all that I can. Yet we cannot deny that this is a terrible thing."

She batted her eyes and a large new tear fell from each one as she managed to choke out the word, "Agreed."

"There is another to consider," the D'Tor of Vandor began, "what of this paladin with whom the other travels?"

"He," she gulped and tried again, "He loved another."

"Oh, no, no, child. That's not what I meant, bless you. No, I meant, that he too is in danger."

"Oh," she replied in kind, "Of course. I – I have not told you all of him. I was trying to protect him. I did not know you."

"And now?" the D'Tor again echoed himself from earlier.

"He is no mere paladin. He is the Paladin-Prince, Bengallen of House Hastenfarish."

"Prince in the Light!" the D'Tor exclaimed, "The rumors that he survived the attack on his homeland and rallied the Frontier peoples against a horde of goblins and their dragon, all true?"

"More or less."

"And one of his companions is this Caanaflit?"

"It is so," Deerdra replied.

"By the Holy Family!" the D'Tor shouted, "He must be warned. His men, oh, his men must be made to know that he yet lives. Oh, by the saints and their mercies!"

The senior priest rallied in excitement, the spell of sadness that hung between them broken. Though they held each other's hands still, he took hers and kissed it.

"He has soldiers here," Deerdra elaborated, "He has sent for them. Sent a woman, of which both the Prince and Caanaflit spoke highly, Bethany."

"The Priestess Bethany?" the D'Tor asked.

"Yes."

"Here, in the city?"

"She was last known to be here. Now tis unknown."

"But things unknown can yet be discovered," the D'Tor mused, "With apologies, child, I will have to make finding Sister Bethany my priority, that and speaking with the Morralish military leaders. Then, the whole of my focus will be to determine what has happened to you and what, if anything, must be done to undo it. I will not rest, child."

"Take me with you," she kissed his hands and pleaded, "He will find me … and even knowing what I know … there is no room for secrets between us now. Even knowing what he is, I still bear affection for him. I only know him to be good. He rescued me."

"Because the truth was so clear, I could not see it," the D'Tor paraphrased scripture, continuing, "I understand. We will hide you, then. I will join you when the other matter is settled. I have a paladin under my personal employ. He is an old veteran and I keep him shaggy and weathered as suits his current endeavors, but judge him not on appearance. Few men in this life are so pure of heart and clear to purpose. You were wise to come to me rather than the Primarch of Dinnothyl. A shadow has fallen upon the Antori Imperium, one that has reached even to the Cathedral of Din. Not unlike the shadow that has fallen upon you. They would have, unwittingly, submitted you to the Imperator. Where as I, as a servant of Vandor, have a greater level of political autonomy and am possibly the only man in Antoria who can help you. God help me. I say it."

"We say it," Deerdra replied solemnly, but changing her tone, added, "A single oversight not withstanding, I told you, your Holiness, that I am very smart. I am aware of the dangers of this city and its empire."

"So you are," the D'Tor said, patting and releasing her hand, "Your change of clothes is likely waiting. I'll send the Paladin Ulric Fortigurn at once. He will spirit you from the city and I shall soon to follow."

"Thank you," Deerdra sighed.

The D'Tor put up his hood and placed his hand on her shoulder, saying, "You are most very welcome, child."

As he left the room, a young, novice priest entered, crudely clutching an exquisite blue garment.

She could read the knowledge that he carried upon his troubled brow. She could see the fear in his eyes. His white-knuckled grip confirmed it.

"You have listened?" Deerdra asked.

He was surprised, but answered honest and sure, "I heard some things at first and so I listened more carefully."

"That means you'll be coming with us."

"M'lady, I – I..."

"You heard?"

"Yes."

"So you know?"

"Yes."

"So you must come with us."

"Yes, m'lady."

Patting his hand and taking the garment from the novice priest's clutches, she instructed, "Now turn about so I can have some privacy. I'll tell you when to turn back and help me with the laces."

Turning about he again uttered, "Yes, m'lady."

Chapter 21
Claiming Honor

In all the ancient stories, Prince Aethumir of House Farish had a marvelous suit of enchanted armor called the Runes of Torchlight. Its own legend tells that the Runes of Torchlight was forged for the Farish Kings, Aethumir's grandfather's grandfather, in the fires of the last dragon, by the dwarf king's master blacksmith, centuries before the current historical era.

No finer suit of mail or armor had or has ever been crafted. Thus its rune etched golden plates shone as a symbol of the dwarf king's ringing endorsement that the Farish should be the rulers of men.

The armor was apparently stripped from Prince Aethumir at his death, presumably stolen by the orcs that killed him. The engraved runes, among a hundred other purposes, prevented both the armor's destruction and the wearing of it by anyone who was not descended of the Farish lineage.

Evidently, this platemail suit had been in the keeping of the Iron Claw Orc Clan for all these many centuries. Until this day that the Ironclaw Chieftain made war upon Woodhaven and Aethumir's descendant, only to fail. So it was that the Runes of Torchlight was recovered from the enemy and the ancestral relic restored to its proper line.

Malcolm tightened the last two straps.

"Suppose it must have been some ancient iteration of my clan that slew your noble ancestor. Apologies, Your Majesty."

"Possibly," Bengallen mused, admiring the striking reflection that stared back at him from the polished steel mirror, "but we must remember the dual natures that riddle both our lines. Remember, those same orcs that slew Aethumir were led by the orc who fathered Pathron, who himself grew to man and wed Aethumir's daughter, fathering Aethumir's heir, and beget the Hastenfarish line. If this suit of armor has been held by the same orc tribe – Ironclaw would fit the legend – then it also means that we share a common ancestor, in my Hasten lineage and your orcish one. The father of Pathron was an Ironclaw Chieftain and you, my thane, are thus my kin."

"You treated me as such when there was no way either of us could know this, my Prince,"
Malcolm, then at ease, remarked, "You told me that very story."

94

"I was moved to make you my brother and ward of my house," Bengallen replied, "Vandor moves us with His Divine Love. He has His purposes; if we but heed God's beckoning, such things are oft made clearer to us."

"You say it and I say it," Malcolm gasped, placing his hands together at his chest and bowing his head in a gesture of prayer.

"We say it," Prince Bengallen concluded the prayer in agreement.

Prince Bengallen and Thane Malcolm stepped out from behind the rubble that had stood between them and the victorious leaders of the battle. Everyone so assembled audibly gasped as the light of the evening sun blazed in reflection off of the brilliant armor. It was a golden armor, with many uncustomary features beyond the runic inscriptions scrawled across every inch, such as shield-like oval disks built into its gauntlets and chainmail at the flanks attached to hinged abdominal plates for added mobility.

Thane Caanaflit came forward to greet the Prince.

"It was a brave thing," Bengallen said to Caanaflit as they approached each other.

They closed in a few more steps before Caanaflit could kneel, but Bengallen embraced him as he began to do so, holding him up.

Caanaflit replied, looking beyond him at the smoldering carnage of the ger, "Looks like I missed the real heroics though."

"Nay!" Prince Bengallen dismissed, releasing Caanaflit from his embrace, "Leading a cavalry charge at our most desperate hour to turn the tide of battle. Caanaflit, my friend and thane, Lords of Morralish live and die dreaming that they might do such a thing. A thing of legend. Bards will write of it in their songs. Children will reenact it in their games."

"And I'll pay them all to ensure that they do!"

Malcolm chuckled and Bengallen replied, "Such a cynic."

"What now?" Caanaflit asked, remaining pragmatic.

"We bury the dead, recall the citizens, and meet with our dwarven allies."

"Is anyone who didn't stay and fight for their city-state still entitled to citizenship?" Ruffis asked, arriving with Alpona.

Alpona bowed his head and sighed, "It is always the bravest who die."

"Well," Bengallen added, "Most laid down their lives in defense of those who could not fight. We can only honor them in how we treat those for whom they have sacrificed. The brave die well. Those less brave yet live to be so inspired or to find a way to live with their shame."

"So simple, then?" Caanaflit challenged.

"Tis over now," Prince Bengallen replied, "It can be no other way than as it is. You think of a better way before the next battle; I stand ever ready to receive your insights. Take not such unfortunate thoughts with you from this battlefield, however. Those people need to believe in their heroes. Some died so that others could live. That is a selfless and noble thing. That is what Woodhaven needs now. That is what we must show them. I celebrate the honored dead. I know they feast with their ancestors in heavenly halls prepared for them. Worry not for the dead, but for those that survive to live after them. Tis them before us now. Leave this place in glorious victory or stay here forever."

Caanaflit wondered if he was *speaking metaphorically or delivering an ultimatum. Probably both.* Bengallen did that a lot. *Only Caanaflit could ruin so grand an entrance with so few words,* he thought of himself in chastisement.

Prince Bengallen continued forward confidently, newly clad in the ancient armor of his ancestors and clutching the head of their enemy. The leaders of this battle gravitated toward their Prince as he moved through them.

The full entourage together turned the corner of the ruin and looked out with pride at the gathering crowd. Woodhavers. Spearpointers. Dwarves. They all looked to Prince Bengallen.

For what? For leadership or courage? Nay, the battle was won. They looked to him for meaning amid so much carnage.

Prince Bengallen, grasping Blagrogk's head by the hair, raised it aloft and shouted a wordless cry that shot through the crowd, echoed, and faded. Beside him, his mighty thanes took up their places, Caanaflit and Malcolm, to his right and left, followed by Shomotta and Alpona, then Ruffis, and Sira Roselle and other distinguished fighters as well.

Taking the cue, they raised their bloody weapons high and let loose a
cacophony of shouts and roars that were picked up and rejoined by the whole
of the assembly. Dwarven battle horns sounded, not with command signals,
but with long blasts of victory. All the emotions of success, grief, and relief
were made as sound and given outlet. Some also wept, others laughed, yet
others clanged their weapons and stomped their feet until, at last, they were all
as one in the sound unique to this place, this day, this victory.

Prince Bengallen tossed Blagrogk's head aside and held out his right palm to
calm the assembly. They did so and again Caanaflit marveled at the
mysterious power the Paladin-Prince had to command an audience with
naught but a gesture.

"This is your victory!" Prince Bengallen shouted, continuing, "I have no
grand speech prepared to mark the occasion. Apologies!"

A skittering of laughter played though the crowd as Bengallen paused.

Allowing for it, he continued, "There is plunder about and tis yours for the
taking. Whatever leaves this field on your person this evening is yours. Forget
not there is work yet to be done. Your brothers and sisters bled and died here
today. Honor them! Aid the wounded. Gather the dead. Speak of their deeds.
Some went ahead of us today, to heavenly halls prepared for them by their
ancestors, and they will see the face of God. Worry not for them now. Live a
life that honors their sacrifice – today and for the rest of your days. Remember
this victory. Remember the cost. Remember the honored dead!"

"The Honored Dead!" Malcolm shouted.

"The Honored Dead!" the assembly thundered, and again, "The Honored
Dead!" they blasted a third time.

Caanaflit leaned into Prince Bengallen and spoke, "Not the grandest speech,
but pretty darn perfect."

"Thanks for the rehearsal," Bengallen replied kindly, "and for letting me
know what everyone else was thinking."

"As always, you are welcome, my Prince," Caanaflit said, relieved to know
that he had not truly soured the Prince's mood.

Chapter 22
Slaying Men

Illwarr the Manslayer rose through the gladiatorial ranks of Napua with blinding speed. Skin dark gray and thick like rhinoceros hide to the untrained observer. Looking down into the arena, he mostly looked like one of those "orc-things," but this was far from accurate. Most people did not even take note of his size until presented with the perspective of the men sent against him. Illwarr was nearly twice as tall as most of the men he fought.

He was purchased from a traveling wizard in exchange for a handful of old elven lore books that the owner, the grandson of a scholar, had inherited. Scholarship was a luxury to a lanista, an owner of gladiators and operator of their training house, itself called a ludus. This lanista, his name long forgotten, could ill afford luxuries of any kind. His rivals owned the city's greatest champions. Their fighters were in much demand, while he struggled to keep his own fed and strong.

Then came Illwarr. The mysterious giant monstrosity had slain the stock fighters of this lanista's competitors creating a new demand for fighters which his owner was ready to fill with his own stock of fighting slaves. Even Napua's gladiatorial champions, one-by-one, Illwar had slain on his way to the top until there stood but one gladiator left to rival him.

Ornandez was the former city champion. He had earned the title by defeating the previous champion, Costus, and lost it by losing to the more recent champion, Stratos. Yet when Ornandez, beloved by the city, lost that fight, he was given mercy and lived to fight another day. It was the same, earlier, when he had himself defeated Costus.

They both had become crowd favorites for executing criminals ad gladium and for a time supposed that would be their lives. They were wrong. Even before Illwarr, they were wrong.

Costus and Ornandez were both Southlanders. Though the New Freedoms established in their homeland, the islands south of Thalos, made it unpopular to fight Southlanders as gladiators, it was still done from time to time. Moreover, the spirit of those freedoms, originally ignored by each man alone, as something inconsequential to slaves, had become a thing living between them as they grew in camaraderie, fighting side-by-side in later times.

Thus they began to thirst for lives beyond the arena. They dreamed of freedom and shared their dreams between them. They even dared begin to speak to others of their cause.

There was a heightened civil unrest in the Imperium in those days. Heavily-armed and highly-trained freemen, mountain folk, in a single day, had been transformed from welcomed mercenaries to mistrusted refugees. These hard men, all were soon to learn, had some starkly different moral notions about the imperative of freedom.

Costus and Ornandez wondered if the time was right. Many signs suggested that it might be. No sooner than they began to spread their whispered dreams, a house slave, a non-gladiator, came to Ornandez and told him of men who had come to Napua to help the slaves win their freedom. These men sought to turn the gladiators to the cause, to be leaders in the rebellion. Such things had been tried before, tried and failed, but the time did seem right.

This slave became the go-between for these mysterious men. The gladiators reported their numbers and received the status of the movement. They had even begun to make strategic plans together for the day of liberation and what would come after. Then came Illwarr.

The creature blazed his way through the gladiator ranks, killing over one-hundred men, including Stratos, the city's champion. Yet because of his foul and inhuman visage, there was reluctance to name Illwarr their new champion.

So they began to fight him against former champions, the handful that still lived. Until, at last, Costus slain before him, only Ornandez remained.

The dream of freedom began to fade. So many who would have stood beside him were crushed, not under the figurative heel of oppression, but under the literal heel of this actual monster.

Ornandez turned his thoughts toward his own survival. Clearing his mind of all but blood and glory, he stepped out upon the sands of the arena, its last champion.

In a four-tier tournament, the morning began with a series of free-for-all fights, with the lone survivor of each moving on. Those surviving gladiators would be put to a series of one-on-one competitions until only two remained. Everyone wanted to see Ornandez and Illwarr fight. The distribution of men had been intentionally arranged, therefore, in a manner that ensured these two, should they survive, could only face each other in the final round.

A four-tier tournament was an exhausting endeavor. They had fallen from favor because the final match was so often unspectacular. The men who progressed that far were usually so exhausted by the end that they cared too little for the fight and welcomed death as surely as a nap.

Yet no one had ever seen Illwarr show fatigue and everyone knew that Ornandez had won a four-tier before. Someone was trying to help him or, mayhap, make as much coin as possible before Illwarr moved on to fight in the Grand Arena at the Imperial Capital.

Six men entered the arena. Ornandez entered from the south, another from the north, and two each from the east and west. The honored guests had not even arrived. It was barely morning. Five men would die with hardly an audience to take notice of either their efforts or their passing.

The opponent's were criminals, except for a single fellow professional gladiator. The two acknowledged one another and immediately went after the scabs.

The weapon of distinction in the Imperium was a form of short sword, called a gladius, fast and versatile in the hands of a skilled warrior. Ornandez, who fought dual-wielding a pair of them, killed both his opponents in a single attack. One was stabbed, pierced through the neck, both paralyzing the man and causing him to drown in his own blood. The other was gutted, thrust to the abdomen, blade twisting on exit, dragging out viscera as it went. The attack was lazy, simple, and would not have been considered artful or skillful at all, save to acknowledge the fact that one man slew two with the single attack.

The other gladiator held a spear and charged one of the lesser fighters. His opponent attempted to knock the spear away with an axe swing, but underestimated the gladiator's skill. The strike found purchase, in thigh rather than ribs, but it was enough to disable the lesser fighter. The gladiator withdrew his spear, turned about and hurled it at his second attacker. It took him solidly in the abdomen and knocked him to the ground.

The thigh stabbed man swung his axe wildly as the gladiator approached him. Catching the axe at the shaft, the gladiator wrenched it from the man's grip, and cleaved open the flailing man's head with the weapon.

In what amounted to a long moment, there were only two remaining. Gladiators, they were, men hard trained for battle and wills bent toward glory. Lives and dreams beyond chains and violence were as dashed and broken as the bodies of the slain. The sands of the arena wore away the hopes of men as surely as the windswept sands of time would wear away even the stoutest stone. Then and there, all was for blood, for glory, and for victory. They would kill to retain the only things their fates had left them.

Ornandez wanted to save his strength, this fight had to end soon. He glanced at the men he had slain, confirming that they had not brought to battle anything worth throwing. He saw the other gladiator make a move to retrieve the spear, so Ornandez ran him down, closing the distance.

Facing away, the gladiator pulled the spear and could turn only in time to deflect Ornandez's charge. Yet the sword bit deep into the wooden shaft. Ornandez pulled away, yanking the spear from the other's grasp. At the same time, he chopped downward with his other sword, but it too was blocked, this time by the shaft of his opponent's axe.

Ornandez turned his wrist forward. The blade of his sword went flat against the axe shaft, slid down, and sliced off his opponent's fingers. The axe fell to the ground and that same sword stroke continued its downward trajectory into the other gladiator's hip.

The man fell to his knees and punched Ornandez in the groin with his bloody half-hand. Grabbing sand with the other, at the same time, he threw it in Ornandez's face. The man would not ask for mercy or a quick death. While Ornandez respected it, in a way, he *did not need this today*.

The other gladiator found the axe again as he grasped in the sand. Though hobbled, he stood with the axe held before him. Ornandez eyes were clearing by then, seeing the easy finish.

Ornandez, the last gladiatorial champion of Napua, walked up to his opponent, calmly. His opponent swung. At the last moment, Ornandez crossed his swords and caught, scissored, the other man's axe between his gladius blades. With a turn of the wrist, the disarmed the man a third time. Bringing the crossed swords back about, he placed them to his opponent's throat, and drew them against one another.

A torrent of blood flowed down the man's neck and two separate fountains sprayed the man's fading life all over Ornandez. In his mind, he yelled *glory*, but his tone made it more of a question than a declaration. He was numb.

For the crowd, he cried out like an animal and they responded in kind. In truth, however, he felt nothing. Ornandez could lie to himself all he wanted, but this was not his life anymore.

He dreamed of freedom. Yet in the midst of dreaming, yearning, he killed a man that might have rallied to his cause. This was not his life.

Two more to go and then, one way or the other, it would end.

Chapter 23
Hearing Word

Sarragossa, a Drileanian boy no older than thirteen, had been freed from slavery by Morralish soldiers in Antoria. These same soldiers had heard the rumor that Prince Bengallen was alive in the Frontier. Since that was the only place a runaway slave had a chance, these soldiers sent the boy there and asked him to seek out the Prince on their behalf.

There, he had traveled with the supply train that lagged behind the Spearpointe Company on their hard ride to Woodhaven. They arrived three days after the battle. The boy had told his tale to any that would listen. So he was forwarded through the ranks, at last to Sira Roselle. She, along with Malcolm, brought the boy to Prince Bengallen and Caanaflit who were catching up and taking their lunch at Bavin Hall.

The Prince motioned the boy forward and invited, "Speak."

"Your Majesty," the boy gasped with relief, and swallowed before reciting rehearsed words, "I have come far to seek amnesty under your banner, but I do not come into your service with empty hands. The sons of the mountains have not forgotten the virtues by which they were raised. Nor have they forgotten their monarch and would gladly serve him still, if such a man yet lives to so command them."

As Sarragossa took another deep breath, his eyes widened, realizing that he had forgotten something. The boy fell to his knee. Dashed so against the stone it looked painful, but if it had been, the boy's face did not betray it. Kneeling before Prince Bengallen, Sarragossa handed up a rolled parchment.

The Prince came out from behind the table, touched the boy upon the head. Accepting the parchment, he paused, looking to a server.

"Get this boy a room. Here. Fresh clothes, warm meal, hot bath."

The server took the boy, but Caanaflit called to him before they were gone.

"Child, what is your name?"

"Sarragossa," the boy answered.

"No surname?"

"No, m'lord," the boy answered again, "I was born a slave. Separated from my mother before I could learn it."

"You're a slave no longer," the Prince interjected, "Take a well-earned rest."

In the days that followed the Battle of Woodhaven, the evacuated citizenry returned with little dispute or disruption to daily business or life. To their credit, those that had not stayed to fight were rebuilding the wall or aiding as they could, before the sun rose upon the next day.

The dead were honored by those that held them dear, including the deaths of two Knights of the Spear, Sir Jason and Sir Vix, nine of their soldiers from the Spearpointe Company, and two score other volunteers from Spearpointe, in addition to the thousands of Woodhaven's own.

Those council elders who could write set aside time to record the deeds of the fallen for future generations. They crafted a document which would be read by many, but required to be so by all newly accessioned councilors before they took office, common and noble alike.

Brunsis the Minotaur was named the Hero of Woodhaven. His unique appearance, as it was, had symbolized that Woodhaven was aided by outsiders who were under no obligation to stand with them. Furthermore, the minotaur had taken it upon himself to focus on aiding the wounded and so, quite incidentally, a great number lived to tell of his bravery.

These things combined with Brunsis' genuine combat prowess made him a symbol of strength and victory for the Woodhavers to rally around. They made him one of their own and gave him a place of honor among them. Thus was a feast held to formally celebrate the Hero of Woodhaven.

Only after all these things had come to pass did Prince Bengallen meet at last with the Dwarven Envoy. What stories they had to tell each other.

The five-hundred or so dwarves had set up a camp on the north side of town. They were invited, many times, to live in the city that they had helped save, but the Dwarves insisted that it was a strict custom of their army, when mobilized, not to "occupy" the sovereign domains of another. That they were granted permission to inhabit the land north of the city was enough.

Dwarves lived long lives and were typically patient, but they still knew the value of timely knowledge. So there was great relief and excitement when

Prince Bengallen himself, and not Caanaflit or Alpona with the Prince's apologies, finally arrived in the camp to meet with them.

A small but sturdy table had been procured for the meeting and was placed at the center of the camp. There were no walls, the sides open, but a high tent roof covered it. Dwarves had no problem functioning out under the open sky, which is not to say that they had any appreciation for it either. They chose to be under some sort of cover when at all possible, part-habitual superstition, part-aesthetic preference.

Malcolm came to one end of the fine table. Two dwarves stood at the opposite end. Other dwarves gathered all around to observe informally.

Thane Malcolm called, "His Majesty, Throne-Lord of the Kingdom of Morralish, and Accepted Sovereign of the city-states of Spearpointe and Woodhaven, Prince Bengallen, House and Clan Hastenfarish, The Prince in the Light!"

Sira Roselle stepped out and, taking up the other side at their end of table, she proudly displayed the sky blue Hastenfarish banner with white griffin ascendant.

Prince Bengallen, clad in the Runes of Torchlight, came forth and stood behind the centered chair provided to him.

Bengallen noticed the chair and the table, of what quality they were. He remembered how, in the days leading up to this, Caanaflit and Alpona reported the dwarves desire to know how the Prince would arrive, who would accompany him, how many titles would he use, and whether or not the table and chair were nice enough. *Indeed they were.*

"Your Highness, it is my honor to introduce to you Lord Throdi, a son of King Odemkin of Dwarvehame, himself Lord of the Southern Ridge and Ambassador to the Fey Courts," one of the two dwarves announced.

Prince Bengallen's eyebrow raised at that last title, ignoring it for the moment, he spoke less formally.

"With apologies, good herald, your Lord and I have already met, upon the field of battle – correction – the field of victory. Myself and the people of Woodhaven owe you all a great debt. Lord Throdi, I apologize again that I am here to increase that debt and, a third apology, that I did not accord you as a fellow prince upon that field, if I had known, of course."

104

"Please be seated, Your Highness," Lord Throdi invited, using the differential honorific before himself sitting, he continued, "There is no need for apology. Your letter gave us additional time to prepare for a threat against not only your kingdom, gods' mercies, but the whole of Uhratt. We owe you for that, more than you know. And with my own apologies to your own herald there, you owe us nothing for killing orcs. You'll always find a dwarf ready for that fight. So, what do you say we quit apologizing, have a few drinks, and you let me entertain you with a good story and some better news. Then, if we aren't too sodded, we'll discuss the future."

"I like you, Throdi," Bengallen said, taking up the cup before him, a dwarf immediately there to pour his drink, as he continued, "Call me Bengallen. This is my trusted Thane, Malcolm, and he probably likes killing orcs as much as anyone, so he shan't worry much over apologies either. The other is my paladin novice, Sira Roselle. Tell me, Throdi, do you have any paladins among your soldiers here?"

"Several, of course."

"Might she train with them? Our company is not always as pious as I would have it be for her training. It would do her good," Prince Bengallen asked, taking a swig from the cup.

"We don't train women as paladins," Throdi said, holding up his own cup to be filled, "so it would do us good as well."

"Sira," Bengallen called, "I mean no disrespect, but I do think this is important. Please hand off the banner to Malcolm and have one of these fine folk take you to their paladins."

"Of course, Your Majesty," Roselle replied dutifully, stepping over to Malcolm and handing off the banner with poise and confidence, in the proper way.

Prince Bengallen watched the dwarves and they watched him and them. They were all learning a lot that day.

"Will another son of King Odemkin not be joining us?" Bengallen asked his host, "I have greatly enjoyed Lord Traldor's company and have come to call him friend."

"No. A retinue of his men came down with mine. They've returned ta report of the Battle of Woodhaven," Lord Throdi answered, making a request, "I have important news, Prince Bengallen, but we'va waited this long so I'd like ta tell ya the whole story, in order, hif ya'd indulge me? Much has happened."

"Certainly," Bengallen agreed, drawing another drink from his cup.

Lord Throdi told the tale:

Prince Bengallen's report had been forwarded to the Dwarven High-King, Hrouthgrum, who read it personally before appointing King Odemkin of Dwarvehame to address the concerns raised therein. Forthwith, they sent two full battalions to Morralish to investigate the claims and sent word throughout the Dwarven Mountains that conscription would be levied. Before either was completed, King Odemkin sent his reply to Woodhaven. A reply that Prince Bengallen, hunting the Beast of Spearpointe, did not receive until many months after it had arrived.

The dwarven soldiers investigating Morralish were attacked and soundly, terribly defeated. The survivors fell back to the Temple of Vandor and used a secret passage to a tunnel that accessed the Dwarven Highway. The passage was only used by Priests of St. Mordin, its doorway only known to their elders. Blessedly, such a priest had been sent with these soldiers and was one of the few survivors or there would have been none.

That was not the greatest blessing, however. In the High Temple the dwarven soldiers found something they had given up on finding. Other survivors, citizens of Morralish Prime who had retreated to the Temple, were still there, holed up, filthy and starving, but alive, some of them.

Nearly two thousand Morralish refugees from the Temple were escorted to Dwarvehame by the surviving military expedition. Few priests had survived. His Holiness the Exarch was not among them. Many had joined the battle, fighting and healing with might, medicine, and magic. Their fate remains as much a mystery as anyone else's.

Blessings were followed by curses. The consecrated ground which had held the undead hordes at bay failed. Something must have happened after the survivors left. Best guess was that the dwarves entering and not leaving drew suspicion and thus greater numbers of unholy enemy turned against it. That, coupled with abandoning the temple, emptying it of the faithful, weakened the consecration enough for it to be defiled or broken by the dark arts of the enemy.

What we know for sure is that undead legions began pouring into the Dwarven Highway. This happened days later and the enemy moved quite slowly. So while they posed no threat to the survivors and refugees evacuated straight to the capital at Dwarvehame, they had begun to cut off various outer villages, cities, and mines from one another. With Prince Bengallen absent reply, King Odemkin recalled his emissaries from Woodhaven and left only a small retinue with one of his sons, Lord Traldor.

Though it took the work of all the dwarven people, of the entire Dwarven Mountains, the threat was pushed back. Captured lands were reclaimed and the way was sealed off. If the undead army had managed to come through without the dwarves knowing, they could have never held them to the highway. They would have sprung upon city after city by surprise, wiping them out.

Dwarven soldiers saw the state of Morralish Prime and the things there. King Odemkin knew what this undead army could do. Though many were cut off and suffered long months and many more died in battle, when it was over, the dwarves had not lost a single city that was not taken back.

It was Prince Bengallen's warning that made this possible. The lives of the expedition into Morralish that followed were not spent in vain. The dwarves already owed loyalty and love to Morralish, but by decree of King Odemkin, they would owe their lives to its monarch, the Prince in the Light, as well.

The Morralish refugees were taken to the Elven Lands along with many dwarves unable to fight. Those dwarves had begun to return home, but the people of Morralish remained. The hope was that they would be released into the Antori Imperium, where so many of their kinsmen were stationed with the Expeditionary Forces. The unrest there, however, largely tied to those same soldiers, began to suggest that continuing to add to them would be unwise.

At least, without at last meeting with Prince Bengallen, reporting these things and hearing his council. There was a thought that once he recalled his forces, that they might escort these refugees home as well, but no recall has since been sounded. It was about this time that Prince Bengallen and the Dwarf-Lord Traldor met in Woodhaven and he sent his retinue back to Dwarvehame with confirmation of the Prince's life and deeds.

"So we march down 'ere," Lord Throdi continued, "Ready for one fight, and findin' another oon entirely. We're on the other side of the river fer dayz. I tried to send wurd. Lost a few good dwarves. Dinna use magic cauze, to my knowledge, orc gather like that only under that sway of some sorcerous mind.

One that kinny discern such magic. Ne'er seen so many follow one of their own. Anyways, we dinna have enough soldiers to take out so massive a horde, not yet, so we waited fer yer attack."

"Your aid and its timing saved many lives, Lord Throdi," Prince Bengallen accepted, "Woodhaven is forever in your debt. I would ask more about these survivors from Morralish. I had begun to doubt such existed."

"I thought I warz to tell it all whole?" Throdi deflected.

Prince Bengallen, too happy to push the issue, relented, "By all means. I had not realized there was more."

"I'm not just 'ere on behalf of the dwarves and my father, King Odemkin. The elves and dwarves er' committed ta containin' this blight. If the Prince in the Light fields an army to retake his lands. Th' elves and the dwarves will throw in our full support, soldiers, equipment, supplies, all we canna spare and then some."

Bengallen and Malcolm both caught themselves forgetting to breathe. As the Dwarf-Lord paused for a drink, they both inhaled sharply. Bengallen was about to speak again, but Lord Throdi had one last thing to say, before opening up the conversation.

"We've not been idle. I canna preten'ta' know why the gods and angels allow such terrible t'ings ta happen. What I do know, yer words saved more dwarves than anyone will ever know. I believe tha' despite what happened to Morralish, you whar spared for a reason. That ya find that armor on the day of our arrival is a sign. A clear a sign as dwarves can ask fer. You are the Prince in the Light. You are the leader against this threat. You have the pledged aid of elf and dwarf that no man has had since Holy Brother Din himself warz flesh, and afore him, not since yer own ancient ancestors. Tis a terrible t'ing we face, but ya seem to be gettin' pretty good at face'n terrible t'ings. We're behind ya. To whatever end, we'll follow the Prince in the Light."

Chapter 24
Sporting Fight

To the moaning displeasure of his audience, Ornandez's second fight was rather brief. Though his prowess spectacular, the common man hardly knew the difference. They wanted long, bloody fights. Killing efficiently and effectively took a lot of skill, but there was little showmanship in it.

Ornandez had come up against another gladiator, though this one of middling skill. How he made it to the top of his free-for-all must have had a lot to do with luck. Both men wielded gladius short swords, though his opponent fought in the traditional gladius and shield, or "sword and board" manner. Their blades clashed several times before both men backed away. Coming back together once more, they crossed blades and locked in the moment. When Ornandez's opponent brought up his shield to protect his face, Ornandez, seeing the miscalculation, sliced into the man's leg with his second sword.

As the man brought his shield down, instinctively, Ornandez stepped around him, slashed his opponent across the bicep, and stabbed him in the armpit from behind. The man lost all control over his arm and dropped his shield, but had sense enough to spin about. Ornandez stepped back to the spot he had stood before, counter his opponent's turn, slicing the back of the man's sword hand. The other gladiator dropped the sword. His left arm smote, his right hand ruined, he had no options.

The gladiator gaped at Ornandez. In the pause, the crowd hissed. The two men said something to one another. The defeated gladiator hung his head and Ornandez removed it from his body, swift, clean.

The other three fights at this tier of competition were much more entertaining. Illwarr was proving his usual bloody spectacle. He had taken to the performance as well, drawing out his kills more and more dramatically. His next opponent would surely die as well, leaving only Sciosphek, a freeman Antori citizen and prize-fighter, between the inevitable clash of Ornandez and Illwarr.

As a freeman, Sciosphek's battles were only to the death if he got himself killed and though he had lost before, it had only been a few times. His victories, from throughout the Imperium, as well as his travels, were many. The winner's coin was not so heavy a purse here, so it must have been word of this Illwarr creature, the novel challenge, that drew him to Napua's main event.

Once a freeman himself, Ornandez had seen Sciosphek fight gladiators, a dozen at once, and an ogre as well. He knew that Sciosphek would spare a gladiator, if the crowd allowed, and that he too stood a chance against Illwarr. If only the two could have faced the creature as one, victory would have been certain.

Ornandez and Sciosphek, with no conversation or prompting, saluted one another in the old way, long abandoned, and in an odd way, so noble a gesture cast a pallor on the event. Who wanted to see two noble champions kill each other?

Someone did. A cry shot from the crowd, "Stab'em in the rork'n face!" And the whole of the ever increasing audience echoed with cacophonous laughter and blood thirsty noise. An ignoble end to a fine moment shared between finer men. Tragic.

Sciosphek wielded an axe and a bladed polearm, a shortened halberd, that could be used as either a single edge sword or a spear. He came at Ornandez fast, with a whirling series of chops. Right over left over right over left, axe and halberd crashed down against an equal succession of blocks, rushed and sloppy, by Ornandez's gladius swords. Until, at last, Sciosphek hooked one of Ornandez's blades with the underside of his axe and stripped him of the weapon. The crowd collectively gasped, adding the stillness of bated breath to the moment.

Daringly, Ornandez leaped toward the lost gladius, dodging the next flurry of attack. He hit the ground rolling and sprung up to his feet in a single motion, both blades securely grasped. The crowd went wild.

They had loved Ornandez in their own rude way. Illwarr and Sciosphek were curiosities, indulgences, but Ornandez was their last champion. They wanted him to win.

Women bared their breasts at him. Men cheered his name. Ornandez initially took up a defensive stance, but remembering who he had become, ran at his opponent instead.

Sciosphek turned and thrust out his polearm, like a spear set against the charge of cavalry. Ornandez knocked it downward with his gladius, barely, but enough. Forward, he closed the distance, stepping on the polearm with his right foot. Pushing it to the ground and himself up from it, he kicked

Sciosphek in the throat with his left. The audience continued to roar.

Though the bladed head of the polearm had broken off, the prize-fighter managed to hold on to its shaft and swung it around in front of himself, wildly, as he reeled back and tried to breathe. Ornandez stood watching, one gladius held flat, inches out from his chest, defensive.

The other pointed at his opponent, daring, mocking. He was posing for his audience. He was a gladiator.

Sciosphek grinned. In the crowd, only the sharpest eye could see it. He said something to Ornandez, who stood unmoved. Sciosphek hurled the shaft at Ornandez. He batted at it, right, moved left, and it bounced to the ground beside him.

As it did, Sciosphek put both hands on his axe and turned them in an odd way. It split into two separate, but thinner, axes and he came whirling at Ornandez once more.

Oranadez was not about to let Sciosphek hook his swords and disarmed him again. He focused, therefore, on strafing right and deflecting blows from the side. The gladiator was able to round his opponent more quickly than the prize-fighter could turn himself. After several strides, this put him behind his opponent.

There, Ornandez crossed his arms, slashing the other man across the back of both thighs. When Sciosphek finished turning, about to retaliate, Ornandez raised his swords, uncrossed his arms as the axe came down, and caught it in the scissor crossing of his blades. Before he could pry the axe from the prize-fighter's hand, however, the second axe came down across a gladius and hooked it, pulling it from Onandez's own grasp and freeing the blocked axe at the same time.

Onandez backed away quickly. Sciosphek, hobbled, took two steps to press his uncertain advantage, but fell to his knees. His legs simply did not work, their muscles cut too deep. As Ornandez walked back toward his opponent, to his surprise, Sciosphek hurled an axe, two axes, at him.

Off his guard, Ornandez narrowly dodged the first, but the second took him in the arm. The crowd OOH-ed and Sciosphek laughed. Ornandez cradled his wound and knew that this would be the cause of his death.
Any hope he ever had, of defeating Illwarr in the coming battle, actively bled from him.

Sciosphek could not make it to the next fight. At this point, he had not needed to injure the man that would. That was a spiteful choice.

Ornandez burned with rage and screamed at Sciosphek. A few, keen of hearing, made out the words.

"Now who will stand against him!?"

Sciosphek said something back, tried to stand, collapsed again, and spat at Ornandez.

Such a turn. What began with the pageantry of honor, respect, and nobility would only end in a violent spectacle of hate, rage, and jealousy. It was everything that gladiators were, whether or not anyone wanted to admit it.

Sciosphek put up a hand to block Ornandez and the champion's sword flayed the outstretched arm. So ruined, Sciosphek shrunk down onto himself.

Ornandez poked him in the guts with his gladius, stepping to the right as the languishing prize-fighter fell over, defeated.

The crowd went crazy. They were thrilled by the change in these men. They loved the drama and, while unexpected mercy sometimes delighted and impressed, the crowd was far more taken with the breaking of men: Body, mind, and spirit.

Ornandez retrieved his second sword and walked back to Sciosphek. They glared at each other.

Raising the reacquired gladius, Ornandez waved it at his audience to stir their frenzy. Once their roar swelled to his satisfaction, he thrust with his uninjured arm, stabbing Sciosphek in the heart with the left-hand gladius. Upon the impaling blade, Ornandez raised his victim from the ground and swung his other gladius, cleaving the man's head from his shoulders.

Thus passed Sciosphek of Jourance, freeman and prize-fighter, from this life, in bitter and brutal defeat.

Chapter 25
Singing Faith

He heard her humming. He had once enjoyed her humming. Such a wonderful thing in such a terrible place. Later, it began to unsettle him. It highlighted the tragedy that she was here. *No one should be here.*

This was a place for no one. All the people here were no one, had ceased to be anyone. Except her, s*he was someone. If her humming was that lovely, what must the rest of her be like?*

So he looked. He was not supposed to. He was the guard of no one. He was not supposed to look in on anyone, as there was nothing to look at. She changed everything. He took his key, a found key, that no one knew he had, acquired on one of his forays into some long abandoned portion of the prison and opened her cell.

She was filthy, but she was certainly someone. He could see her beauty, despite the dirt and whatever else that was all over her. She looked at him and his heart melted. Her eyes penetrated his soul, nearly.

"You, yer'a witch?"

She started to speak, coughed, and found her voice.

"No. Not even a little bit."

"You can lie to me, witch," he called to her, "but yer spells won't wohk here."

"I've noticed," she replied, "Was there something you wanted? Why have you opened this door?"

"You, yer music."

"Oh," she replied, "would you like for me to sing to you?"

He bit his lip and gave her a sidelong stare. She thought he was not going to speak. That he would turn and leave. At last, however, he parted his lips.

"Yes," he said simply.

"You think I'm a witch," she began, "but I would not let a witch sing to you.

Accordingly, I must inform you that I'm no witch. Quite the opposite. If you will hear my song, you will know tis holy. I am a Priestess of the Church of the Holy Family. I am a singer – in the style of the Blessed Mother. My name is Sister Bethany."

"Ere?" the guard questioned, "A church sister, truly, 'ere?"

"Not for my own sins," Sister Bethany replied, "A terrible plight nonetheless... What is your name?"

"Jonn," he shared, almost dismissively, "Then why?"

"To sing to you, mayhap," Bethany offered with a smile, "No, Jonn, because my words are dangerous. Powerful people had bet against their truth and would not face their losses."

The guard frowned and put his hand on the door, taking a step back, he asked, "Are you going to sing?"
Bethany sang:

Some say a light once shone,
Others that a darkness came,
But here was bright and beautiful
Until the inky blight, so terrible,
gave taint, and hate, and shame.

All the innocence of creation,
once of light-blessed peace,
stirred fear, and lust, and greed.
Each a wake of destruction, so,
For wisdom and love there need.

A light dimmed. A darkness at bay.
Divided, each to search his soul.
A Father to riddle out wisdom.
A Mother's love for the goodly sum.
A Son, our brother, a family whole.

Thus let the stars bear witness,
To what men so oft deny
And neglect by the light of day;
for to shine in the dark of night
is far more precious in its rarity.

114

Out from dreams and disaster,
Was born the world now known.
Virtue calls, courage and charity.
Heroes rise with hope and clarity,
Through the dark our light is shown.

Jonn, the guard, stood speechless.

"That is a very powerful song," Sister Bethany explained, "Sung properly, in a place not warded against magic, the Church mysteries teach we Sisters of the Songs how to call forth the powers of the created world and shape them in accord with the Divine Will."

"What about now?" the guard asked.

"Tis no different than any other day; I submit myself to God's plan for my life," Bethany said confidently, brushing aside some strand of matted hair, "What about you?"

"I serve the Imperium," he whispered with less confidence.

"Does the Imperium serve the Holy Family? Does it sing the Mother's Song? Do you feel God's plan working through you?"

"I – Well... I thought it did. I thought it would. I – I..."

"You see me. You hear me. And now you know it does not," she paused, asking him, "The Divine Will, are you brave enough to seek it out?"

"I – I don't know."

"But don't you?" Bethany asked, continuing, "Life has a melody, Jonn. A rhythm of notes that guide your existence, if you would but play in harmony with God's plan. We become song rather than noise."

He gazed at her, baffled, his face twisted in denial.

"Clearly, our lives aren't fated."

"No," the Sister admitted, "There are counter-melodies, and dissonance amid consonance, and certainly cacophony, that clamoring arrhythmic discord. There is chaos in the cosmos – or so it would seem. Yet, just as music is an arrangement of sound into something beautiful, the plan and purpose of the created order is there for us – whether or not certain men will hear or heed. The song is being sung. Tis there for those with the courage and inspiration to find their place in the choir."

"Even here?" Jonn asked, once again enthralled and earnest, "You and I in a place like this? Where is your god?"

She spoke softly, smiling again, to put him at ease as she stood, "A benevolent creator loves that which also creates. I arrived here by following His plan. Now... Now I am improvising. Difficult though the circumstance, this may yet be my cadenza. I live my life, make my music, in the ways taught to me. I have faith enough to make room for that. Until an upbeat again signals my cue, I stand ever ready."

Sister Bethany stood at eye level with Jonn, taking a step toward him.

"What now?" he held out a hand as though to stop her.

She slowly took his hand, gently inviting, "You tell me."

Chapter 26
Dying Well

Time for the main event at last, Ornandez walked out onto the sands of the arena. His arm not only bandaged, the wound had been cauterized as well.

Not standard fare for a gladiator between fights, but Ornandez must have insisted it was necessary and someone must have been willing to listen. Otherwise, he appeared as he always did, modestly decorated leather armor and twin swords.

Illwarr came out opposite him. Nearly twice the size of the Southlander with whom he would do battle, Illwarr thrust his fists in the air and roared to the reply of the crowd. Fists, unlike the orcs with whom he was oft mistaken, with no mere nails, thick and sharpened, but genuine talons, horn-like bone that emerged from the ends of his fingers.

He had two pair of teeth like tusks, but the rest were a mouthful of needles and razors. His skin, hairless and dark gray, thick, not merely with muscle and callous, but appeared more akin to a rhinoceros' hide. Neck broader than head, legs like tree trunks, spine self-armored by protruding bones, muscle and vein grotesquely bulging from every inch, save the slab of fat at the belly, ears and nose like a bat, and eyes blazing orange bright. Illwarr was a horror to behold.

Mayhap, some rare form of ogre or troll, it mattered not. To the men who faced him, Illwarr towered, a demon come up from some hell to devour his opponent, body and soul.

Ornandez felt fear. He did not show it. Crossing his gladius blades, he turned about and pulled them apart, saluting the audience, including a large collection of nobles with the governor, who had finally arrived, crowding into the small pulvinus.

Ornandez shouted the words, "Morituri Te Salutamus!"

We who are about to die salute you.

The governor, as a placeholder for the power and glory of the Imperator and the Senate, gave Ornandez a solemn nod, an old custom. He hoped it was a blessing. It was not.

117

From the general crowd, each fighter received equal response. They did not truly favor one over the other, only the thrill of the final fight to come. Custom and honor be damned, they wanted blood.

The gladiator was tired and sore, but had been worse on both accounts in past battles. We can never know if he truly thought he could win, but he clearly came prepared to give the quest for victory every bit of his breath and inch of his life.

The champion gladiator charged the opposing creature, ran straight at him. Illwarr raised his arms up to clobber the oncoming attacker, but at the last instant, Ornandez dropped into a slide, diving feet first between Illwarr's legs, and cutting him at the ankles as he passed through.

He did cut the creature, but only barely. Worse, Ornandez did not pass completely through. Rather he was grabbed by the head and flung, arse over ears, into the air, landing some feet away. How his neck was not broken from the grapple, toss, and fall seemed like a miracle. His armor saved him from the creature's claws, save for a thumb that sliced the gladiator at the left ear and hinge of his jaw.

Before Ornandez was standing, Illwarr was barreling forward in a charge of his own. The gladiator rolled right and sprung to his feet. As momentum driven Illwarr passed him by, he counter attacked the huge creature.

Ornandez, impressively, had managed to hold on to both of his swords and was instantly poised to strike. He lashed out with both blades, bringing them across each other and back again. In a flash, four slashes were inflicted upon Illwarr's bicep, in addition to the clips at his ankles. All the while, Ornandez's head was still swimming from his collision with the ground. A disadvantage he could ill afford.

Of those six blows landed by the gladius blades, only the one at the creature's left ankle and one at the front of his left bicep, actually drew blood. The creature's hide was even thicker than it appeared.

Illwarr wheeled on Ornandez. Reaching his right arm across himself and over the gladiator's defenses, the creature punched Ornandez on the top of the head. The already dizzy gladiator lost all sense of up and down in that moment and Illwarr's claws went to work.

A flurry of flashes, claw to blade, claw to blade, again and again, until the left gladius missed its parry and creature's talon found purchase upon flesh.

Likewise, the right sword was knocked from the gladiator's grasp and Illwarr again tore meat from Ornandez's bones. He swung his remaining gladius before him and rolled backwards. Distancing himself from the creature, he glanced down and took inventory of his wounds.

The gladiator's left thigh had two deep gouges. His right hip was nicked and his right forearm was cut to the bone in three places. Hands and legs all still worked *for all they good they'd do* him. There was nowhere to run. Illwarr was between the gladiator and his other sword. There were no options.

Thus Ornandez stood his ground. Smallish, wounded, holding his short sword before him defensively, it was impossible for the gladiator to appear courageous or defiant. He did not. As sure as he tried to pretend anything but, Ornandez looked, more than anything, like a frightened child holding out a stick to protect himself from a much older and larger bully.

The bully could smell fear, or made the audience believe that he could, turning about and slowly storming toward the tiny gladiator. Illwarr was smarter than he appeared. He betrayed the fact by how quickly he took to the drama and theatrics of the arena. He did not kill quickly, when he could avoid it. Illwarr stirred the crowd. They hated him, loved his fights, feared him, but cheered whenever he appeared, all according to his design.

Illwarr stood before Ornandez, menacing. The gladiator did not so much as flinch. This frustrated the creature who roared and beat his chest, but got no reaction. In anger, Illwarr swung, not at Ornandez, it was too soon for the kill, but at the gladiator's sword.

Ornandez allowed himself to be disarmed, accepted it, and took the chance to dive forward, between Illwarr's legs. He got through this time.

On the other side, the gladiator grabbed up the sword he had lost earlier and, right as Illwarr turned about, he turned as well. Ornandez leaped high off the ground, both hands tight on the gladius, and stabbed the creature high in the abdomen as he came down. The sword plunged into the creature's meat, to the hilt, and its blade carved a wound down through its guts.

Illwarr roared again. Not the bass filled thunder of his performance roar, but a dissonant howl that rang with pain and terrible offense. Ornandez had hoped for a killing blow and mayhap it might have been, but not instantly and not soon enough for the gladiator. Illwarr struck down Ornandez, clawing down the left side of the gladiator, cleaving his face, shoulder, arm, and chest with a single blow.

Ornandez collapsed to the ground and the crowd OOH-ed with pain as though they too could feel the blow. Illwarr struck at the man again, plunging his claws into Ornandez abdomen, wrist twisting sharply. The crowd OOH-ed again. The gladiator groaned and gurgled, vomiting bile and blood.

Illwarr lifted his skewered opponent from the ground, licking the gladiator's blood from his forearm as it oozed down from exposed entrails. The crowd went wild, hooting and hollering, screaming, and began to call for death.

From within, Illwarr grasped Ornandez by the spine and with his other hand grabbed his neck. With a snap tug, the monster tore the man in half, anointing himself in the viscera that spilled forth, baptized in the blood of Napua's last champion.

Ornandez was slain by Illwarr in violent spectacle such as the people of Napua had come to expect. For all his effort, the fallen gladiator only succeeded at making his opponent's victory all the more astonishing and celebrated.

"So passes Ornandez of the Southlands, gladiator of the first order and would-be freedom fighter, from this life in violent spectacle; what a waste," a man in a green cloak, hood pulled up, said to another man much alike to himself. In the next moment, the crowd erupted in cheers for their new champion, Illwarr the Manslayer.

Chapter 27
Changing Plans

There were a handful of men in green cloaks. So alike and clustered, they stood out starkly. They alone remained seated and silent, standing out all the more, had anyone at all had been paying attention. No one was.

Yet among themselves, a man, unhooded, bald of head and grand of beard, stood up, and so they all stood too. His face was grim. Theirs were almost apologetic. He spoke to them, over the frenzied crowd, "I've had about enough of games and the failure of hope this day. Let us leave this place and revisit our plans in private."

They walked out together. Their leader before them. They did not weave through the mob. Noticed or unnoticed, consciously or subconsciously, others made way for them as they passed. As an arrow flies, in an unwavering straight line, they left the arena.

The streets of Napua were relatively empty, the arena having been filled to capacity. With both ease and speed, the group made their way out of the city, returning to the farm house that had become their base of operations.

They were northmen, Van-blessed mountain folk, and soldiers of Morralish. Yet they wore green, rather than blue, with no visible sign rank among them, save for their leader to whom they deferred.

The Forest Phantoms they were called. No ordinary soldiers, they were also rangers all, and each with a special trade besides. Their leader, a paladin, as was another of them, though the second was a brute of enormous size. A third member of their band was lithe and handsome, with a silver-tongue, and keenest senses. Also there were two wizards, one an alchemist, apprenticed to the other, of obvious elven-blood, who was himself an artificer, more scholar than warrior, but more than able to hold his own. The leader favored a greatsword, the other paladin simply wore spikes on his gauntlets, the smaller man carried two light axes, the alchemist fought in the Antori way, sword and shield, and the part-elven wizard wielded a unique staff adorned with a crystal.

It was they who thought to use Napua's gladiators to incite a slave rebellion. They had watched that hope snuffed out before their very eyes, that very day. If Antoria was to be their new homeland, changes had to be made. As men of both war and subterfuge, they had leaned on what they knew. Alas that plan had evaporated and the question stood before them, like a thing in the room.

"What now?" the handsome, blonde axe man gave it voice.

"We hav'va'tha single greatest weapon in all the Imperium tat erra disposal," the giant paladin with flame red hair answered, "We use it'ta kill Illwarr, turn it loose on all who pra'test the fact, free the slaves, and use them ta keep the city in check. Their voices 'ill carry much weight wit'tat clear and demonstrated threat available ta back'em up."

"Really?" the bald and brassy bearded man, their leader, questioned him, "Strike first and ask questions later?"

"I was thinkin' strike feerst and let 'ta Van-god sort'em oot, ak'shoo'ly, Chief."

"You think this is funny?" the leader barked, "This is some sort of game?"

"Nay," the larger man replied, "I jus' know we're sittin' on tha mains ta victory, while those men died, while an empire of slavers is prop'tup by the might of good men. 'Sinny'thing but funny, Chief."

The leader rubbed his bald dome in thought, explaining, "If we soldiers of Morralish conquer this city by means mysterious and arcane, it won't be a civil war – t'will be a holy one. Our brothers, soldiers of Morralish across these lands, will be exiled from the Imperium. We'll be branded heretics by the Cathedral of Din and the Holy Family, son to father, will be torn asunder. None of us can abide this slavery. You know my mind, tis why I brought us here. Yet what you would do, puts more lives than our own and those of a slave rebellion in jeopardy. It could murder the world! Paladin or no, you don't want that blood on your hands. We'd all be damned right along with our irrelevant intentions."

"He is right, Sir Quain," the sagely wizard approached the huge man and spoke in conciliatory tones.

"I know 'ee's right," the massive Sir Quaindraught accepted, though with a hint of impertinence, "He's always right. I just haddinna thought'tit'trew."

"And now we have," said the slender blonde man, shaking off the thought of it all, "Next."

"I heard tell," the short-haired alchemist began, "just before we came here, that someone had come to the city looking for Prince Bengallen. Had claimed he survived the attack on our homeland. That it could be re-taken and this man had come under royal order to beseech our generals to rally us home. We've been out of touch for a while. I know we haven't seen anything ourselves, but it doesn't mean something might not be in motion, something known only to the senior commanders."

"Sternus," the blonde man corrected, "You are telling it wrong. Some folks are saying that a dragon destroyed Morralish Prime and, having survived, the Prince and his retinue tracked it down into the Frontier and slew it. That's the story that says tis safe for us all to go home now. Bye-bye. Tis a fantasy spun into propaganda. Those of us that want to be Antori can stay and accept Antori law. Those of us that cannot abide it can reunite with our dragonslayer Prince. All a little too mythic, don't ya think?"

"A little less mythic to us though, right?" the part-elven sage asked them, brow raised.

They all chewed on the silence a moment. They knew something, a great secret that posed many more questions. So each thought. Each interrogated the narrative within himself, what was and was not possible.

"If the Holy Prince yet lived," the leader, called Chief, broke the silence, "the first thing he would have done is call his troops home. I know him."

"Yet we've heard no call," Sternus, the alchemist, reiterated.

"An why da'ya suppose 'at is?" the brutish red-haired paladin asked.

"Because someone does not want us to have heard it," the slender blonde answered, "Ooh, it fits. Why pay us, and a nation it can claim no longer exists, when the Imperium can simply assume us into its own legions. Not all that sinister, relative to the nation that thrives on legal slave trade. Have we been maneuvered?"

"Mayhap, Sir Ihrvan," the Chief speculated with him, "You have the right of it. Spit and holler, it makes too much sense to ignore, but tis all mere conjecture. So we'll have to look into it. We'll seek out the Prince. Find him or no, I'll report to the generals after, share our findings and hear what of their news and orders. Unless we come up with something that would impress upon us the need to do otherwise. Tis a plan at any rate. Take two days leave and meet back here, we'll move out then. No interactions with other Morralish soldiers, we're still operating dark. We don't need any homesick lookieloos stumbling into our business. We've suffered significant setbacks here and there may be more bad news in the days to come. Find what comfort you can, rest yourselves, a long road lies ahead."

Chapter 28
Gathering Thanes

Prince Bengallen gathered his thanes in Bavin Hall at Woodhaven one last time. He addressed them, "Dwarf and elf lend aid, yet the sons of Morralish have not returned to claim their home. I have received secreted dispatch, from junior soldiers serving in the Avigueux Provence, north of the Antori Peninsula. They question their officer's edicts. They want to come home or see if there is home to return to. Yet without higher command, they know naught but to follow their leadership. Some think their leaders conspire with the Imperium for citizenship and greater coin for the continued service of the soldiers under their command. Others believe that their generals are just going through the motions, following orders issued years ago, themselves knowing naught else to do. Yet rumors of our deeds in Spearpointe have spread across the Imperium and the eyes of my men turn north and east as their hearts call them home. So we shall go to them then. We shall enter into the Imperium in grand display, either as Heroes of the Frontier and guests of the Capital or as approaching army drawn from the provinces."

"You'd march on their capital?" Ruffis laughed.

"My patience is long gone," Prince Bengallen retorted, "The time already passed. There is justice to be done and none should dare stand in its way. The sons of Morralish will return home, even must I conquer the whole of the world to see it done."

"So," Caanaflit challenged, "Tis empire then, after all, Exalted Imperator?"

"It must seem so. It may need be so," the Prince explained, waving his arms expansive to his sides, "Necessity. All of this borne of necessity. None of it what I wanted. No one is asking me what I want. Not since before my palace sacked. Not since before my father, my friends, and mentors, and … were slain. Not since before my body cleaved and left to die has anyone asked me what I wanted. I do what I must. If any of you are not ready to do the same, the door lies but some feet away."

No one stood. *Of course they did not. Why must Ruffis poke? Why must Caanaflit question?*

Everyone knew that what they were doing was important. Each action filled with meaning. Bengallen was a moral man. The Paladin-Prince would have ridden alone, straight back into his conquered lands, if he thought for an instant it would accomplish anything. He had nearly done it anyway.

These were not secrets. That the Prince only dealt with the problems before him and did only what was right and needed was no secret.

Yet he continued to answer to the skepticism of lesser men. For better or worse, and it was truly debatable and debated, he had yet to find the force of will to be king.

"Who shall go with you, Your Majesty?" Malcolm asked.

He had thought to volunteer, but thought twice. Inviting another remark from Ruffis was unwise and the question placed his Prince in the position to command rather than accepting offers. Malcolm was learning.

"My thanes, if they be so, shall ride with me. Three Knights of the Spear, Sir Garrus, Sir Caldun, Sir Bohr, and the Antori squire, the one that rode with Sir Jason and Sir Vix, Felix – Felix Invictus," Prince Bengallen instructed, continuing, "Plus two other men from Spearpointe, of their choosing, and six others from Woodhaven, you may choose them. Oh, make it five and Brunsis, the minotaur. He and I never spoke as intended. Invite him to travel with us for as far as he might care too."

"I'll see to it personally," Shomotta at last spoke, "Any further command?"

"We leave at dawn," the Prince said simply, "Make your preparations."

Prince Bengallen stood and they all stood with him, though Ruffis, again, did so lazily. Shomotta offered a slight bow, Alpona and Malcolm followed suit. Caanaflit wore his contemplation on his face. As Bengallen turned to the hearth fire behind him, the others filed out.

"Thane Malcolm," Prince Bengallen added, "Would you send in Sira Roselle?"

"At once, Your Majesty," Malcolm replied as he exited Bavin Hall and immediately he saw her, banner in hand, standing sentry at the door. There he spoke to her, "I am going. You are not. His Majesty will tell you himself, but I wanted to tell you first."

"Why?"

"I only know that you were not on his list."

125

"You did not question?"

"Tis not my place to question."

"Tis not?" Roselle questioned him again, "Are a throne-lord's thanes not his advisors?"

"Rosey, he did not ask for advice," Malcolm explained, "Hear him. If you would have His Majesty reconsider, I – nay, we will go to him together."

"I would not have us parted," the lady-knight gasped, "Not now. Not so soon."

Malcolm pressed his forehead to hers, kissed her briefly.

"The Prince would see you now."

Roselle, eyes still heavy, entered Bavin Hall where Prince Bengallen motioned to the empty seat beside him.

"Sira," Prince Bengallen addressed her as soon as she was seated, "I need someone here, eyes and ears, my word and will. I need that to be you."

"Your Majesty," she began, "Should I not bear your standard before you and apprentice under you? Would not a thane better –"

He cut her off, "My thanes are not from the Frontier. You are. Spearpointe and Woodhaven have their own leadership, their own ways, and they should run themselves without a thane of the throne scrutinizing their every decision. I've promised them a certain amount of autonomy. Yet, a soldier, one of their own, here to protect, learn, advise. That will be more palatable, more appropriate. These are my orders. Besides, you are learning much from the dwarven paladins, yes?"

"I am," Sira Roselle agreed, "and I will heed your command. You bestow upon me a great honor, Your Majesty. I appreciate the explanation and hear the wisdom in it. Tis my pleasure to serve and I am humbly grateful."

"Rebuild the Spearpointe Company and coordinate with the local watchmen. Strengthen this new alliance between Spearpointe and Woodhaven. Mayhap Frontiersmen in need of work can help rebuild the walls here. In the months ahead, more dwarves will come, some soldiers of Morralish even, you are my standard-bearer, you know my mind. I trust you to represent me to them. That I have you and can count on you, Sira, for that I am humbly grateful."

Chapter 29
Speaking Elvish

Parting company, Prince Bengallen went to the Temple in Woodhaven. There, an elf, also grateful in his own way, had come to temporarily reside.

"Ess ham thoo ooh haff fissotat –" Prince Bengallen began in Elvish before he was interrupted.

"With respect, Your Highness, I can speak the common Antori tongue, as well as that of the mountain folk, well enough and your Ilufaen is quite terrible."

Bengallen was not feeling the gratitude, but began again, assuming it was there, "I am told you have visited with the dwarves. That a contingent of them are to journey home with you."

"Then His Highness has been told truths."

"How long had you been in captivity?"

"Why does His Highness concern himself with this detail?"

"Is not a liberator entitled?"

"Why would one suppose he is? Do you now claim the power over me that was held by my captors?"

"No. There is much changing in the physical and spiritual worlds. It would not be my place to teach them to an elf, but if he knew of them, I would seek his counsel."

"His Highness should have started with that," the elf said, "You are Bengallen Hastenfarish, the Farish were once at one with the elves, elven-blood is in your veins, but when your kind sought the throne of men, the time was not right. So we elves retreated from what is now called Morralish, save some few advisors. They would pass from this world in the centuries that followed. We all know the fate of Aethumir. Yet you come to me in his armor, would entreat me as advisor. I am the wrong family. I am no kin to the so-called 'elf-lord' Hal'shar. I am kin to the great Chamberlain of the Antori beginning, and I have no love for Morralish Kings, their mutts, or paladins besides."

"Speak to the Mother with that tongue?"

"Tread lightly, prince, you'll not want to blaspheme the Mother to an elf."

"Which is why I did not. I invoked her name. We are both bound to her as Holy Family. You do not have to love me, brother, but our great Mother does. In the name of Divine Love, I ask your aid."

"Clever," the elf relented, " and you did save me. To answer your first question, more than three, less than four years. I know from the seasons passing, not the days. I've answered one question. His Highness may ask two more to make it three in the name of the Holy Family ... and the ties that bind."

"I would tell you, again, that much has changed in the world. You may come to regret your rudeness. If you have been captive so long, I am unsure you can aid me. Yet, as I have two more questions: What is your role?"

"I am a diplomat."

"You jest."

"I do not."

"The Frontier city-states of Spearpointe and Woodhaven have accepted me as their overlord."

"Bravo."

Prince Bengallen, having announced himself thus with no change in the elf's demeanor, inferred that this diplomat must not have been sent to the Frontier, or Morralish for that matter. Thus Prince Bengallen asked his third and final question, "To whom were you sent as a diplomat when you were captured?"

"The orcs," the elf stated plainly, "To the most feared of orc chieftains, I delivered word from my people and spoke with him on their behalf. My subsequent enslavement his only reply. I will now return to my people and tell them what has transpired. Worry not, the dwarves will report on your behalf. They think you're a swell guy. They just love the cheese out of you."

Prince Bengallen smiled then. The elf was clearly off put by it. The Prince, wordless, simply stared, grinning ear to ear. When at last the elf uneasily stood, Bengallen spoke, "I have you."

"Pardon."

"You were sent to the Chieftain of the Ironclaw Clan?"

"Yes."

"You know we have slain him?"

"Yes and I am grateful, but there is a limit to my gratitude."

"You know that a thane in my service slew Blagrogk's eldest son not six months ago?"

"I know of his death as well. Now if His Highness—"

It was Prince Bengallen's turn to interrupt, "That thane in my service is also a son of Blagrogk. He is half-orc, called Malcolm. He is my thane and my friend. If you are truly a diplomat sent from the elves to speak with the head of the Ironclaw orc clan, then it would be my privilege to introduce you to Malcolm Ironclaw, that you may resolve your quest."

"You jest," the elf echoed Prince Bengallen's earlier surprise, appearing to enjoy the banter.

"I do not," the Prince replied, "Not at all."

Chapter 30
Attending Affairs

Sira Roselle approached Thane Malcolm and placed her hands in his. He kissed her gently, placing his brow atop her forehead.

She spoke softly, "I am staying. You leave soon?"

"Very," Malcolm replied in like tone, "We leave now, for Spearpointe, Prince Bengallen will briefly attend to affairs, await the rest from Woodhaven, and then we trek across the Frontier to the Imperium. Half the journey is the one I've already made thrice in little over a year. Such is a life of quest, I suppose, but all this to and fro was something I must have missed in the stories. Though, thinking back, it was clearly there."

"Even now," Roselle playfully chided him, "Your head full of stories."

"Especially now," he said, lifting his voice, "As I leave this, you, I have to remind myself that all I ever wanted was to live those stories. I don't want to leave you, but we'd both regret it, resent each other even, mayhap, if we were to go against our liege lord to be together."

"Our love would not exist if not for the faith he has placed in us," Roselle agreed, "to let him down now, would surely tarnish what we share. How I want you to be wrong. Yet if we did such a thing, we'd no longer be the people we fell in love with."

"Am I convincing you or you I?"

"Fitting that we'd have to convince each other."

"Give me your permission to see this through," Malcolm asked, "and I shall give you mine."

"Thane Malcolm," she addressed him, pulling her face from his own, but locking eye contact, what for serious, "Be the man I love, do your duty to our lord and leader, and return to me, proud and victorious!"

Surprisingly, in that moment, Malcolm understood Alpona's critique of Prince Bengallen's reluctance to order Sir Jason's charge, but he pushed the thought aside and replied in kind, "Sira Roselle, be the woman I love, do your duty to our lord and leader, fly his banner, be a symbol of his authority and protection. I shall return to you."

They embraced and kissed again. Propriety be damned, he kissed her well and long with no care for passersby. She reached up and placed her hands to the back of his head, sustaining the intimacy of their moment a little longer.

Uncoupled, Sira Roselle whistled and her horse, the great Thumu, trotted over. She began to mount the steed and Malcolm aided her. Their hands lingered, one in the other, one last embrace, as he stared up at her and she down upon him. At last they released one another and she began to fumble with her riding gloves.

As Malcolm began to turn away, he noticed she dropped one. He turned back to pick it up, but she was already wheeling the horse about. Leaning down to pick up the glove off the ground, Malcolm noticed it was fine and new, nothing she had used before.

He began to call out to her as she rode off, but she was holding the other glove, unworn, in her hand, above her head, waving it as she went. Thus realization dawned on him, it was a favor, like in the stories he loved so much. She had bought such fine and impractical gloves, not for riding, but as the ladies in the stories. It was a token of her affection left to her champion. Malcolm blushed.

Tenderly parted from his love, he had one final task prior to signaling for the Prince's departure. Thane Malcolm passed beyond Woodhaven's walls into the dwarf camp, where many were preparing to leave on journeys of their own. One among them was an elf, who, seeing Malcolm approach, pulled out a chair for him at a small table. As the half-orc came within speaking distance, the elf made a slight casual bow and spoke, "Malcolm Ironclaw, I am Zyrus, an emissary of my people. The words I bear are for the Ironclaw Chieftain, do you claim this birthright and hear me?"

"I would hear your words, good diplomat," Malcolm began, sitting, "but I claim no lordship over the tattered army that, defeated, has fled this place?"

"Why have you come then?" Zyrus asked, joining him at the table.

"My prince bade me come and hear you. So I do."

"It is your business what you share with the Prince of Morralish," responded the emissary, defensively, "Your loyalties are no concern of mine. The orc, however, are. Not only those that imprisoned me, or those that besieged these

131

walls, but what of the women and children of the clans? I speak also of them. When you deny your birthright, do you also think of them?"

"No. I did not."

"Even the Forgotten are sometimes remembered," Zyrus added, cryptically, "and that is precisely why I have come. As I understand titles, to those entitled to them, they can be picked up and put down at your pleasure. You are entitled to Chieftain of the Ironclaw, if you would agree to wear it, for just a little while, I will discharge my duty."

Malcolm, grim faced, nodded.

The elven diplomat continued, "From your father's corpse there was loot taken. A bauble, it would have appeared as nothing more than a trinket of wood and stone, was taken. Hold it in your hands and speak the words: 'The Ironclaw Chieftain listens on behalf of the Forgotten.' Do this, then, when next you've drawn near to the Dreadwood, another will come to you and speak words. Mine was merely to extend the invitation."

"Where is the item of wood and stone?"

"It was taken from me by your father, without hearing my words, when he enslaved me," Zyrus answered, "He thought it a talisman of protection. He wore it. Perhaps your Prince has taken it as fair plunder. Perhaps your wizard studies it. Perhaps one of the rogues will sell it. I have not seen it."

"I know of this talisman," Malcolm replied, "my brother, a warlock, tried to convince my father to let him study it. They argued over it. To my knowledge, they never spoke again."

"Perhaps he knew what it was."

"Regardless," Malcolm said, "I know of it. I shall find it."

"I sincerely hope that you do," Zyrus offered, standing, "If there is nothing else you'd ask of me, a journey lies before myself as well."

Malcolm bowed, casually permissive, adding, "Gratitude."

Chapter 31
Tasking Troops

Lord-General Kellus Anderason, second in the Morralish Third Army Regiment only to his High Lord-General, assembled all the officers of the third and fourth battalions to a counsel. There had been much gossip and rumor of late, and with that High Lord-General come and gone, the ranking knights assumed they were being assembled to be set to right. They were correct, but the right of it would come as a surprise yet still.

"My fine commanders and captains," the General began, "it seems I may have acted in error. You have heard the tales being told, yet few of you know of the Thane who delivered such tidings before they became commonly told."

"What tales and tidings, m'lord?" an anonymous officer's disembodied voice burst from the assembly, asking.

"Tales that the Prince of Morralish has survived and risen to challenge in the Frontier," the General clarified, "of which everyone now has opinion. This was, in fact, prefigured by a Thane, allegedly in our Prince's service, who did recall us to the Prince at Spearpointe. This Thane was, himself, prefigured by a Priestess, unknown to and not encountered by me, who made similar claims to the General Council in Antoria Royal. I had dismissed privileged word of the one, under advisement. I dismissed fortuitous encounter by the other, of my own lapsed judgment, with the intent of not spreading false hope and retaining our focus on the missions and finances that keep us paid and fed. In the time since, as you all know well, no requests come from Antoria and hope of the Prince's survival, false or not, has spread on its own. I am forced to reconsider the evidence known to me as well as my stance on it."

A knight ranked captain, stood and spoke into the silence even as many commanders who out ranked him did not, "It seems rather clear to me, my lord. The Stone's Pryde should make for Spearpointe."

"I'm inclined to agree," the General replied, forthrightly, "but you yet know the whole of it. When our High Lord-General came, he told me what he meant to be a secret, but one that I cannot in good conscience keep from you a moment longer. All available generals are to convene to discuss their regiments being absorbed into the Antori Legions. I am to have departed already. By now, our High Lord-General has or will soon realize that I will not be joining him."

"Not all the generals were invited," a hooded man said, standing.

Annoyed by the presumption, interruption, and lack of formal address, the General began to rebuke the man, "First, you'll address me as 'lord,' second, unmask yourself, and third, how the hells would you know?"

The man threw his hood back, he was older than General Anderason, but no one around him indicated recognition.

He said with a smile, "Because, your lordship, as the High Lord-General of the First Regiment, Summit Vanguards, I have come from Antoria Royal to seek you out on related concerns. Yet this is the first I have heard of such a gathering."

It quickly became clear to all that Lord-General Anderason recognized the senior general of the prominent regiment, gaping unconsciously as his superior spoke.

Anderason abruptly gathered himself, bowed his head, placed his fist to his heart.

"My lord, I would gladly hear your counsel."

All the men in the room stood immediately at those words, but the surprise guest gestured them to sit, putting them at ease.

"General Anderason, you seem to know more than I do. I thank you for the information and appreciate the honesty with which you entreat the men. I had also come to the conclusion that it was time for us to leave. With these battalions the furthest out and closest to home, I came here to ask you to prepare a supply depot and assembly point for soldiers departing from the Imperium to Spearpointe and, ultimately, points north. As enlightening as your words are, I suppose, I would still ask you to do the same. Tis apparently a subversive order, one which your own High Lord-General might oppose, but at this point, I'm guessing that isn't a problem for you?"

"Not at all, my lord," General Anderason replied, "We'll draw up initial plans and figures tonight. Set the men to task in the morning."

"Excellent."

"I would add," Anderason added, "Lord Harkon, it is nice to know I am not alone in this."

"General Anderason – no – all you, knights and paladins, officers of the Third, Stone's Pryde," High Lord-General Harkon addressed them, "We are not traitors. We are the betrayed. Ours is now the work of getting to our Prince. Ultimately, hopefully, avenge ourselves and our slain kinfolk against whatever terror befell our homeland. Tis a worthy thing. Your general, there, says so. I, High Lord-General of the First, say so. A Thane of the Prince has come to your door and said so. A Priestess has said it in the capital of foreign nations. Your Prince, miraculously survived, if you dare to believe it, has said it. Tis a noble cause, just and true. Let any who deny it be cursed as traitors and cowards too! Ours is the genuine task of our people. I say it!"

"We say it!" the officers of the Third Regiment concurred in unison.

Chapter 32
Minding Spearpointe

With immediate concerns resolved and other affairs in order, Prince Bengallen and his retinue rode south to Spearpointe. Their stop in Burntleaf was uneventful, save for some argument between Shomotta and the Tavern Master. No one ever seemed to determine what it was over or how it was resolved so quickly. Regardless, Prince Bengallen, his chosen companions, and other reinforcements from Spearpointe, that had not yet returned home, only stayed the single night and continued, straight away, for the smaller Frontier city-state at first light.

They arrived to find the Autarkic Frontier City-State of Spearpointe once again in mourning. Its Lord-Mayor had died in a hunting accident. The good people awaited the return of his nephew and heir to begin the election proceedings. It was anticipated that none would run against the handsome, popular, and heroic knight, but alas, the news of Sir Jason's own death in the Battle of Woodhaven only complicated the situation in the days before their arrival.

Elections in Spearpointe typically went thus: A foreign noble of superior station developed enough business interests in Spearpointe to warrant living there. Unable to tolerate the lordship of his lesser peerage, the new noble called for elections. Depending on the quality of the current Lord-Mayor, the business interests of the challenging noble, and the fame and title each wore, people voted where their interests lay. Most often, but not always, old mayors were ousted and new ones installed.

Upon a Lord-Mayor's death, however, his heir would make a call for an eligible noble to seek the office and a time would be given for them to compete for the love and favor of the citizenry. Occasionally, more than one would respond. It fell to them to work out between themselves, however, which one would finally stand for election. If no one stood against him, which was more often the case, the late-mayor's designated heir was simply confirmed by a plebiscite, a yes/no vote of the people requiring only a simple majority.

Yet, in this instance, there was neither a Lord-Mayor nor an heir. A peculiar species of madness descended upon the lesser nobles that made up Spearpointe's gentry. A sudden thirst for power parched them. Favors, bribes, even gangs of loyalists, to this one or that one, clashed in the streets, resulting in many injuries and even a few deaths. Despite Prince Bengallen's way with people, the city remained on the brink of chaos after his arrival.

Maintaining order became a daily struggle.

His simple hope was to appoint Caanaflit as an interim mayor, but the canny rogue advised against it, "It would look false upon Your Majesty's promise to let the Frontier manage its own affairs," and he, of course, had the right of it.

They lost more than a week to the election that followed. Never had so many competed at once. The populace was fractured in its divided loyalties and especially unhappy that so little time had been provided for deciding. To ease the citizens' concerns and gain their consent for the proceedings, Prince Bengallen decreed that the winner would only hold the title of Mayor for a year and a day, after which, a plebiscite would be held to determine if he had proven himself worthy to formally become the Lord-Mayor of Spearpointe. If he was not confirmed, he would continue until an appropriate candidate chose to run against him in the traditional way.

The people not only consented, moreover, they found the Prince's edict fair and wise. The days that followed were free of the civil unrest that had plagued the days of recent past. More than anything, silent popular acceptance decreed that the matter would be resolved in this manner.

In the end, Sir Shamus Stoutspear, Knight of the Spear, who had rode with the Paladin-Prince against and had been wounded in the Slaying of the Beast of Spearpointe was elected Mayor. Though his injuries had left him too crippled to remain a proper cavalryman, he had been awarded a high position in the city watch and had served there well, visibly, even during these difficult and uncertain times.

Caanaflit was thrilled by the choice, his overt pleasure only suspicious to those closest to him. Sir Shamus, at least as loyal as Sir Jason, had none of the latter's messy familial ties in distant nations. They who were suspicious, incidentally, pleased enough with the outcome themselves, ignored their own circumspect intuitions.

Leadership of a simple village was not beyond the purview of a knight, but a proper lordship, over so many people, so much land, to a knight who had to give himself a surname, it was unheard of. Yet he was a hero, wounded for the people, serving among the people. He might not win the plebiscite when the voting would be less divided among so many candidates as the principal election had been.

He might later be supplanted by the challenge of a noble lord. For the time being, however, Spearpointe had a Mayor, chosen by them and from among them. Whether or not he had what it would take to become the proper Lord-Mayor of Spearpointe was something he had a year and a day to prove. With the right introductions to the right advisors and a name like Stoutspear, Prince Bengallen was certain he could rise to the occasion. Thane Caanaflit notably agreed, all the more so.

Chapter 33
Teaching History

The journey that first day was rather silent. Each man with his own thoughts and ruminations. Many were still road weary from other travels not so long removed. Yet they had good horses and a drawn carriage, if they needed it. Cradled in a carriage, however, was no way to start a journey such as this. So each man rode atop his mount, eyes to the horizon, the sun overhead, and his meditations his own.

That evening, at campfire, Bengallen addressed them, "Most of you are neither familiar with the Antori Imperium nor versed enough in the Church's history to have gleaned much about it. I know what I know as much from the Church as from political lessons, but I did have a chance to visit once, when I was young. Caanaflit and Shomotta have been there more recently, they can share their insights upon the road. Yet, if you would hear me, I will tell you what I know of the place. Its onset was important to the Church, as well as the Order of Paladins, to which I belong. This is what I know:"

At the dawn of the historical era, moving beyond the fog of the years that followed the Great Cataclysm and the Slumbering of the World, the line of the Dtorian Kings was broken. King Mercos II of House Dtorian died unwed and without an heir. Then came Dinnothyl.

Vandor sent to us his blood, the son Ellenofae bore him, to take the high seat and become the First Imperator. The Din-god, clothed in mortal flesh, wielded the might of Antoria to bring peace and justice to Uhratt. Within two decades, he had smashed the temples of the dead gods in Avigueux, redeemed the ancestor worship that had fallen into decadence in Qallengrad, and banished the demon cults from Thalos. He formed the custodial empire, that has persisted for centuries, from these realms and made allies of Morralish in the east and Hazar in the west. At that time, Dinnothyl, being both half-elven and the son of their goddess, inspired the elves to freely join the Antori Imperium, and they rode with men to root out heresy and blasphemy. This, however, was not to last.

On the eve of his thirty-third birthday, as well as the eve of his wedding, Dinnothyl gathered the Throne-Lords of the three vassal kingdoms to counsel. They betrayed him. They had replaced the palace sentries, formed from the Praetorian Legion, with legionnaires conscripted from their own lands. Out of fear and mistrust, greed and a lust for power, the once-and-would-be kings beset Dinnothyl.

The never-again king of Thalos was said to have taken on the visage of a demon only to be smote and destroyed by Dinnothyl's conjured blade of holy light. The other two, though wounded and the ancient blades of their royal houses reduced to ruined slag, held the First Imperator at bay long enough for their men to overwhelm him.

In flesh, the Din-god took thirteen wounds. Prior, he was pierced once in each of the three campaigns that formed the Antori Imperium and so it was said that he bled for his people.

On the day of his betrayal, he was slashed once by each of the two surviving traitors and stabbed five times by the rush of their soldiers. To crown their act of open rebellion, the traitor kings had Dinnothyl murdered in the cruelest tradition of ancient Antoria. A method outlawed three decades prior, on the day of Dinnothyl's coronation, its use would signal a return to the old ways. Three wicked spikes were driven into his flesh, by which he was nailed to a wooden beam torn from the mast of his balcony's canopy.

The horrid display of the dying man-god was lowered from said balcony. The bloody visage, hung from his own walls, outside of his own throne room, swayed atop his own banner, which quickly turned from pearly white to deepest crimson. The spectacle sparked a series of rebellions that lasted an unbroken century and every minor rebellion thereafter could be traced back to that day.

After the first three days, however, the traitor kings had fled, the palace had been re-taken, and Dinnothyl was brought in from off the wall. This was done personally by his Chamberlain, who was like a Thane that also serves as High Steward, with aid from a mere dozen legionnaires, those who had survived the battle to retake the palace. To their astonishment, Dinnothyl yet drew breath and spoke his final words!

"I have given you my life and my blood," Dinnothyl rasped, "I leave this to you. My father has bid me join him."

There has been a lot of debate about what "this" meant as well as whether the Din-god was talking directly to his Chamberlain, the dozen soldiers present, the whole empire, or everyone everywhere. The tradition of the paladin, for example, was built on a belief that "this" referred to his example, in life and blood, and while it had been addressed to those specific soldiers, it was offered to everyone who would take up his cause as they did. Each paladin can trace his sacred anointing back to a man in the room at Dinnothyl's ascension.

As his last breath left his body, an illuminated mist rose from his mouth. His whole body began to transition into the mystical vapor, brightness intensifying as it all flowed skyward, but not without spreading to anoint every man present: Twelve soldiers and the Chamberlain.

In a flash, he was gone. Only the crown remained.

The Chamberlain, a high-born elf named Kylaess, had his own interpretation of the Din-god's last mortal words. He took "this" to mean "all that was Dinnothyl's" and believed that he, himself specifically, was the one being addressed by those dying words. Thusly, Kylaess took the crown, married the waiting bride, pulled the once-white, then red, banner from the window, and rode out to avenge his god's murder and betrayal. The Chamberlain also took "my blood" to mean Dinnothyl's physical blood, soaked in the banner, and this was why red replaced white as the color of the Antori Imperium.

The Kylaess, who became the Second Imperator, was viewed by history to be passionate, more than naive or literal, in his interpretation of Dinnothyl's last words. Truly, Imperator Kylaess of House Perathyl, a house name he created meaning "ordered by him" in homage to his interpretation, was not given a mote of the time to consider these events as our historians and theologians have since.

Elves were known for their cunning and wisdom and not prone to blood-lust, so it would be unfair to discredit the man on these grounds. Elves were also known, however, for zeal and passion and the Chamberlain who became Imperator was nothing if not a paragon of his race. History has considered these traits, along with the events as they unfolded, and eventually chose to look gently upon Kylaess.

He died a few years later, in any case, and his half-elf son and heir became the so-called Infant Imperator. His mother's cousin was chosen to be his Chamberlain. Too soon after his selection, this Chamberlain had his own young daughter betrothed to the Infant Imperator. The decision and its timing were bereft of propriety and far from diplomatic.

The elves were becoming disillusioned with this decidedly human concept of empire. This shift in governance, along with their complete lack of say in it, became a rallying cry for their own secession. Rebellion on all fronts, the loss of fighting men due to the elves' departure was difficult enough without throwing away more lives in some fight to retain them. Thus the elves were permitted to freely withdraw from the Imperium, leaving as peaceably as they had joined it.

They departed with an iron clad peace treaty, including a standing invitation to rejoin. This was laid out in 'The Filial Accord of the Infant Imperator.' Pleased, the elves did maintain a hardy alliance for a decade or so, but as death counts climbed and the rebellions stretched on endlessly, the waning bond eventually broke.

About the time of those broken ties, the Infant Imperator – grown to man – had a son, Mercos, named for the last Antori King. As the boy came of age, there was growing political pressure to marry him to an elven noblewoman to restore the Imperium. Had there not been three rebellions to quell abroad already, a fourth might have broken out in the homeland when Mercos of House Perathyl was married to Julia of House Tdarius, a distant branch of the ancient House Dtorian, which had married into the Avigueux royalty.

This marriage ended the rebellions in Avigueux and restored Dtorian blood to the line of Imperators. Yet it was also seen by some as a victory beyond the grave for the traitor kings that had slain Dinnothyl.

Dissenters said things like:

"How does the watery blood of human kings matter when the right to rule was already ordained, anointed by the very Blood of God?"

It mattered to the noble human families that surrounded the Imperator. Thus, when Imperator Mecros died an old man, his son became the Fifth Imperator. Having already been wed to a human wife and with human heirs of his own, it became clear that no interest in preserving any elven-blood in the line of Imperators remained. This was the final severance between the elves and the Antori Imperium.

The rebellions would fade and flare, but there was no real peace in the Imperium after Dinnothyl. The so-called "Imperator's Peace" was a thing strictly enforced by war and the threat of war, which was no peace at all, only an illusion thereof. Under such conditions, the Antori Imperium became many different things to many different people. Merchants, scholars, and the faithful flocked to it as the pinnacle of human civilization, to be at the center of all roads, to study in the great colleges, to be where the Son of the Holy Family once lived and died.

Others fled, disillusioned. Yet others, seeing through the illusion, thrived in the cracks of the society, obtaining hard coin by maintaining that illusion through slavery, vice, and corruption. Yet many and more than all of these together were the common folk, who cared little or less for what borders they found themselves within. Hardy, honest, the salt of the land, these were people who sought only to protect and provide for their families until their days were spent.

Chapter 34
Debating Senate

While ultimate authority was in the hands of the Imperator, the laws of Antori Imperium were written and the will of its citizens made known by a collective of elected representatives known as the Imperial Senate. Each senator had to be free of debt, own property within or adjacent to the district he represented, be at least 30 years of age, and male. Exceptions to all of these criteria, however, had been made on a case-by-case basis in the past. Of the sitting senators at the time, one had acquired copious debt after his first election, but twice re-elected, another, serving his second term, had recently reached his thirtieth birthday, three had no property holdings whatsoever, and one was female.

On this particular day, the senate had a full docket of matters to discuss and, having been in session since before dawn, the mood had grown quite dispassionate. Several public ordinances had been passed with little or no discussion. Opponents to them were certain they could simply have them overturned, at some later time, once the problems they had foreseen began to come to bear in people's lives.

"Sometimes you have to let an ordinance pass to see how it will affect people," it was often said of such matters. This was how the Imperium had come to function, if one would dare call it functional at all.

The Imperial Senate was run by a Senate President, elected by the senators internally on a yearly basis, and he was almost always a man of great wealth and title. Traditionally, he was a decorated veteran of the Imperial Legions, but this custom had gone out of favor. In these days it was hard to get a military veteran elected to public office at all, let alone to the senate or its internal leadership.

In the second hour after their noon recess, the Senate President opened the floor for the next matter, "Docket number thirty-two, today's date, 'A Matter of Dispute Between Public Accommodation and the Right to Refuse Clients.' As certain goods and services are to be made available to all persons with the means to pay and yet all free citizens have the right to do only the work that they choose. Is there discussion on the matter?"

"Slave owners," one senator began, "are being denied services from certain premiere artisans, right here, within the capital city, under the misguided notion that slavery offends their moral sensibilities. Never mind that many of their own supplies come from industries that depend on slave labor, quality citizens are being denied public accommodation."

"These are citizens," another senator, more pale than most, long of beard, snow white, with only wisps of hair atop his head, "who feel neither loved nor respected by their fellow citizen. Are we now in the business of legislating love and respect? Love and law are incompatible ventures. Law exists because love is insufficient, it is fickle, and though we all ought love each other better, being forced to act as though we love, when we do not, being forced to behave respectfully, produces neither love nor respect. It fosters only resentment, the opposite of love and respect, and ultimately creates and compounds difficulty for the law."

"Philosophy of law and love aside," the opposing senator, a younger man with chestnut hair and a sharp goatee, retorted, "I'm not saying these artisans should love or respect their fellow citizens, though they should, I am saying that they should not deny them services of public accommodation."

The older senator was quick to reply, "I am told this affront to your sensibilities on public accommodation is most prevalent among bakers and those artists who portray likeness, painters, sculptors, and the like. Is this true?"

"As I understand it, yes."

"Bakers I understand, but I find it odd that portraits and sculptures are even matters of public accommodation at all."

There was a murmur with laughter throughout the senate chamber that passed quickly.

"What is and is not a public accommodation is not up for discussion at this time, Senator Macrobius."

"Fair enough," the elder senator, Macrobius, accepted, continuing, "Have you done much baking, painting, or sculpting? It is all rather time consuming. Baking is work, kneading, hot ovens, you put your life into it. Portraiture is art, a man is inspired by his subject, he puts his soul into it. Sculpting is both. If a man finds slavery morally reprehensible, how can we force him pour his life and soul into tasks that support it? How can we make a freeman, under no contract, to do anything at all and not, in essence, deem him enslaved to another man's desires? Is the government to now enslave its own free citizens against their will, Senator Iscavius?"

144

"No," the younger Iscavius scoffed, shouting, "It is a denial of a public accommodation, over a matter that is perfectly legitimate and legal! It takes the law into their own hand! It is some unelected few punishing law-abiding citizens according to their own morality. No freeman has that right."

"Of course they do not," Macrobius debated calmly, "But that is not what is happening. A citizen is free to express his displeasure with the law when he feels it does not represent him. That, my fellow senators, is why we are so employed. Now, if all the bakers in the city, or throughout the Imperium, stopped selling to slave owners, that might be a problem."

"Bet your ass it'd be a problem!"

"I say 'might' because baked goods are staple to a slave's diet. If no one, literally not anyone, was serving that need, you don't think industrious others would enter into the baking trade to make that money being declined? Yet, I admit, that having so few bakers willing to provide so great a need, even for a short while, would be very disruptive to the public good and, in that instance, we should act. However, we are nowhere near to this issue. I mentioned, and Senator Iscavius agreed, that this issue was most common with bakers and likeness makers, but what was unsaid, was that even among these artisans, for whom this choice to refrain from service is most common, it is still exceedingly rare. In fact, there is – to my knowledge – only a pair of bakers, cousins, and a handful of painters and sculptures inclined to so decline. A mere dozen or so artisans of which any refined city-state, let alone this Capital of the World, is in no short supply. If baked goods and graven images are matters of public accommodation, there remains public aplenty willing to accommodate. There is no need to coerce the hand of a few, when so many others would do the work willingly. Moreover, these are bakers and painters and sculptors who would love new business and would respect, and be inspired by, the client who brought them such patronage. This is not a matter than warrants government intervention, bread and portraits remain readily available."

"Whether the general public is accommodating or not is not the issue," Senator Iscavius, clearly flustered, protested, "That these... these anarchists be disallowed to flagrantly disregard their civic duty–"

Macrobius cut him short, "This matter is, in fact, nothing more than an effort to target these specific men – by wealthy slave owners – using their influence to call upon the senate to punish those who have shown hate and disrespect for their activities. A man is allowed to hate and disrespect the actions of another, to refrain from participation or endorsement upon those grounds, regardless of the legality of the actions in question."

"Order!" demanded the Senate President, "Order!"

The chamber had set to murmuring again, but abruptly came to silence.

Upon the motion of the President, any Senator could be dismissed, forever barred from public service, with a simple majority vote by his peers. It was seldom done. Seldom did anyone give a reason. So when the President called for "order" it was regularly and immediately given.

"Apologies, Esteemed President," Macrobius offered.

"Unnecessary," the Senate President spoke dispassionately, "Your points have merit; clearly there is significant concern over how this matter is resolved. You've also made some allegations as to the insignificant extent and improper motives of bringing this matter before the senate. Those need to be investigated. We shall table the matter until the morning of the first day next week, after the results of verification and inquiry are known."

"Esteemed President," Iscavius beseeched, "It is Senator Macrobius that should be investigated. It is known that he has always been vocal in his own opposition to slavery. Yet he, like the anarchists in question, have been emboldened of late, with the disquiet bemusing of foreign influences. Ideas and men of the lands from which Senator Macrobius ancestor's hail. We must ask where his true loyalties lie!"

"And I would answer you," Macrobius gave reply, "I have only ever had the best interests of the Imperium in mind and heart. If I disagree, it is because I see a better way. You are free to disagree with me. We make our cases. The senate votes. We've done our jobs. Curious that you think it should be otherwise."

The implication of Senator Macrobius' last comment, that Iscavius was in the senate for another purpose, like pushing the will of the highest bidder, was clear to the President, if no one else.

"Enough, the both of you. I'll not have my senators hoisting accusations upon each other like this. There is a proper way to do such things. For the time, the matter is tabled. I now turn your attentions to — gods be good ..." the Senate President trailed off, reluctant, staring at the docket before him; inhaling sharply, he continued, "Docket number thirty-three, today's date, 'The Matter of The Presence of Morralish Forces within the Imperium, the Collapse of Their Native Government, and How Best to Conduct Affairs with Them.' "

Chapter 35
Journeying West

Prince Bengallen's company continued to travel. The rain had become unbearable. There was ice in it, coming down in sheets and torrents. They had traveled along a branch road from the Frontier Road at Spearpointe. It would connect with the branch Bengallen and Caanaflit had once taken before, from opposite the Lake at Burntleaf, eventually leading them to the Old King's Road and, from it, to Andover.

As the Prince recalled, there was a cave at the upcoming intersection and, as they pushed onward, Caanaflit insisted that they were getting close to that very intersection. Most doubted that Caanaflit could determine that in these conditions, but they all thought themselves as hardy as the next man, so none wanted to be the voice that complained.

They were all fortunate in their vanity, Prince Bengallen unlikely to have heeded their complaints, even should they have made them. Whether by fate or luck, however, they soon came upon the intersection, with the cave not so far from it.

"In this weather," Ruffis consulted the Prince, "it's fairly likely something else has had the same idea about this cave. I'll go check it out. Mayhap we've gotten here first."

"Agreed and gratitude," Prince Bengallen accepted, continuing, "I know naught of the bears in these parts, but I should think you would not want to come upon them alone."

"A cave troll, more like," Malcolm added, "and I know you don't want to."

"Even in all this you're too noisy," Ruffis complained, "and the smell of wet orc is unmistakable."

Caanaflit huffed and, before the elf's jibes descended into full blow racism, he dismounted his mare, Hessa, and moving off said, "Fine, I'll go with you."

Ruffis spat. He wanted Caanaflit with him even less, but for the life of him could not think of a tactical reason to dismiss his counterpart. A fact which doubled his displeasure as the two made their way up to the cave.

Relatively speaking, the rain had eased a bit as Caanaflit and Ruffis disappeared from the clear, gentle slope. Only darkness and silence followed.

A few moments passed, more than a few, and they had not reappeared. Shomotta, scanning the hillside, attempted to reach out with his mage's sight, to see them, and it failed. Again he tried and again it failed. Or did he? Had he had tried? Had he not thought to, not needed to? Shomotta's mind was awash with confusion and surprise.

"What!?" Alpona shoved Shomotta, demanding.

The knock cleared the wizard's mind and spurred an instant of thought. An instant in a wizard's mind was as several long moments to other men, and so he began to puzzle it out.

"What?" Shomotta echoed in whisper, instantly to Alpona's perception of time.

"You were making a face," Alpona explained, "you don't usually do that."

"Do I not?"

"Not that I've seen," Alpona insisted, "Not like that."

"I cannot see them," Shomotta's whisper more conspiratorial than tactical amid the rain.

Alpona dismissed, "No one can, sort of the point."

Shomotta looked away from the cave and into Alpona's eyes, disagreeing, "Well, I can. With magic I should, but it seems that I may not."

"What does that mean?" Alpona asked.

"Uncertain," Shomotta began, "It would be easier if you'd let me think."

"I'm sorry?" Alpona offered, himself uncertain.

"Don't be sorry," Shomotta spat, "be silent! Be still!"

Shomotta and Alpona looked back to the mouth of the cave some moment after Caanaflit and Ruffis had reappeared. Shomotta cursed himself for breaking off his observations.

Ruffis and Caanaflit returned to the caravan, the latter spoke, "Both unoccupied and no signs of recent occupancy, the cave should serve us as safe shelter."

The rain continued to pour with no relenting in sight as they attempted to dry themselves in the cave. Rather than push on in such unfavorable conditions, they decided to make an early evening of it and crack into the wine stores. With any luck the worst of the storm would pass in the night and they could make an early morning of it.

"Tis no Waypointe Inn, Your Majesty," Caanaflit began, raising his mug, "but every long journey deserves a respite and many of us have journeyed much of late. We thank you."

"You are most welcome, thanes and allies," Prince Bengallen reciprocated, raising his cup.

All took the first drink. Though Alpona, drinking from his wineskin, had earlier used the rain water, unobserved, to dilute his beverage considerably.

"Ruffis," Malcolm called upon him, wielding an olive branch, "Might you now tell us of your mad schemes and dealings that took down the bridge at Woodhaven? We all owe you much for that."

"Don't mind if I do," Ruffis accepted, in a voice that told Caanaflit he was about to hear one heck of a lie. Caanaflit looked to Bengallen, widened his eyes, and scratched his own chest over dramatically. The Prince laughed, discerning his friend's meaning.

As Ruffis began to set up his tale, the minotaur, Brunsis, went to the mouth of the cave and Prince Bengallen followed. After Brunsis sat, the Paladin-Prince called out to him, "We've not had our conversation."

"Do you not wish to hear the dark elf's telling?"

"I really don't," the Prince answered honestly.

"Where would the Prince have me begin?"

"I want to know about the Baron from Darrkeep, Tolthar Gerring," Prince Bengallen answered, "but, if you would travel with us further, I would like to know about yourself as well. Speak with me for awhile. You have claimed wisdom and I ask that you share whatever you deem fit for me. I will listen and, if you will humor me, I might ask questions after."

"Roll up a stone, sit," Brunsis offered, accepting, "You've surprisingly passed my test of humility and you've bested me in a fight, I suppose you've earned my story."

The Prince sat across from the minotaur and they both looked out into the fading light as it undulated before them, through the pouring rain, scarlet and bruise like a bleeding wound.

Brunsis rubbed his thumb and finger atop either side his protruded snout and closed his eyes. He held a silence, before opening his eyes, breaking it with the sound of his soul:

Chapter 36
Amazing Minotaur

"If you've heard of a minotaur, then you know of my father, known simply as the Minotaur. If you've heard any version of his legend, then you know the essence of the creature. Long have I sought the truth of my father, as I am sure most men do, in some way or another, but never have I found it. As I am sure most men do not.

Best I can figure it, from scouring the lore and interrogating the sages of Uhratt, there was only ever one Minotaur. The King of Thalos had refused the worship of some ancient entity that wanted to be called a god, in lieu of some pact with some demon with similar ambitions. The offended would-be god surreptitiously transformed the princess into a heifer. Himself taking the form of a bull, he then had his way with her.

Scholars have wondered why so many of the ancient tales begin with sex. Let us be honest, the beginning of any life starts with sex. Ignoring this fact comes and goes out of fashion from decade to decade. The fact remains. Apparently, many of the old stories reflect the sensibilities of their own times, not ours.

So the heifer gave birth to the Minotaur, so like a man, yet so fearsome. The king had the creature trained in violence from birth. Thinking the creature was some manner of dark gift, the king sought to make an army of them. This prize heifer was bred to many and many a bull, though year after year she only produced calves.

Eventually, in frustration, the King of Thalos did at last order the heifer butchered for a royal feast. It was only then that he discovered the horror. Loathsomely contained within the heifer's massive size, by means unknown and unknowable, the missing princess had lived. It was as though the body of the cow had been wrapped around the body of the girl. Yet when its head was removed, so had the princess also been decapitated.

Great was the king's shame for the savagery he had subjected his daughter to, for years and years, but also for the child-like bull creature that was his apparent grandson and heir. He made sacrifices of all who knew of these foul things, to his demons, and brokered their assistance in the dealing.

They counseled him that the Minotaur was also the son of an ancient would-be god. Although that entity would have used the creature to take the Throne of Thalos and align it with himself, they could instead use the creature to punish the entity for his transgressions against the king.

A temple to the Demon-Lords of Anzerok was built on a small lonely island in the Sea of Veaul. Beneath its surface, a great maze was built and the Minotaur imprisoned within. Men and women, given over as blood sacrifices to the demons, were cast down into the Labyrinth to be hunted and slain by the Minotaur, who knew only the violence taught to him. In this way, the demons told the king that they would gain power over the would-be god, and strengthen their place in the cosmos.

It was, of course, a ruse. The only entities involved, they that wished to be worshiped as the gods of men, were demons all. Yes, seeking power for himself, he possessed a bull and had his loathsome way with the princess. The reversal, the enslavement of the Minotaur, however, forced that particular demon to join those certain other lords of demons, rather than contest them, under whatever rules such hellish matters operate in conjunction with our world.

My father was thus the instrument of demon sacrifice from centuries before the Cataclysm and the Slumbering of the World. Not so long into the renewal of the world, the temple was discovered and, from there, Thalos fell once more into its demonic ways. Many were sacrificed, countless hundreds, over those first centuries of known history. Until divine blood came to sit upon the Antori Throne and, from there, conquered Thalos.

The Din-god, as Imperator, sent royal ministers to oversee the rule of the conquered provinces. In Thalos, the demon worship, at this particular temple, became a closely guarded secret from the Antori overseers. The Divine Imperator's reign was tragically short, however, and when Thalos got word of the deaths of both its own king and the Imperator, the demon cult assumed power. They immediately captured the Antori overseers to be sacrificed at the secret temple.

They must have scrambled around that maze, like so many before them, until at last, only one remained. She was an elven woman, Qysis. She alone survived.

By wit alone, she survived. Until, starved and cornered, the Minotaur had her, but he was moved. Chasing her, so long, she had done so well, was such a challenge, was the closest thing to a relationship with another living creature the Minotaur had ever had. He could not kill her. He took her in his arms and into his garden.

Erosion, over the centuries, had opened up a hole in the ceiling. Beneath this, in the light, a small grass pasture and other plants had begun to grow. They sustained him when meat had become scarce. His home there was a frightful place, built entirely with the petrified bones of the ancient sacrifices. Yet in the dark world of the lonely Minotaur, it was his place of light and growth.

Returned to health at the hands of the monster, Qysis became his friend. Though primarily educated as a diplomat, she knew the small things of nature and magic that all elves know. She cultivated his garden and transmuted its appearance. The Minotaur quickly grew to love her for the beauty, life, and novelty she had brought into his miserable life, countless centuries theretofore ruled by blood, death, and terror.

Others came. Yet not another sacrifice was made. Men and women lived the remainders of their lives and died of old age, or other ailments, as sort of unfortunate guests of the Minotaur and Qysis. Who, herself, for what reason or by what magic, it is unknown and unknowable, became alike unto the Minotaur. By some sympathy, some symbioses, she became, in effect, a minotaur too.

In time, people stopped coming. As those condemned were not sacrificed, the demons refused to transact in that temple. In their solitude, Qysis at last reciprocated the Minotaur's love, and I was born.

All things considered, as I would come to discover, I had a relatively normal, if not sheltered, childhood. My father was distant, brooding, and unknowable, but he showed affection for my mother and never mistreated me, even if he never loved me as she did. I think in some ways he resented me. He saw in me not only what he was and what my mother had become, but in the potential of what I might also become, remorse for what he had been.

I cannot know that. Yet, in the possibility that it is true, neither can I blame him. Moreover, it prepared me for the future prejudice I would face. Look at me. People assume a lot. I don't blame them either.

I was about ten or so when they came. Knights. Some demon priest had tricked them into descending into the Labyrinth. He told them of a demon that lived there, despite the accords of the heavens and hells that prevent such things.

I suppose there is truth to that. He did it, however, that blood might be spilled in the temple once more in the name of his demon masters. He cared naught for whose blood it was.

The knights, I don't blame them either. Had they met the man I have become, I might have unwittingly joined them in their quest. They slew my father and mother. The Minotaur, of course, put up a fight. Many knights died.

With my father slain and myself abducted by the demon priest in the confusion, I was told later by the man responsible, my mother threw herself on the knight's sword in her grief.

The knight was a Northman, like yourself, who had come into the service of the Baron of Veaul. So far from home, I know not why. He was but one of many people I would meet and learn from in my travels. I've read and heard many versions of my father's life, many tale of the Minotaur, but that is the version I like to believe. You hear me, Prince, that is the best version and its all pretty terrible. I've made an oath never to kill, intentionally, but I've earned my way in the world as a brawler, a fighter. It is a living metaphor appropriate to the nature of my existence.

I've lived with elves, in Antoria, distant relation of my mother. They taught me much, but the road and the struggle of life ever called to me. Rather than resist these urges only to have them break loose, I have chosen a life that indulges them, but under my own terms. I am a contradiction, but in knowing what I am, I have mastery over myself. I have made myself so that there will never be another like me. So that I will never have children and they will not be exploited. You understand my meaning?"

Prince Bengallen winced at the thought and nodded uncomfortably, but certainly. It spoke to Brunsis' commitment.

The minotaur continued, "You may look upon me with your paladin's eye and find my soul made right. I also revisited the demon priest who had abducted me and from whom I had escaped. I had brought knights of my own this time, and paladins and priests besides. We forced him to call up the Demon-Lord, my grandfather, if you will, that set these things in motion. We bound him and banished him to the outer darkness, where things no longer have sway over this world. The day may come when he returns, but it will be long centuries from now and I will be gone, with no line left behind me for him to abuse."

The Paladin-Prince had looked on him so back in Woodhaven, when they first fought, of course, and there was no trace of evil, no voice of warning, of any kind. Not like the vampire, of which he was imparted with heightened recall of its lore and confirmation of its weaknesses. Not like with Caanaflit, where there was only a shroud of darkness. Not like the hearts of vicious men, which give him an uneasy feeling, hardening his own heart against them.

Nothing worse than those insights either. There was no overwhelming sense of atrocity, none of mind rending, sanity challenging horror that kept him from looking upon that Starspawn Beast too keenly. The seemingly monstrous minotaur, seen more clearly, in that mystical way, was remarkably unremarkable. He looked like any man would.

"Have you been so far as to Helmsphar?" Brunsis asked the Prince.

"Not half so far," he answered.

"I heard rumors once," Brunsis continued, "That there were creatures like myself there. And now you understand why this was of concern to me. I made my way there, and though I found many terrible things, minotaurs were not among them. Men and orc live side-by-side, which at first I found rather enlightened, but looked more closely. They enslave all sorts of creatures, trolls, ogres, goblins, even some dwarves and elves. Their treatment is brutal. Among the humans and orcs, there is a rigid caste system. Nothing like the common-noble distinction that you all think so necessary to social order. Worse even than the exaggeration of it in Antoria, with its own slavery besides. Top to bottom, tens of thousands of people bred like livestock to reproduce certain traits. Each family assigned to a trade, forced to it, killed for deviating, killed also if there are ever too many at the same trade. Not exiled, not freed, raised, used, and slaughtered like animals … the whole society as needed."

"By what authority?" the Paladin-Prince gasped, appalled.

"That's just it," Brunsis finished, "No one remembered. Tis just been that way for so long — the enforcers keep enforcing it. So of course they attacked me and penned me up with some ogres. They didn't know what I was, but that seemed like where I belonged. Eventually, the Baron, Tolthar Gerring, from Darrkeep, the only place with whom Helmsphar conducts trade, saw me for different and purchased me. Said his father was dying and that he wanted to see the rest of the world before he came into his inheritance. He wanted to see how the other peoples of the world did things before deciding how he wanted to do things in Darrkeep, once it was his to decide. I became his tour guide. We traveled the plains, the deserts, woods, and beaches of all the rest of the civilized world, save the elves, the dwarves, and the Van-blessed mountain folk of Morralish. We spent much time in the Frontier before moving north. We had not long been in your lands when the dead rose to besiege your great city. I trusted that dastard and he abandoned me there. Whether he knew what was coming all along or had been alerted, he betrayed me, either way. I was his guide and friend and protector for more than three years. When I went to him, at the risk of my own life, he was gone. Not fled in a hurry, but packed up and gone. Leaving only his minotaur behind. I wish I could tell you more. Yet I can only confirm that you are right to be suspicious."

"Can you tell me more of the man himself or of Darrkeep?"

"Alas, I can only tell you, Prince, what he chose to show and share with me.

I've come to believe that he is a very different man, a mask, for the one behind it that I suppose I never knew."

"I'll ask you one more question," Bengallen lowered his voice to a conspiratorial tone, "but that I am asking it must forever be in confidence between us."

"Prince, everything I've said here was to be in confidence between us."

"Agreed," Bengallen began, "The elves enslaved near Darrkeep, in Helmsphar, were they dark elves?"

Brunsis furrowed his brow, thoughtful, possibly disapproving.

"They were not. I only saw a few. Pale, mostly, save one, he was yellow-brown, like distant sand dunes in the afternoon light. He warned me to leave. They killed him for it. I should have listened. Is there something I need to know about any of our companions, Prince?"

"Ruffis is a jackass," Bengallen said bluntly, adding, "Most are knights and soldiers in my service. Caanaflit is my friend. Malcolm is my ward. Alpona is possibly the most skilled fighter among us. Shomotta is a wizard, though I am guessing you've already noticed that. "

"As have I that Ruffis is a jack's ass," Brunsis laughed, "Is that all he is?"

"Oh, I highly doubt that, but at the moment it is all that I know he is. We've yet to meet anyone that knows anything about elves like him, his color, those tattoos. I've met elves with attitude issues, but none so crass. He just doesn't add up."

"Fair enough," Brunsis accepted, "You add him up and come up with anything interesting, Prince, I'd appreciate to be informed. I should do the same."

"Gratitude, Brunsis," Bengallen nodded to him.

"Gratitude, Prince," Brunsis nodded slightly lower.

They returned to the others. A fire had been made. Red cheeks all around suggested several cups. Alpona was telling a fish tale about his friend, Rodjker. God rest his soul.

156

Chapter 37
Conspiring Generals

The Kingdom of Morralish had seven army regiments, each composed of nine generals, one of them being a nobleman holding the title of High Lord-General. The other eight generals were paired, General and Lieutenant General, all or none of which might have been of noble birth, prefixing the title of Lord only in the case where a noble general was also the senior of their pair.

The Fifth Army Regiment, the Peakstars, were believed to be lost, along with their homeland, as they were the ones assigned to defend the Realm in recent years. So the High Lord-Generals who gathered at the Conclave of Morralish Generals in Jourance, on the border of Avigueux and Antoria, a city nestled in the heartland of the Imperium, expected there to be six in their number. Yet there were but five of them among the dozens of other general officers and noblemen who would not miss their opportunity to grab for power.

"Where is the High Lord-General Harkon? Or any officer of the First Regiment?" decried the High Lord-General Hrothmond, himself of the Second Regiment.

"There are things we wish to discuss that a paladin might not have the temperament to hear, so the First Regiment was not notified of this assembly," General Leidtenfrost, the recently appointed commander of the Sixth Army Regiment, answered.

Lord-General Hrothmond looked displeased and replied, "If there are things to be said here, things that would offend a paladin's sensibilities, then mayhap they should not be said at all."

He expected cheers and applause for his moral bravado, but only the lonely approving clank of his own Lieutenant-General was heard.

General Leidtenfrost spoke into the silence, "Our great king is dead Our homeland is defeated and poisoned. The Imperium has offered us and our select soldiers a place among their legions. In a traditional sense this is treachery, disloyalty, but the situation we face is far from traditional. We are foreign men in a foreign land. Our ranks and titles mean nothing the instant the Imperator rescinds our invitation, withholds his coin, and cancels our contracts. On that day, my good generals, our unfed, unpaid armies of mountain folk become an invading force of barbarians, in effect, even if not in deed. No one likes the sound of it, but it is the hard truth. We are here to discuss and consider nontraditional solutions to our nontraditional problems. If his lordship, General Hrothmond, would like to go convene with the Paladin-Generals of the First Regiment, to consider more traditional avenues, then we grant you take your leave of us."

The Lord-General Hrothmond scoffed when the other general referred to the sons of the mountains devolving into invading barbarians. He scoffed again, at the fact, that he scoffed alone. Once it was his turn, he spoke again, a dire cadence in this voice, "I'll speak for the traditionalists then. I move – that we assemble all our regiments – at Three Gods Pass – and march every son and daughter of the mountains back – to those very mountains – from which we sprang – and reclaim them in bloody contest – with whatever foe we find there."

"Everyone here," General Leidtenfrost replied, almost nonchalant, "except you, apparently, knows that the whole reason for this Conclave is to prevent that very thing. You sound like the conscripts. I say we choose the elite from among them, to serve us here, and let the rest go or do as they may."

The Lord-General Hrothmond scoffed, a third time, at the murmurs of agreement that rumbled throughout the hall.

After their murmuring faded, he replied, "Well, it sounds as though your minds are all made up then. I guess we aren't here to discuss anything after all."

"And again your intuition fails you," General Leidtenfrost sneered wickedly at the other general, "There are a great many details to be worked out."

The day unfolded in like manner.

Later that evening, a smaller gathering of only the five senior commanding generals was convened. No personal aids, only the men themselves.

"Brothers," Hertvork Leidtenfrost addressed, "Forgive the hour, but important word has just arrived. I have bid you assemble that you may be the first to hear of it and that we might discuss it before hearing from the others."

Prince Bengallen was alive. Strein Hrothmond knew it in his heart and held his breath in hope that word had come at last. *This could change everything.*

He was right, of course, Prince Bengallen was alive. He was right, also, that such news would change everything. This, however, was not word of the Prince's survival.

A man in dark red, stark against the sky blue cloaks of the Morralish generals, entered the room.

"It is my honor to introduce," General Leidtenfrost began, "the Legatus of the Antori Fourth Legion, Claudious Darix Terriatus. He comes with tidings."

"Good evening, good generals," Legatus Terriatus spoke formally, "As you know, the laws in the Antori Imperium are drafted by representatives, themselves elected by its landed citizens from all provinces throughout the Imperium. Our Senate has voted on the 'Morralish Refugee Act, revision four' and it has passed with near unanimous consent. There is a lot to the document, and I have brought a dozen copies for your review, but allow me to brief you on the points of note."

The faces of the Morralish generals were grim, but all, Hrothmond included, nodded with interest, consenting.

"Please continue," Leidtenfrost invited.

Terriatus informed them, "Generals and commanders of noble birth will be given land and villas in the Western Plains. The size of these farms will be decided by the number that accept them, their relative military rank, and whether or not they immediately retire from service upon acceptance. Those retiring will be accorded the rights and privileges of a retired Antori Centurion. Those who remain in active service may select one-hundred men of their own choosing, from their current commands, to form new Antori units – over which – they shall serve as Centurion."

Hrothmond was outraged. *Antori Centurions were less than Morralish Captains by rank*. Though that was not why he was outraged. That made sense.

Antoria neither wanted six new legions, nor did it need to offer the Morralish generals a retirement befitting them. Morralish was not within the Imperium. *Lorded lands there, cut-off and left to who knows what fate, were suddenly irrelevant. To lords as these, any land at all was better than the alternative. That too made sense.* What enraged Strein Hrothmond was how spoon fed these so-called discussions were being thrust upon them and, again, how readily his peers accepted it.

"What of the tens of thousands of men unselected?" General Hrothmond demanded.

"Any that wish to join the Imperial Legions may present themselves. Any accepted will be assessed, accordingly given rank and up to a five year service credit toward retirement. As with any legionnaire, they would only need to serve an additional five years to earn their citizenship—"

"And how many of them?" General Hrothmond angrily interrupted the Legatus.

He knew the number would be small. He knew where this was going. He wanted to hear him say it.

"A few thousand," Legatus Terriatus admitted, "no more than four, no less than three."

"That still leaves tens of thousands of men who have served us loyal and well — to be abandoned," Hrothmond pleaded.

"With the dismantling of the Morralish Expeditionary Forces in the Antori Imperium," the Legatus began again, "the Senate has agreed to divert some of the money saved from that expense to the funding of provincial militias. Your men are welcome to join them or do whatever they wish. Those within the Imperium, who have not found their place within it, will be branded as refugees and, thus, will be required to sell themselves into bondage or be exiled from all lands of the Imperium."

"Break them up. Steal their best. Then tens of thousands to be killed or sold into slavery for breach of exile as befits the occasion!" Strein Hrothmond alone spoke the silent implication.

Legatus Terriatus and General Leidtenfrost nodded in resolute confirmation.

General Hrothmond spit on the Legatus' boot, chastising him, "Who are you to make any such decree against any son of the mountains?"

His apparent rival, General Leidtenfrost, answered, "The Fourth Legion currently serves in defense of the Antori capital and Legatus Terriatus was, of past service, an Antori Senator rather than a soldier. He is, appointed by the Senate, a special envoy uniquely fit to work with us, to see this transition occur as smoothly as possible."

"You've sold your people out, Hertvork," General Hrothmond called him out by name, "and the rest of you have clearly bought in. If you are the generals of Morralish, then I am ashamed to call myself one. Take your meager retirements, and your one-hundred traitors, and your title Centurion. I spit upon you all! I resign my commission and return home, to find what pieces of my people I may and help in whatever way I can. Any man, of any regiment, who would go with me is free to do so. I'm no longer a general, so I'm not commanding your men and your men aren't slaves, not yet, so you cannot stop them."

He had no idea what he had done. A spider's web had been spun before him and Strein Hrothmond walked right into it. He was of noble mind and heart, as well as title, and his good and forthright intentions were well known by his colleagues. So, of course, they knew he would not stand for any of this.

"Lord Strein Hrothmond," the Legatus called and a clutch of red caped legionnaires, swords drawn, poured into the room behind him, "For defiance of the Imperator's Peace, as outlined in the Morralish Refugee Act, I brand you outlaw and place you under arrest."

Realization dawned. He had been played, and a different peace washed over him. They wanted this to happen and they want the crusty, old general to throw himself into the fray, so that they would have no choice but to slay him, resisting arrest. It would sadden the other generals, but it would have appeared necessary. He would be of more use alive. So rather than throw his life away, he surrendered.

Placing both empty hands before himself, Strein Hrothmond stated clearly, "Though I served at the behest of our common faith and my foreign king, I have fought for the Imperator's Peace as much as any of his own citizens. If I am to be branded an outlaw in defiance of something I've made my life's work, I'll not prove you right with a rash act in this moment, but force you to make your case in the courts."

Hrothmond caught the disappointed glances Leidtenfrost and Terriatus shot to one another, confirming his suspicions. He was a fool for not seeing it sooner, but, in that moment, he had chosen wisely, discretion oft times being the better part of valor.

Chapter 38
Perceiving Magic

They had taken an old road across the river from Spearpointe and it connected them with the path Ben and Flit had once taken to and from a certain tower. They would not take that spur to the tower this time, though both felt the pull of nostalgia and curiosity. This time they would continue on to the Old King's Road and connect with Andover. This way was faster and, though the Frontier Road to Mayfield was safer, this was not a band that would lose time to fear.

They met but a lone traveler on this road. He was elderly and had an ill-favored look about him. He asked to trade his spare cloak for fresh foot wrapping as the cloak was too thick to be cut down as such and still get his foot in a boot.

Initially, Caanaflit thought to pass the man by. Yet he was accompanied by Malcolm on this day's advance and the half-orc thane, well-versed in lore, warned against it.

Thane Malcolm took the lesser of the man's two cloaks as trade for mostly fresh socks, a luxury item, and gave him a couple salt-cured trout from his ration. The old man's dark countenance faded and he insisted the half-orc ask some favor of him. Malcolm thought upon it, so little it seemed the man could do.

At last he told the man, "If you ever find yourself in my position, trade kindly with the fellow then in yours."

The old fellow agreed and gleefully put on his dry socks as Caanaflit and Malcolm rode on.

As they went, Caanaflit commented with gentle mockery, "I suppose that some magical cloak now. Speed and invisibly or some such?"

"I supposed that it is," Malcolm replied.

Re-donning his certainly magical helm, as though to punctuate his point, they rode on.

Caanaflit gnawed upon his words.

At last they reached Andover. Hunting, fishing, some trading, a drunken evening or two, and a strange old man besides, it had thus far been a rather uneventful trip. They had made good time, reaching the town late into the night. Prince Bengallen decreed that they should rest the next day there, in addition to refreshing supplies and trading out a few horses, then spend a second night, leaving early the next morning after.

The first morning, as Ruffis and Shomotta awoke before the others, the wizard found a sought after opportunity.

"Ruffis," Shomotta addressed him, "You vanished from my sight when you went in that cave with Caanaflit."

"I suppose I would have," Ruffis explained, "some of the magic bound to me aids my concealment, even from supernatural means. The more I am hidden, the more powerfully the magic conceals me further. That cave was pitch black."

"You can extend this power to others?"

"I don't have any control over the magic tattooed upon me," Ruffis explained, "I am actually very poorly gifted in the mystic powers of my people. It was why I was raised separate from them. I can evoke a little here or there, but nothing of consequence. These marks upon me, my father's work, are well beyond me."

Shomotta was shocked again. Ruffis was not lying. He was not good at lying. He believed what he was saying was true. Though, to Shomotta's wizard's sight, once that he examined the elf fully, saw the opposite.

Those white vines that crawled across the dark elf's body, they were spellwork for certain, but they funneled and withheld a power far beyond the tattoos themselves, something originating from within. The arcane markings masked the power behind them, but looking around them, behind them, upon examination, the power within Ruffis was terrible, cascading. Magical energy broke upon the tattoos like a waterfall upon a lake, but the waterfall was hidden and the lake's depth deceptive.

Shomotta chose to leave it for the time being, another mystery for another day. There might well be a good reason for the containment of that power, and for Ruffis himself to not know of it.

Shomotta chose, instead, to pursue his original line, "So it would surprise you to know that Caanaflit also disappeared, in the same manner as you did."

163

"When I was with the Deep Eyes," Ruffis responded, "I tried to will my concealment to others. I wanted to share it. We even had a spelly guy, like you, who said I could do it. I tried. I never did. I liked those guys. I can't believe that it would start working now, to help someone I dislike."

"It occurs to me," Shomotta suggested, "that Caanaflit might be possessed of his own powers. He has little memory from before our meeting. Perhaps he has powers of which even he is yet unaware?"

"You think he used the magic bonded to me?"

"Or mimicked it. Or interacted with it in some other way," Shomotta offered, asking, "Do you understand how the various parts of your tattoos work?"

"Not even a little."

"So it is also possible that you also are under magical effects of which you are also unaware."

"Likely even."

"He may be the same."

"My father did this," Ruffis said, gesturing at the white swirl on his face, "to protect me. If Caanaflit is the same, the markings of his power are not visible and we don't know who or why they are upon him. My father died before he could pass on his secrets, but I know he was saddened by the visible toll this spellwork cost — that if he could have hid these marks, he would have. He simply could not."

"If Caanaflit is possessed of some hidden power," Shomotta emphasized their speculation, "They might be of an origin completely different than the arcane markings your father placed upon your body. You are not wrong, however, that their concealment from us, and very possibly him, is certainly unknown to us, and again possibly him. That is of concern to me."

"I already don't like him," Ruffis huffed, "I'll add it to the list."

"Thank you for your honesty, Ruffis," Shomotta continued, "I don't dislike Caanaflit, but I think he'd be the first one to admit that he should not be trusted. The both of us then, should be up on our toes. He and Alpona grow friendly and the warrior might be developing a blind spot for the rogue."

164

"Agreed," Ruffis nodded.

"Forgive me if this is an inappropriate request," Shomotta slid one topic to another, "but that I might better understand the magic that is bound to another, for the concern at hand, as well as my general education, might I study the tattoos upon your body?"

Ruffis grimaced, "I don't mind you asking, so long as this isn't some excuse for you to get your eyes and hands on my hot body."

Shomotta smiled and replied, "You have hinted before that you know my exploration of sensual pleasures go beyond most social conventions –"

Ruffis interrupted, "That sure is a lot of words to admit that you're gay."

"It is not so simple as that," Shomotta replied, "however, rest assured that I have no intentions towards you, Ruffis, not in that way. Yet I would very much like to learn more about the magic upon you."

"I'm fine with that," Ruffis agreed, "but if you stare at this beautiful black specimen long enough, you might find yourself otherwise enchanted. Then, if you go trying to cast a spell with my magic wand, I promise no restraint and make no apologies about the ass kicking you'll get."

"So you threaten to bash me, then?" Shomotta summarized.

"Exactly."

"With that sort of attitude," Shomotta resigned with a sigh, "my interests will definitely remain nothing to worry yourself over."

Chapter 39
Denying Respite

That evening they had gathered at the bar of whatever nameless tavern in which they were staying. At first they were all together, but as time wore on they broke down into their usual company. Alpona, Ruffis, Caanaflit, and Shomotta were playing some sort of card game.

Ruffis was desperate for a chance to show up Caanaflit. Caanaflit who was himself merely biding time until he could next get the best of the dark elf. Bengallen was with the knights, save for Squire Felix, who was himself with the soldiers. Brunsis, the minotaur, terrifying to the locals, drank alone.

When Caanaflit caught Ruffis cheating, their table exploded into conflict, and Alpona noticed Malcolm was nowhere to be found.

He had entered the bar that evening. He had drank with both the minotaur as well as Prince Bengallen. Alpona was sure of it. Yet he had slipped out at some point.

The Prince alone was the early-to-bed type, some leftover affect of his lordly station. So Alpona did not believe the half-orc simply off to find his slumber. Leaving the chaos without a word, it made a stronger point to repudiate their trifling by brooking no comment, Alpona left the tavern only to find Malcolm sitting on a bench two steps outside its doors.

"Alone?" Alpona began, noticing the slender leather glove in the hand of his fellow thane, "Plenty of time to be alone out upon the road, if you want it. Surprising that you'd take the time here, the only town since Spearpointe."

"Do you think a woman could ever love Brunsis the Minotaur?" Malcolm asked.

"Stop. Start over and say what you mean to say."

Malcolm bulked, his eyes widened at his friend calling him to truth so abruptly. They had spent much time together, Malcolm with Alpona more than any of the others, and so the Zli-jahi warrior alone might understand the truth of it.

The half-orc met him halfway, "I have taken Sira Roselle as a lover. Pledged to each other, we were married in the old way."

"Gimme a moment," Alpona stammered, "That is about 180 days opposite to where I thought you were going."

"I don't understand the expression?"

"The world is a disk, 360 days in its rotation," Alpona said simply, holding his hand flat and drawing an imaginary circle around it, "I thought you were in freezing winter, but your words tell of flowers in spring," he concluded, moving his pointer finger from one side of the circle across to the other.

"Ha," Malcolm laughed half heartedly, "I see. Tis so."

"You're missing her then?"

"Aye," Malcolm agreed, "but that is only the surface of my thoughts."

"Then allow Alpona to cast stone and break the placid waters," he offered boisterously, taking a seat next to his friend, "Here I splash and wait to see what rises to the surface!"

"There are two things," Malcolm, reluctantly grinning at his friend, replied, "Unrelated except by this lady's favor clutched in my hands. I don't know where to start."

"Start with the glove."

"She dropped it after we said our good-byes. I think she bought it just to leave it to me, like a lady in a story. Anyway, she left it in such a way that I could not simply hand it to her and waved the other in acknowledgment as she rode away."

"Well, that's rather adorable. Rightly so, I don't see wh—"

Malcolm interrupted him, "In the moment before, we kissed. There were people about. It was a nice moment, so I pretended not to notice, and she either didn't, or pretended as well, notice the looks those Woodhavers gave us. We risk our lives to save theirs. Yet they would openly show disdain for our affection of one another? I am sure some other thanes and knights have noticed our inclination toward each other, and to their credit, they've been fair, but those lesser men, to turn up their noses at us. It bothers me."

"A few things," Alpona began, "One, hadn't noticed you and Sira Roselle so I

167

wouldn't suppose that any thanes or knights have your approval. Two, I suspect some will have no compunction against voicing disapproval when they do know. For what it's worth, I think it's great, the pair of you, finding each other in all of this. I've never really loved a woman who loved me back — not properly. Lusty nights of passion notwithstanding. Three, for as many as we saved, Woodhaven lost a lot of folks and gained a shattered sense of security besides – to an orc horde – of all things. I'm not saying they have the right, but it's understandable, if they don't want to see your orcish visage sharing a tender moment with anyone."

"And there is the tip of the other matter?"

"The attack? You don't think?"

"Don't you?"

"Well, I – er – ah — didn't give it much thought," Alpona stammered, clearly concerned.

"I wasn't just an orc in Woodhaven after an orc attack," Malcolm protested, "I was the man, orc or otherwise, that brought that attack down upon their city."

"We can't know that."

"I wish we could claim that," Malcolm hung his head, speaking towards the ground, "I shamed my father and killed his chosen son. You cut off his rorking hand! We kicked the wasp's nest and then ran. Don't you think they followed us?"

"I think they followed us here, to Andover, maybe. But no one here was attacked by orcs or even heard of the horde passing by," Alpona heartily disagreed, "Perhaps scouts tracked us so far as Spearpointe, but how would they have known we went to Woodhaven. Hell, why not attack Spearpointe, already wounded and far less defensible? How could they have reported back and moved the horde so quickly? I think they had their own reasons to come after Woodhaven. That forest clearing might have already been underway before we even arrived at the Ironclaw settlement. I think fate put us in Woodhaven to stop them."

"Prince Bengallen wanted to knight me," Malcolm replied, tangentially, "After the Battle of Woodhaven, for it, for all my quests, but I told him I did not deserve it. Before, he silenced me when news of the attack came. I was to suggest then that it was our fault. He must have thought it too or he could not have known what I was about to say. He told me that I was a knight, whether I would be knighted or not, and that when I was ready, so was he."

"I see," Alpona said, placing his hand on Malcolm's shoulder and nodding his own head, "I see."

Malcolm waved the lady's glove in his hands again before looking back to Alpona.

"This favor,in the stories, tis what a lady bequeaths a knight when he leaves court to go upon a quest. A part of herself, her faith and admiration, a token to take with him. I am beholden to these quests and the values that knights should embody. Tis all I've ever wanted, but my first quest ended in failure. I freed men and women from slavery only to see them safely to the hands of new masters. Now my biggest role of my greatest battle, I cannot stop but think, was to have caused it. I wanted nothing more than to be a knight who served a worthy king. Everyone seems to think my time has come — everyone except for me."

Alpona's eyes appeared as though he would weep, but his mouth curled to a smile as he spoke, "Malcolm, my friend and fellow thane, we don't live in the stories. The people in the stories didn't live in them either. They suffer set backs and doubt, but we only know of it, if it serves the telling. A ten thousand years from now, when they read of Malcolm and Alpona, they'll only know this moment, if it serves some greater purpose. All the little moments, our discussions on the road, your reluctance to face your father, my sharing with you my concerns about the Prince and our other companions, those things won't be recorded. History will forget them, and they will have no place in our legends to come."

"I know that," Malcolm said, reflecting Alpona's smile.

"I know that you do," Alpona chuckled, clearing his face and voice before continuing, "When a man nears his goal, it rarely happens the way he envisioned. Moreover, if he did not think to ever have attained it, the prospect can be frightening, a secret fear, even from himself. Were you a knight, what would you want next from life?"

"I would want to be a good knight," Malcolm said with conviction, "With apologies to my humility, I would want to be the best knight, or the best I can be anyway."

"Your father and brother and clan have paid for their injustices with blood,"

Alpona began, a darker tone in his voice, "You are free of them. Their victims avenged. You have taken a wife, a good wife who will reinforce the virtues you share. You are all the things a knight should be, and among we thanes and knights of this company, you are already the best of those things. You've earned your place. Whatever else there is to do, you have done that. You are a great knight, with or without the title. Whether or not you take it, however, this is not the end of your story. Malcolm, this is merely the beginning. You need to ask yourself, what in this world, this age, Sir Malcolm will desire for it. Not merely how well you'll serve your king, but what things, given a whisper's breath of a chance, Sir Malcolm, Thane Malcolm, Lord Malcolm would do for, what gifts he would give to, the people of Uhratt? I can think of no finer thing for a young knight to think and pray upon, but I am not of these lands and perhaps I do not understand knighthood. Were you a young Zil-jahi, given a named sword and marked a warrior, it would be the first thought of your private mind, when you think upon yourself."

Malcolm chuckled, "We are all made better as the madman fades and the wiseman comes forth. You have the right of it."

"Just another place I've been before, my friend. Just another place I wouldn't let you go alone. You can miss your wife. Shame on you if you didn't. These other burdens, they are the past, they cannot be changed. Your character is your destiny. Embrace your shining future."

Malcolm folded the glove and tucked it back into his belt pouch.

Springing to his feet, holding out a hand to Alpona, he agreed, "So we shall!"

Alpona took Malcolm's hand up, ignoring the fact that the constant aching in his bones received an honest momentary relief from the assist, and he agreed, "So we shall."

Not so long after Alpona had left the table, Ruffis had as well, making some sort of scene in the process. This left Shomotta and Caanaflit alone at the table. Shomotta was cleaning up the cards and redistributing the last round's coin. All the while Caanaflit stared at him, watched him, silently.

Once all was to right, Shomotta began examining each card. One can only assume he was looking to see if the cards had been marked. Finally, Caanaflit leaned back and, low in his chair, attempted to catch the wizard's eye, speaking, "Shomotta, are we not friends anymore?"

Shomotta raised his head up slowly and looked Caanaflit firmly in the eye,

170

"Were we ever friends?"

"I went looking for a friend once," Caanaflit reminded him, "and I found you. I brought you into this company."

"As I recall," Shomotta replied, "You were looking for an old friend – I have since earned my own place in this company."

"Certainly, that none could doubt or deny," Caanaflit agreed, "I would say that you have done that and then some."

Shomotta was still as stone, nothing but the bottom of his mouth had moved for speaking, and he continued, asking, "What are we talking about then?"

"That's just it," Caanaflit opposed Shomotta's firm manner by speaking playfully, "we never talk any more."

"I speak when I have something to say."

"So you simply never have anything to say – to me – anymore?"

"I do not," Shomotta admitted, "You're ways are not my ways. The way you are always playing everyone. The way you are trying to play me even now. Caanaflit, there was a time when we might have been friends. I've found others with whom I hold more in common. I don't mean for it to be personal, we are simply of different natures."

Caanaflit made the silliest appalled face, placed his hand to his chest dramatically, and challenged, "Are you saying you don't like me any more? That is personal. I am offended. Whatever did I do? What can I do to make it up to you?"

Shomotta quirked his lips.

"Putting Ruffis in his place is one thing, but you challenge and taunt him at every turn. You say things to people, the Prince, Malcolm, Alpona, myself, here and now, not as befits the conversation, not what comes naturally, but constantly you try and turn everyone to your favor. You pull everyone's strings – or you try – all the time."

"Taken to reading my mind again, have you?"

"As a matter of fact, I have tried. You have found a way to block me. Not with magic, but with numbers," Shomotta admitted, continuing, "Always you count, adding and subtracting, computing interest and percentages. The surface of your thoughts, always numbers, a code, a screen, I do not know. That you are intentionally concealing your true thoughts from me, however, is undeniable."

"That I have found a way to again conceal my private thoughts, a right all men take for granted, this raises alarm?"

"No," Shomotta sighed, "Alarm was raised when I saw how you interact with your friends. I continued to be concerned as I continued to observe your incessant manipulations. So I tried to read you, as much to allay my concern as confirm it. That you'd gone out of your way to thwart me was disconcerting."

"Well, well, well," Caanaflit giggled, "You are wrong again. That is something I learned a long time ago. Before my memory loss. You see what happens is, I remember the things I'd learned before, but only when the need arises. Once remembered, however, I don't forget. The counting is something I do to keep my mind sharp, tis a habit now, was a habit, I suppose. If it protects my mind from invasion, news to me, but all the better. I don't know how you got the wrong of me, but I am loyal to the Prince. Anything I do, not for my own edification, is in service to him. Now, mayhap, you don't know the whole of what we're up to, he and I, but you'll have to take that up with His Majesty."

Shomotta, not buying it, not completely, not for an instant, put his own mind hard to work. He prepared the mind reading spell as Caanaflit spoke.

Gesturing under the table, he whispered the word "Cromentolaus" before asking the question.

"What was your role in the Lord-Mayor's murder?"

Caanaflit's mind, as perceived by Shomotta, stumbled.

... zero plus zero is zero, zero minus zero is zero, zero percent of two is zero, zero plus two is two, two minus one is one, one percent of two-hundred is two ...

After the momentary interruption, however, he returned to more impressive calculations.

... seventy-four percent of four-hundred and forty-four is three-hundred and twenty-eight and six-tenths.

Simultaneously, Caanaflit spoke aloud, "That tragedy? You think I had something to do with that? Now I'm truly hurt?"

Shomotta listened to the stumbled maths in Caanaflit's mind, stymied for a lie that parted from his lips, before pressing.

"That's what I thought. You are too good a liar for all that. You didn't think anyone knew. You lingered in Spearpointe, why?"

At this point, Caanaflit's mental defenses were back up, so he lied easily, "I had business to attend to. As I said at the time. I own stakes in a number of vendors and am patron to a few bards besides, so they tell the right tales. There is nothing to say that I have not already said. I did what I do. What I told you I was going to do. Until, that is, you contacted me with that device. Then I was rather busy rallying your reinforcements."

"Of course," Shomotta accepted superficially, "Whatever was I thinking?"

"Alright," Caanaflit stood, playing more flustered and indignant than he actually felt, "You don't want to talk to me, then don't. Not my friend, so be it, but keep your crazy ass notions to yourself! Alright?"

"I would not speak of things I cannot prove unless the Prince were to invite me to do so."

"I assure you, he will not," Caanaflit barked.

"And this is the problem."

Caanaflit stormed off, surprised at feeling the barest fleeting empathy for Ruffis, in such moments, as he went.

Chapter 40
Remaining Cohort

Sira Roselle had only been back in Spearpointe a few days. She was resting in a guest room at the Mayor's Mansion, the home of her friend, the new Mayor, Sir Shamus Stoutspear. Though she had not taken to sleeping in, she had not been leaving her room until time for the noon meal. This morning, however, a relentless rapping began to strike her door before she had fully roused from slumber.

At last the lady-knight attempted to modestly, yet hastily, cover herself and breach open the door a crack. A messenger boy, adorable little sword on his hip, stood there and blinked at her.

"Yes, lad?" Roselle invited his words.

"Sira," he began, "There are soldiers, they say of Morralish. They wish to speak to whatever Marshall or General represents the Prince's military force here."

They're in for a shock, she thought privately, replying to the boy, "Request the banquet hall from the Mayor's men. Invite him to join us. I'll come as soon as I can."

"With apologies, sira," the boy said, "The Mayor has already drawn them together. He has sent for you."

"Not even the real Mayor and he thinks to do my job as well. I can't go down there like this. They'll simply have to wait," she protested, followed by a long moment's silent pause, before repeating herself to the boy, and closing the door on him, "I'll come as soon as I can!"

No time for a bath, she did put on her armor, with a blue tunic that proclaimed her both a soldier of Morralish and a Knight of the Spear, before running a comb through her hair until it agreed to lay down. Leaving her room, she grabbed up the griffin banner.

In as short a time as she could manage, Sira Roselle presented in the Mayor's Hall. The Mayor introduced her.

"Knights and good men, tis my honor to introduce you to Sira Roselle Taversdaughter, First Knight of the Spear, Standard-Bearer to Prince

Bengallen Hastenfarish, and Paladin Apprentice to the same, recently returned from the field of battle, His Majesty's victory — at the Battle of Woodhaven."

A lot can happen in two years, she thought to herself, raising her hand, palm out, in salute.

"Sira, with equal esteem, I introduce to you," the Mayor continued, "The Forest Phantoms, elite men-at-arms in service to the Morralish Expeditionary Forces. Their Commander and Chieftain of the MacRoberts Clan, Sir Yeruh-meer, a Paladin of Vandor. To his right, a fellow paladin, Sir Quaindraught. To his left, the knight Sir Ihrvan. Their companions, the wizards Kinnik and Sternus."

Chief Jerumir rubbed the temples of his bald head, returned Roselle's salute, and spoke with a confident voice, though one less rugged than his appearance.

"I take it you're not the general, but if you are indeed the standard-bearer, sira, I suppose there there is much you can tell us."

"Commander, Sir, er, ah," Roselle fumbled for words and so chose to simply ask what she was thinking, "How would you prefer I address you?"

"You can call me Snuggles — if you've got good news," Jerumir joked, "but my highest title is Chieftain, tis like a Lord but without all the money. The boys call me Chief, you may do the same."

"Chief," Sira Roselle tried it on, "I would first have you know that your orders from His Majesty are to remain in Spearpointe and Woodhaven, aiding with defenses as needed, and preparing additional soldiers, as they return, to re-take Morralish Prime."

"I like where your head and heart are at," Jerumir replied, "but I would first have you know that we're not about to do anything of the sort."

"Were no' e'zactly garrison-the-fort types," Sir Quaindraught added with toothy smile.

"There are no soldiers returning," Jerumir continued, "and we have come to find out if the rumors of our Prince's survival are true and, if so, why no recall has been sounded."

"His Majesty, Prince Bengallen lives," Sira Roselle spoke this with passion, "If you have heard of the great Beast – he and his mighty thanes have slain on

175

behalf of the people of Spearpointe – or of the ten-thousand orcs vanquished at Woodhaven, under his leadership, then you have heard the truth of it."

"Ooh," Sir Ihrvan, the silver-blonde, spoke up, "Hadn't heard about the orcs. Which number do you suppose the truth, the ten or the thousand?"

"Many brave men and women died!" Sira Roselle contested, "You'll not mock them in my presence, sir."

"Apologies," Jerumir offered, placing his hand on Sir Ihrvan's shoulder, "How about we all have a seat. I believe there is a meal coming. Forgive my men, sira, we work very closely together and I give them a certain latitude with their opinions. We've not sat in a proper hall among allies and would-be friends for some time."

As the others took seats, Roselle rolled up the banner and sat it upon an empty seat against the wall and away from the table. Once she had done so, she joined them.

"Apology accepted."

Chief Jerumir went on to explain the Forest Phantoms to Sira Roselle and the Mayor. An elite unit that operated outside the normal command structure, working with whomever needed their talents the most, as directed by the King himself, or – absent his command – as their Chieftain saw fit. He was not sure anyone was getting orders, or – if they were – from whom they were coming, so they had come to Spearpointe seeking the Prince himself.

"Is it true he slew a dragon?" the elder wizard, Kinnik, asked, drawing Roselle's attention to his more than merely human countenance.

The lady-knight laughed.

"We all had just about decided dragons were real, but no, t'was a primordial demon. Those creatures called Starspawn, rather hard to describe, but huge, inky black, dozens of tentacles, and as many large teeth."

"They were a known nuisance long before the Slumbering of the World, but this is the first I've heard of one on this side of history," Kinnik remarked, a twinkle in his eye.

"Well," said Roselle, "We had a hunter with us who was known for having killed a Chimera, apparently not many of those around any more either, as

176

well as a trio from the Far Continent, one of which was an elf with skin as black as the Starspawn's and a bloody centaur besides. We've had to rethink the line of myth and history out here on the Frontier of late. You can see why we were nearly ready to believe in dragons once again."

She noticed it on their faces a second time. Both times that she mentioned *believing in dragons*, they all pursed their lips. They must have thought *the Frontier-born lady-knight a lunatic*, she worried. *All anyone can do, however, is tell the truth and asked to be believed.* Unless she was missing something. *If Caanaflit had been there …* but he was not.

"Though the centaur people on the Far Continent are known to men who study such things," the elder wizard said cumbersomely, "We've seen things too. More than trolls and ogres, mind you, consider us open-minded."

For their part, they must have believed something of what she told them. They encouraged her to continue. Sira Roselle told them of the Beast's killings, the hunts, the goblin attack, the relationship between the two, the Order of the Spear and the squires of the Prince, and His Majesty's mighty thanes. She told them of Prince Bengallen sending the Priestess Bethany to recall the sons of Morralish and believing they were returning, of discovering they were not, of initially refusing to abandon the Frontier to investigate, of treating with dwarves, securing their aid, and saving Woodhaven on top of it all.

"Dwarves and elves, allied to the Prince in the Light, make way for Woodhaven. The Prince himself now travels to Antoria to personally recall his soldiers. Our job is to secure Spearpointe and Woodhaven, build up their supplies and resources, to aid in the push north and the reclamation of your homeland," she concluded.

"Sira can tell a story," Sir Quaindraught shouted, "I'm bloody well sold!"

Sira Roselle thought of her half-orc husband then. *How he loved his stories. The knight's praise was higher than he knew.* How good to know that she, the wife of a man who loved stories about knights, was just confirmed by a knight as someone who could tell stories well.

"So His Majesty is upon the Frontier Road?" Chief Jerumir asked.

"I didn't say that," Sira Roselle countered, "How can we prove to each other that we are who we say we are."

"I had decided to take your word as a knight, at this point," Jerumir said plainly, "I'll see to whatever tests you'd put me to, as knight and paladin, but the only one who knows us both in common is His Majesty, the Prince. Between the fall of the Kingdom and the secretive nature of our band, I doubt I can allay such concerns."

"Would you reveal yourselves to our local priest?"

"I would."

"If he trusts you," Sira Roselle offered, "I'll take it as confirmation of my own sense to trust you."

Over the next hour, they shared a meal. They asked questions about each other's stories and the people that populated them, but Sira was careful not to discuss anything beyond the Battle of Woodhaven. The Forest Phantoms, in kind, neither discussed their recent covert dealings in Napua nor their suspicion of certain Morralish generals in Antoria.

They did not wait long after their meal for the priest, Brother Thom, to arrive.

"Oh, good, you're bald, sir," the priest voiced his observation as he entered into the room.

"I am," Jerumir accepted, amused.

Brother Thom came to the table, next to Chief Jerumir, and pulled a black candle and a vial of oil from his bag.

"This is a holy oil, you see," Thom explained, "It will only burn in the presence of evil. This candle is evil, well, more of a allegoric evil, but will serve for the purpose of this ritual. I will anoint you with the oil and you will speak. If you tell the truth, some small part of the oil will evaporate, having protected you from evil. If you lie, it will corrupt the holiness in the oil. Then when the candle touches your head, the oil will ignite."

"My baldness?"

"Oh, right," replied Thom, "It can be hard to get all the hair thoroughly coated in the oil. Smaller searings can make it hard to tell if the words were lies or if the candle just got a pocket of hair unprotected. But as you are bald — so there'll be none of that."

"Yer momma told ya not ta worry about it," Sir Quaindraught teased, rubbing Jerumir's head.

Sira Roselle burst out laughing, but cut herself short for decorum's sake. *Just because it was okay for them to joke with each other, didn't mean anyone else should be laughing at them.*

"Go on and laugh, sira," Jerumir commented with laughter in his own voice,

"This is all being done for your benefit."

"Apologies, Chief," Roselle offered with a smile still playing about her lips.

"May our Father's wisdom, Mother's voice, and Brother's truth protect the righteous from the flames and snares of evil," Thom said as he liberally smeared the holy oil over Jerumir's head before he lit the candle. It burned a solid red as he asked, "Who art thou?"

"I am the Paladin Jerumir, Knight of the Church, Soldier of Morralish, Commander of the Forest Phantoms, and Chieftain of the MacRoberts Clan."

Brother Thom placed the flame to Jerumir's head. Nothing happened.

Thom asked, "Whither thou comest?"

"Napua, a coastal city, on a plateau in the mountains east of the Antori Peninsula."

Flame, head, nothing.

"Why dost thou cometh?"

"To seek what fate of our great Prince, Bengallen of House Hastenfarish. If he lives, to learn of his location. To rendezvous with and advise him of our situation and receive his orders or blessing to pursue our own aims."

The candle burned its red flame. It touched the Chieftain's head a third time. A third time the oil protected him, in his truth, from its searing heat. The man was truthful in his telling.

"Sira," Brother Thom addressed her, "I have done as I have been asked. We're all among friends here. Being so, might I have some of these leftovers? ... So that I can give my own ration to the poor."

"Please, Brother, join us," Sira Roselle invited, motioning to an empty seat and waving a server over, directing, "Have all this packaged for the Brother that he may share it with others."

The server went off to fetch a crate.

"You shouldn't do that," Sir Ihrvan said, "You just took his lunch from him and gave it to the poor after eating so well yourself. They sort of hate that."

"A fine gesture," Brother Thom added, food mostly swallowed, "but he has the right of it."

"Regardless," Jerumir redirected the discussion, "If the Prince is not upon the Frontier Road, by what way has he gone?"

"I didn't say he is not, Chief," Roselle reminded, "I merely said that I did not say. They took a route, across the Umber River, that puts them on the Old King's Road, to Andover. If you've come by way of the Frontier Road, through Mayfield, you would not have crossed their path. Now, I know naught of traveling such distances and cannot claim to know if they have come to that place where the Old King's and the Frontier Roads merge on approach to Three God's Pass. I have never traveled half so far in all my life, but I doubt you can catch them up at any rate."

"A natural doubt," the younger wizard, Sternus, at last spoke, "But we have our ways."

"Then I wish you luck and would keep you no longer," Roselle stood and offered her salute.

The Forest Phantoms stood as well, Jerumir, Quaindraught, and Ihrvan returning her salute.

"I do graciously thank the Mayor for his hospitality and Sira for her time and vital information. Please give my apologies to the Constable for breaking protocol and not including him here. I have neither intentions toward Spearpointe, nor an inclination to stay. Haste is my excuse, if he will have it."

"If you would return," the Mayor invited, "Spearpointe shall welcome you with open arms."

With that, the Forest Phantoms left as quickly as they had come. No sooner than they were out the door, the Mayor asked, "Should we have them followed?"

"No," Sira Roselle said in a matter of fact tone, "I'm going to advise against that. If we have anyone that could both keep up with them and stay hidden, then surely we have something more important for him to do. Besides, they'd find him out, sooner or later. Those aren't the kind of men I want to piss off."

"Agreed," said Mayor Stoutspear and Brother Thom simultaneously.

Chapter 41
Comprehending Darkness

The bright moon shone, high at the top of the sky, midnight. While Prince Bengallen's thanes sat around a fire, telling stories, *how did they have so many stories*, and staying up too late. Another of many late nights on the road, the Prince, himself, walked about alone in the moonlight. Though he valued his sleep, on this particular night, he was drawn to the bright moon.

It gave him a cold comfort to think that his people and his love might be gazing up at the same moon. That, in its fullness, they might be as one. Recent knowledge that at least some of his people had in fact survived, not only the soldiers stationed abroad, but farmers, merchants, villagers, women, children, the past, present, and future of his people still intact, gladdened his heart. His struggle persisted as no mere matter of retribution, justice, vengeance, but also of restoration.

The wizard, Shomotta, found him and, speaking from a slight distance, inquired, "Do you study the stars, Your Majesty?"

Prince Bengallen lowered his face and invited his thane forward, answering, "Please, join me. I appreciate them aesthetically, but I know naught of their names and neither am I familiar with their movements."

Shomotta came closer and spoke, "Light with darkness. Darkness with light. What does your Church teach you about the moons?"

"Our spiritual gifts," the Prince began his reply, "are born of the Light, of which all lights are but dim reflection. So these gifts are inclined to thrive in the light of day. As the bright moon, waxing, floods the night sky, the Light holds more sway. The more tis spiritually alike to the day."

"What of when the bright moon is diminished?" Shomotta asked, "What of a night where it is eclipsed completely?"

"Evil lives in the dark," Prince Bengallen answered with grim certainty, "Its sway swells as the bright moon wanes into obscurity."

"This is true," the wizard-priest agreed, placing his hand into the bag on his hip, "but it is somewhat more complex and yet also more completely explicable."

"Is it?" Bengallen paused, asking only after observing Shomotta remove an object from his bag.

"Would you like to see something … cosmic?"

Bengallen smiled, "Of course."

"You have seen my spyglass?" Shomotta asked rhetorically as he assembled the shaft around the lens, "You have not seen through it."

The wizard placed a red-tinted cap over the lens and handed it to the Prince.

Peering through, he asked, "What am I looking at?"

"The moons."

"The bright moon is full. There is only the one visible and I yet see it well."

"Hum-ha," Shomotta laughed, insisting, "Look."

Prince Bengallen held the device to his eye and noticed the cap made the stars look red, less sharp, but also less luminous. As he turned his head about, struggling a moment to find the moon, he had to pull the spyglass away to align his sight. He winced at the bright moon's comparative magnitude without the lens.

Placing his eye back to the device, he found it, the moon, red and muted, large through the spyglass. What he saw next was haunting. The Prince awed in wonder rather than rush for an explanation.

There were moons, plural, in the sky. Not one, or two, but three moons. He could see a dark disk – *or were they spheres* – to both the left and right of the bright moon. Only magnified and in the muted light could he see the black silhouettes, otherwise drowned in the wash of light emanating from the bright moon. These dark moons were also far smaller than they appeared on the nights when their cycle obscured and eclipsed the bright one.

"There are three moons?"

Prince Bengallen's voice raised with each word as he continued gazing upward through the spyglass.

"Four, actually," the wizard added, explaining, "A third dark moon is completely to the back of the bright one when it is full."

"Wha—?" Bengallen began, "Whi— What?"

"When we fought the Starspawn," Shomotta began, "You knew of the First Discord."

"Yes," Bengallen replied, turning his face from the sky to his friend and thane, "The remaining fragments of our ancient scriptures remark and reflect upon it."

"This world was created with two suns," Shomotta continued, "As one sat, the other rose, and the world was filled with light, a perfect harmony. Then came discord into the world. It was darkness and chaos and horror. It could not be undone, but here the created order reigned. The discord was divided into three parts and consigned to the second sun. Its power keeps them in place. Yet so doing, the three discords, called the dark moons, absorb and at times obscure the light of what was once our second sun, now called the bright moon. Thus it became less bright than the sun and darkness was revealed to the world. Most of all that exists is darkness and chaos, and now, in our time, even here amid the concordance of order and light, a place has been made for darkness and discord, that we might yet be spared from its complete dominion."

Bengallen gasped, reflecting aloud, "So fragile. Tis this what makes it all so beautiful?"

Shomotta considered.

"It is what makes us glorious. Every moment, of every life, every ray, of every light, amazing, sacred, holy so long as it holds the darkness at bay. The evil men do, so monstrous it might seem – feel – is as nothing faced with the eternal stretch of inky chaos that lies beyond our world."

"Bleak."

"You are firmly of the Light, my Prince. These things may attempt to assail you, but if the whole world were swallowed up in darkness, you would be among the last to vanish. You are not so near to it and, as such, you feel it less keenly. Myself not so far from you, I can but hope. The plight of the common man, however, he does not even understand the precipice on which he stands. Yet with every step, he feels the shaky ground upon which he treads and the draw of the abyssal maw, yawning at him."

183

"Beauty with horror."

"Light with darkness," Shomotta repeated his earlier words, "Great evils of the world, nameless forgotten things, false gods, and that fallen angel besides, have been banished and consigned to those dark moons. One might ask 'why not all evil' and though I cannot claim to have unraveled that mystery of the cosmos, I imagine it might be a bad idea to unite too much evil and darkness with the discord of its origin. Perhaps better to let the world work out as much of it as we can on our own."

"Keeps me in the paladin business, but so bleak a reality is detestable," Bengallen rebutted, "I can conceive of a light without shadow."

Shomotta allowed his grim countenance to crack a bit, a smile. He liked to hear Prince Bengallen say such things, but pushed back on philosophical grounds nonetheless.

"Light, yes, but shape, and form, and substance?"

Bengallen insisted, "Because we have not seen and cannot conceive of another way should not mean that it cannot be so."

"Is it true that paladins feel no fear?" Shomotta asked, shifting the conversation away from debate and more toward his own feelings rather than his reason.

"In a sense," the Paladin-Prince answered, uncertain as to where the conversation was turning, "I know of terror, that which is to be feared, and why, but the emotion of it — it simply does not grip me. The fear finds no purchase."

"Even knowing?"

"Yes, even still."

"Would that I had been a paladin then," Shomotta mused, "It is a wizard's business to know too much. The fear becomes somewhat — calibrated to the depths of understanding, but it very much remains. You paladins may know the tears of the world, feel its need and sadness spurring you to set to right and deliver the Light, but we wizards know why the world is weeping. And for all our power, we can only live with the fear that it is so much greater – than all of us – and all of the power we should ever hold will never be enough."

184

"You saw something," Prince Bengallen spoke his realization aloud, "When your magic brought you to the brink of death, you saw something."

"I did."

"Well?"

"I should tell you," Shomotta accepted, "but not before you contemplate these things."

Prince Bengallen's impulsive youth and appreciation for theology and philosophy told him to press the issue. Yet his training and experience in those same matters gave him sense enough to know that the wizard-priest, operating more as the latter part of that distinction, was correct.

Instead, Bengallen asked, "So suns and moons I shall think upon, but what of the stars? What are they then?"

"Hope," Shomotta answered simply, but pausing to think upon it for a moment longer, explained further, "We might be the first world, but we might also not be the last. Each star out there holds the promise of a new world, not unlike our own sun. They are, each one, hope for a future beyond even what we may know or can even imagine."

"Not so bleak."

"Not so bleak at all."

The two parted company. A good note to part on. The only thought, Prince Bengallen decided, from their conversation that he could find sleep thinking upon. So he did, leaving the contemplation of darker matters for the light of day.

Chapter 42
Finding Hope

Lord Strein Hrothmond called to his guard, "What prison is this? – I demand to know! – When do I plead my case? – I wish to make correspondence!"

Not only did the guard, departing from the noontime delivery of gruel, ignore him, but he did not even hear all of his words. Before the imprisoned lord could finish, the guard had come to the end of the hall and closed a solid door behind him.

Strein Hrothmond played with his food as much as he ate it. In truth it was hardly fit for either, but sitting in the floor, palming his meager bowl, his mind wandered. So pleased that he had defeated their trap and did not let them kill him. Yet he could not help but wonder, *compared to rotting in this place, would that have been the better message after all.*

Imprisoned, he had naught to do but think. He reflected on the Conclave of Morralish Generals, *what a farce,* and wondered what he could have done differently. He speculated as to what had been happening in the time since his imprisonment and his imaginings were terrible and disturbing, save for one.

He held a single hope that, somewhere out there, *the Line of Hastenfarish was not broken* and that *the Paladin-Prince would reveal himself to remind the men of their loyalty. Mayhap it had already happened.* He wished he could believe that.

"Pisst!"

Strein Hrothmond immediately thought of his children. Never had so simple a sound stirred his heart so greatly since he bounced babies on his knees. He tried not to think of them as adults anymore. *Where were they when the kingdom fell? What were the grandchildren doing?*

Instead, of late, he remembered them only as babies in his wife's arms. It was simpler, safer. He had enough to drive him mad there in that prison. He did not need to help it along, thinking on the horrors that befell his homeland and family.

"Pisst. Pisst."

He heard it again, a conspiratorial sound. He had enough conspiracy aligned against him. He smiled with glee, however, at the thought that someone might recruit him into one.

"Yes," he replied softly.

A young guard, different than the one who came before, unlocked his cell.

"You can count?"

Strein nodded.

"Aye."

"Count to thirty, slowly, then go to the end of the hall and out the door. Only one other door, from there, will be unlocked. Go through it to another cell block. Many cells, all but one is empty. Got it?"

Lord Strein Hrothmond, former general, had a hundred questions.

Strein the prisoner had none and again replied, "Aye."

The moments ticked away to his counting, one through, at last, thirty. He skulked down the hall at first, before realizing that all the other cells were empty. *This was a forgetting place.* If not for him and some possible few others, it *would soon have been itself forgotten.*

Exiting the guards' door, he came into a half circle room. One door on the flat wall, six on the arch, and an empty desk and chair in the middle. He went to the door on the flat wall first, *the likely exit, locked.* He went to the desk, it had no drawers or papers of any kind, only a lone *hook for a keyring, missing.* He tried a couple of the other doors and the third one opened, *success.* Strein closed it behind him.

His stomach was in his throat and his spine tingled with electricity as he moved down the hall of cells. *What was there to find?* As more and more of them proved empty, his anxiety spiked. Finally, in the next to last cell on his right, he saw her.

"Pappa!" the Priestess called to him.

"Bethany?" the words fell from the old general's mouth uncertainly, like the croak of a dying man.

"Yes, father," Sister Bethany confirmed to him, opening her unlocked cell, "please come in, before anyone sees us."

She took him by the hand, pulled him into the secrecy of her squalor, and hugged him tightly.

"Oh Bethany," he began to weep, putting his hand to her face, "look at you. What have they done to you?"

"Nothing that a few good baths and hot meals can't fix," she reassured him, "I'm alive and so are you, in these days, that counts for much."

"Indeed," he agreed, calmly asking, "How did you know to find me here?"

"Well," she smiled and he saw his beautiful daughter shining through the mess she wore, "I've been her a bit longer than you. I've befriended a guard, Jonn, and he told me a 'knight from my home country' had been brought here. That he would help me see you, but, of course, neither of us knew that you were — you."

They laughed and hugged again. They forgot, for a moment, their predicament. That moment did them more good than all the planning in the world.

It appeared that some magic persisted in the world that could not be suppressed.

"It feels odd to say it, here, like this," Strein Hrothmond said to his daughter, "but clearly the Holy Family favors us. They're not through with us yet. I say it."

"We say it," she prayed with him.

Chapter 43
Thinking Through

Just beyond the halfway point from Spearpointe to Three Gods Pass, "The Gateway to the Imperium," Prince Bengallen's company came upon a small convoy headed east, opposed to them. They were only lightly guarded, but their guard was well armed and armored, a few of them clearly Morralish soldiers, less clearly, possibly more.

Caanaflit and Malcolm rode ahead to greet them, identifying themselves as "Thanes in the service to Prince Bengallen" and demanding to speak to the one whomever led the convoy.

The convoy halted. A merchant, in fine but worn clothing, waddled out to greet them. He explained that the Morralish soldiers among his convoy wanted to return home and had signed on as guards to get the convoy so far as the journey was shared. In exchange for the protection of their martial prowess, they would benefit from a strengthened number and receive food and basic provisions.

Away from the ears of the guard, the convoy leader was informed that all soldiers of Morralish had been recalled to the service of His Majesty Prince Bengallen. After the brief rundown of events, the convoy leader, young for a merchant with such influence and finance, expressed apology for incidentally leading the soldiers astray, and asked if he might negotiate to keep them on throughout the journey.

Caanaflit groaned. Malcolm insisted. The young merchant and two ethnically Antori guards, as to avoid the confusion Morralish soldiers might face, were taken to see the Prince.

"Your Highness, thank you for receiving me. I had no knowledge of your edict and have come to beg terms that might keep my family and friends, your own future subjects, safe in our travel through the wilderness of this Frontier."

"The Frontier life is not for the faint of heart," Prince Bengallen began, "Why do you leave the safety of Antoria to find your fortune here? Why leave your Imperator to live under my banner and law?"

"Nothing so political on my count, Your Highness," the merchant leader replied, "In fact, I've spent most of my limited fortune just getting here."

189

Bengallen's eyes narrowed as he echoed questioningly, "Not on your count?"

"It seems that they are all blind in the halls of power, Your Highness," the young merchant said.

Prince Bengallen quirked his mouth, indicating partial understanding, but asked, "Your meaning?"

"They don't see the foundation of the empire. Rent and crumbling, they don't even see it!"

Bengallen's brow lowered, potential understanding faded to confusion, demanding, "What? To what are they proverbially blind and failing to see? What do you suppose is the foundation of the empire?"

"Apologies, Your Highness," the merchant offered with a bow of his head before continuing, "I too am guilty of it, in my own way, I suspect. I speak of the slaves, of course. We don't generally speak of them, notice them, considered tacky, you see. Generation after generation trained from birth to ignore the slaves that make so much of their – our – lives possible. Anyone with slaves that live better than freemen are oblivious. Those with wretched slaves ignore it. Most that don't own slaves don't care. Power and wealth conceal the problem, but don't resolve it. And now — Now th'ole scheme is about to fall apart. Thanks to all your boys in blue."

"Come again?" Caanaflit interjected.

"Morralish soldiers always found slavery distasteful, nothing new in that. Usually, though, they kept it to themselves, minus the odd word, here or there, with too many cups on the floor. Now, with the prospect of settling down in the Antori provinces, the option to purchase citizenship, the desertion and other disappearance of certain of their cohort, your boys are talking about a lot of things — very publicly. They don't approve. Adding lots of new ideas to the conversation. A conversation that the powerful aren't listening to. Slaves been whispering about their freedom since as long as there have been slaves, but now — now there are freemen, and warriors at that, not just whispering, but shouting about freedom and justice for all. Lot of guys with half-a-courage might find the other half in that."

Bengallen looked to Caanaflit, who shrugged in reply, adding, "Not the sort of thing I'd have missed. If your men are stirring up trouble, we're talking the last few months. When Shomotta and I were there last year, if we saw anything, it implied the opposite."

Shomotta nodded in agreement.

"And that is why you are leaving?" Bengallen asked.

"Yep," the merchant said simply, elaborating, "Gonna get scary. Soon and quick. Don't know who will win. Don't know that I care. Just don't want my wife or children to get killed in the chaos. Not afraid or unsympathetic. I don't own slaves, but I am not a fighter. My only responsibility is to my family and my limited wealth was enough to relocate them to the Frontier, safely, and make an honest go at a life out here. Took on these others to limit my own costs while makin' the trip possible for them as well."

Prince Bengallen looked the man in the eye as he spoke, his own countenance unreadable, stare unbroken, even as the Paladin-Prince made a reluctant reply.

"Two years ago, I would have cursed you all for cowards, demanded my men come with me, and tried to shame the rest of you into returning with us. I would have been wrong. In what wares do you trade?"

"My father left me coin so I was a grocer. I purchased, transported, and prepared larger quantities of agricultural goods for small quantity purchasing. I have no illusions that I might have to adjust my business, but I'll find a need and see it well filled."

Bengallen broke eye contact to shoot a glance to Caanaflit, who visibly pondered a moment, tapping his finger against his chin, before looking skyward and cocking his head to the left.

"Spearpointe or Andover."

The merchant looked back to Prince Bengallen, finding his face and tone more relaxed.

"If you want to live in one of the city-states, you'll find Spearpointe most likely to need a grocer. There are lots of smaller communities though. Among them, Andover is not too far from here actually — seems to be the best choice. When you arrive, grant the Morralish soldiers additional provision to continue their journey so far as Spearpointe. There they will find a small military force led by a Knight of the Spear, my knight. Your borrowed Morralish soldiers will report to Spearpointe and there await my further command. Do this and you, your family, and the rest of your company have my blessing. Go in peace."

The merchant took a deep and formal bow.

"Most humble gratitude, Your Majesty."

After he and his two guards were some distance away, Caanaflit mused, "Your Majesty is as benevolent as he is wise."

"Indeed," agreed Shomotta.

Bengallen walked with them back to their horses.

"The Frontier has lost many of its finer men of recent. Today it has gained one instead. One that will now want to be loyal."

Late that same night, Alpona caught Caanaflit rummaging through Ruffis' things, indiscreetly.

"Do you truly trust him so little?"

"It matters naught," Caanaflit replied, "look at all that I have found."

"It matters," said Alpona, "would your own packs be empty?"

"Look," Caanaflit insisted, avoiding, "Here is a ring of the Prince. This other thing, whatever it is, clearly of dwarven make. This metallic ball belongs to Shomotta, I've seen him use it for his magic, dangerous that he might not have it when he needs it."

"Long ago, as I think about it now, when my master taught me the way of the sword, many things did I witness," Alpona began, "There were many students of many things at the monastery and I was the most skilled of none. They had come from many homes, families, brought many things, but I came from nothing and brought nothing. My family, foreign and of abject poverty when at last my father died, gave me over to the monks to raise. So I insisted on learning the sword, despite having many other skills yet to master, many other lessons still to learn. Out of wisdom or pity, or maybe one is in the other, a master began my training in the art form for which I have become renowned, even among this frontier of these distant lands."

Alpona paused, a heavy breath of nostalgia inhaled and hovering on his lips. Caanaflit knew his ally was not finished with the tale, but took the moment to close Ruffi's rucksack and move a pair of paces away from it.

Apona continued, "Long had the other students suspected me of stealing and now that I had been given a great opportunity, something that stood me out from them, they watched me jealously to discover their proof — and so they did. A small copper coin, left unattended in another's room, the door open. A trap, I was soon to discover. Caught, the ones that ensnared me, dragged me before my master, recounted my misdeed, and requested that I be cut-off from the monastery."

Alpona paused again, looked up, looked down, as though searching for something he needed to finish. Caanaflit took a few more steps. Alpona turned to him, proceeding with his telling.

"My master merely sighed and walked off, ignoring us and not breaching the topic in the days that followed. In those days my peers conspired against me, however, adamant and observant, they learned of my secret place, my cache of pilfered property, my shrine to the tiny things of the world that I did not own. My master was escorted there and I was summoned thereafter, to stand before him, in shame. Yet again, he disregarded my inequity."

Caanaflit began to speak. He thought he knew where this was going and never could hold his tongue for a story. He was wrong. Alpona knew he was wrong, held up a finger, canted his head and hushed the rogue before resuming once more. To his credit, Caanaflit hushed.

"This caused great discord among the other monks, student and teacher alike," Alpona stated, initiating his conclusion, "A large number of them actually gathered in protest and threatened to leave the monastery if action was not taken against me. But wisdom flowed from my master and he said to them, 'You are all so righteous and so wise, as to know good from evil. This you have learned from me and perhaps there is nothing for me to teach you. Yet this poor savage does not even know right from wrong, let alone good from evil. How can I impose a fair justice upon him? From whom shall he learn, if not I?' "

Chapter 44
Continuing Senate

In Antoria Royal, the Chambers of the Senate, the Senate President presided, "Also, 'A Matter of Dispute Between Public Accommodation and the Right to Refuse Clients' continues to be tabled for yet another week, as accusations and findings continue to resolve under investigation. A report detailing these investigations remains available for your reading with my executive clerk following today's session. Before we get to the docket today, I have granted Senator Macrobius the floor to speak his concerns about current events. I will give him the time to make his statement, then you may ask questions or make a motion to move on to other business. Senator."

"We cannot continue to ignore the wind," Senator Macrobius, a notorious philosopher, stood and began, "Only a fool denies the blowing wind simply because he cannot see it. Doesn't mean it is not there. Listen, you can hear it. Lean against it and you can feel it. The wind has changed, brothers, are we brave enough to change with it?"

There was a long silence. The illustration was clear enough or too clear, mayhap, if perchance you enjoy your puns. In truth, no one was completely certain what, precisely, he was referring to.

"Was he done?" many of the other Senators whispered, "Had he cracked?"

"Is that it?" the President asked.

Macrobius nodded, sitting.

"Our entire economy is dependent on slave labor," a wealthy senator took the bait, "Are you suggesting that we simply abandon it and watch our society collapse?"

"I merely acknowledged the wind," Macrobius replied, "Yet, as you have asked, I will answer: A wiseman does not build his house upon the sand and thus need not fear its collapse."

The other senator glared, red faced, but without retort. Another protracted silence filled the chamber.

At last, the President broke it.

"If there are no other questions for Senator Macrobius — then I invite you to docket number one, today's date, 'The Private Purchasing of Public Parks and the Resultant Loss of Free Speech Forums.' Shedding the maintenance expense of public parks is a cost cutting measure narrowly approved by this Senate last year. While bids for private ownership have added revenue and successfully decreased spending, many citizens have complained that new owners often censor the activities and discussions that are had there, most requiring permit for speeches. The Imperial Senate has been asked to consider repurchasing these parks to better provide for the freedom of speech. Is there discussion on the matter?"

"We approved the sales," a senator began, "I suppose we can suspend selling the remainder, if it is the will of the people, but I do not see how we can force them to be sold back to us."

"We can," another senator answered "because we're the government!"

"I don't see the problem here," Senator Iscavius redirected, "By selling this land, the government has not infringed upon the freedom of speech. The people are just as free as ever to speak what they will, but likewise, land owners are free to set the terms of the usage of their land. This is the problem of the would-be speaker, not of the government."

"I disagree," Senator Macrobius interjected.

Iscavius sneered, "Of course you do."

"The Imperator's word is law," Macrobius began, "our decisions are as nothing without his ratification. Yet, we exist, as a Senate, to represent the will of the people. To be their voice in the government. The First Imperator, a god in the flesh, granted the people certain inalienable liberties. If we do nothing else, as the voice of the people, we should ensure those freedoms. I consent to you, Senator Iscavius, in part, the government, here, is not the one infringing upon the freedom of speech. It is the land owner's rulings and the would-be speaker's problem. Yet these would-be speakers are citizens, are they not? They are granted freedom of speech, are they not? Just because the government is not, itself, doing the infringing upon a citizen's freedom, doesn't mean we, as the part of the government for the people, may relinquish our duty to the people, to ensure those freedoms. If one citizen imprisons another unjustly and without commission, is it not the government's duty to free the man? Even as the government did not inflict the infraction against the man's freedom, the government exists, in large part, to ensure and restore guaranteed freedoms. How, then, are we not just as obligated to restore this particular freedom, when one citizen denies it to another?"

"Because it is the other citizen's land."

"If a boy pisses on your villa, Iscavius, do you have the right to piss on him in return? To geld him?"

"No."

"No one is denying anyone else the right to own land."

Iscavius replied with question of his own.

"But what is the point of owning it, if one cannot set the terms of its use?"

"We are nation of land. As a nation, we have laws," Macrobius answered, "Our very business is, from a perspective, to tell people what they can and cannot do with land owned within our borders. To dictate the terms of participation. There is plenty of unruled land in the Frontier or in the Western Plains for men to claim and use without rule of law or terms."

"But we can only go so far!" Iscavius insisted.

Macrobius mused, "Ensuring basic freedoms, such as speech, doesn't seem so far to me. You seem quite willing to infringe upon the rights of businessmen, pressing them to serve those they would not. Public accommodation is not even a freedom guaranteed to the people. Why not, then, infringe for the sake of our most basic freedoms, like speech?"

"Do not confuse the issue?"

"I am not the one who seems confused."

A skittering of laughter echoed through the chamber, but the stern brow of the Senate President silenced it quickly.

"You say we speak for the people," Iscavius began his rebuttal, "So I speak for the men who bought that land. They had reasons for buying that land. It came with the right, as any land, for the owner to set its terms of use. I think it unfair, illegal, now with their coin spent, to change the terms of ownership, after the fact."

"Why," Macrobius asked, "Senator Iscavius, are you implying that the

196

monopolizing of these former places of free speech by a certain ideologically aligned citizens was done specifically to limit public exposure to opposing ideologies?"

"No! Of course not, I said no su–"

"Then what is the harm in ruling that parks located within our glorious city be designated 'Free Speech Zones' and offering a refund to any recent purchasers who don't like it? Of course, taking such a refund, they'll essentially be admitting that they had intended to circumvent one of the most basic rights granted us by our First Imperator. Yet, since you don't think that is why they bought them, it should not be an issue."

The first senator to speak on the topic spoke up again.

"I like it! No one is saying they can't own the land. No one is saying people can't exercise their free speech there. If the purchase was of right intentions, both sides win. I move for a city ordinance to be drafted, declaring all parks 'Free Speech Zones' and allowing refund to park owners so displeased, to be voted at earliest convenience."

"I second," Macrobius added, "and move that the young senator who proposed the ordinance be the one to draft it. Time to let him get his feet wet."

"I second that," agreed the 'because we're the government' senator.

"Both motions have been seconded," the President announced, "All in favor of Senator Galaebe drafting a city ordinance to be voted on next week, declaring all parks 'Free Speech Zones' and allowing the government to refund and reacquire any park who's current owners do not wish to comply, say 'aye.' "

The chamber resounded, "Aye."

"Those not in favor say 'nay.' "

A meek pair of 'nay's squeaked in reply.

"Motion carries," the President announced, "We look forward to formally hearing the ordinance next week and voting on it, Senator Galaebe. Moving on, docket number two, today's date ..." and so continued the work of the Imperial Senate.

Chapter 45
Traveling Magic

All this long journey, Malcolm had kept his eye out for the small stone and wood bauble that the elf had told him about. Yet he never saw it. At last, he had a suspicion and approached Caanaflit, asking, "Would it be safe to assume that you have taken inventory of everyone else's belongings?"

"Good afternoon to you too, Malcolm," Caanaflit replied with a playful grin, "Why, whatever do you mean?"

Malcolm played along and made an exaggerated sad and grumpy face, "There was something of my father's that should be mine. I did not look for it when he was slain. I was in shock, really. I expected to feel something when he died, when the Prince flung his severed head about — remorse, grief, relief, something. I felt nothing, and my wits were not with me. I am sure someone there, and so someone here, had claimed it, but I know not who."

Caanaflit's face went flat and he asked, "Alright. So seriously then, what are you looking for?"

"A trinket of stone and wood."

"Worn about the neck, like a talisman?"

Malcolm almost said yes, replying, "Possibly."

Caanaflit's grin returned, "Wouldn't you know?"

"Seriously, then," the half-orc began, "It was taken from the elf we freed and he wants me to have it.

"Why?"

"I'm not even sure."

"Not a hint."

Malcolm sighed, "He said some cryptic words. Told me to say some other words once I have it. Somehow, it lets some other elves know that an orc leader – my father dead, that'd mean me, apparently – is willing to treat with them."

"Fascinating," Caanaflit said.

A pause stretched between them.

"Well?" Malcolm asked.

"Oh, yes, Ruffis has it."

"Spit."

"I know. I know. Who wants to deal with that? I'll just steal it back from him. Tis your own after all, yes?"

Malcolm gave it the briefest thought, before replying in the affirmative, "Yes."

"One moment then. Wait here."

"Now!?"

"Yes, now."

"Alright," Malcolm accepted, leaning against a tree.

Ruffis was hunting, as was everyone else, as Malcolm and Caanaflit should have been. Caanaflit walked right up to Ruffis' pack. Reached his hand in without looking and produced the bauble.

It is fair to say that Malcolm did not actually see Caanaflit pull the item from his own sleeve. Malcolm did not catch the actual sleight of hand in the moment, but that does not mean that he did not know exactly what had happened.

The stone and wood bauble had been tucked away, of course, on Caanaflit's person the whole time. Having indeed inventoried everyone, he had claimed the item long before this moment, for safekeeping. Of that, there should be no doubt. Whomever might have had it originally – and so it must not have been Shomotta, who when asked had no idea what it was – ceased to be relevant.

Caanaflit had a known interest in such things. After many weeks on the road, however, it had done nothing for him. Then came Malcolm, playing the role of the naïve half-orc, and allowing the rogue to draw precisely the right information out of him.

His curiosity once again piqued, all of a sudden, Caanaflit knew exactly where to find it. Along with the promise that the item might yet do something interesting after all, he produced it for Malcolm, speedily.

Caanaflit was too clever, too often, too much so for his own good. Sometimes, that made him predictable. There would come a day, when Caanaflit himself would realize this and make an effort to prevent being so exploited. This day, however, came and went long before that one. Thus, Malcolm had won his prize.

A warm wind blew through the woods where they hunted. An ill omen, or so it felt to all. Two-by-two they returned to camp, empty handed, except for Ruffis and Alpona, who had not returned at all. As evening came and they should have long since left this place, Shomotta cast bones and other talismans, gazing into the fire for augury. Long moments passed, yet the wizard bespoke no foretoken.

He had used this same magic to help them prepare for the orcs at Woodhaven. Bengallen and Malcolm had seen him do it. Once that spell had been prepared, Shomotta spoke quickly and with clarity. To them, their friend looked and felt different this time, as though he saw something, but was hesitant to speak it.

Finally, Prince Bengallen addressed him, "Shomotta, what do you see?"

"I see," he replied, "What I see, I do not understand. It must be interpreted, but I haven't yet—"

The wizard's last words drifted off as he continued to stare into the fire.

Malcolm looked to Bengallen and Bengallen back to him. They both looked to Caanaflit, who shrugged, and to the others of their cohort. Blank stares all around. They were all out of their depth.

"Men," Shomotta finally spoke, "Riders like the fingers on the hand. The hand, not to be confused with the will that moves them. They come to here. They are supposed to be here. And wings! By all the gods and angels, my Prince, wings of colors three: black on the inside, made brown by nature, painted blue by men – bat's wings. That is all I see and feel."

"Where are Ruffis and Alpona?" Prince Bengallen asked.

"In the sky. They shall return."

Chapter 46
Swelling Ranks

Jonn had come far and risked much over what, in hindsight, were remembered as so few days. To the south-east of Llaris, between a prominence in the shoreline of Lake Orube, which completely surrounded the city-state, and the Dreadwood, there was a Morralish military encampment.

Formerly home only to the First Army Regiment, it had also become refuge to twice as many soldiers from several different regiments. Though the truth of the Morralish Refugee Act had not been made known to most of them prior to their arrival, these were the men and women who had, nonetheless, seen the proverbial writing on the wall and knew their only hope was under the fair justice of High Lord-General Harkon, himself a paladin.

Except the High Lord-General had been gone for some time. He had gone away, abruptly, to parts unknown, on secret mission with only half a battalion of men. He had no idea as to the swelling of his Regimental Headquarters with these deserters who, non-ironically, called themselves Loyalists. At first, the good men of the First Regiment took them in with an uncertain forgiveness in confusing times. Yet as their numbers grew and their High Lord-General remained absent, the present leadership became increasingly uncertain of how to proceed.

It would be treason to continue to encourage this behavior, but how could they turn away confused brothers and sisters who only meant to be loyal? Many began to wonder, with so many coming to them, if there was some terrible conspiracy about. Did any among them know about it? Were they complicit in it? Had their general taken men to investigate this very thing? Even if it were so, it did not provide a clear directive as to what to do with the ever growing population.

No one was happy with the state of affairs. How could they be? Their homeland reportedly destroyed. Their King and lords, family and friends, dead. No orders from their clients and hosts in the Antori Imperium. Disillusioned soldiers came there for guidance with none to be found. Their own general gone, his return unknown and destination uncertain. The ever growing thought of living out the remainder of their days in these foreign lands, where their values and laws were so different. It was a dire time in the camp of the First Regiment.

Then came a Llarisean prison guard named Jonn.

"Say what you came to say, boy."

"Begging your pardon, sir," Jonn replied, "I am not a boy. Proved, moreover, by my willingness and success in traveling two days, alone, overland, with little sleep and less provision. Forgive me if my newfound pride and confidence are inconvenient to your posturing, sir, but how do I know you are the one to whom I should speak?"

"Ooo …" the burly man growled, continuing in gruff manner, "Yes, I like this beh, er, fellow. Finally, one of the right sort among all these prissy foxgloves about Llaris. Suppose I was posturing a bit. Usually works real well on yer sort. I'm the senior general present, Lord Kenneth Cardness. Yer name?"

"I'm Jonn, m'lord," he answered, "I was led to believe that many of the leadership here would be paladins. Are you a paladin, m'lord?"

"I'm not," the Lord-General Cardness replied, "But Sir Falkist, my captain here, is. So you have noble general and paladin captain, b— Jonn, will you now speak yer piece?"

"I have another 'noble general' of Morralish and a priestess of the Holy Family, besides," Jonn said with confidence, "in my custody. Imprisoned unjustly. I am inclined to release them, if I can find a worthy lot of mountain folk to take them on."

The men in the room that passed for their hall, began to whisper to one another as Lord-General Kenneth Cardness grinned widely. When he spoke they quieted, none would miss what would follow, "You got any names to go with such a wild claim?"

"The man is High Lord-General Strein Hrothmond, former commander of the Morralish Second Army Regiment," Jonn stated plainly, "the woman is his daughter, a priestess, Sister Bethany."

There were no whispers then. A stillness hung in the room until Paladin-Captain Falkist moved closer to the general and spoke in hushed tone, "I say true, my lord, General Hrothmond's daughter is well known a priestess. She held some favor at the Temple of Vandor in Morralish Prime. She had attended a religious conclave near here as its representative. I know this because I was in the paladin honor guard for the event. I know not why she would be imprisoned, justly or otherwise, but if he lies, it is a very well-informed one."

202

"As are you, sir," Lord Kenneth acknowledged, before turning back to Jonn, asking, "By what token do we know you speak the truth?"

"I have none," Jonn admitted, "but I only came to see if this place was safe to bring them. You need not trust me, m'lord, nor do anything at all. Just be here, for them, when we return."

The Lord-General considered a moment, then gave reply, "Sorry, Jonn, 'fraid that won't be the case. You see, I have a literal army of mountain folk with nothing to do and you just informed us that there is a prison unjustly holding two of our countrymen, one a superior officer to myself and man of legendary renown, the other, his own daughter, a holy priestess and favored daughter of the mountains — No, Jonn, I'm certain we shall not be here."

"Why not, m'lord?"

The Lord-General Kenneth Cardness stood, fist in the air, and proclaimed, "Because we shall march forthwith to this prison, besiege its walls, and free our unjustly imprisoned countrymen. We'll send a message, straight to the heart of the Imperium, and the Avigueux Provence besides, that we are to be dealt with justly! That to trifle with mountain folk is to prick the hand of Vandor and the fist that follows will strike, just as surely! I say it!"

"We say it!" boomed throughout the room.

"Fill yer belly now, Jonn," Lord Kenneth offered, sitting, "You will return to this prison with my finest scouts, my army only a little ways behind."

"Gratitude," Jonn offered, "m'lord, but wouldn't it be better for me to get them out secretly? It would be safer."

"Of Llarisian schemes, this method befits," Kenneth explained, "But we of Morralish are of a different mind. Much has transpired here, unknown to you. We've enough of plots and schemes. Put simply, this is how we do things, and we all could use the reminder as to who we are."

"As it please, m'lord."

Chapter 47
Telling Tales

It was in the wee hours of the morning when they at last returned, a large goat on a spear carried between them. Sir Garrus MacMourne and the lone survivor of Sir Jason's charge, the squire, Felix Invictus, had stood the watch and stepped out to greet them. Alpona and Ruffis wore poorly disguised grins, quickly discarding their attempt to suppress them.

"Well met, my Thanes," Sir Garrus welcomed them back, uncertainly, "There was some worry, but the wizard said you would return."

Ruffis face became unamused, "Oh, spit, he didn't ruin the surprise, did he?"

Felix answered, "Apparently not; know we naught of a surprise."

"He saw something," Garrus amended, "Cryptic, he spoke about it. No one understood."

"Excellent!" Ruffis cheered, with a bounce.

"Apologies for the concern," Alpona offered, making two slight nods, one each to each of the men.

"I suppose you want to wake everyone up in some big fuss then?" Garrus MacMourne asked in his cranky elder voice.

"No," Alpona declined, bouncing the speared goat, "Help us with breakfast. There is no danger. We have time."

One at a time, men woke and made their way to the warmth and savory smell of the fire and its cooked goat. Alpona and, especially, Ruffis greeted the men with exaggerated joy and hospitality as they cut and served goat to each man.

"Glad to see you well, friends," Malcolm replied to their presence and kindness, "and gratitude for the warm and hardy meal. He is a rather large goat. Well done."

"He was once the king of his mountain, sure," Ruffis said.

Malcolm scanned the horizon. There were no mountains within a day of them, let alone to be ascended, descended, and returned from.

"Don't think about it too hard," Ruffis jeered.

"Don't mind Ruffis," Alpona reminded.

"I try not to," Malcolm accepted.

In the next moments, Prince Bengallen joined them.

"What is this?" the Prince said expansively, "My brave thanes spend the night away from camp and return with glorious feast. You must tell us of your great hunt, that we may truly enjoy this meal."

"Of course, Your Majesty," Alpona acknowledged, cutting a long slice of loin and thigh for the Prince, "but if you might indulge us, we'd rather not go straight at it. We would ask you of Morralish past and fill our encounter with context befitting Your Majesty."

Prince Bengallen took a bite of the fresh goat, savory juices fresh in his mouth.

"Certainly," the Prince agreed, between bites.

"What can you tell us of a certain Knight-Captain," Ruffis asked, "a paladin by the name of Yeh-rooh-mear?"

Prince Bengallen loosed a single laugh, but readily grew nostalgic.

"Paladin Jerumir, now there is a name I have not heard in years. I find myself wondering how you might have heard of him. Yet, tis your feast and I agreed, so I'll tell you what I know of Jerumir."

Everyone, save Alpona and Ruffis, looked confused. Everyone, including them, paid attention.

"He was the son of a mountain clan's chieftain, the MacRoberts," Bengallen nodded to Malcolm on that beat, but otherwise continued his telling, "I knew Sir Jerumir when I studied to be a paladin at the Temple. He had no children of his own, so when he came every few years to assist in the instruction of the novices, he took to some of the younger of us in a fatherly way. I was older than these, his visits not aligning us so. Yet my mother died when I was very young and I had no siblings. So I, similar to Jerumir, took to some of my younger fellows in a brotherly way. This Knight-Captain and I became fast friends in that. Normally, it would have been discouraged – our standing as paladins so removed – but I was Prince of the Kingdom and he the prince of his tribe, within my kingdom. Thus we were granted a certain latitude in our affiliation. Some years later, he and his band fought with my father, the Paladin Di'gilcrest, and myself at the Battle of Drileans. I saw him only once after that. He was again at the Temple, as an instructor, and I made a point to visit with him. Was there something specific you wanted to know?"

"No, Your Majesty," Alpona accepted, adding, "What of this band of his? If I may ask."

"You may," the Prince answered, pausing to chew up another fresh bite of goat before continuing, "As I mentioned, a Chieftain's son, Jerumir was granted a certain latitude. This also included his military service. His band of adventures weren't initially recognized as part of the kingdom's formal military — knights-errant, if you're familiar with the concept. They were bloody well effective pursuing their own aims, however. So proven, a place was made for them. A place sort of between things, again, with a wide latitude."

"Were they sort of like a Black Company?" Caanaflit interjected a question.

"Yes and no," the Prince answered, "Those companies are a concession – of sorts – to the generals who insist that they need such things. There is a lot of military and ethical debate that goes into that conversation, as to whether or not they are necessary. Sir Jerumir's men were something different, smaller, different standards, higher, more diverse in their skills, but I suppose there is some similarity in the degree of freedom and unconventional means by which they pursue their goals."

Once Prince Bengellan clearly finished, but before Caanaflit could say anything else, impetuous and impertinent, Ruffis shouted him down.

"No! This is our thing, Caanaflit. You don't get to take it over. We're asking the questions!"

Bengallen shrugged helplessly at Caanaflit, who rolled his eyes, sighed, and walked off.

Ruffis, so self-satisfied with the role reversal, forgot to ask his next question.

"I knew the Paladin Jerumir," Prince Bengallen reiterated, "He was – is, hopefully – a fine man. The likes of which we'll need when the sons of the mountains return home."

Something cracked in the tree branches overhead. Caanaflit, some feet from the camp, stopped in his tracks and turned to look. Everyone except Alpona and Ruffis looked up.

As though it were some cue, Alpona asked, "As paladins, you shared much training with the priests, correct, Your Majesty?"

"We did."

"Was this Jerumir a good preacher?"

Prince Bengallen spat the food from his mouth, in a most undignified way, as robust laughter followed. Calming himself, but with amusement still plain in his voice, the Prince answered, "For all – the compliments – I'm all too glad – to pay the man – that would not be among them."

"At least you haven't taken to the politician's lying tongue!"

A voice shot from the south as a cloaked silhouette approached.

Caanaflit cursed himself, distracted by the story, then his annoyance, then the sound in the trees, as he looked upon the approaching figure who had escaped his notice. *A rare feat.* Everyone looked to the man as he drew back his hood, revealing a bald head, large with brassy beard.

Prince Bengallen stood and uttered, "It cannot be."

"Tis I," Chief Jerumir called, "Your Majesty, I come to pledge you my allegiance, lend you my aid, and bring you word from the Imperium – as well as take your word there – if you would so charge me."

The man spoke as he approached. Outside the camp's perimeter, he fell to one knee and bowed his head.

Bengallen met him there and solemnly touched Jeremir's head in benediction. Formalities complete, the Prince crudely pulled the Chief to his feet, embracing him fully.

They both laughed. A tear fell from Prince Bengallen's eye. Caanaflit returned to his seat at the fire. Ruffis glared at Caanaflit knowingly as Malcolm approached Alpona.

"You arranged this?"

"This," Alpona replied, "this is only a little."

"How so?" Malcolm asked, "Why the game?"

"That was Jerumir's idea," Alpona, mumbling, shrugged.

"Man knows how to make an entrance," Ruffis supplied.

Prince Bengallen and Chief Jerumir rejoined the men at the fire. Jerumir continued to speak, "If the rest are half as good as those two, you've got a fine lot here. They interrogated me well before they agreed to lead me to your camp. Before we're getting into all the 'this and that' of what is going on in the world, Your Majesty, there is something I have to show you. Something that I wanted you to see me, first, before I showed it to you."

"Sure," Bengallen, lost in the moment, agreed.

"To the south, the clearing, this way," Jerumir motioned to the rest of the Prince's companions.

They all came to the edge of the clearing. It was empty, save a tall, seedy grass. Looking about, all noticed those long, green blades sway as a blast of that same warm wind blew again.

Shomotta, his face alight with realization, looked to the sky.

A dragon.

The Forest Phantoms had grown suspicions of the Antori Imperium long before the fall of Morralish. Yet they only had so much latitude in their authority to pursue their own aims. They could not, for example, take it upon themselves to conduct active espionage against the Imperium that might endanger their alliance or lead to war.

They could, however, gather the evidence that came to them and prepare a case against the Imperium, to present to the King, that he might sanction more aggressive actions. So they did, until, that is, word of the death of their King and the occupation of his capital had come to them.

They immediately assumed Antori involvement and, acting on the suspicion, were quick to discover the plans for the dismissal and integration of Morralish soldiers on contract to the Imperium. On its own, it proved nothing, other than taking advantage of the situation, but it did prompt further investigation.

Their ongoing espionage efforts resulted in, among many other things, discovering one of the most closely guarded secrets in all the Imperium, allegedly, unknown even to the Imperators themselves: The Demesne.

The Demesne was the code name for a warfare research laboratory built into the cliffs below the city of Napua and accessible only by sea. There were no limits, no rules or ethics followed, to the experiments conducted there.

Alchemy, engineering, arcana, bloodlines, even contact with the denizens of the hells and heavens, alike, were attempted in ever evolving rituals. There was no good or evil, right or wrong, to the men of the Demesne. Advantage in war was their only truth and highest purpose.

The Forest Phantoms considered that this secret laboratory might have developed whatever terror befell Morralish. They thought, mayhap, even that Morralish Prime had been a test run for some new warfare they might unleash upon all the capitals of man, elf, dwarf, and all the races of the world. Antoria, after all, called itself an empire and it had not expanded for more than two-hundred years.

As it turned out, something of the kind, a terrible weapon, was sold to the Perzi Empire, to be used against their enemies in Aramar'tip. For though they had developed such a weapon, they could not use it themselves. Every realm not subjugated to the Imperium had a peace treaty with them.

Yet, the ongoing hostilities in the great deserts provided a much more fertile ground for testing weapons than sowing peace or plenty. If any Morralish allies assisting Aramar'tip were harmed in the process, well, that could only be traced back to the Perzi Sultan, with whom Morralish had no formal diplomacy.

That was in the deserts and great care was taken not to attack Morralish forces directly. If the Demesne was involved with the sacking of Morralish Prime, the Forest Phantoms not only found no evidence, but what they had found actually made the Demesne less suspect. Yet what had they found?

From where it came was not discovered by the Forest Phantoms during their second and final infiltration of the secret laboratory, but the Demesne had acquired a dragon. Gargantuan and ancient as the dragon herself, the myths and legends were tested within the secret caverns, her nature observed and mysteries unraveled, one-by-one.

The Demesne discovered, for example, that massive feedings cause the dragon to enter into a reproductive term and produce eggs. So long as they gorged the dragon, she continued to produce eggs and, unlike most creatures, the dragon was asexual. Her eggs would, without father, contain young and hatch.

They discovered ways to accelerate the growing and hatching process, but despite all their experiments, they never discovered how to circumvent the need for hosts. No matter how premature or prolonged the hatchling's exit from her egg was, each larval dragon required another living creature to live inside of for a lengthy period of gestation.

Furthermore, they had discovered that the more premature they hatched a dragon, the more characteristics of the host creature the new dragon would take on, when at last it burst forth from its dying host. It was in this way that they created the dragonmen. It was these dragonmen that were sold to the Perzi Sultan. He, in turn, loosed them upon the Holy Order of Marzi Clerics dedicated to Saint Amar, thus greatly weakening the spiritual and cultural strength of Aramar'tip and, in turn, the independence of the Hazar Desert from the Perzi Empire.

That atrocity had already been set in motion, if not already occurred, by the time the Forest Phantoms had discovered it. They made a point to inform the ambassador from Aramar'tip to the Antori Imperium. Though what good or ill it may have done was still unknown and unknowable to them.

By the time that the Forest Phantoms raided the Demesne, having reconnoitered it thoroughly, the dragon had long since ceased cooperating. She was bolted to the ground with a device at her end to roll eggs away from her and a device at her front to force feed her a mince, massive quantities of pureed plants and whole animals, no doubt some optimal brew, laced with alchemical narcotics that dulled her senses.

They had abandoned ever using the dragon as a weapon herself. Attempts at magically controlling her mind, even when drugged, had produced only marginal success, nothing sufficient for combat dependability. She had become, like everything else there, a tool, a foundry for their other experiments.

Sir Jerumir had dreamed of the dragon each night since he had first laid eyes upon her in their initial probe. He, in part as a paladin, in part as a freeman, could not abide the conditions in which she had been kept. So, when they returned, they disconnected her feeding trough on the outset of their infiltration. After a final pass through the facility, they liberated the increasingly alert dragon upon their departure.

While attempting to free the powerful creature, the Forest Phantoms were discovered. During the fight that ensued, the dragon, partially freed from her bonds, emancipated herself fully, bringing the structure down around them.

Yet her hide was tough and her stride long. As the caverns collapsed, the dragon shielded the Forest Phantoms beneath her chest and wing. Afterwards, at the sea, allowed the men to ride upon her as she swam to shore.

How intelligent was the dragon? It remained unclear. Certainly she had mind enough to perceive her rescue and morality sufficient to return the favor.

She could not fly, not at first, but the Forest Phantoms watched over her, despite the protest of some. Gradually, she regained her strength and abilities. Throughout her recovery, the wizards tried to read her thoughts, but her mode of thinking was far too alien, not unlike an animal. They could only ever glean her most basic intentions, inseparable as they were from her emotions. Though complex, she bore love for those men that had saved her and thus became a member of their band.

"You are spitting me," Ruffis interrupted Jerumir's telling with his own disbelief.

"Nay," Sir Quaindraught also interjected, "I figured we'd free her, she'd go bleedin' mad. We'd put her down and I'd be addin' dragonslayer to mah accolades. But nay, she's fast become as much family as the favored dog. More so."

The dragon raised her head, looked at Ruffis and the red-haired paladin with knowing eyes. Flicking a lash of tongue from her mouth, as though to make a pithy protest, she laid her head back down upon the rising slope before her, comfortably, and closed her eyes once again. Everyone watched in amazement as the serpentine motion of the dragon, who had remained stone still during Jerumir's telling, flowed with a calm grace, returning to rest.

"Apologies, friend, I am without words," Bengallen said.

"As am I," offered Caanaflit.

"Likewise," agreed Alpona.

"Indeed," Shomotta concurred.

Prince Bengallen looked to Shomotta, his friend's heavy voice shaking him from awe.

"Shomotta, my friend, if you must go now, return to your home, I certainly understand. You owe me – us – no more than you have already so freely given."

"Thank you, my Prince," Shomotta accepted, "It is good to know your heart. I will return home, but not yet. I sense my path is with your own for a while longer. I continue to walk it with you. Yet, when the time comes, I appreciate your understanding."

Prince Bengallen nodded solemnly.

"Will you be joining us then, sirs?" Malcolm asked.

"At least fer a time," Sir Quaindraught replied, "as it pleases His Majesty. Yer Malcolm, yes? We heard about you in Spearpointe. You seem the right sort, despite bein' part-orc an all."

The red-haired paladin slapped Malcolm across the back in an over rough, if not comradely, way. At the same time, an unspoken sentiment, a secret of understanding, passed between Thane Malcolm and Prince Bengallen.

"Thanks," coughed Malcolm.

"How was Spearpointe?" the Prince asked.

"In order, Your Majesty," Sir Ihrvan supplied, "aside from some refugees from Woodhaven, which we dinna learn too much about. Your garrison commander, fine woman, hosted us at the Mayor's mansion. Met him, the local priest too. Had a little churchly fun. Right nice lot."

"Gratitude, sir, glad to hear," Prince Bengallen accepted.

Chapter 48
Embracing Opportunity

Lord Strein Hrothmond went back to his daughter's cell. Their guard, Jonn, afforded them this opportunity whenever he worked the evening hours. They embraced as always, but Bethany had remained standing, whereas it had become their habit to sit.

"Our visit must be short and I know naught how many more," she told her father.

"What has happened?" he asked quickly, his face turning from gay to grim.

"Good news," she assured him, "Jonn has risked much and gotten word to mountain folk, displeased with the changing tides, that we are kept here. They need a leader. They will come for us."

"Our captors shall kill us if they fail."

"Father," she said, "These days together have been a reprieve, but I would not live like this forever. You can only untangle my hair and tell me stories of mother for so long. You said to me, 'our Holy Family is not through with us.' They yet have plans for us. We serve them in caring for each other here and we will serve them by caring for our brothers and sisters lost out there in the changing world."

"Indeed, daughter, indeed," he relented, "The gods will for us be done. The church has taught you well."

"And there is more. I did not tell you, because I did not know if they would interrogate you," she began, pausing before continuing "His Majesty, Prince Bengallen Hastenfarish, lives. I know where. I can bring him to us and he can lead us – all of us – home. I saved him from the doom that befell our people. I know much and more and I will tell you all, father, once we are free of this place. As dark as things seem, there is a light that shines and we can, nay, must remove the obstacles that obscure it."

"You say it true?"

"I say it!"

"We say it," her father accepted her oath, making it prayer.

Chapter 49
Plotting Rebellion

There was much that needed to be discussed and some location secured for the discussion. Traveling several more miles, they at last spotted smoke. This led them to the farm of a man named Sebastian. Whether he had no surname or that was his surname has been forgotten. Sebastian's Farm, however, would become a historical landmark. Prince Bengallen, his retinue, and the Forest Phantoms convened in Sebastian's barn and held, what history would call, a war counsel.

Seven Frontiersmen, soldiers of the Spearpoint Company, had traveled with the Prince's retinue as guards and support, tending the horses, making and breaking camp, and tending to the various necessities of the operation. Outside the barn, they kept watch, ensuring the privacy and security of their superiors.

Within, the Prince and his thanes, knights, and other agents shared and correlated all of their knowledge of current events. The Fall of Morralish Prime, the Beast of Spearpointe, the Battle of Woodhaven, and the state of the Imperium, all as best as anyone knew, were discussed at length. Everyone became familiar with everything. Few held little back, even in personal matters.

Caanaflit played details about his amnesia, certain emerging skills, and his resources in Spearpointe fairly close to the chest. Ruffis was similarly ambiguous in regards to his own past. Yet, where questions were dodged, Prince Bengallen vouched for the both of them. His word was literally law and readily accepted as such. Less significantly, Alpona continued to hide his failing health, Malcolm, his marriage to Sira Roselle, and Shomotta, his own intimate predilections. Barring those few exceptions, and few others, those assembled openly shared who they were, what they could do, where they came from, and why they were involved. Much was learned.

It is worth noting that the Forest Phantoms, to include the half-elf wizard, Kinnik, had never seen a dark elf. Moreover, much to Ruffis' chagrin, Kinnik would prove to be annoyingly curious about him. Shomotta also took time to discuss, primarily with Sir Ihrvan and Sternus, the report of these dragonmen, sharing with them the massacre of his order, at their own temple, as well as the regional superstition not to speak of dragons "lest you call them forth."

On the sharing of information went until, at last, they all settled firmly on Illwarr the Manslayer and the Forest Phantoms' most recent activities prior to seeking out the Prince.

"Interesting," Caanaflit replied, "and they, the slaves in Napua, they present as genuinely committed to revolt?"

Jerumir answered, "It was at the brink of things. They really did believe, as do I, that if it had happened, the Morralish soldiers garrisoned nearby would have aided and protected them from slaughter by the native Antori law enforcement. No one seemed to want to be the instigator, however. That is where we thought the gladiators might serve as heroic symbols to rally behind, if they were the ones to start it."

"Agreed," Caanaflit approved, "It was a good plan. Is a good plan, so long as new gladiators could earn their stripes by toppling this Illwarr in the appropriate contest."

Caanaflit looked to Malcolm, then over Alpona, with an eyebrow raised.

"If it were that easy," Alpona worried, "then they would have done it themselves."

"We considered that," Sir Ihrvan explained, "but the easiest route would have been to unleash Sky upon them and we're not ready to announce to the world that dragons are real. While we aren't well-known, we are known well enough, and mountain folk at that. Too great a risk that our own sudden enslavement and rise amongst gladiators, a ruse, might have been discovered – thwarted – or, worse still, we expediently murdered in our sleep."

"Besides," the sagely wizard, Kinnik, spoke, "we yet had greater duties and loyalties to be fulfilled. If this is His Majesty's wish, we would gladly descend into the world of gladiator and take on this task."

"No, you had the right of it," Prince Bengallen agreed, "You're long time in Antoria and experience with my military commanders is a resource best used in another task."

"Still," said Caanaflit, "Tis a good plan. With a slave revolt on, it would be hard to divert any native Antori military attention to the withdrawal of Morralish soldiers."

"Morralish soldiers," Bengallen added, "who wouldn't consider killing slaves and could not be coerced to do so without a clear directive from their King, which would never happen."

"I can do it!" Malcolm interjected. Caanaflit grinned and Alpona groaned.

"Say true?" Chief Jerumir asked.

"I killed a troll and I've become a much more experienced warrior since then," Malcolm offered as justification, "Your Majesty, I hate slavery. I had seen how my father treated slaves. I freed many of them, only to have them sold back into Imperial slavery. Let me do this. I will gladly slay this Illwarr and champion the slaves of Napua."

Caanaflit spoke up, "Rather than abandon him to actual slavery, myself – and possibly others – could go with him. I can pose as his owner, sell him, begging your pardon, and keep an eye on him as a freeman, as well as re-assess the slaves' inclinations. If anything goes wrong, pick a few locks and we leave to catch up with you in Antoria Royal."

"Not bad," Shomotta agreed, "but I would not abandon Malcolm to the slave pens alone. I would go with them, to be sold as well. My magic may also provide useful advantage."

"Indeed it would," Malcolm accepted, expansively, clasping his hand onto the wizard-priest atop the shoulder.

Smiling wide, Caanaflit asked, "Your Majesty?"

Prince Bengallen looked to Sir Jerumir who nodded in approval, turning next to Alpona.

"Alright, I guess we knew this moment was coming: Orders. Alpona, I want you to go with them as well. If one of you should fall, I trust the others to avenge him."

"It is an honor," Alpona accepted, pausing to bow at the waist – mayhap a bit exaggerated in its formality – before continuing, "to serve you, Your Majesty, and to stand by my friends in the task of their choosing."

"Your Majesty," Jerumir added, "as none of them are northmen, there'll be no suspicion or obvious connection to Morralish. We've explored and invested in this scenario. This will work. I think they're just the right sort to get it done. Meanwhile, my team can get you to all the right people within the Imperium and, then, we can lead our people home. If the Imperator has a problem with that, we but wait for the slave rebellion to swell."

"This should improve our odds greatly, Your Majesty," Caanaflit added, "I've kept the concern to myself, as I didn't have a better idea, but I have imagined your forces trying to return home, yet assailed and suffering attrition from harassment attacks by the Antori Legions. Not so much to prevent the withdrawal, but to retaliate and punish you for it. I truly think this scheme the Forest Phantoms have hatched makes that far less likely."

"Maybe I'm just new to all of this," Brunsis the Minotuar came forward and spoke, "but what about the slaves?"

"Can they win?" Sir Garrus MacMourne, the eldest of the Knights of the

Spear, added.

The squire, Felix Invictus, an Antori native, chimed in, "Absolutely not. I don't think this does anything but get a lot of civilians, slave and citizen alike, dead."

"I think they can," Sir Jerumir spoke, undaunted, "Especially with initial regional protection from the Morralish forces garrisoned near Napua. Remember, the slaves don't have to win any ground, they only have to unite and flee."

"Unite," Felix insisted, "against their owners, most of whom are peaceful Antori citizens, farmers, tradesmen, merchants, artists. Soldiers clashing over military matters is one thing, but indentured servitude, slavery so-called, is a fundamental institution in the Imperium. Escaped or slaughtered in the attempt, what you are advocating is no mere distraction. It is death and chaos on a level you cannot imagine."

The Paladin-Prince's eyes narrowed as he spoke, "Don't be so sure, Felix."

"Apologies, Your Majesty," Felix continued, "What happened in Morralish is more terrible than we know, I'm sure and I'm sorry. Yet the Antori Imperium is vast, four realms, and the Imperator's Peace a force of order in them all. The death and disorder that a slave rebellion, even a failed one, will bring is of a magnitude — a scale unequaled by anything we've seen. Unconscionable and unimaginable!"

"Slavery is wrong," Malcolm replied all too simply.

"If," Felix irately replied, "this was about ending slavery, there are safer venues. The Senate could be beseeched — but this isn't about slavery. You merely need a distraction and freeing slaves is but a pretense, a convenient moral high road for you to tread upon."

"Yes and no," Sir Jerumir disagreed, "We are presented with two truths, slavery is wrong and the Morralish soldiers should be informed of their homeland's need and sovereign's call. I want both those things, genuinely. Do I want them equally? No, I want my own battered and oppressed people's needs met, first and foremost. If, however, liberation can be offered to another people in the process, I am very concerned with offering it to them. In fact, if we all die right now and the Morralish soldiers are absorbed into the Imperium, this slave rebellion is going to happen. Tis only the late King Lionel's word and will that insisted the Expeditionary Forces honor Antori law, including slavery. Tis not something we have – not something allowed in our homeland – not even something people think about, not for hundreds of years. If they are to make Antoria home, ending slavery will be at the top of the list, and we don't have much use for the Senate either, so it will be violent."

King Lionel. Prince Bengallen had not heard his father's name so invoked since before his death. It caught him by surprise. Mixed feelings of familiarity, pride, longing, and responsibility swirled about him, pulling him briefly from the moment.

Felix, on the other hand, was furious. He felt talked down to. The arrogance and self-righteousness was unbearable to him. He rebuked them all.

"Who are you to say what is right and wrong and to be so certain as to know the future?"

All the Forest Phantoms jumped to their feet, hand's to weapons or beginning arcane gestures. Sir Jerumir waved them down, but not before everyone else had jumped to their feet as well. Prince Bengallen motioned for everyone else to sit.

Sir Jerumir replied, "Me? I know my brothers and sisters, but that's beside the point. What about him, Prince Bengallen, with whom you've rode and sworn fealty? The Morralish soldiers are his to command. As for the slaves, I'm a paladin and I do know right from wrong. I make no apologies for that."

"Oh," Felix rebuked, "I've rode for the Prince alright and watched friend after friend die and die and die. Pardon me, again, if I am not so eager for more death."

Felix stormed from the barn. Jerumir went to catch his arm, but Bengallen caught the paladin's own.

"Leave him be. He was mortally wounded on my account against the Beast. He was squire to Sir Vix, they rode in Sir Jason's charge, he its lone survivor. He was moved to serve me, our shared just causes, once. If he is so moved no longer, he has already done so much. I cannot dare ask more of him."

Jerumir nodded humbly, accepting, "Aye, Your Majesty."

"Even though he left," Brunsis voice thundered more than he meant it to, drawing everyone's attention, "doesn't make his point any less valid."

Following, Alpona spoke up, "Does the Church allow for slavery?"

"No," Prince Bengallen said, plainly, "Like my father knew, however, the politics with the Imperium are complex. One Imperator or another had persuaded the Primarch of the Cathedral of Din to provide a special dispensation for indentured servitude during a difficult economic time. T'was a way to both secure the feeding and sheltering of a rapidly impoverished

218

population while also acquiring cheap labor to stimulate the economy. Yet there is a saying, 'you cannot unring a bell' and so it was that there has been slavery right under the Church's nose ever since."

"Temporary slavery?" Alpona asked, uncertainly.

"Initially," Bengallen answered, "One to five year contracts, then they started adding extension clauses, then offspring clauses — Every slave can buy his freedom, out of his contract, theoretically, but tis a farce. They have no access to money beyond what their masters allow them. So how can they?"

The faces in the room turned sour. Slavery was wrong. The injustice in it was plain to them all.

"So this is the Prince's chosen course?" Brunsis asked.

"After my troop recall," Prince Bengallen responded, "Antoria's military strength will be weakened. Our mercenaries, the Morralish Expeditionary Forces, make up more than half of Antoria's military might. They've leaned too heavily upon us. When we leave, with only the Legions and local law enforcement to contend with, the slaves will have the best chance at freedom they've ever had. That they ever will have, I say it. Tragically, some will die – such is war, tis terrible – but tis the only window of opportunity that they've ever had since Antoria first instituted slavery. That they are slaves is the fault of the Imperium, not ours. Sparking a rebellion, at the time of a Morralish troop withdrawal, tis the only justice we can afford them. Our own homeland remains occupied by some monstrous force. Our own people — exiled, enslaved, and worse. My army must go home. If the Holy Family can use that fact to mutually benefit the slaves of Antoria and correct the Church's ancient misstep, I say it. Yet, I am bound first, my sovereign responsibility as Prince, by my allegiance to my people. This is our course."

Without further comment, Brunsis returned to his seat.

Chapter 50
Leaving Senate

The Imperial Senate had convened once more and had come to the conclusion of the first hour's business.

"And finally," the Senate President added, "I read the findings regarding Docket number thirty-two of the fourth day, of the sixth month, Summer of the 944th Year Since the Awakening, 'A Matter of Dispute Between Public Accommodation and the Right to Refuse Clients:' Of the accusation that Senator Iscavius was using his office in bad faith, representing special interests rather than the general good of the Antori people, investigations have proven terminally inconclusive. Of the accusation that Senator Macrobius was using his office in bad faith, acting at the behest of foreign interests and influences, investigations have proven the claim false. Of the accusation that the number of incidences of client refusal is grossly insignificant to the number of craftsmen and artists who continue to provide for the public accommodation, investigations have proven the claim true. Conclusively, less than 25% and, possibly, as few as 3% of craftsmen and artists, whose goods and services are considered matters of public accommodation, are refusing clients based on disagreements pertaining to existing law. While the investigative committee recognizes the right to disagree with the law, and sympathizes with the craftsmen and artists in question, there remains the concern as to 'whether or not it is a violation of the law, to conduct one's business in a way that discriminates law-abiding citizens over matters, such as slave ownership, that are themselves protected and administered under the law.' Does anyone wish to review the details of these findings?"

Though Senator Macrobius was curious as to what details supported a 'terminally inconclusive' finding, he knew that it was in poor taste to question the work of an investigative committee during an open session. That doing so, in turn, could lose him votes today and he could afford to lose none. Thus, the Senate Chamber silently awaited the President to move them forward.

"Alright," he began, "Docket number one, today's date, 'A Matter of Dispute Between Public Accommodation and the Right to Refuse Clients.' Are we prepared to vote at this time?

"I move that we vote," Senator Iscavius suggested.

"I second."

"All in favor of voting, say 'aye.' "

"Aye," loudly.

"All opposed, say 'nay.' "

Silence, though Macrobius had hoped to debunk some more bad argumentation, apparently no one cared to argue the matter further.

"The 'ayes' have it," the President pronounced, "By show of hands, those in favor of universally enforcing public accommodation and banning the refusal of clients on moral grounds, for all trades exercised within the Imperium, so indicate by raising your hand."

Senator Macrobius damned the corruption of the Senate. *All that time investigating was merely time for Iscavius to purchase votes. Men, who had applauded sound reason in weeks passed, raised hand to sky right alongside those, who would not know sound reason, if it were inscribed on the Senate Chamber walls by the hand of a god.*

Which they in fact had been. The basic Freedoms of the Antori People, then and there being eroded and circumvented, one new law at a time, were plainly written where all of them could see. Macrobius looked at that wall and shed a single tear.

He did not hear the declaration of the vote, nor the men who voiced concerns as to how the new legislation would be worded or enforced. His mind drifted, reflecting on his career. His brief stint in the Legions. His time as a peace officer. His election to magistrate and ultimately his decades of service to the Senate.

Had it all been merely the illusion of justice? Had a life of sincere service to the Imperium been but a farce? Only ever becoming increasingly clear to him, every aspect of life in the Imperium, public, private, civil, religious, military, domestic, foreign, free, slave, moral, cultural, and legislative, all indicated that Senator Macrobius had wasted his life in a vain pursuit of a better world.

Yet he kept glancing to certain senators, those small few who had not raised their hands. *If freedom had a future in the Imperium, they were it. What might an old man do for them?*

The President's voice came thundering back into Macrobius' awareness, "— as of tomorrow morning, then, any baker who refuses fair contract to produce

221

for a man's slaves or any likeness maker who refuses to paint, sculpt, or otherwise render the likeness of a slave owner – or any subject of their choosing – shall be dragged before the local magistrate in chains to plead their case. If sufficient legitimate reasons cannot be given, to exclude now moral differences, the person in question shall be fined. If one is unable to pay, he shall then be subjected to indentured servitude to the offended party until restitution is made."

This was to be done, as law, and called justice, called the will of the people. This Senate was a farce.

Macrobius shed a second tear.

"Moving on," the Senate President announced, "Docket number two, today's date, 'The Private Purchasing of Public Parks and the Resultant Loss of Free Speech Forums.' I call upon Senator Galaebe to read the formal wording of the proposed 'Free Speech Forum Restoration Act' and call for a vote there after."

Senator Galaebe wrote a fine piece of legislation, in fine tradition of the Imperial Senate and the Freedoms of the Antori People. He had even included concessions to win over potential naysayers, excluding certain governmental buildings and their immediate vicinities. *An unfortunate, but prudent exception.*

Moreover, Galaebe had not voted with the rest in the previous action and was proving, with each word, to be a place for Macrobius to hang hopes for the future. Until, that was, the vote was called.

Macrobius, Galaebe, and only four other senators, those same four who voted together previously, had raised their hands, voting to provide the people these venues for free speech within the city.

So few, the vote failed.

All the pain of the previous vote came slamming back upon Macrobius' tired, old heart. With this new grief heaved upon it, thrice he shed a tear.

Senator Macrobius abruptly stood and began walking down to the floor of the Senate Chamber.

"Senator Macrobius," the President called out in rebuke, "Return to your seat! You have not been recognized or dismissed!"

"Begging your pardon," Macrobius replied, continuing his trek, "It has become all too apparent that I have not been recognized. Yet, I believe, I have also been dismissed for just as long — and quite enough for today. I assure you. I – or my wisdom anyway – are we not one in the same? Thus, I place a vote of no confidence upon all future proceedings of this senate until such a time that I am removed from office or given reason to return."

"You cannot do this!" Senator Iscavius shouted.

Macrobius crossed the floor and dragged his fingertips across the engraved words of "The Freedoms of the Antori People," carved into the far wall, as he passed them by. Everyone else there might ignore them, but he would not.

Pausing at the exit, Macrobius declared in reply, "For the time being, Iscavius, I am a free man still. I can and I do!"

Senator Macrobius left the Imperial Senate.

Chapter 51
Crossing Purposes

Sir Garrus found Felix that night at a small fire with two infantrymen from the Spearpointe Company. Felix had surrendered his arms and armor and was pulling the tack off his horse.

The knight spoke as he approached their triangle, "Is this where we're planning the mutiny or the desertion?"

"Desertion, sir," one of the Spearpointe soldiers answered, a little too briskly, pointing to Felix, "Er – uh – but not us, just him."

"He's only taking the horse," the other added, "thought we'd let him go, sir."

"Well," Sir Garrus replied, stepping into their firelight, "that depends entirely on which direction he is going."

Felix kicked the leather cuirass atop the pile of gear before him and answered the indirect question, "I don't aim to be disloyal. Yet I'm suddenly in a position where I cannot continue to be loyal, not in good conscience."

"I remember you, you know," Garrus began, "You weren't from Spearpointe. Sir Horcifer had to transfer you to the Spearpointe Company after he took over Sir Petros' mercenaries, after he put the Southlanders' own champions in charge. Seems that even an exiled Legionnaire thinks himself too good to serve under a Southlander. Why were you exiled anyway? Why wouldn't you serve under the storied Southland champions? Why are you leaving now? Are pride and bigotry that important to you?"

"Oh, spit!" One Spearpointer shouted as the other ran off toward the barn.

"Dare you, sir?" Felix Invictus strode toward Garrus MacMourne, shouting face-to-face with him, or would have been, if the old knight had not been half a foot taller than the Antori.

"Dare, I do," Sir Garrus said mockingly, adding in a serious tone, "Put your armor back on."

"You don't want to fight me old man," Felix warned, "Already late for the grave, you really want me to hurry you along?"

"Your lips are flapping," Garrus, otherwise like stone, commented, "Use them to answer my questions or shut up and stand to. Those are the only two options I'm giving you."

"Now I am to be your slave?" Felix laughed, something maniacal and unhinged growing in his voice.

"This ain't about that," Garrus dismissed, "You're free to leave and I'm free to kill you, if you turn your back to me. I've not thrown this knight-thing around much, but I think I've found the time and place. Deliver! Break word or life. Your freedom is to choose."

"The Din-god came to the Antori people!" Felix shouted, eyes wide, "We are his chosen people. All you mongrels and half-breeds and cavemen, playing at knights and nobles, all think you're better than me. I am the blood of Antoria! I am your better. If it is pride, it is gods given!"

"But you are not an Antori citizen, are you?" Garrus pushed him, verbally and physically, "They exiled you. They – kicked – you – out. Why?"

"All I ever did," Felix's crazed anger began to sound with equal parts grief, "was promote my race. Do what was necessary to ensure our future."

"The Hells did you do?" Garrus grabbed Felix by the shirt collar, insisting, "What in the Nine Hells – did – you – do?"

Felix, sobbing then, declined to answer, offering instead, "No! Palmer, Vix, Jason, Allille, Russo, all dead. I don't recognize your authority!"

Garrus pulled the Antori closer, but Felix broke loose of the hold and grabbed up his sword from the pile, backing away.

"Confess," Garrus demanded, wishing one of the paladins were in his place, "Let it go, boy. You did some wrong and you have suffered for it. The loss of our allies is a tragedy to us all. I rode with them too. They were my brothers too. Tis all meaningless to you, if you can walk away now. Worse if you turn against us. Will you dishonor the honored dead?"

"No!" Felix, sobbing and shouting, cried, actually taking a clumsy sword swipe at Garrus.

"What is this!?" someone shouted.

Sir Garrus and Squire Felix, singular focus widening, both realized that Thane Malcolm, Sir Bohr, and Sir Ihrvan stood among them. Others were surely on their way.

"All rorked up," Felix continued to make no sense while holding his sword aloft before him, "None of this was supposed to be this — so rorked up."

"Take him down," another voice shouted from further back.

Two crossbow quarrels appeared, one landed in Felix's neck, the other in his arm, causing him to drop the sword.

As Felix toppled over someone else called out in the darkness, "Who gave that order?"

Half the Prince's retinue had gathered there, but it was the Prince himself who asked again, "Who gave that order?"

No one answered as Caanaflit, crossbow in hand, stepped into the firelight.

"Who gave the order?" the Prince asked a third time.

"I thought it was you," Caanaflit lied.

"Oh, spit," the Spearpointer said again.

Most of them merely stared at each other, waiting for someone to take responsibility.

The paladins, Prince Bengallen, Sir Jerumir, and Sir Quaindraught, between their limited healing gifts and proper field medicine managed to save the man's life. The damage to his throat, however, robbed him of the ability to speak. Furthermore, in the days that followed, he would also refuse to communicate with them in writing.

The crossbow bolt double shot, signature Caanaflit, he readily admitted to firing. What he did not immediately admit to, however – a fact not discovered until years later – Caanaflit himself, in the darkness and confusion, had called out the order to take Felix down. Caanaflit, certain that Felix would send word of their plan to the Imperium, refused to hesitate. He was not about to let so great a plan collapse under one man's misguided designs, the mercy of knights, or the forgiveness of paladins. So he took the matter into his own hands.

Even though Felix survived, Caanaflit's will was done. Unable to speak and having attacked a duly appointed knight, Prince Bengallen had Felix imprisoned at the next suitable town, Valleyview, leaving behind two of the Woodhavers to assist in guarding him. All were given strict orders not to allow Felix to put pen to paper or write or inscribe anything at all until after "the Grand Army of Morralish marched back through these parts" to collect them.

Valleyview hardly boasted a populace significant enough to require a proper jail, but it had one. While some worked out the arrangements with the Constable and others took an evening's respite from the road, Ruffis and Alpona took a walk through the community, looking for whatever there might have been to find. There was, of course, nothing. The world was full of such places and they meant no one any harm.

"I'm not keen on this," Ruffis changed the subject.

"About leaving him here," Alpona replied, not realizing, "Did you see something I didn't?"

"No," sighed Ruffis, stopping his stroll and continuing his words, "You all going off and I'm straying with Prince-y Pants."

"This again?" Alpona groaned.

"No," Ruffis said again, "Not again. This ain't just me not liking him. This is me and him traveling together, with a bunch of his boot-lickers, while you go off with the others to be big rorking heroes or whatever. Kind of sets me up for failure."

"Set up for failure or given a chance to defy the odds?"

"Don't..."

"What?"

"Don't do that," Ruffis insisted, "That silver-lining, problems are opportunities but — don't. This feels wrong to me."

"You're an elf, Ruffis, and an unusual one at that," Alpona stated the obvious, "There is no telling what will happen if you are sold into slavery with us. You would attract buyers with no interest in gladiators at all, let alone ones willing to keep us together. Even if that goes right, people start asking about you, our connection to the Prince might be discovered. The rest of us will blend in well enough, at least for this, but you can't. You can't go with us. Not like there was some other option and someone here chose to stick it to you anyway. It is simply not an option. You cannot go with us on this one."

Ruffis narrowed his eyes and scrunched his nose.

Alpona widened his eyes and cocked his head sideways.

"Oh," Ruffis said.

"Oh," echoed Alpona.

"Well, then —" Ruffis began, trailing off.

"Well, then —" Alpona prompted him to continue.

"I thought it was something else. I still don't like it, but I get it. I guess I won't make my big protest speech. The one where I tell the Prince off and go with you in spite of him. No sense being more unreasonable than everyone already thinks I am."

"I'm glad we talked," Alpona accepted, chuckling, "You are exactly the right amount of unreasonable. Yeah, no sense in messing that up."

"Yeah," Ruffis agreed and resumed their perambulation.

Chapter 52
Pointing Spear

In Spearpointe, Sira Roselle Taversdotter had traveled to the small Temple of the Holy Family and attended the priest's morning devotional prayers. It was neither Vansday nor a holy day of any kind. She simply felt the need to be in holy company. She lingered after the service. The aged Brother Thom was delighted to have her stay on for lunch.

"Brother Thom," the lady-knight addressed him as they walked indoors, "I want to thank you for your help."

"You should have just told me that he was a paladin," Thom said, "They don't much lie. If he needed to lie, he could have confessed to me, and I could have vouched for the necessity of it."

"My inner voice told me he was not a bad man," Roselle said, asking, "but what if he lied about being a paladin?"

Thom crinkled his nose and avoided answering, "Aren't you a paladin?"

"I am a novice," she replied, "I have studied. Books, and with the Prince, and with dwarven paladins even, but it takes years to contemplate the higher mysteries, as you know, let alone put them to use with any competence."

"You're more competent than you know, confident, on the other hand —" the priest mused, shifting abruptly and asking, "Are the higher mysteries meant to be used?"

The question caught Roselle unprepared.

She was silent for a long while before answering, again a question was used for an answer, "Are they not?"

"'Tis good that you do not answer with haste," Thom replied, "Better that you admit you do not know. 'The pursuit of wisdom begins with the confession of ignorance.' That is from the Wisdom of Vandor."

"But are they not?" Sira Roselle asked once more.

"Our scriptures are fragments," the venerable Brother Thom began, "'Tis commonly believed that The Wisdom of Vandor, even the Song of Len, were once collected into completed works, like the 'Life of Din,' but were lost to us in tumultuous times. All that remained were fragments, bits and pieces remembered and passed on. How is it then that we have any higher mysteries at all? There is a fourth work, one that predates them all. This work was studied by a monk named Vandor and it contains within it the mysteries of the cosmos, complete and total. The mind must be prepared for such a thing and Vandor, older than myself, had spent his entire life preparing himself. So when that fallen angel came into the Lands of Uhratt, Vandor, enlightened by his book of mysteries, was one of only two things that could stand against him."

Sira Roselle's eyes were wide. This was a perspective on the story of Vandor's Ascension that she had never heard. So, encouraging him to continue, she asked, "One of two?"

Thom laughed, answering, "One need not books to learn. Ellenofae had, independently, delved deeply into the mysteries of the cosmos by contemplating her own existence, her own acts of creation, watching them unfold and create on their own. She is older than any living thing. She had the advantage of time. So her Song is of the lessons learned. Even now the Mother sings still, new discoveries, for an understanding of the cosmos is an unending endeavor."

"They were fated to come together."

Thom laughed again, "You are wise. Prince Bengallen chose well."

"Does that mean that fallen angel — was he also fated?"

"Who can know but the gods," Thom answered, "but that is a distinct possibility. As tragic as it might seem, as terrible as his influence has been, if – and I stress if – the cosmos had to unfold that way and the only alternative is to not exist at all, then I could accept that — Anyway, Vandor made notes as enlightenment came to him, just as Ellenofae sings of what she has learned. While only fragments of these things are available to all people, for the spiritual growth and edification of all, complete versions were retained by certain clerics and it was their place to decide who should know what. So the fullness of the scriptures were distilled into hundreds of volumes of lesser works, some only available to the highest clergy offices, others to priests according to their age, interest, aptitude, and character, others to paladins, fragments for the faithful, and somethings known only to the Exarch, the Primarch, and the Listener alone. While it is true that the complete versions have been lost, the higher mysteries are drawn from these other secret, rare volumes entrusted to their holy guardians."

"Lies?" Roselle asked, "The truth of our gods, our faith, the cosmos itself is kept from the people, the faithful?"

"The higher mysteries are protected," Thom continued calmly, "as are the people from them. As I said, 'One need not books to learn.' Some mysteries have been puzzled out by various entities over time, through intense observation of the created order or experimentation with eldritch powers. Often enough, the solution of one mystery leads to the solution of others as well as to the discovery of yet more mysteries to be solved. Some have gone down that path without the proper character, morality or motivation. They gained a level of power and immortality that allowed them to place themselves over us, as gods, and with we mortals below, unequipped to thwart them. The Holy Family cast them down at the beginning of our known history and while they could do so once again, they would not want their own works or faith to be responsible for such an unfortunate thing. Nor would they completely deny us access to such a potent defense against evil. Thus, they entrusted their highest knowledge to a select few and bid them dispense it only as needed."

Sira Roselle reeled with the revelation, but was coming to terms with it when she replied, "So the higher mysteries are to be used, but only by the worthy and in a limited capacity."

"Precisely," Brother Thom confirmed, "I could prevent my own aging. I could save the life of every terminally ill person in Spearpointe, everyday. Though not both, I suppose – the toll it would take – nonetheless, I could do so. Yet tis not my place to institute unlimited immortality in Spearpointe. The population would grow, babies and pilgrims alike, until I could not sustain them. As people grew older and sicker it would become harder and harder. I would have to pursue greater power, desperately. I would have to teach others, eventually too much to the unworthy or ill-prepared — then they could wield that power over Spearpointe, eventually, even the world. Mayhap I, tainted by my desperation, would be driven to tyranny. Who am I to cause such things? So a mother brings me a sick child and I may heal her. A boy brings me a sick grandfather and I may not, but if I do, I tell him tis temporary. We all have our time and, if we get a little more, we should use it only to prepare for the inevitable."

"Can you actually make a whole city immortal?" she asked.

"No," Thom smiled, admitting, "Not I. I am not so gifted. I never sought that level of understanding, nor did I show much aptitude for it. There are those that could, however, and that is the burden such knowledge and power places upon them."

"My gods —" Roselle uttered.

"Precisely," Thom said again, continuing, "One could lie about being a church priest or a paladin, I suppose. Woe unto he. Because of the potential power and responsibility we have discussed, anyone with the knowledge and ability to play the part, but without the exacting moral character to be worthy — such a man would be hunted down by every paladin and witch hunter in all the Lands of Uhratt. Come to think of it, I can't recall such a thing to have ever happened. Not in my own years or what history I know. They either aspired to too little or their destruction was kept very secret by the Church. This is why one of the earliest mysteries you must master is to see men's hearts. Supernatural evils will always reveal themselves to this power – they have no defense against it – but even the souls of mortal men and women will yield some inclination as to their character."

"So had you known Sir Jerumir was a paladin," Roselle figured it out, "and his soul told you he was a good man, you would have trusted every word he said."

"Precisely," Brother Thom said a third time, smiling again, "Good men can be led astray. To be good and to tell truths or lies to one who might be your enemy are not the same thing. So the candle ritual is useful in such situations. Yet, had I known he was a paladin, I would have trusted his intentions, whether or not his words true, and respected his right to any lies he felt the situation warranted. As it were, the candle ritual had already begun and in it we saw that he was truthful to us in all things, but for today — Today, you clearly came here for a lesson and have received a most important one."

"So I have, Brother," Sira Roselle acknowledged and gave a slight curtsy, "Thank you."

"You can think more on it later," Brother Thom instructed, "For now, help me with lunch and tell me of Prince Bengallen and Thane Caanaflit. I've never got a decent account of what happened in Woodhaven – something about a million orcs or whatever – Caanaflit lived here for a time, did you know that?"

232

Chapter 53
Remembering Forgotten

The dragon, Sky they called her, was a fearsome and majestic creature. Standing on all fours, her chest cleared the ground by more than the height of tall men. Her tail lashed out, though often loosely coiled, was near again the length of her torso, neck, and head combined.

Jaws apart, men could walk into her mouth. How many men? No one wanted to measure. Her eyes were mostly golden where a man's were white. In them there was no appreciable iris, but her pupils were slitted in the manner of a serpent.

Above her eyes, like pronounced eyebrows, were twin ridges in the shape of her skull. They ran up her elongated forehead. Sprouting twin black horns, emerging along the same line, each one curved down, along the back of the creature's head. The horns continued to curve along the jawline, turning around, framing her head, before straightening a they swooped forward. They ended in two points several feet to the front on the creature's face, a few feet to the side of either ragged nostril. These horns began as twin spirals, almost like a ram's horns, if not for straightening at the front. Where they could doubtless do terrible harm. Even so, her four claws of black talons and great maw of black fangs appeared every bit as dangerous.

Sky's scales, the visible potions, were mostly rounded triangles, though about her head and joints, many were shaped according to function. Also, notably, her underbelly had an almost braided look, where large, long, flat, smooth structures banded across her chest and abdomen. Those massive scales looked more like an insect's carapace, though touch revealed a texture alike the rest of her hide. A hide of brown scales painted light blue with a treated clay to provide airborne camouflage as well as proclaim the Forest Phantoms' patriotism.

Around Sky's elegant, flexible neck was a leather collar. Similar straps were about the tops of her legs and the base of her tail. Suspended between them, and supports upon her torso, were ten dangling harnesses, designed for transporting men.

"We 'ad five done up for the lot of us," Sir Quaindraught explained, "afore Chief took to ridin' up on the top, an' five back-ups besides. We'll run the four of you down to Napua, then come back and get the Prince and his guard for the Capital."

Malcolm, still uncertain, spoke, "We ride – under her? Dangling?"

"Yeah," the ruddy paladin replied enthusiastically, "Big guy like you'll be fine. She gives a smooth enough ride once above the clouds. Tis the smaller guys that need to worry, crosswinds might blow'em 'round a bit."

"Dangling?" Malcolm asked again.

"Suspended in the air," the tone of Caanaflit's comment neither an answer nor a reiteration of the question.

"Fascinating!" Shomotta embraced the idea.

"Strap in, lads," Sir Quaindraught ordered, "you'll be fine!"

With the notable exception of taking flight and the rigorous climb skyward, wherein both Caanaflit and Shomotta haphazardly emptied their stomachs, sailing among the clouds on dragon's wings was a rather pleasant experience. She would glide, coasting, for long stretches of time and, having descended ever so slightly over that time, would flap her wings but once or twice and return to previous heights. She made something so near impossible for men, even with magic, seem simple and effortless. Flight was truly part of her nature, the sky her natural habitat.

The cloud cover was merely patchy that particular day, as Malcolm marveled at the world stretched out before him. How peaceful this perspective made the world appear. The farmlands faded, as they pushed onward, and the forest grew thick, in an unfamiliar way, as they passed over the Dreadwood and possibly the Elven Lands hidden therein.

Had he fallen asleep? He was uncertain, unexpectedly finding himself once again on solid ground. Malcolm and Ellenofae were alone in a beautiful garden of colors, the likes of which the half-orc had never seen.

> Blooming vines crawled up and down
> the tall trunks of every tree with flowers,
>   crimson, cyan, ivory, and gold.
> Woodlands all of green and brown
> where gentle breeze blew petal showers,
>   of pinks so mild, and purples, bold.

Amid such beauty, Malcolm, initially standing before her, knelt. She placed her hand to his chin, gently guiding him back up to his feet, lifting him as though he feather light and her hand silken soft.

"Are you truly a god?" Malcolm asked in whisper.

"Who do you say that I am?"

A question, Len's answer.

"A Queen. The mother of your people," Malcolm replied, "in spirit if not in truth. A sorceress and wizard of great power. Unknown and unknowable. I dare only to presume and speak as you have so invited."

She looked at him and smiled. Her beauty was crushing. A man might forget his vows, but before he did, She spoke again.

"There is love in your heart. I can feel it. Such a thing. There is much love in the world. Tis easy to forget. People love their families, their friends and neighbors, their brothers and sisters in faith, and even their gods, whatever they may be. The love a man and woman bear for one another, true love, where mere lust is bound into the service of nobler affections, it looks, and feels, and smells different. It sounds different – in the voice of one brought before me – who's heart belongs to another. I can hear it."

"I have taken a wife. She has taken me for husband."

"So formal," Ellenofae laughed, continuing, "In Helmsphar, they do not even know those words. In Perziton, each man takes at least three wives, more if he can, or he is not considered a man. He remains a boy forever. Orcs —"

"Apologies, great lady," Malcolm dared to interrupt, "I do not need to be told of orcs. I am firmly committed to the oath that I have made."

She sighed.

"Of course you are. I hear it there in your voice again and it was just the point I was about to make. Not that you need me to tell you. I merely intended to show you that I know it as well. Respect it. Love you for it. I have sung about your love. Your want for it. Her want for it. Your finding it in each other."

"So you are a god then?"

"Persistent."

"I was not raised in the Holy Family, but I am familiar with its faith. My Prince has shared his own revelations with me. Now, I stand before you. If not to impart revelation," Malcolm prefaced, asking, "then why have we met here?"

"You have done well. In so many things, you have done so well," She whispered, "Is this not revelation?"

"I have too much respect for — too many things and you, yourself, whatever you are, a great lady, for me to ask again."

"I have every intention of answering your question," Ellenofae explained, "I am trying to create a context between us. One into which an answer can be given. Do I make you uncomfortable?"

"You want to be my friend?" Malcolm asked in words that carried laughter in their syllables.

"Yes."

"And you wonder if I am uncomfortable?" he continued, "From all I know and by your own telling, don't you already know my heart and mind? Ha! Can't you read me like a book, even without divine powers?"

"I am choosing to not." Len said, "A friend, as you put it, would not."

"Indeed," Malcolm drew the 'ee's out in the word, giving him a moment to think.

"I have been called a god," She finally began to answer, "Tis a word and as such solely depends on definition. Is a tomato a fruit or a vegetable? Is a bean either? I am the first of my kind, of all of my kinds. I am the first fae creature. All the other fae, the elves, the fairy-folk, and those of the Forgotten alike, are my descendants. As the singularity of their propagation, am I not a god? Likewise, I am the first woman. All other women, human and fae, were cast from my mold. I am their template. Am I not their goddess? I am the first creature to study the cosmos. From which I, myself, was the first thing to hear its music, any music, the music of the spheres. I recorded what I learned and heard in that first song, a song still playing, a song unfinished — I hear it still. How am I not a god of music and knowledge?"

Malcolm stood in silent awe, nodding in agreement.

"When the Van-god fell in love," Ellenofae continued, "it was with me. I bore his Son. Half-human. Half-fae. When our Son, Dinnothyl, died, he ascended to the Father. Without him there would be no Holy Family. Without me there would be no Holy Family. More? I was called goddess, in the language that I created, before any other languages existed, let alone found their words for 'god.' So, from many perspectives, many definitions, I am a god."

Malcolm hung his head in shame. He dared not speak.

"Yet there is only one truth," She concluded, "That truth is God and, lo, I am not He. He wore the mantle of Vandor when he came to me. It was Vandor who loved me so, yet the man was but a part of God. Likewise, our Son lived his own life, but he has become one with his Father and they are singularly God. I am the Mother of the Holy Family. A husband needs a wife. A child needs a mother. Yet, I am a creation. I, a creator, was myself created by the One who created the cosmos. The One that wanted to be our God and so made us alike to Himself, able to create. He made Himself alike to us, for a time, and yet never ceased to be Vandor thereafter. He allowed Vandor to give part of Himself, to make a Son, to create as we do. Having lived as a creation of His creation, as a Son who lived his life and completed his work, now the One that created the whole has become one with all His peoples. Through Vandor and Dinnothyl and through the work of all the faithful children of the Holy Family, we have a One True God. In turn, He has a role for us all. I am a mother."

Malcolm stammered, struggling to comprehend, but quickly opting for simplicity.

"Thank you."

"You are most welcome, my friend," She said, smiling at him once again.

Malcolm loved and hated her smile. He loved it and he hated how much he loved it.

"Yet I feel," Malcolm spoke only to prevent any more silence between them, there was too much in it, "as I am to become a friend of a woman so great, you have more for me."

"All of that was for your Prince. If he ever doubts himself, you will tell him what you have heard and that you learned it from my own lips. His vision will clear. You are correct, however, to the matter, I have more to tell you. What I have told you is known to many and should someday be known to all. What I tell you now is a secret. Few remember it. Long forgotten. I tell you and trust you, my friend, to only share it with those worthy of your own trust and confidence."

Malcolm nodded again. This time less in awe and more with a firm understanding. So great a secret surely required context.

They had it then, so he accepted, "I make your secret my own and will guard it with my life, Most Holy Mother."

"It is your secret already. Though unknown to you, tis yours," She began, "The orc were not always as they now are. They are of my forgotten children. Stolen. Abducted. I created orders of fae, many times, many kinds, all with a purpose, a role. Elves have learned to fight well enough from men and dwarf, yet they were never meant to. I saw the chaos. I heard the First Discord. I sought to create an order to stand against it. The Thalnok were my warriors. To protect the rest of we fae. To keep us safe as we each played our role. Yet discord is insidious in a way I had not known. I learned far too late. It led many astray. One of them, one I had set high beside me, stole the loyalty of my Thalnok, and those others loyal to me were abandoned, defenseless without our warriors. Chaos reigned. My songs were slow to restore order. When next we looked beyond our wood, dwarf and men were filling the world and had already taken up the task of combating the discord spawned chaos and darkness on their own. A darkness that had changed my wayward children, from a vanguard of protection, into instruments of destruction."

"We are fae?" Malcolm gasped.

"We it is now? Is it?"

"I – We – Wha-?"

"I am Mother — even of the orc. Sometimes, even the Forgotten must be remembered. It would be to my shame and regret, if not for you: Malcolm. I see you becoming what I made your line to be. I see you reclaim the birthright of your people. I very much am your friend. Millions look to me for hope and yet tis you that have given hope to me. The discordant darkness might have tainted your bloodline, but you have chosen the path of light. You have proven that what one chooses is greater than one's origin. Tis with pride and gladness that I see you now at Prince Bengallen's side."

All at once, Malcolm thought he was falling. He felt the nothing beneath his feet. He felt the wind blustering all around. He reached out, grasping his harness as he started awake. He looked down and saw the forest giving way to the open plains, as he and his companions continued soaring high above them.

Chapter 54
Descending Thanes

The older wizard, the half-elf Kinnik, slipped loose from his harness and went tumbling toward the distant ground. Night had fallen and so he disappeared before Caanaflit, Alpona, Shomotta, or Malcolm could even call out to the others.

Lungs filling with panicked swell, they paused, when they heard the paladin leader, Sir Jerumir, called Chief, yell, "Go!"

This time, his lieutenant, the burly Sir Quaindraught, pulled loose from his harness. What looked like haphazard tumbling, Caanaflit noticed, was actually intentional. A third "go" marked the third to fall, Sir Ihrvan, and he too turned his face intentionally downward. *It must allow more control over the fall.*

"You're next, hero," Chief slapped Malcolm on the arm, pulling apart a clasp on the half-orc's harness, "trust me."

Chief Jerumir pulled a second clasp, they did not come loose easily, and only Malcolm's iron grip upon the suspension cords kept him attached, dangling from beneath the dragon, flying at unknowable heights. He paused only to give the paladin a serious look before reluctantly letting go, plummeting.

Shomotta was ready when Jerumir looked to him. His clasps were already opened as he hung by grip strength alone. The eager wizard-priest released following a chuckle from Chief Jerumir and the informal command of, "Well, go on then."

When Jerumir turned to where Alpona had been, all he saw were the dangling straps of his undone harness. The man had already taken it upon himself to slip away.

"This is stupid," Caanaflit said to the Chief, when at last his turn came. He had already unfastened one buckle, hand resting on the second clasp, *ready or not.*

"You'll love it," Sir Jerumir said, twisted almost backward in his own harness, "trust me."

His friends gone before him, without further hesitation, Caanaflit pried the second clasp open, falling loose. It took him a moment to get the hang of it, but he found, right away, the benefit of falling face first. The air itself tossed him about, wheeling and spinning him, dizzying. Finding the proper plummeting angle was a relief. One not known to Alpona, Shomotta, or Malcolm. Caanaflit chuckled, passing them by, each tossed about at wind's whim in the waning moonlight.

As he zoomed past two of the Forest Phantoms, who had spread themselves out, catching the wind, not unlike a ship's sails, Caanaflit became concerned. He tried to do likewise, but merely ended up, again, in that nauseating spin. As he passed the wizard, Kinnik, also, concern became fear, but only for a moment.

Passing the mage, the bracer that each man had been given, which had been attached to the top clasp of the harness, began to glow, faintly. So doing, Caanaflit could feel that arm, or the bracer more accurately, wanting to fall slower than the rest of him. The further he fell, the more this magical effect slowed him, bringing his hand over head and his feet dangling toward the ground.

Likewise, as each man passed the wizard by, his armband would glow, slowing and righting his descent. The other thanes, who had mostly continued to whirl about uncontrolled, were never to have passed Kinnik, as they did not nosedive. This was why the Forest Phantoms' second wizard, Sternis, the younger alchemist, always came down last, to failsafe the others.

Were there a problem, he could plummet after his comrades, catching up to them, and activating the bracer of anyone who had not passed his counterpart, Kinnik. Malcolm, Shomotta, and Alpona all experienced this. Once all devices were active, the two wizards would rendezvous, indicating everyone between them was safe, and only then activating their own.

Upon landfall, each pair of boots hit the dirt as gently as downy feathers. The two mages were first, followed closely by three of the thanes, the other Forest Phantoms, and at last Caanaflit. The first to have his armband activated fell more slowly, for the longest amount of time, and was the last to land. Malcolm and Shomotta took a knee and there remained for sometime, casting off the last of their respective vertigo. Alpona wobbled about, but was making an effort to stay on his feet.

Caanaflit, however, having got the sport of it, or near enough, rushed toward the group, shouting, "Absolutely – unbelievable – amazing!"

"On yer feet, lads, like the others," Sir Quaindraught insisted, looming over Malcolm and Shomotta, "You'll want to walk it off. Tis the only way, truly."

Caanaflit touched his bald head with his right hand, walked toward Alpona and touched his friend's with his left, asking, "When and why did you shave your head?"

"Just before we left. I've lived filthy, like a slave, before" Alpona answered, allowing himself to lean against Caanaflit's hand for a moment, concluding with a lie, "I don't want all that hair to keep up with."

"We look like a matched pair now," Caanaflit laughed, "Tis a little odd. Like looking through a distorted mirror."

"You wish," Alpona forced a laugh and, still dizzy, walked off in a circuitous way.

Sir Ihrvan approached Caanaflit, saying, "Chief's bald too. Not like you're the trend setter."

Caanaflit smirked, replying, "Twas sort of unique to me in our little band though. Just seemed a strange choice for him. Strange … Anyway, tis his own head."

"So it is," Ihrvan agreed, "From here, I'll take you four to town and make the right introductions."

"The rest is up to you," Sir Jerumir added, "We'll be headed back to aid His Majesty's journey, once Sir Ihrvan gets you set-up here. May the blessings of the Holy Family be upon you: wisdom, mercy, and strength. I say it."

Caanaflit had not yet come into a habit of praying, but it was expected. Having barely established rapport and past the precipice of such a thrill, Caanaflit neither sought to offend the paladin nor dismiss his well wishes, thus he spoke, "We say it."

Finally, Malcolm and Shomotta rejoined them. Malcolm addressed Jerumir, "You've not asked about it yet. I suppose now is the time."

Sir Jerumir MacRoberts, Chieftain of the MacRoberts Clan, looked, not at Malcolm, but at his sword, and spoke, "I figured you'd address it, when you were ready."

"I'm honored," Malcolm said, "that you didn't simply demand it from me the moment you were told what it was, back at the Sebastian farm."

"I recognized her long before that, Thane Malcolm."

"And now?"

"The Dawnsong has come to you," Jerumir began, "rightly through the knight you squired. Tis a powerful and storied blade, if she did not want to be in your keeping, she would not remain so. Her history is classically tied to my family, yes. Yet her legends are our own. How ever you have found each other, on great quest and in regal company, I would not suppose to stand in the way of that. The Dawnsong sings of justice and order, from the dawn of time when the world was right. A great wrong has been done in Morralish and you are to be an instrument in its righting. There is a harmony between you and that sword. Not deaf to such things, I can hear it."

"And yet," Malcolm said, "Am I to pose as slave, I cannot take such a blade with me and would not risk losing it to theft or, Mother's mercy forbid it, my defeat."

"And so..." Jerumir invited Malcolm to continue.

"So I would leave the Dawnsong in your keeping. Were some ill fate to befall me, then at least it would be returned to the MacRoberts line. Should I succeed, however, I do not feel our work together is yet finished, and I would have it returned to me."

"I humbly accept this honor, my thane, to carry the Dawnsong in days ahead, in your stead, at our Prince's side," Sir Jerumir held out both hands, ceremoniously, continuing, "Just as it would be an honor to restore the Dawnsong to her chosen champion and quest, when next we meet again. Just as I hope, someday, when there is a King in Morralish once more, you, Malcolm, will come and feast with my clan, tell my people of your adventures, and be honored to return their ancestral blade to them."

Malcolm saw the story in it. He loved his stories, and this had the makings of a great one. So Malcolm handed over the ancient Dawnsong, agreeing, "This is our bond now. We shall see such days come to pass. Even should either of us fall. Our oath, upon this blade between us, this sword returned home, once Morralish has been restored and I take up a new purpose ... in this life or the next. I say it."

"We both say it," Sir Jerumir echoed, "and I say also that I am glad to call Thane Malcolm Ironclaw, ward of my Prince, also my friend."

"We say it," Malcolm humbly concurred, releasing the greatsword to his new friend, bound by oaths made.

Chapter 55
Securing Supplies

"Tis an ambitious, but solid strategy, my Lord Harkon," General Anderason agreed, "We'll do our part."

Harkon's grim face cracked an unfamiliar, but easy, smile, and he replied, "I know that you will, you are a good man and a fine soldier. If I had only met you sooner, I'd have had you trained a paladin and had you for my own regiment."

"Not so sure I'd have made it up to general over there."

"And as it turned out," Harkon mused, "we needed you right here where you are. Funny how things work out."

"Faith, Lord Harkon," Anderason added, "I have faith they will continue to do so."

"Faith and hard work," Harkon further amended, continuing, "We'll need to set up a midway station and keep a sizable amount of supplies there. I'll get plenty of soldiers there to garrison it before its supplies become too much a target. In the meantime, I want its future stores to be secured. Visit all the coastal towns on the route to Napua and offer honest coin for stock goods. Napua will be your best bet though. Tis big and can be resupplied by boat from the Capital herself, so Napua won't be afraid to sell down to its final fish and last grain – if the price is right. They can always get more. Buy it all if you can."

The amount of gold entrusted to General Anderason for this task, and from him to his officers, was obscene. The bank notes were even more so. It was more than enough to become a lord, enough to make the purest heart question his most holy vow. If anyone had known that so few carried so much, an army would have spontaneously formed from the dregs and highwaymen across the countryside.

Yet though they few, the officers that would bear this moral burden and strategic resource were paladins all. All save for one man, a single wizard among them. The odds that these select agents could hold their own oaths true and, if needed, even defeat far greater numbers than themselves were entirely in their favor. The quality of the paladin is beyond reproach and the worth of even one wizard should never be underestimated.

243

Chapter 56
Selling Slaves

Ordering drinks proved initially difficult. It was clear that this establishment was intended for established patrons. Their table was passed by over and over again. Caanaflit, at the bar, observed transaction after transaction without so much as a glance in his direction. At last, the barkeep had gotten into a long conversation with a weasel-faced man about the rising cattle prices.

Caanaflit became so interested in their conversation that he forgot he was frustrated. Yet, Alpona had not, and joining him at the bar, said, "You are clearly the leader of men, important, at least as this room goes. You stand our leader, ignored, while he would suckle that man's worm."

"Do not worry yourself," Caanaflit dismissed, "We have but one purpose here. Let him choke upon it."

"Your expletives ever impress!" Alpona laughed.

As the Zil-jahi warrior returned to the table, Caanaflit considered their purpose, eventually calling out in Antori, his Qallen dialect suddenly strong, "Barr-kept! Barr-kept!"

The barkeep paid him but a glance of notice and returned to his conversation.

"Barr-kept! Barr-kept!"

"Barkeep," the man behind the bar emphasized, "I'll get to you in a moment."

"Bark-heap! Bark-heap!"

"What!?" the barkeep growled, marching over to Flit.

"I am the son of a foreign lord," Caanaflit lied, "the guest of a local man whom I am meeting here, a patron of yours, at his request. What should I tell him of the treatment and service – me and my men – received here after our long and weary travels – at this unkempt bark heap?"

"Ah-apologies," the barkeep stammered, "Ya-you should have said something sooner."

"I shouldn't have had to," Caanaflit grumbled, "and I am saying something

244

now."

"I'll bring drinks right over," the barkeep bribed, "first two rounds – on the house."

"Three!" Caanaflit insisted, "Tis been a very, very long journey."

"Sure, right over."

Caanaflit came back to the table and addressed the others, "Likely with spit in them, but free drinks are on their way."

Spit or no, three rounds and then some later, the conversation flowed freely, if not unfocused, between them.

"I still haven't figured it out," Alpona announced to the table, drawing a long swig from his draft.

Shomotta raised an eyebrow, he had not seen Alpona drink like this since before they slew the Starspawn and, with care, he inquired, "Figured out what?"

"The beards," Alpona said, more like he was making declaration than conversation, "You don't keep much of a beard. Neither does Caanaflit nor the Prince, but in the Frontier, most the other men of strength and standing do. Now, here, in Napua, in this Imperium, I've not seen beard one."

"True," Malcolm grunted, slow to take notice, his own cups littered around him.

"This," Caanaflit chimed, "I have also noticed and discussed with Bengallen in our earlier adventures."

Alpona, though drinking, motioned Caanaflit to continue.

Shomotta agreed, "Enlighten us."

"There isn't really a rule," Caanaflit began, "Some boys beards come in earlier than others, often they play at growing one, their sideburns, little chin goats, patchy face mops, and the like. If they get too long or unkempt a parent will put an end to it. There are cultural standards, however, more rigid in Morralish though often enough followed in the Frontier. The right to a true beard, to begin one's life-long great-beard, if you will, is tied with becoming a

245

man. Now manhood, in Morralish custom, is not tied to age or means, not necessarily. There are three life transitions, any one of which entitles a man to a proper beard. Primarily, becoming a father to a son. Tis a role change, the new father must now model manhood to his son and the growing beard is a symbol of this. Secondary beard entitlement comes when an eldest son buries his own father. Again, the beard is a symbol for the role change; he is now the head of his house and an equal among his uncles, have he them. The third and least common cultural entitlement to a beard is for a son to distinguish himself in some craft or trade that is different than his father's own. Yet again, the beard symbolizes a change in role. In this, the man has become independent of his father, potentially an equal to other men in his community or extended family, and of his own accord."

"Why don't you and the Prince have beards then?" Malcolm asked; his intention to focus, though the haze of his drinking, was plain in his affect.

"I was gonna say that," Alpona barked.

Shomotta nodded, acknowledging his own curiosity.

"The Prince," Caanaflit continued, "Had begun to grow a beard, among the woodcutters where I found him. He removed it when we set out. You see, he is not a father and, in the technical sense, neither has he buried his own father. Moreover, when he took up the sword once more, he was again in his father's footsteps. So the Prince has decided that he should not grow a beard until he sits securely on his father's throne, having duly honored the man's memory. Tis the closest thing to a funeral he can offer him. Far greater a thing, as I see it."

"And yourself?" Alpona asked.

"It wouldn't feel right to me," Caanaflit concluded, "shaking my mane in everyone's face while standing next to His Majesty, face bare. Yet that is not the whole of it. Just as I sometimes go about with hair on my head, I have beards that I sometimes wear. I say true, you have all seen me, at least once, with hair and beard, yet did not recognize me among the long-haired, bearded masses – and that was the point. To be both bald and clean-shaven is a rather distinct appearance. To then be other than that, at other times, lends me a great deal of indistinguishableness, anonymity, useful to certain aims."

Alpona leaned in, over the table, whispering over dramatically.

"Clever."

246

Malcolm grinned, rubbing his chin, thinking of a beard.

"Now," Caanaflit interrupted the odd moment, "If you'll excuse me, I believe that my appointment has arrived."

Caanaflit confidently strode across the drinking establishment, a fine, new, silk cloak of burgundy and gold billowing out behind him. As he approached an olive-tan man with wavy hair, one of the man's bodyguard's intercepted him.

"Are you the bald man?"

Unable to help himself, Caanaflit touched his forehead with two fingers, his eyes widening with surprise, then horror, as they slid up to the top of his skull.

He stammered in mock concern, "Buh-buh-by the g-gods, I am!"

The bodyguard sneered, more to stifle his own amusement than annoyance. The wavy-haired man had either heard Caanaflit or gotten the gist of it and motioned that he should come forward. The bodyguard allowed Caanaflit to do so, putting one guard to his back, flanked by one to his front.

Undesirable, rude even, but when in Antoria, one plays by their rules.

"I hear you've come with slaves to sell?" the man asked.

"I hear Napua is in need of slaves?" Caanaflit replied.

"Only the philosophers," the man stated, "Answer questions with questions. Are you a philosopher?"

"It is entirely possible," Caanaflit said, lightly with amusement in his voice, "that I have been unduly influenced by a few. Yet, as you stated the obvious in the form of a question, I thought it perhaps some custom for me to do likewise."

The man's eyes narrowed for a moment, examining Caanaflit, before widening, brightly, his mouth blossoming also into a smile. He exuberantly welcomed Caanaflit to his table.

"I am Cerro Darisi, a native son of Napua. I like you. I can tell already. Please, sit at my table and tell me your name and of your slaves."

"I am Kaaneth," Caanaflit lied, "Third son of Lord Tzargo, himself a second cousin to the Tzar of Qallengrad. To impress our royal relative, my father bled coin while attending court, foolish wages on foolish matters, and now I am left to undo his mess."

"They swindled him, eh?"

"They did indeed."

"We call that the 'country cousin' around here," Cerro elaborated, "Under the guise of introducing some relation or associate, that you don't much care for, to city life, as though you did, you will yourself take advantage of their inexperience."

"Yes, we've recently become familiar with the idea."

"So you are now selling father's slaves, far from home where no one will notice, to recoup coin, and save face."

"I was coming to the Academy in Antoria Royal," Caanaflit shared more of Kaaneth's fiction, "and though my tuition paid for my entire course of study, my father's inattentiveness has left me without a single coin for day-to-day living. He gave me, instead, slaves to sell, and I heard Napua, more than most, needed strong slaves."

"And you heard of Cerro Darisi how?"

"I heard you had a shot at fighting in the Capital's games," Caanaflit explained, honestly, "Until some great beast slew all your men. That you might be invited still, if you could produce men to slay the beast in turn."

"The Academy, eh? So you're smart?"

"—er than most," Caanaflit amended.

"So you know a little something about the worth of your slaves," Cerro said, unclear whether a question or comment.

"Given what has happened," Caanaflit lied, "I've taken a recent disliking of dishonesty. While I've clad them as warriors, for my protection in my travels, and they are certainly a strong lot, but they are merely farmhands. I'm not going to sell them to you as something more than, only to have you come looking for me later."

"Smarter than most, indeed," Cerro noted, "I'll give you one gold coin for each man and one more for your trouble. Four gold coins could last a thrifty

248

man four whole years at the Academy."

Cerro laid out four gold coins on the table, one-by-one, and Caanaflit acted impressed as each one was produced, accepting with the last, "A generous offer. No finer will I find. Gratitude."

"Let it never be said," Cerro proclaimed loudly, "That Cerro Darisi is not a patron of higher learning."

Caanaflit passed over the forged documentation and collected his four coins.

"They're over at my table, there, sodded. They know they're being sold and haven't any fight in them now. Reality, sobriety, and a day's rest should reinvigorate."

"Oh," Cerro grinned, wickedly, his face turning grim, "We have our own ways of awakening the killers in men."

Caanaflit assumed the others would go with Cerro without incident. It was the plan after all. Still, he had hoped to hang around and watch. Noticing that he had been followed from the bar, however, he figured his time would be better spent entertaining his tail by living up to his tale.

Caanaflit had told a story, claiming to be someone. If he did not act like that person, whatever suspicion that had pinned the tail on him would only be confirmed in Cerro Darisi's mind.

So Caanaflit wandered through the city a bit. It was different than anything in the Frontier, sure, but it was not impressive to him. In every way, Napua wanted to be Antoria Royal. Top to bottom, the place had no sense of itself. It merely reeked of people who wanted to be somewhere, something, someone else.

Columns and columns, every building, even small, unimportant ones, boasted white columns, with gold accents on the crenelations of those that could afford them.

"An enterprising wretch could make a small fortune scraping gold leaf off buildings at night," Caanaflit muttered to himself idly, passing through a pair of such columns as he entered the brothel.

He paid for companionship, but had no indulgent intentions. He shared a laugh and drink with the tawdry courtesan, telling her of the man following him and his need to be out of the streets for a while. She accepted this, even appreciated the break from her own busy day.

Biding his time, Caanaflit told her of his adventures in the Frontier with Prince Bengallen, the parts he wanted made known anyway.

"What's the difference between biding your time and wasting it?"

"I should not think that you would need that explained by the likes of me."

She smiled in realization.

"Faith enough."

By the time he decided to depart, she was throwing herself at him, nearly literally. Yet he bid her "good evening" and returned to the street.

There, Caanaflit was loathe to discover, his tail pursued him still. Worse, there were two of them. It was *awfully early into all of this to be killing people*, but he supposed no other choice. Caanaflit ducked into an alley, quickly, and there dove behind a crate.

"Spit!" one swore.

"Yoo see'em?" the other asked.

They had only stepped into the alley, but they were looking. Caanaflit could not afford to be found. He had the opportunity for surprise and took it. Leaping from concealment, he stabbed one man through the bottom of his jaw, the long dagger finding its way deep into the gray matter within the victim's skull. With his right hand, he palmed the side of the other man's head, bashing it into the head of the man he had skewered. Both men limp, he pulled them forward, toppling them behind himself, a few feet further into the alley.

Caanaflit spun about, pouncing on the man merely stunned, and placed the dagger to his throat. He had intended to offer the man life. Life for information. Life, if he ran away, far away, forever, but the faces said it all.

The two men were the slave bodyguards of Cerro Darisi, the slave buyer. He had given so generous an offer because he had intended to simply rob those coins back from his happy customer. Caanaflit supposed it was simpler than negotiating, yet it angered him greatly.

"You want simple? I can do simple," Caanaflit informed Cerro's brute, coldly, as he pulled his dagger across the man's throat, "There. Simple."

Chapter 57
Opening Gambit

It was the first battle of the rebellion, what historians would call a slave rebellion, but there was not a slave among them on this day. They were men who politicians schemed against, men who would not sit idly by while foreign legislation relegated them to a status that left them no choice but to become slave or outlaw. Those men and the men who would not sell them out, men who believed in freedom for all and would not abandon their subordinates to such a fate, went on the offensive.

The men that opposed them that day were a sorry lot, from a tactical standpoint. Individually, however, they were not to be underestimated. A small clutch of Llarisean and Dileanian prison guards garrisoned the secret prison, called the Oublitille.

It was a forgetting place, where freedom was not taken away by law, but the law circumvented entirely. Wherein the prisoners had committed no crimes. The guards there were healthy, well fed, paid, and equipped, but their prison was supposed to be a secret. Their numbers were few and they had no preparation for this. They were trained to prevent an escape. They were not prepared for an army to besiege the walls and invade the halls of the Oublitille.

The prison was a simple, if not castlesque, structure. It was two towers with parallel walls stretched between. The towers contained blocks of cells, while the area protected between the walls boasted quarters and courtyard for the garrison.

Lord-General Kenneth Cardness had personally led every soldier, not native to the First Army Regiment, from their encampment to the Oublitille. Battalion upon battalion of men, who had come to seek refuge and alliance as Morralish Loyalists, poised themselves against the prison that unjustly held their countrymen. They outnumbered the guards of the Oublitille by nearly one-hundred to one, and they made a rather impressive show of the fact.

Truth told, General Cardness had hoped to win the fight without loosing a single arrow or unsheathing a single sword. Fielding his more than five thousand against their less than one-hundred, he anticipated a swift surrender. Yet the guard of the Oublitille were a selected group of devoted fanatics and, before terms were even discussed, every guard that could find a nook in the crenellation or window below the rampart began firing arrows from it.

Damn good bowmen too. Almost every arrow found purchase. Four score brave soldiers of Morralish died in that first volley and as many more were wounded. There would be no negotiation after such, only the solitary decree, "Attack!"

The gates were assailed by men beyond counting. At such close proximity and with covering fire of Morralish's own archers, the bowman guards were suddenly of no effect. With sword and axe the assailants tore through the wooden doors, exposing the iron drop gate within.

The lowering pulleys of the gate had latched, it fastened when it was lowered. A system that normally had to be disengaged for the gate to rise again. Clearing the debris, they lined up, shoulder-to-shoulder, and lifted with all their might, prayers in their hearts, blood boiling within their veins, carrying courage to and from those hearts, until at last it gave.

The combined force of the mighty men of Morralish bent the mechanism, allowing the gate to rise and fall freely. Some few remained, holding it aloft as their brothers passed beneath, into the courtyard, until others arrived with beams, from a yet-to-be-fashioned siege tower, to hold the gate up.

The Morralish Soldiers poured into the Oublitille, like ants upon a fallen beehive. By numbers alone they took the courtyard, driving the defenders back into the prison towers and dividing them. Yet from the towers, they once more began to rain arrows upon the sons of the mountains, who could do naught but take what shelter they could find.

Jonn revealed himself once more to the Morralish commanders, telling them which tower their countrymen were being held in. The prison held relatively few captives in those days, compared to its design. For convenience, all were kept in the eastern tower, alone warded against magic.

No mercy was granted, not after so much initial bloodshed, not after firing before hearing terms. So a wizard and twenty strong men were sent to the back of the western tower. By brain and brawn, the will of the twenty-one, they disassembled and eroded the base of the tower, collapsing it all to rubbled shower, along with whatever guards were inside.

Its fall the signal, those within the courtyard rushed the eastern tower, hammering down its doors and flooding into its halls. Likewise, men, from the thousands of more outside, rushed in to replace and maintain the occupation of the courtyard.

The dam had broken. The soldiers of Morralish, with worthy cause, flowed and filled the objective with the righteous retribution of their steel and will.

This was not their homeland. Their countrymen within, but two in number. Yet at last they were afforded the opportunity to right this one wrong done to their people. It was symbolic of the worry for home that laid heavy upon their hearts. Aimless determination and impotent rage had found a target and taken aim once again. Made potent once more, they themselves become the bowstring pulled and loosed. Though war and death the result of their arrow's flight, the tension had been great; its relief was immeasurable. They were warriors after all.

So great was their number that most the guards, falling before them, could not land a single stroke against them. Level-by-level, the tower's prisoners were freed but few new prisoners were taken. Until, at last, the top cell block was entered. The last of the guards had fallen back to this place.

Even at the end, they dared to hold Lord Hrothmond and Sister Bethany with knives to their throats, like some rough hostages to be bartered. Yet seeing so many of their own number defeated and so great an opposing force, swelling in number before them, the remaining guards did naught but fall to their knees and beg mercy for their lives.

Despite such a tragic initial loss of life, the Morralish Loyalist Army took few casualties overall and had freed their wrongly imprisoned countrymen. Resources would be plundered and prisoners interrogated, but not in that moment. In that moment, they rejoiced and thanked the Holy Family for their victory.

"High Lord-General Hrothmond?" Lord Cardness asked, "We've not had the pleasure, I am the Lord-General Kenneth Cardness, and this must be your daughter, the Sister Bethany. Tis my honor to meet you both."

"We are they," Hrothmond replied, "but on such a day the honor is ours. You have honored us greatly in this rescue."

Cardness gave a slight bow, addressing the priestess, "Sister, men came looking for you. They claimed to be thanes of the Prince. They claimed that he yet lives. Is it so?"

"Indeed it is. Indeed he does."

Chapter 58
Becoming Gladiators

They were, each of them, bruised more than they cared to be. The initial assessments and training were of little consequence to men already trained so well. This had allowed them to avoid the lash, for the most part, but the whole ordeal was all excessively rough and had begun to take a collective toll on their bodies.

Five other slaves had begun the training with them, four of which had survived. Three of those men were beaten and broken, almost to nothing, and they had become the clock by which the training day was measured.

Sore as they were, Alpona, Malcolm, and Shomotta, knew the brutality was coming to a close. Those other slaves had proven themselves worthy and trainable. To push them beyond the doors of death, after so much investment of time, energy, and, most importantly, coin, would be wasteful. For, when all was said and done, the business of slaves and gladiators was a literal business and, ultimately, about one thing alone, profit.

The fourth man with whom they trained was something like themselves, a soldier of some kind. He looked Thalosian, but refused to speak to the other slaves directly. He was always the first one awake. It was no different that day.

When Malcolm joined Alpona and Shomotta in the training yard, this man was there already. The other three, beaten and broken, however, had not yet been forced from bed.

The training yard was different that morning. Rather than logs, rocks, and obstacles, it had sparring stations and a crate of weapons. Those gathered were already examining them.

"These swords," Alpona said in disgust, "are made of tin, copper, and pig iron."

"Oh, that can be fixed," Shomotta offered ambiguously.

Before Alpona or Malcolm could ask the wizard-priest to elaborate, Cerro Darisi, their owner, came before them along with their trainer, called Doki.

"Well," Cerro began, "I see you've all found your way up and out this morning. I have good news for you. The last two fully trained gladiators that I owned have fallen in battle to a glorious death. So now I must escalate your training. Whatever you may have told your previous masters, we have observed that you four have some skill already, and you will henceforth train separately from the others. We'll leave those three to recover today and focus on your abilities. Hear me, to lie to me further is a swift death. Show me what you can do and I'll begin fighting you in the arena. There you can find accolades or at least a worthy demise. The choice is yours."

"May I speak, Doki?" Malcolm asked in the proper way.

"Yes, yes," Cerro answered dismissively before the doki could respond.

"What is to keep us from simply slaying you with these weapons, here and now?" Malcolm asked, a mischievous gleam in his eye.
As Doki tightened his hand on his lash, Cerro laughed and replied dismissively, "You'll note that those weapons are made of base metals. No blending. No alloys. No steel. There is a magic here that protects me from the base metals. Nice to see the fighting spirit finally showing through though, orc. It well confirms my suspicions."

They fought each other in mock tournament all day. The thanes were careful not injure each other. Neither did they demonstrate their complete prowess. Getting into the arena was what this was all about for them, and they did what they had to do for that goal.

The fourth man, however, fought for blood. He had laid at least one wound on each of them and, if these fights had been real, one of them would have had to have put him down or die pulling their punches. At last the moons rose. The long day of combat training came to a close.

"I am Alchesus," the Thelosian spoke at last, his accent confirming his ethnicity, "did you say that you could change the metals on those weapons?"

"Yeah," Malcolm was also curious, "didn't you say that?"

"Not technically," Shomotta answered, "but sand has a deceptive hardness, the hardness of stone, and I can use magic to lend the sand's hardness to the blades. Will you tell this to Doki or Cerro, Alchesus, or are you friend?"

"Hells no," Alchesus replied, "One, I say we use your magic, kill them, and get out of here. Two, I am yet enslaved and in no rush, then, to add a wizard's ire to list of woes."

"Indeed," Shomotta uttered his familiar phrase, but grim in tone and wearing a theatrical scowl.

"The Antori Imperium has kept slaves for centuries," Alpona prefaced, "What makes you so keen to slay your master and escape, while most accept their servitude?"

"I wouldn't be so sure that anyone accepts their enslavement beyond a chance for freedom," Alchesus mused, "As for I, sold into slavery, and worse, by my own brothers almost two decades ago now. I owe them a debt of blood. I'd be home to see it paid, if the chance were to avail itself."

"You would kill your brothers?" Malcolm asked, thinking of his own slaying of his brother and father.

"Yes, I –" Alchesus began to answer, his mood changing abruptly, "I need not explain myself to you. Lend me aid in escape or leave me be."

Malcolm looked to Alpona, who nodded solemnly, then to Shomotta who did the same in unspoken agreement.

Malcolm answered, "We have become slaves, intentionally. To kill the great monster that rules the arena and, thereafter, inspire all slaves to rise against their masters. We cannot help you in the way you would have us, not yet, but we would gladly accept your aid, when the day comes, that our causes are one. We do not intend for the wait to be long and, from the words Cerro spoke today, neither does he."

"Freedom fighters," Alchesus laughed, continuing, "I should have known. Hear me, brothers, I fought with the Southlanders, against Thalos, in the Alcyone Civil War."
"There's a story there," Malcolm suspected.

"In my youth, a Southland woman, Vulez, washed ashore near my fishing route and I rescued her. Without informing my family, I sailed her south and home. I nursed her to health over the voyage and we fell in love. Her father bade me stay with them, but after a year of bliss, I became ensnared in the troubles, in the war. Captured, Vulez and I were turned over to my brothers, our father having died in the conflict. They had not the heart to slay me. Yet, sick to madness over father's death, they violated and killed my wife. For some days, they kept me in irons. As their minds returned to them, my presence and grief ever shamed them for their misdeeds. I was the shadow of their guilt, a reminder of the vile darkness their despair had turned them to. So they cast me from far from their sight. Sold me to slave. I accepted it, at first. Broken, it was easier, to have no will of my own, no mind, no memory. Yet now, more than a decade later and faced with death as a gladiator, I see the world clear and true once more. I must avenge Vulez's death, even to slay my own kin."

Initially, no one said anything. No one knew how to reply to that.

"We know of the Southlands and the New Freedoms," Alpona offered, "we are kindred spirits in more ways than one. Would you not rather fight for freedom than vengeance?"

Before Alchesus could answer, Malcolm added, "The two are not mutually exclusive."

"You speak true," Alchesus accepted, "Aid you I shall. Then after, I go my own way, for my own purpose."

"As all free men may do," Shomotta concluded.

Chapter 59
Marshalling Forces

The Morralish Loyalist Army returned to the encampment of the First
Regiment to find it flying the standard of its High-Lord General once more.
Immediately, the Generals Harkon, Hrothmond, and Cardness, with select
others, including Sister Bethany, convened in council.

"I find High Lord-General Strein Hrothmond, and his daughter, marching a
heavy regiment to my camp, but the men are not his own. Where is the
Second Regiment?"

"High Lord-General Vantis Harkon," Hrothmond replied to him by name and
title, "the Second Regiment, as far as I know, remains encamped at the Qallen
southern border. These men here are a loyalist army, fled from their own
commanders to seek the counsel of the wise and fair Morralish Lord, Church
Paladin, and Army General that is yourself, Vantis Harkon. Your worthy
subordinate, General Cardness borrowed them to free my daughter and I from
unlawful imprisonment."

"You are the Sister Bethany?" Harkon asked, "The priestess that I have heard
whispers about in every Morralish Army Regiment from the Great Deserts to
Three Gods' Pass?"

"Humbly, I suppose that I am, my lord."

"Then the other rumor is also true? You are envoy from our Prince Bengallen,
Dragonslayer and Mayor of Spearpointe, who's mighty thanes have also been
shunned by every Regiment?"

Bethany looked confused.

"Our great Prince was alive. He did send me here to recall the Expeditionary
Forces. Yet, only he and I, another man, and a trio of dwarves knew of his
survival. He was to remain anonymous in the Frontier until reinforced. I
suppose that was too much to ask, I gone so long. I know nothing of dragons,
thanes, or mayors, but I suppose His Majesty, as a paladin, if not as a prince,
would have been compelled to participate in the wellbeing of those around
him."

"By the gods three," Harkon swore benignly, "A small band of dwarves came
here too, hours before I spirited away with many of my officers on our fact

finding mission. They told me not only that Prince Bengallen had survived, but that others, Morralish refugees in all directions, had as well. We went to see what the other Regiments knew. Now, after so long a journey, I return to have my answers delivered straight to me."

"Confirmation, my lord," Bethany offered, "If we but heed Vandor's beckoning, things are oft made clearer to us."

"So it seems," Harkon agreed, "Confirmation here and my time abroad saw other plans put into motion as well. We must be swift and decisive now, agreed?"

Hrothmond and Cardness agreed. The other generals agreed.

Even Bethany agreed, Harkon had been speaking to her after all, "Agreed, my lord, your other tales are of interest to me, however. I would hear them, when there is time."

"So you shall," Harkon offered, elaborating, "upon the road. Yet here is one more, most recent, to tide you over. The Prince comes to Antoria. To march through the Triumphant Gate himself with laurels upon his brow. Though he not an Antori citizen and though Spearpointe not part of the Imperium, it has citizen and economic interests there. Whatever our Prince has accomplished – be it slaying dragon or taking office – it has earned him a hero's welcome to Antoria Royal. Many believe he will use this formal visit to negotiate for us and make us all imperial citizens. Yet others say he will announce the Morralish troop withdrawal. Serving all these decades, I know the Hastenfarish mind, as well as the discernment of a fellow paladin. Sister, you traveled with the Prince, know him personally, what say you?"

Bethany smiled and spoke her heart, "As we've discussed, he sent me here to recall the sons of the mountains, to return to those mountains and reclaim them for their people, to find what justice we may or avenge our loved ones against the dark forces that stole them. In truth, he had a mind to ride north on his own and settle the score, personally. If he thought for a moment that he could have, he would have too. No, my good Lord-General, my brother, if His Majesty rides west, it is not to broker a new deal with the Imperium. He rides west only as a detour north."

"We must make ready," Harkon replied, "Much of the Third Regiment is encamped near Three Gods' Pass, the Frontier edge of the Imperium, making ready for the Grand Army's march home. General Hrothmond, I assume you are still fit for duty and ready for a command?"

"As a matter of fact," Hrothmond replied, "I was imprisoned and relinquished my command in support of you, General Harkon, and your exclusion from the council of generals. Those generals, without your protest and having silenced mine, have sold out our men and women to the Imperium."

"I've learned well of this traitors' council and we here shall act in defiance of their decrees."

"In that case," Hrothmond accepted, "I am ready to serve."

"In that case," Harkon echoed, "I'm putting you in command of this new Regiment, they rescued you after all, you belong to them, their symbol. General Cardness will take my place at the head of the First. Combining both, formally, with General Anderason's elements of the Third, we shall become, formally, the Morralish Loyalist Army. If there are no objections, I'll command the combined army until His Majesty arrives."

"Alright, lords and good soldiers," General Cardness addressed his fellow general officers, "We've finally got a mission. One I think we can all get behind. Much to be done. Go do it!"

As the subordinate generals left the tent en masse, to give their orders, spread the word, and begin the movements of the battalions under their respective commands, Bethany spoke up again, suspicious, "Swift and decisive indeed, my lord. What, pray tell, do you intend to do with this Loyalist Army?"

Only she, General Harkon, and her father remained.

"Nothing too drastic or unwarranted," Harkon answered, "As General Anderason has secured the Great Road at the Frontier east, we shall, battalion-by-battalion, garrison the road, from his forces in the east, across to the west, to the very doorstep of the Imperial Capital herself if need be."

"Don't you think the Imperator will notice?" Bethany asked, "Garrisoned troops out the widow of his Antoria Royal palace and all the Army stretched into the east beyond?"

"Well I rather hope he does," Harkon stated plainly.

Before Bethany could retort, her father, Lord Hrothmond, interrupted her.

"Daughter, you've done much, but this is a rather brilliant plan. The Imperator has no options. Recalling his legions takes as long as recalling our regiments, but we'll be a month or more ahead of him. He'd be a fool to empty the home guard from the city. Even if he did, they couldn't take us. We'd just fall back, east, where he has next to no reinforcements. The further east any Morralish battalion may regress, the more battalions it would then be reinforced by – and that much closer to home besides. The Imperator's only option, which won't go the way he suspects, will be to move other Morralish forces, in the field, against us. Our brothers will be reluctant to slay us at the Imperator's command. They'll outright refuse if His Majesty, the Prince, has returned and declared his intentions as we suspect."

"Precisely," Harkon agreed, "this is also why, to ease your concern, Sister, those men to be deployed nearest Antoria Royal will be the last to take up their positions."

"So leave the generaling to the Generals, got it," Sister Bethany offered with an honest smile.

"In a sense," Harkon said, stifling a laugh, "but do speak your concerns and ideas. You are definitely a part of this, Sister. No one here is dismissing you. Please understand that you need not doubt me. I was the one they left out of the traitors' council, after all. They were concerned I'd do – well – something just like this."

"Of course, my lord," Bethany accepted, "Gratitude."

"And mine to you and your father," Harkon added.

"Plenty of gratitude to go around," Hrothmond replied, "I say it."

Sister Bethany, in the manner of the priestess, elaborated her father's suggested oath into a sung prayer, full and lovely,
"Bonded are we, by faith and fidelity,
  to our homeland, just and right,
  to His Majesty, Bengallen, Prince in the Light,
  to brothers and sisters, near and far,
  by what we've done and who we are.
  May Holy Family bless us anew;
  their wisdom, mercy, and justice to do.
  So say we and say it true."

"We say it," the Lord-Generals agreed in unison, "true."

Chapter 60
Counting Coins

Caanaflit was neither about to leave his friends behind, nor take the attempt on his life lightly. It was a slight. So, retaining the guise of Kaaneth, a lesser noble from afar, come to make his fortunes in the Imperium, Caanaflit began to explore the business options available to a man with four large gold coins in his pocket.

On the Frontier, a good year's wage would net a gold coin half the size were it paid out all at once. Enough money to feed, clothe, and house a family for the whole year, if spent wise and well. A single man in his thirties, even his early thirties, could retire on four gold coins of this size.

Caanaflit understood that, even a large gold coin, would not go half as far as a small one, not within the Imperium. Moreover, of course, Cerro Darisi – no retiree, early or otherwise – had no intention to part with them but for a single evening.

Yet, they were valuable. *More than a year's rations could be attained, new wardrobe of the finest silks and linens, more outfits than days of the week, or a fine suit of armor, well, maybe not so fine, but a suit of armor anyway.* Caanaflit, however, needed none of these things. Goals within goals, plots within plots, Caanaflit had to think a long moment about what exactly he did need. *Slaves, of course, the time and attention of slaves.*

Interestingly enough, Caanaflit as Kaaneth had already insinuated himself into the slave trade, earning himself these sizable coins. Compared to the hoard he had squirreled away in Spearpointe and the huge diamond with the banks over in Antoria Royal, these coins were nothing to him.

Caanaflit rented, therefore, a fine room for Kaaneth for one, with fine meals and appointments for himself, two. Breaking a third gold to copper, he went about bribing slaves for information. By the end of the day, he knew not only who needed what kinds of slaves, but most of the rivalries between the wealthy and noble houses of Napua. By the end of the week, he had bought and sold over three dozen slaves. His four large gold coins, used up to the last, had become ten in fewer days.

Over that week, he learned so much more: Which slaves lived well enough for their own tastes, which were abused, and all level of preference between. Caanaflit tried to take mercy and morality into account as he moved slaves between owners, but was not always able to do so with a bigger picture to consider. They were all to be freed soon enough.

To that end, he also learned more about the slave owning public. Even families barely one step up from poverty themselves often had a house slave, called ancilla. Moreover, *the only people in Napua who did not own slaves were those so poor as to be on the brink of selling themselves into slavery. It was an unsustainable system.* Caanaflit took a moment to contemplate and struggled to understand *how it had not collapsed already.* The moment before his heavy purse jangled, the answer revealed.

Many of the nobles were also putting on airs. They sold slaves to him because they could not afford to keep them. Most lived far beyond their means, had exhausted their inheritance, and were waiting for some scheme or another to come to fruition, potentially, they prayed immodestly, returning their home to solvency. This was far more commonplace than even Caanaflit had suspected, but it fit well into his own scheme, playing nicely with uncovered rivalries.

This brought him easily into the second week of his plan. He made friends with the city's gentry, particularly the desperate, hungry ones on the brink of financial ruin. He learned about their rivals, their wealth and habits, concocting each day, new ways to rob them. Caanaflit paid each struggling noble some pittance for their silence and trouble, though in truth, those that aided him were far more satisfied by the wound inflicted on their supposed betters, than making any coin for themselves. He also continued to move slaves from one owner to another. In many cases, he had manipulated the situation so thoroughly as to buy slaves with their master's own coin. Thus it was that, by the end of the second week, Caanaflit's ten large gold coins had become fifty-five.

Chapter 61
Surviving Contests

During these same two weeks in Napua. Prince Bengallen's other thanes, Malcolm, Shomotta, and Alpona, had completed their accelerated training and had fought their first battles in the arena. Fortunately, the city's supply of gladiators had been exhausted and Cerro Darisi had secured criminal executions for his new batch of fighting men. Bengallen's thanes were prepared to survive the arena, killing whomever they must.

They wondered, nonetheless, if some or all of these so-called criminals were, mayhap, not fully deserving of death. Yet someone was going to execute them. Taking on that burden themselves put them in a place to do the greater good later or so they hoped

Moreover, they were also glad enough not to be immediately pitted against other fighting slaves, what few remained, who might also dream of freedom. They knew, however, that if they did not stand against Illwarr soon, other gladiators would be trained and their moral dilemma would compound as many of them would be precisely the type of kindred spirits they were here to liberate.

As fate had it, their first matches were ironically appropriate to themselves. Malcolm was dressed and billed as a demon. The arena was decorated as a certain fiery hell and a questionable rapist, the type of criminal Malcolm loathed most, was dropped in, to give the city a morality lesson via preview of what may await violators in the afterlife.

Shomotta was pitted against a Perzi renegade, a coastal highwayman who preyed on unguarded travelers. Although the fight was billed as brothers fighting over a woman, Shomotta ignored the theatrics. With such recent news confirming the Perzi slaughter of his holy order, he considered slaying an evil man cut from his enemy's cloth as an indulgence due neither contemplation nor doubt.

Both fights were extremely straightforward, much to the crowd's dismay. Hours to decorate the arena as a flaming pit and Malcolm slew the rapist in nearly as little time as it took the orator to introduce the match. Sure the rapist, armed only with a dagger, ran from his pursuing demon, but Malcolm cared not for the chase. Once he had ran the condemned out from cover and into a straightaway, the half-orc simply hurled the trident, in the manner of his renowned spear throwing abilities, killing the rapist on impact. The crowd chanted and pleaded for Malcolm to mutilate the corpse, but though dressed as a demon, he was ever a good man, a hero. The villain slain, the battle won, justice was done and so, for Malcolm, the encounter had ended.

Next, platforms were set-up all around the arena, along with various ropes and scaffolding to cross between them. Lowering a slave girl, touted as a "desert princess," onto the central platform, three monstrous lizards prowled beneath. The announcer called them "dragons." They were not.

The orator instructed each man to "rescue" the princess as they were dropped into the fray at opposite ends of the elaborate display. At the outset, as the renegade sprang forward, Shomotta waited. To the audience, he appeared to be praying. In fact, he cast a spell.

To his wizard's sight and to him alone, the safest, if not the most direct, route to the central platform became apparent. As the renegade powered through, frenzied, taking risks, setbacks, nearly falling a dozen times, Shomotta wandered through almost casually. He also watched his opponent, careful not to get too far ahead of him.

As the renegade crossed a one-rope bridge, to get to the central platform, Shomotta again cast a spell. One that provided for a momentarily enormous burst of strength and speed. At this point, his platform was much closer to the central one. So he rushed forward, leaping, landing, rolling across the central platform, and passing by the pseudo-princess in a single acrobatic push.

Springing up, crossing to his rival, Shomotta slashed. Barely a foot between them, the rope cut away, the Perzi renegade swung down, into the vicious maws of hungry creatures waiting below.

The people hooted and cheered, delighted by the man ripped apart, his flesh and bone alike consumed by the huge lizards. Almost unnoticed, Shomotta took the slave girl by the hand and escorted her back the way he came. There, Shomotta was bound in chains and removed from the arena.

Unknown to him, until much later that evening, once he had been secured and removed from the contest, the arena guards cruelly kicked the girl over the side. So that the crowd might enjoy the sight once more, she too was ripped to ribbons of red-pink ruination and herself consumed.

Alpona and Alchesus had been selected to fight together. In the story fabricated for their battle, they were billed as officers of the Imperial Navy, dispatched to hunt down and kill pirates. In truth, the Brigantine Bunch, a pirate family, had been slain by the actual navy, but some few of their crewmen had survived to be captured.

As the orator told it, however, the arena served as their island fortress. Alpona and Alchesus, having chased them across the sea, would disembark to hunt down these alleged leaders of the Brigantine Bunch.

They were given two bronze, medium-sized, round shields, diameters approximately the height and width of a grown man's torso, while a single gladius and trident were made available. Alchesus chose the three pronged spear for himself, leaving the short sword to Alpona. For armor, Alchesus secured a hide shirt, which looked to have been taken from some enormous lizard, with sandals, while Alpona wore a wide leather belt that protected most of his abdomen and flanks and a pair of boots. Their garb and equipment represented nautical and soldier themes, respectively.

The Brigantine Bunch, in truth five unnoteworthy pirates, all wore tattered silks. Their leader had been given a leather vest and fancy hat, both black but trimmed in white, to mark him out from the rest. The pirates dispersed themselves to make it harder to track them all at once.

Alpona and Alchesus were fielded together, into the midst of their ready opponents, from the eastern gate, or as the announcer claimed, "the brave sailors disembarked their vessel on the eastern shore, having discovered the pirates' lair."

The pirate leader wielded two sabers, while the men to his right and left each held only a single rapier. Another pirate swung a flail, a spiked ball hanging from a length of chain, while the last of them, the woman, had a saber like the leader. To his theatrical credit, the supposed pirate leader did point his sword at the gladiators and shouted monstrous obscenities at them.

"The way they've spread out," Alchesus noted, "I think they'll try to separate us."

"We fight together then," Alpona agreed.

They charged the pirate leader together. The leader swung one sword at Alchesus, who blocked with his shield. Alpona saw his chance, swinging his own sword, but the blow was parried. This pirate demonstrated some legitimate skill in fighting with two weapons. *It must have been why he was chosen as the leader.*

The pirate deflected Alpona's strike and, rebounding, came at Alchesus with his second saber in the same motion. It smacked near the top of the blocker's shield, tipping it, and allowing the first blocked saber to slide past. Deftly, Alchesus leaned back, avoiding the blow, and thrust his trident, counter-attacking his opponent. The pirate leader again impressed them, dodging the thrust and catching the shaft of the trident under his arm.

The pirate twisted, attempting to disarm Alchesus, but the Thalosian's grip was strong. Instead, he slung the pirate to the side, pulling his weapon free, and raised his shield just in time to block another blow. Even off kilter, the pirate pressed his attack. He even caught his footing in time to bring his free sword up behind Alchesus' shield, but was blocked by the shaft of the trident.

Another opponent ran in on Alpona, turning him away from the first fight. Alpona caught the first thrust against his shield, lashing out with his own sword in response and wounding the opponent in the ribs. Undaunted, the pirate struck against Alpona twice more: The first, an upward swing, which Alpona again took against the shield, and the second, a clumsy thrust, which the thane parried with his own sword.

Yet Alpona pressed his opponent, off balanced by the parry. With his left, Alpona slammed the shield into the fighter's face, stunning him, and with the right, without hesitation, he stabbed him in the throat.

Alchesus continued to trade strikes, blocks, and dodges with the pirate leader until he at last caught the pirate's leg with the barbs of his trident. With a twist of his waist, Alchesus tripped the opponent. The wounded pirate leader, untangled, began to roll away. Before Alchesus could pursue, however, yet another pirate charged at him.

This pirate was a female, supposed to represent the mother of the Brigantine Bunch pirate family. She was a big woman and, missing her sword thrust, simply tackled Alchesus, bowling him over and disarming him in the process. The Thelosian rolled over onto the pirate woman's saber, flat against the ground, trapping it beneath himself, and in the same motion, punched her in the face.

She released the sword, hit Alchesus back, and the two of them simply traded punches for a moment there on the ground. Alchesus looked, and felt, like he was getting the worst of it, so he rolled back, pulling himself out from under the pirate woman's legs. Freed, he arched his back, springing his bottom half up from the ground and grappling her about the neck with his legs.

Immediately, her hands went to pull him off of her. Even as she stood up, her struggle to break free was to no avail. As she opened her mouth, to bite him in a sensitive spot, he felt her hot breath upon him and flung his head and shoulders backward, toward the ground. The astonishing feat of strength and agility pulled the woman right off her feet, over his back, and sent her face first back into the ground. Alchesus himself landed on his back roughly, but with one roll right had his trident and with two rolls left, secured his shield.

Alpona defended him from the fourth pirate to have run into their melee. The pirate thrust his rapier down at Alchesus, but Alpona put his own shield to the ground to defend his ally. The pirate placed his free hand atop Alpona's shield, however, using it as a lever.

Bringing both his own legs off the ground, he tumbled onto Alpona's shield arm. The thane's arm buckled, his face went into the dirt, blinded to all the action and violence behind him.

Alchesus sprang to his feet but, as he turned to aid Alpona, the pirate leader, also standing, returned to continue their fight. Alpona, though seemingly defenseless, knew what he was doing. Sword and shield firmly in grasp, he began to roll. He could only discern enough to roll away, but reflexively he did so. Rolling would give him a few glances at the battlefield, remove him from the immediate threat, and give him half an instant to think. All more than he needed.

First, he saw the pirate who had toppled him. Sure enough, the rapier point thrust at the ground, would have been in Alpona's skull, if not for the roll. Next, he saw Alchesus and the pirate leader again squaring off. With his third roll, he saw two things, the flail wielder poised to strike at Alchesus' back and that he was about to roll into the pirate woman.

Alpona tucked on his fourth roll, putting a knee in the pirate woman's throat. Standing from the kneel and twisting himself as he did, Alpona hurled his shield like a discus. It spun in the air, barely arching, and surprisingly, even to Alpona, intercepted the flail strike, mid-swing. The length of chain bent at the shield's edge, the attached spiked ball knocked against the shield, and the knock unbalanced its wielder.

Incidentally, Alpona had stomped the face of the pirate woman. As he pushed off to run toward the flail-wielding pirate, his heel gave her jaw and neck an awkward jerk and her hand, about to grab his leg, immediately fell limp. Rushing forward, Alpona laughed as the flail pirate, still unbalanced but charging forward, tripped and tossed himself into the dirt.

Alpona continued forward. Arriving at the opponent, he punted the man's face as though it were some small errant pebble on a city street.

The pirate's body flopped over to his backside as a torrent of blood and teeth sprayed through the air. As Alpona turned around to assess his ally, Alchesus, and the ongoing fight with the pirate leader, he found, instead, the remaining rapier-wielding pirate charging at him. The blade, which might have pierced Alpona's chest had his back remained turned, instead went through his arm.

The pain was remarkable. Not simply a hole, clean through his bicep, but it rubbed the bone, slicing through meat as it stabbed inward and again as it withdrew from his flesh.

As the pirate withdrew his blade, Alpona sundered the man's hand with his own sword. The pirate uncontrollably dropped the rapier and, cradling his ruined hand with his whole one, opened his mouth, probably to beg for his life.

Horror on his face, the pirate's head tumbled from his shoulders without making a sound, as Alpona decapitated him in a single slice. The crowd roared, gasped, and roared again as a blow from a flail bashed against the back of Alpona's leg, slightly below the knee.

Alchesus and the pirate leader continued in pitched battle. The leader proved to be surprisingly adept. Yet, despite this, he had four holes in him and Alchesus, bruises and a little cut aside, had none.

Somewhere in the fight, and even he could not remember, Alchesus had lost his shield again and had taken to wielding the trident with two hands, defensively. He had rung the pirate's bell with the back end of the trident, only to catch a wild saber slash in the forks at the front of the weapon.

Again, Alchesus had underestimated his opponent. He thought him more stunned and swinging wildly. Yet, when the saber was locked within the trident's barbs, the pirate turned his wrist, the blade of his sword, levering Alchesus' weapon lower. The pirate leader brought his other saber against the trident, sundering it near where the forks attached to the wooden shaft.

This both notched the wood and moved the weapon even nearer to the ground. Alchesus shifted his weight and stance to raise his weapon once more. The pirate stepped on the notched shaft of the weapon, breaking off the forked trident. This left Alchesus with naught but a wooden staff.

Alchesus knew that they were both getting tired. The out and out fight was taking its toll. The pirate leader had some success with surprise ability and maneuvers, and Alchesus decided it was time to offer up a surprise of his own. He dropped the staff.

The pirate leader, righting his own body, balanced himself from forcing the fight so low, his swords again poised to strike. Unarmed, Alchesus grabbed both the pirate leader's wrists, one in each hand. He spread his opponent's arms wide, stepped in, and brought his own forehead crashing into the pirate's face. He did this again and again and again. Five blows, headbutts, until the pirate, his face a ruddy ruin, released his swords and fell limp.

Alpona turned to face his attacker, the flail pirate, near and about to strike again. As Alpona wheeled, he felt something tight, pulling in his leg.

Had the blow ruptured the muscle? Mayhap it was only a significant bruise or had the muscle been torn loose from the bone? Mayhap it was simply numb from the impact, but whatever was wrong, it left Alpona essentially crippled on the battlefield.

Sword still in hand, the thane parried the onslaught of blow after blow. He could not step in to press his attack as the flail had superior reach. Neither could he move right, or left, or back to draw his opponent in. Alpona, effectively immobile, remained alive by only his reading of the pirate's body position and own deft sword work, wrenching his wrist and elbow more and more with every strike.

But for how long?

A splinter – a long, thick splinter – explosively ruptured from the flail pirate's chest. His opponent ceased his barrage of attacks. Behind him, Alchesus stood, the broken shaft of his trident in hand, driven through the pirate's heart.

He released the staff. The last pirate collapsed to the ground. As Alchesus went to aid his wounded ally, they both heard it: The crowd, screaming and cheering as though they had all gone insane!

Chapter 62
Interesting Company

"But if the Prince comes, then so does he and he sent me here," Deerdra pleaded, "He is skilled too. I cannot hide from him."

"I thought you were very, very smart," the old, white maned man replied, sipping from his mug before and after the comment.

"I am smart ... smart enough not to be a fool. He will find me. Us."

"This man, this Caanaflit, is he really so bad?" the old man began to question her, pausing to scratch a bit of rust from the armored gorget around his neck before continuing, "Has he harmed you in some way? Been unfaithful to your wedding vows? Or are you mayhaps nervous after so long a separation? He rides with the Prince in the Light, aids him in his quests, surely he is not so terrible."

Deerdra glared at him and took a swig of her own drink. She was disappointed. This was supposed to be the storied Paladin Ulric Fortigurn, but for over a month, he had been little more than a drunken tour guide of the worst places in the Antori Capital.

Having swallowed her drink and thought her thoughts, she answered the aging warrior, "His loyalty is as strong as the situation requires it. I know what he is. I knew it then. I was fascinated, charmed, he is charming in his fashion. And no, he did not harm me, not in any way that we knew. I know who I am now, what I am, and knowing that, I cannot let him find me. I have responsibilities that superseded any oath to him."

"I do not disagree," Ulric acknowledged, continuing, "Would he truly demand you put aside your destiny for his sake? Is he such a man?"

With no pause between them this time, she replied with a cold certitude, "He most certainly is."

"Then the time is come. In the morning we leave for Avigueux and I will have you introduced to the courts, formally. We'll let him know that you are there, but there we can involve ourselves in the intrigues of the court and make all manner of shadows slide and move. Your intellect and their resources will hide us far better than the Holy Church can. I will ever remain with you and protect your person under the guise of a mercenary bodyguard."

Deerdra looked at him strangely.

"After all this time, all of a sudden, a plan."

"I've been planning," Ulric replied with mock offense, "I have made correspondence, all in undecipherable codes, of course, with my allies there."

"You have?" she challenged, continuing, "Because all I have seen you do is drink too much and drag me around to all the most distasteful cesspools this otherwise beautiful city has to offer."

"That was the old plan. Now we have a new plan."

"Wait, wait, what? That was the plan."

"You say you have submitted yourself to the wisdom of the Church," Ulric began to explain, "but you also confessed to still harbor feelings for this Caanaflit. This last month must have seemed all rather foolish to someone so smart, and you had every reason and opportunity to run off. You did not. That is to your credit."

"We've wasted a month so you could test me?"

"No. I've been testing you. You've been testing yourself. We've also spent a month getting lost in the city. If you up and vanished, and this Caanaflit is as good as they say, that is a red flag. He would then have cause to come looking for you. If you slowly fade from the city's memory, however, and we seep out of the city, along with the filth of any other cesspool, there is no alarm and no clear point of departure from which to begin a search."

For the second time this year, Deerdra felt like an idiot. This was neither a feeling to which she was accustomed nor did she wish to become so.

"So you've been learning me while the city forgets me?"

"Tis a rather perfect way to put it," Ulric accepted, then drank.

"Well," she took two large swallows from her mug before continuing, "now I want to know more about you."

"I was an Antori Witch-Hunter. Then I got old. I lost my hand and the Church retired me. I had briefly taken up monastic life. T'was expected. It did not suit me. I went on a quest for a relic from the forgotten times, the Sunstone, and I did not find it. Though the priest who helped me with my research had become a D'Tor of Vandor by the time I had returned. So rather than go back to the monastery in disgrace, he put me to work as his eyes and ears among the common places in the city. Those places where propriety prevented him from frequenting."

"So I had you right then," Deerdra remarked.

"Ha, ha! Is that so, little lady?" Ulric, amused, asked.

"You are more interested in being interesting than holy."

"That is true, but for all my life, being holy has given me the opportunity to be interesting. So I persist in my virtue and duties."

"So, despite your crass and grim demeanor, you are a good man?" Deerdra asked plainly.

"I am a Paladin. I am beyond reproach. I'll die before harm would come to you. By tradition I swear it. I made my oath to the D'Tor and to the Holy Family, and by my oaths I live until I live no more."

"So you say it," she quipped.

"I say it. By Van and Din the whole church says it," Sir Ulric Fortigurn affirmed; a sound that resonated with her soul.

"We say it," Deerdra accepted, sealing his oath and prayer in good faith.

Chapter 63
Converging Plots

Caanaflit, frequenting the various places where he would drum up business, when what to his unsuspecting eyes should appear, but the swirl of blue cloaks, Morralish soldiers in Napua, drew near.

"Sirs," Caanaflit called, standing and approaching them, "brave sons of the mountains, what brings you to fair Napua? Wine mayhap? Or women?"

"We are paladins," one of them said, and Caanaflit thought mayhap the man was going to leave it at that, before the grim-faced paladin continued, "Acquiring supplies for our new garrison, we need a lot. If you're selling wine, we'll take some moderate amount. We'll not have your slave whores, and do not offer them to us again. We are also looking for fair deals on mass quantities of cheeses, nuts, unleavened bread, pickled fish, and other stored goods, if you might point us in the right direction, good man."

"I can get you a great deal on barrels of olives, I know a guy. You'll have to pay someone to pickle your fish; people here just sort of catch what they need and can sell fast around here, tis not really an export."

"We'll take some wine and olives at fair price. How much can you provide?"

"My friend, so blunt," Caanaflit said, laughing, "you really don't have the tongue for this sort of work. If you would come back to my rooms, and speak with me privately, I can likely barter all your needs on your behalf. Save you some money and make some for myself besides."

The paladins stepped away three paces and whispered, consulting one another. Caanaflit pretended not to listen.

"You called us 'sons of the mountain.' We don't get a lot of that around here. What was that about?" the heretofore silent paladin asked, holding his hand aloft and muttering his incantation thereafter.

"Oh that won't work on me," Caanaflit said, smugly, "Bigger and better have tired. Other sons of the mountains, men I call friend and ally. Again, I would be glad to speak with you further … in private."

The paladins looked to each other again, facial affects confirming Caanaflit unreadable. They both shrugged their shoulders, giving the greatswords upon their backs a reassuring jostle.

"Lead the way."

A short journey to Caanaflit's private quarters, the day had only begun.

"You are Morralish Paladin's then?" Caanaflit asked, "Third Regiment, Stone Proud?"

One looked to his regimental emblem on his shoulder, the other spoke, correcting, "Stone's Pryde, yes."

"Yes, yes," Caanaflit agreed, "I actually knew that, I merely wanted to see if you'd correct me. So we are all friends here, or we should be, allies for certain. I am a Thane of your Throne-Lord, His Majesty, Prince Bengallen, Prince in the Light."

Caanaflit had hoped for smiles and playful slaps to the arm, instead, their scowls deepened.

The one that did most of the talking spoke again, "So you are confident in our identities, but how are we to be so in your's?"

"Prudent," Caanaflit remarked with genuine admiration, "I am without anything to confirm my story. I am now on a secret assignment for His Majesty, but when last I visited the Stone's Pryde, on His Majesty's behalf, my very formal documents of introduction were well ignored anyway. I have knowledge, but I doubt you know much about the Prince personally. I've met another of your Paladin Order, the Chieftain of the MacRoberts clan and leader of the Forest Phantoms. If any of that means anything to you."

"It means a great deal," the paladin replied, "Either you are this Caanaflit character I've heard about or you are quite the excellent spy."

Caanaflit allowed his eyes to light and joy to climb across his face, saying, "Yes! Yes, I am Caanaflit and also an excellent spy, but, again, ally and friend to the good mountain folk!"

"So it would seem," the paladin accepted, but not without suspicion, "what is it you can do for us?"

"A lot," Caanaflit answered simply, elaborating, "much and more. You merely seek to supply your garrison, and that I can do. For far less than you are prepared to pay too, I assure you. Yet, I am about His Majesty's business here, and I think we can help each other to mutual benefit. As a show of trust, I will tell you trust-worthy paladins what I am at here. If you believe me and deem it worthy cause, then we shall work together. If not, then we keep each others' confidence and return to our independent endeavors. Fair?"

"Verily so," the paladin answered, softening his demeanor, "We shall hear you."

Caanaflit poured each of them a cup of wine.

"So here is my plan..."

Chapter 64
Gladiating Malaise

The other thanes of Prince Bengallen in Napua continued to endure their burden as gladiators. As they each man recovered from his respective injuries, he fought other battles, new injuries, more recovery. Clearing out the prisons of all deemed worthy of execution ad gladium, their bodies had survived, but theirs had become a burden of conscience.

They began to worry. Mayhap not all those pitted against them were deserved of the death penalty or, worse still, some were possibly innocent altogether. By their own hands or another's, however, their opponents were sentenced by the city of Napua, by the rule of the Imperium, if there was fault or guilt, it lay with the foreign government around them — or so increasingly reassured each other.

Had it only been one or two, these men of violence could have accepted that justification easily, but as each man's body count in the arena climbed, each wrestled, in his own way, with the spectre of doubt that grew in his mind. No man was ready to abandon the others, but it was only each other and their mutual agreement to this course of action that kept any one of them from executing a bloody escape.

Of the five who had begun training with them, only Alchesus remained. One died in training and the others had fallen in the arena, bested by criminals who themselves only ever won a day's reprieve, to be slain by Malcolm, Alpona, or Shomotta with each new tomorrow. Yet the tomorrows had become not so unlike the yesterdays to them. Each victory tasted only of ashes.

This was, of course, exacerbated by their treatment. So skilled and willing, they mostly avoided the lash, but they lived under the constant threat of it. They lived very little, for they had no lives except to train. Most days, after sundown, their time was their own, but what of it? In the pen or in their cells, there was little talk and much sleep.

Their days were hard, and they were always tired. Yet their muscles grew and reflexes sharpened. For as awful as the whole ordeal genuinely was, these mighty men had become only all the mightier for it.

Yet their behaviors, or lack thereof, baffled the lanista and the doki. Small coin was awarded for victory, a sum more for a good showing, but they made no use of it. Slave whores were brought to them, a few coins for an evening's

277

companionship, and they were always declined. As often as they could afford, they would pay for better food, especially meat, or some wine, but they even ceased to seek the comfort of wine in those last days.

They were the strangest gladiators Cerro Darisi had ever seen. He did not like them. He did not trust them. He distanced himself from the business. Eventually, they stopped seeing him altogether and all decrees, battles, and other matters came to be handled via the doki alone.

Yet they were victors all. They had the skill of champions. Men of their kind were in short supply. They were willing enough to fight and, with no alternative, he apparently remained willing to put them to contest. Until at last it came, thee contest, the one they had all been waiting for.

Illwarr the Manslayer had not slain a man for a long time. They gave the criminals over to these new gladiators, and the crowd had grown bored of watching the monster eviscerate animals. These new gladiators had established themselves well. It was the perfect time, as such things go, for the local magistrate to sponsor games honoring the nobles of the city.

In truth, the magistrate had decided that he could stand having a monster as his city's champion no longer. He had seen these men fight and believed that together they might slay the horror. So he went to his four wealthiest friends and had them pay to have each of the four gladiators named after one of their families in the coming battle.

Not only would he be rid of this loathsome and embarrassing Illwarr, but whichever gladiators survived would bring great honor to the noble house for which they would be named. Thus great favor from said houses would come to the magistrate who had made the opportunity available.

Regardless of its reasons, the final contest was upon the thanes and they were more than ready for it.

Chapter 65
Recruiting Loyalists

The Mountain Spring was a large drinking establishment on the northeastern wall within the Imperium's capital city of Antoria Royal. It was bedecked in all manner of Morralish themes and samples of the culture and life of the Van-blessed mountain folk. While it may have begun as a folly, a pretentious kitsch for the locals, two decades ago, the Expeditionary Forces had, over that time, re-made it into a place of their own. It thrived. It had expanded greatly and had a bunkhouse out back that was practically a barracks.

Nearly every Morralish soldier, top to bottom, came here when they took leave to the city, and the common soldiers, who could not afford finer accommodations, kept the bunkhouse full most of the year. It was no exception the night that the Lord-General Strein Hrothmond and his daughter, the priestess, Sister Bethany, arrived.

"The Antori have a term for that, m'lord," the Morralish sergeant said, "They call it a Fifth Column."

"People who would betray the local good for that of the Imperium?" General Hrothmond sought clarity.

"People," the soldier clarified, "who would fight against their own to curry favor with another. Like if there were a rebellion on, those within the rebel controlled city, who would act on behalf of the Imperium rather than the rebels."

"This isn't exactly the same," Sister Bethany interjected, "You said 'their own' but who is that? Should the slaves of the Imperium consider their masters 'their own' kind? Should men and women descended from the mountain folk, resettled within the Antori Imperium, consider the Imperator and his legions 'their own' when they would misuse, abandon, and neglect the sons and daughters of the mountains?"

"Call it a Sixth Column, then," General Hrothmond concluded, "Frankly, I care little, but you see what we are after."

"Is a mighty gamble, m'lord," the sergeant considered, "Not your aims, but seeking this sort of aid. All it takes is one person, only one, who might betray the Imperium, yet chooses to remain loyal to them. If he gives word to a constable or a magistrate, wouldn't just jeopardize your fifth – and sixth –

columns now would it? They could have a dozen legions tightening nooses around twelve Morralish units, far afield, those most isolated from the reinforcement of their superior regiments, before the week's end."

"He is not wrong," Bethany agreed.

"Tis a chance we need to take," Hrothmond insisted, "We have a moral imperative. If we are withdrawing from the Imperium, there will be panic, confusion, unlike Uhratt has seen since the Great Cataclysm. The slaves will suffer unduly. We have to give them the chance to rise up. They will need help, more than the military can provide. I know our former countrymen are sympathetic to the plight of the slave; it cannot sit well with them. Moreover, we have soldiers, officers specifically, who will have been tempted by the Imperial Senate's decree. Leaving might not be enough to sway them, not now. Yet if we remind them of what Morralish is, what we stand for, by giving the slaves a chance of their freedom, then we may win them back."

"He's not wrong, either," the sergeant spoke to the priestess, echoing her own words, "that's why I brought a friend."

The Morralish sergeant motioned to his right as the old greybeard turned around to face them, offering, "I am Senator Macrobius. I have left the senate for what it has become. I am myself of Morralish descent and am prepared to leave the Imperium, for the same, if there is a place for me among my fore-father's people."

"If you can help us reach out to like-minded people," General Hrothmond stated, "you'll find a place of honor among us."

Before anyone else could respond, the front doors of the Mountain Spring flew open and praetorian legionnaires began piling in. One of them decreed, "Strein Hrothmond, you are under arrest for treason against the King of Morralish, breaking the Imperator's Peace, murder, conspiracy, and terrorism against the Imperium! No mercy shall be shown to those who aid this man!"

General Hrothmond pushed Bethany into the sergeant and stood, walking toward the praetorians, legionnaires assigned to the Capital's defense. Macrobius took the priestess and the sergeant by the hands and pulled them through the disturbed crowd, in the opposite of everyone else's attention.

"I am unarmed," Hrothmond explained, "I was simply enjoying the company of my countrymen before I faced my return to prison. While I've only ever served the Holy Family and my King, I know that doesn't count for much in the Imperium any more."

"Silence, dog! On your knees."

Strein Hrothmond looked around, the confused faces of his countrymen and the determination of the approaching praetorians, wading through them. The sight told him that this was the right path. So he did not take up a silence as he knelt, "I got what I wanted. No sense in denying you. Bear witness, brothers, Antori justice and the hand of the Imperator's Pea—"

Flogged with a club over the top of his head, Strein Hrothmond's voice was cut short. Pummeled so, collapsed to the floor, blood gushing from his mouth, one had to wonder if his life had not been cut short as well.

"What is this!?"

"What did he do!?"

Demanding shouts were joined with derisive, antagonistic comments, choice expletives, and cries of "No! No!"

"Swords!" the centurion called to his praetorians, who readily followed his command, pulling gladius blades from scabbards at their hips.

They drug Strein Hrothmond's limp body from the Mountain Spring, a pair towed him and ten surrounded him, a dozen legionnaires with swords drawn. The mountain folk did not attack, but the event had visibly upset them.

Many were the men who knew the name Strein Hrothmond, knew him to be as fine a lord and leader than any had ever been. A fair, brave, and honest man with a good name should not be treated so.

For swords to be pulled on them all, even as not a single man among them did a thing to stop it, compounded the insult. It was disgusting and they had allowed it. Dismayed, it felt as though the Imperium had spat on all the mountain folk and not for the first time.

It would be on every soldiers' tongue or in his ear before the dawn.

Chapter 66
Feasting Thanes

There were two nights between them and their coming battle with Illwarr the Manslayer. So they at last decided to spend all that small coin of victory on some celebration. They deserved it. These might be their last nights, and though they would need to sleep with clear heads tomorrow, every man should have the right to make merry and drink drink before he faces his death.

They hired three women, but dressed and treated them like proper ladies. Malcolm abstained from companionship, but served as host. A table and feast were brought before them, even a wine porter and serving boy to attend their enjoyment of the meal.

The thick and savory smell of roasted meat was in the air. The bitter and sweet tastes of brewed beverages clung to lips and breath. At the beginning of the evening, the attendees constrained themselves, all playing the game of courtly behaviors. Malcolm saluted each man's bravery, recounting each one's deeds.

Things devolved soon after. Not terribly, but this was life, what little might be left of it, and none of them had lived it so well for quite some time. The underfed slave whores could only play at being ladies for so long. With so much food enticing them and drink severing ties with inhibition, polite behavior gave way to hungers. The mighty men followed suit.

It was as though they had all forgotten themselves. Not in this moment explicitly, but in the days passed. Slave and thane alike had come to think of themselves as the roles they were playing. Yet, as Malcolm recounted each man's story, they began to remember who they truly were.

Alpona's study of the ancient and secret Zil-jahi fighting arts, his survival on a deserted island, and his wielding Flammerung against Starspawn and Orc Chieftain alike had been an inspiration to Malcolm. Shomotta's study of arcane and divine mysteries, his journey across many lands and peoples, and his unique ability to lend eldritch might to their causes, enhancing weapons, calling lightning, and teleporting them behind enemy lines, had made the impossible possible before Malcolm's very own eyes.

Even Alchesus' was hailed for serving with the Southlanders in the pursuit of freedom and facing a hard life, choosing to survive, to fight, to dream of freedom ever still. These were things that Malcolm could relate to, more than ever amid their current plight. So he was honored as well. Being treated, fed, and doted on so well and proper and being in the company of such storied men, gave the slave women a sense of worth too, a thing long absent from their wretched lives.

Slowly, but surely, the feast continued to take on qualities more base and natural, a vigorously celebratory tone, nonetheless. So Malcolm, having eaten and participated to his limit, excused himself. Not so long thereafter, however, Shomotta came and found him. Wordless, he entered Malcolm's cell and sat with him.

Malcolm spoke first, sitting on his crude slab of a bed, "You should enjoy yourself."

"So should you."

"I did, as your host, and now my mind is elsewhere."

"Is this not how orcs might get on in such times?" the wizard-priest asked, leaning his back against the wall and lazily sliding down to sit on the floor.

"Tis," Malcolm agreed, "That might be part of the problem, but there is more. Tis simply — not what I want."

"Mind? Ha!" Shomotta playfully scoffed, "Heart! Your heart is elsewhere. The knight woman, she carries Prince Bengallen's flag, you have traded affection … and now?"

"We had, I – I …" Malcolm trailed off.

Shomotta smiled and closed his eyes, offering, "Say no more. Love, I can see it now. You are beautiful to each other in ways no one else can understand. It is right that you forgo the loins of another, in favor of the memory of her's."

Malcolm gulped and replied, "The sentiment is appreciated, but I'd rather you not discuss her loins."

Shomotta opened his eyes, laughing again, "So strange. Men can buy whores, total or for the night, and no one finds shame in it, but even hint at sex with a loved one and all is taboo."

"First," Malcolm disagreed, "I would find shame in buying and selling whores. Tonight's exception being that we were buying friends, who simply happen to be whores."

"Now you sound like Caanaflit."

"Second," Malcolm grumbled, ignoring the comparison, "Emotions and intimacy are private matters between loved ones."

"Whatever the relationship?" Shomotta asked, challenging.

Malcolm considered a moment, "I suppose."

"Are we not loved ones?" the wizard-priest asked, moving forward, onto his feet, closer to his fellow thane, but remaining low, squat, at eye level, continuing, "Can you not share words of your love for this woman with me? Can I not think about it and be happy for you, for both of you? That in the midst of so much violence and tragedy, you could find beauty and hope. Do you love me so little that I cannot be entrusted with the knowledge of your greater loves?"

Malcolm looked clearly uncomfortable.

Despite the implication of his body language, however, accepting words parted his lips, "I never really thought about it that way. I suppose I do bear some love for you – for many of my Prince's thanes and warriors – but I never thought of it as love before. So you think this love, brotherly love, means I should share word of my other love with you?"

"Yes," Shomotta answered emphatically, "As I love you a little, it makes me happy to know someone loves you a lot. Among the Hazar people, my people, we share these things with those we care about. We care that they are being cared for and have someone to care for. Not every physical detail of any sensual liaison, no, but that they are having them, that they are good, that they have helped one or all persons grow, if not in intimacy with each other, at least in intimacy with oneself. Yes, I want to know that my loved ones are being well loved."

"Tis an interesting perspective," Malcolm admitted.

"To confess, however," Shomotta amended, "I have noticed how this is not the custom here and have done poorly at modeling the way of the desert to you men of grass and mountain in this regard."

"Yet you push me now," Malcolm noted.

"You reminded me of who I am tonight," Shomotta continued, "with your kind words. I can never thank you enough for that. Then you departed. The true me, awakened, saw the opportunity and that is what you should know about me, Malcolm; I am not one to pass by opportunities. I thirst to experience life, in all its kinds and ways. I have had sex with pretty whores.

284

The Marzi Temple retained some of the most beautiful women in the world to service the priests. I have consumed my share of food and drink, though it sometimes amuses me to have more. What I am really after, ever searching, are new experiences. I have never talked about love with an orc. I have never shared this kind of intimacy with you. You are my friend, Malcolm, now that we have spoken of private things, know that you can call upon me anytime."

"Right," Malcolm said, not knowing what else to say, "Thank you, Shomotta."

"You are most welcome, indeed," the wizard-priest accepted, standing up from his haunches and turning to leave.

"Wait," Malcolm interjected, having thought a moment, "The Temple of Saint Amar supplied prostitutes to the priests?"

"Well, no," Shomotta stopped, turned back, and leaned against the narrow doorway, beginning to explain, "The Marzi worshiped whom you call Saint Amar as a god in his own right. Amar, the divine entity, the ascended warrior-mystic, is recognized as a saint in the Holy Family church. Their stories tell that he supported them in the war with the old gods. As the direct worship of Amar is small and we do not proselytize converts, the Holy Family church, specifically the Cathedral of Din in Antoria Royal, allows us to continue in our ancient traditions, unaltered by the Church."

"To include ..." Malcolm prompted.

"To include the initiation of poor, attractive, uneducated virgins into somohumrado, roughly translated 'wives of the temple.' Their sexual availability and domestic skills allow the priests to focus on spiritual pursuits. They even aid in some. It is hard to explain, but it is a great honor to be chosen. It is a better life than most of the women chosen could eve–"

Shomotta's difficult explanation was cut short by a nearly naked Alpona appearing in the doorway behind him.

Towel clutched to waist, panting, he explained, "The girls – they know – many slaves – know – Caanaflit – that sneaky – Caanaflit ..."

Shomotta stood up, demanding, "The hell are you saying?"

Malcolm stood and countered, demanding, "Catch your breath. Make sense!"

Alpona cursed himself under his breath. He grew weaker and sicker all the time even as his fellow thanes were stronger than ever. He knew the wine did not help.

Yet there were times when he could not help himself. It made the pain go away.

At last, he caught his breath enough to continue, "There is supposed to be a signal. 'After the death of Illwarr, you'll know it when you see it,' is what they're all saying. The slaves here are ready to rebel. All, they're all waiting to rise up and all they are waiting on is, well, us."

" 'Caanaflit, that sneaky Caanaflit,' indeed," Malcolm echoed, elbowing Shomotta playfully.

"Well," Alpona began, awkwardly, "I had to tell you, but, now, er, uh, I, uh, gotta go, you know …"

"No, I don't know," Malcolm lied, grinning ear-to-ear, looking to Shomotta, "Mayhap you should stay for a while and tell us all about it."

Shomotta sighed whimsically, clasping Malcolm on the shoulder before leaving the cell.

"He's not serious?" Alpona asked Shomotta as he passed by, then turned to Malcolm, "You're not?"

"No. Go! Go now," Malcolm insisted, laughing and gesturing at Alpona's near nudity, "Get – all of that – out of here."

So that night it was love that saved them. Each one had been on the brink of his own darker depths. Yet each man fell to slumber with the easy comfort that comes from accepting yourself and any love that comes to your heart.

Malcolm's love for Roselle, alive in its long silence, broken, at last allowed to breathe in words. Shomotta's love for new experiences, finding them again all around him. Alpona's love for life, onto which he grappled quite vigorously that particular night. Wherever he could find it, each man felt love, and brushed his burdens aside.

Chapter 67
Whispering Secrets

That night, Sister Bethany, on the other hand, was plagued with nightmares. She heard herself, over and over again, warning her father, "I agree with Lord Harkon, father, you really shouldn't be doing these meetings personally."

Yet each time he gave her the same reply, "How else can they trust the offer, if not from me?"

Still fully dark, she awoke. The dark moon had completely eclipsed the bright one, as happened a couple of nights every month, and morning had not yet broken. She turned over, said a brief prayer for her father, and tried to return to slumber.

Succeeding, her dreams chose a different scene for her torment. Her father bravely faced his arrest, pushing her aside, as others spirited her away. They had so recently come to know freedom once more, but he again faced imprisonment or worse.

"It was not a new idea," Senator Macrobius spoke into Sister Bethany's room.

"I'm sorry," she replied, drowsily.

"No," he said, "I am. I heard you stirring. I thought you awake. I wanted to talk to you."

"Come in then, I am covered."

The old senator entered her room. His room that he had provided to her more accurately.

Sitting in a chair across from the bedside, he continued, "It was not a new idea, to lead the slaves in revolt. There are Antori citizens, some Morralish descendants, mostly not, just people who cannot abide slavery, who believe it goes against the example of the Holy Family. There was a plan, on some sixteen or seventeen years ago now, to free the slaves in a civil war. The leaders were found out, rounded up, given over to death, public and gruesome, in the Grand Arena as slaves themselves. That talk has grown quiet, but not altogether silenced. Those men became symbols, especially the ones that did not die right away. Who fought and other gladiators laid down arms before them, refused to fight their would-be liberators. There are still

287

whispers and those that do the whispering now know, all too well, whom they can and cannot trust."

"There is already a Fifth Column," Bethany realized.

"Not that we thought of ourselves as such," Macrobius amended, "but to your aims, we could be. There is a spider's web cast among the shadows of the Imperium. Gossamer threads of light, reaching out to one another, connected even amid the darkness. We are waiting for the right time, conditions, to act. If we rise up now, will the Morralish soldiers join us in the cause for freedom? Will they stay and fight with us or will they use us and our slaughter as a mere distraction for their own departure?"

Sister Bethany could not answer. She had held like concerns of her own. She knew her father would fight for the slaves. She knew others would. She wanted to believe that Lord Harkon would, that Prince Bengallen would — if he might arrive in time. Yet she was a priestess and only a Morralish General could answer that question. Whether his answer be truth or lie, only such a man had that authority.

"I cannot say with authority," she admitted, "but I believe they will. I believe in them. I believe in Morralish. I believe that the Holy Family moves hearts and souls, that their divine love fills us and, overflown, we are compelled to share that love."

"Love at the end of a spear?" Macrobius asked.

"Love for a slave is to see his bonds cast off," Bethany answered, "If one stands in the way of love — well, men ought to know better than to stand in the way of love."

"So you say," the old senator smiled, " and so they should."

"Is there any way to free my father?"

"There may be."

"If you will promise to see about freeing him," Bethany requested, making it a bargain, "I will see about a proper alliance between the regiments of the Morralish Loyalists and your – does your movement have a name?"

"All either of us can do is commit to try. If you can agree to that, then I can agree to that," Macrobius agreed, adding, "and there are those who have called us 'bakers and likeness makers.' If you need to call us something, you can call us that.

Chapter 68
Battling Monster

In Napua, three thanes of Prince Bengallen Hastenfarish, under the guise of gladiators, entered the arena. They entered as men, to slay a monster, to become champions, legends, freemen conquering bondage, a sign, a symbol to the slaves of Napua, to all the slaves in all the world, that a men can rise up against their masters.

They would be as steel struck upon flint. From the spark thus issued, flames of freedom. An insurrection across the whole of an empire, a brightly burning signal fire to the wayward soldiers of Morralish, that they might carry freedom's torch into their homeland as well.

The formal arena contest was to be conducted in the ancient tradition of ancestor worship. Although, under the light of the Holy Family, they no longer called it that. Each of the four gladiators would be given the name of a noble family of Napua and one of its prominent ancestors. In this way, the affected believed, the spirit of the ancestor fought with the gladiator, adding to the spirit's glory and that of his house, even after death.

In truth, it was an excuse for nobles to flaunt wealth while vying for the naming rights. Ultimately, so that they could win the favor of peers, merchants, and the common folk alike, if their proxy won his fight.

Illwarr had slain too many men, even two at a time. The city had endured a monster as its champion for far too long and so four were chosen. To the people of Napua they were the gladiators of Cerro Derisi and they were the only surviving fighters of note.

Though each man was told the noble house he would represent, so much disdain for the fights had grown in them, at this point, none bothered to remember or care. Thus those names can no longer be recounted. Suffice to say that, regardless of anyone else's schemes or reasons, these men were at last sent into the arena of their own volition and for their own purpose.

The monstrous gray creature, thick of hide and twice as tall as Shomotta or Alchesus, had a clipped, smashed nose, like a pig's snout, and feral eyes like a wolf. Illwarr had taken to being armored with iron bracers and a collar, wrists and neck his only obvious vulnerabilities.

Released, Illwarr charged at his enemies, sent out together from the opposing east gate, like an enraged bull. He had developed a love for killing, the roar of the crowd, and a taste for man-flesh. The latter of which he had recently been denied for a time.

Malcolm and Alpona dodged to the left, Shomotta and Alchesus to the right. All cleared the path, but as Illwarr passed them, he swung his mighty arms wide, knocking Alpona on the back of the head. As the others put distance, Alpona flopped to the ground, body sprawled. Illwarr, noticing this, twisted about, and stepping forward, reaching down for the grounded warrior.

Malcolm was on it. Each gladiator had been given a spear, an Antori gladius sword, and a round shield nearly three-feet in diameter.

Malcolm, running back toward Alpona, tossed his spear with the expert precision for which he was known. Releasing the spear, his hand continued forward, drawing sword from belt in the same motion. The spear landed on the back of Illwarr's grasping hand and pierced it. First blood and it had stopped short the creature's snatch for Alpona.

Shield forward, Malcolm ran upon his friend, leaped over his body, and came at Illwarr as fiercely as the creature had come against them. At distance, right as Illwarr began to raise his hand, Malcolm jumped again. The spear lodged therein was at an odd angle to the ground, neither perpendicular nor parallel. It was perfect.

Shield first, Malcolm's momentum slammed into the butt of the spear, driving it further into Illwarr's hand, pushing it clean through, sprouting out from his palm. The creature, stunned in pain for the barest instant and with so brave an assailant unchecked in proximity, lost two fingers to a swift slice from Malcolm's gladius sword, as the thane stepped back to aid his friend.

Shomotta and Alchesus responded in kind. Both turned and let their spears fly, striking Illwarr in the hip and thigh, respectively, the same instant as Malcolm took his fingers. The creature thrashed and frothed with rage.

Malcolm could not immediately roust Alpona, but it did not matter at that moment. As Malcolm was between them, Illwarr ignored the unconscious Zil-jahi warrior in favor of the slashing half-orc. Malcolm feigned a move left, confirmed the creature's focus, and bolted right. Illwarr, stutter-stepped and pursued.

Also ignored, Shomotta and Alchesus rushed in behind. Alchesus, grabbing Alpona, pulled him clear. Shomotta, increasing his speed briefly with magic, replayed Malcolm's tactic.

Shield first, he threw his hastened body into the spear in Illwarr's thigh, pushing it clean through. This hobbled the creature, who stopped in his tracks, allowing Malcolm to put more distance between the two of them.

Illwarr howled in pain and impotent rage. He had never faced warriors such as these. Their strength – or their weapons – more easily penetrated his naturally armored flesh. Immediately, as though deciding to take a break, Illwarr began to remove the two spears that fully penetrated him.

Looking at the spearhead in his hand, he saw something odd. An ordinary iron spearhead, as ordinary a spear as they had sent anyone into the arena with, but the whole thing, point and shaft, had been encased in some clear, thin layer. To Illwarr, it looked like glass. Magically crystallized sand, in fact, the technical difference minimal, but not inconsequential.

He had to pull each spear all the way though his body as the magical encasement prevented him from snapping them short. He embraced the pain, however, emboldened to maintain his titles, Manslayer, Champion, more than ever.

Illwarr looked left, he looked right, but suddenly, he did not see anyone. No opponents in the arena and no spectators in the crowd. Turning again, he saw it, the pallid mask, the face of the only man he believed could kill him. In a panic, Illwarr threw both spears at it, but they passed through, harmlessly, as the mask came at him. In the last moment, Illwarr hunkered down, cowering, arms raised to face, to defend against whatever attack was coming.

The crowd saw something other. The crowd saw Shomotta aiding Alpona, but it was a pretense to disguise the casting of a spell. The crowd saw Malcolm and Alchesus regroup and make a run, side by side, swords over head, at Illwarr. The crowd saw, from their perspective, Illwarr miss them terribly with those thrown spears and, afterwards, something they never thought to see. As only Illwarr saw the illusion of the pallid mask, it appeared to the crowd that the Manslayer cowered before the two charging warriors.

When each of their magically encased short swords crashed down upon the creature, Malcolm finished off Illwarr's maimed hand and Alchesus flayed a long strip of flesh from the creature's opposite forearm. With that, the spell was broken and Illwarr again flung his arms outward, landing another knock to an opponent's head.

This time, his metal bracer smacked Alchesus flat in the face. The Thalosian warrior went down, cold, even as Alpona finally came to.

Illwarr put all this weight on his good leg, leaping toward the grounded Alchesus. The monster stomped the man, once, twice, thrice with blinding speed and ferocity before aid arrived. At once, Malcolm slashed at the creature's good leg with his gladius and Shomotta again ran upon him, driving the remaining spear, lodged in the creature's hip, through, deep into bowels and viscera.

Vomiting blood, Illwarr wheeled about, only to discover that Malcolm had cut something vital, and both his legs had been hobbled. Swinging at Malcolm and Shomotta, interchangeably, Illwarr had remained blind to Alpona's recovery and approach from behind. He had lost his spear and shield at the outset, but made use of his gladius and free hand.

Nearly a foot of spear still jutted from the creature's back and, arriving there, Alpona grasped it, hoisted himself up. He scurried up the creature and placed his foot on that same peg.

Illwarr bucked. He reacted to the man climbing his back. Severally wounded, however, it was too little, too late. Alpona had already gripped the iron collar around Illwarr's neck and, though he lost his footing as the creature thrashed, he easily regained it when the creature righted itself.

Both legs wounded, Illwarr nearly toppled himself jerking about. Balance restored, Alpona inverted the gladius in his grip as he hoisted himself further up, raising the blade above the creature's neck. With all his might, he drove the point downward, stabbing the tiny gap behind the lip of the collar, deep into the creature's meaty neck. So thick, the blade's tip barely exited the other side.

Leaving the blade stuck fast and releasing the collar, Alpona leaped off and ran toward his maimed ally. The collar slid up, pressing into the gladius' protruding hilt, twisting the embedded blade, and tearing Illwarr's flesh from within. This contortion bound the weapon within the creature's neck in such a fashion that it could not be pulled free.

Illwarr dropped to his knees, grasping in futility at his own back, unable to grasp the small sword impinged by the armored collar with the large taloned fingers of only a single hand. Shomotta kept his guard up, carefully watching the dying creature flail, as Malcolm too went to Alchesus.

It was only in that moment, needing aid for their friend so badly, that they remembered the crowd. The crowd was stone sober and dead silent. They were completely awestruck with how handedly these relatively new gladiators had broken the greatest terror to ever reign in their arena.

Alpona called for help, it echoed. Malcolm called for help, it echoed. They both threw up the missio, the sign of submission, defeat, the plea for mercy. Alchesus was still breathing but they knew not for how long.

Shomotta kept watch on Illwarr, studying his eyes. When the creature heard the calls for aid his eyes snapped left, in their direction, and Shomotta alone knew there was at least one assault still left in the monster. The wizard-priest was ready.

As Illwarr turned, blood pouring from his mouth, Shomotta ran at him a third and final time. Upon the remaining bit of spear, no more than a foot sticking out above and behind Illwarr's hip, Shomotta performed the shield bash a third and final time. Pushing the spear full through, it burst forth from his abdomen, to the front of his opposite hip. The creature chortled, a hiccup-like sound, as it teetered towards Malcolm and Alpona.

Enough warning, Alpona snatched up Alchesus' gladius sword, allowing the monster's own toppling momentum to throw its face into the blade. Alerted, Malcolm also turned around, barely quick enough to see the death blow and pull Alchesus clear, just in case there was any more fight in the creature.

There was not.

Thus died Illwarr the Manslayer, Champion of Napua.

Chapter 69
Evolving Scheme

Alpona took Alchesus into his arms. Defensively flanked by Malcolm and Shomotta, the four ran back to the eastern gate.

The crowd went wild. Rabid-bat-spit-crazy, they screamed and hooted. Women tore their gowns, exposing their chests, men began to argue with each other over bets, and a mass hysteria descended on the arena.

The thanes were worried for Alchesus. They worried that their gate might not open. They worried that, for vanity's sake, they might have to wait out the crowd, for silence, so that the orator and their noble patrons might be heard and victory formally declared.

Yet, surprisingly enough, the gate lifted as they approached and they carried Alchesus through it without delay. Following the victory, the gladiators were ushered to their owner to be rewarded. They came into the arena's arms room and, turning the corner, one-by-one, saw Caanaflit.

He explained, "I re-acquired you awhile back after bankrupting Cerro – and his friends – purchased most of his assets, either directly or indirectly. But you had intended to kill Illwarr, and I didn't want to get in the way of that. Then, an opportunity fell in my lap, to get us into the Imperial Capital, an invitation for Illwarr, or the heroes that slay him, to compete in the Grand Arena. Much has changed. I've reported the military strength of Napua's civil and legionary defenses to Morralish Soldiers garrisoned north of here. They know who we are and actually believed me this time, Shomotta. They're going to invade Napua, aid the rebel slaves to withdraw back north to their encampment, but not before we are clear. The slaves that I have not purchased and freed already should all, by now, be aware of the military support en route or are near enough to someone who will know. If they aren't ready to rise against their masters when the time comes this evening, they never will be. The sooner we get out of here, the sooner it comes."

They all sort of blinked at him, dimly.

"Greetings, Caanaflit," Malcolm said, "good to see you."

"This is my friend," Alpona added, nodding to the bloodied man in his arms, "Alchesus."

"Indeed," Shomotta uncertainly acknowledge the moment.

The blue cloaked man with Caanaflit, apparently an officer in the Morralish army, had already approached Alpona, helping to lay Alchesus on the ground.

Caanaflit looked at the wounded man, asking, "Will he survive?"

The Morralish officer placed a hand on Alchesus forehead and another on his abdomen. He was a paladin and, as such, had studied the higher mysteries of the Church, gaining a modest ability to heal the human body through faith and force of will. His hands glowed briefly, faintly, and Alchesus stirred slightly.

"Someone need set his bones," the paladin answered, "but I've stopped his bleeding and stabilized his injuries. He should survive."

"Follow me," Caanaflit said, "I have secured a ship for us. They'll likely have someone on board that can be of further aid."

With no further hesitation, they all ran from the arena. The streets were abandoned in its vicinity. Caanaflit, via the rumor mill, had promised "an encore performance, a spectacle of violence to rival the felling of Illwarr" and so the crowd in the arena had remained there, ironically, eagerly awaiting more.

Though the promise would be fulfilled, it would not be what they had in mind. They would not be entertained.

Unhindered, the thanes made it to the edge of town, a cliff with various stairs cut into the face of it, for the climb down. A great deal of commerce came and went by sea, so the stairs were well maintained and made for easy passing. At the bottom, at sea level, the band shot across the stone port, out onto a wooden boardwalk, turning down a pier, and Caanaflit ushered them to embark upon a vessel of his choosing.

On board, Alpona immediately called for a medic. A dwarf woman of ruddy complexion came up from below decks to answer the call. As Alpona bent down to lay Alchesus upon the deck, the dwarf woman placed her hand on Alpona's shoulder and asked, "Can't say I'm fond of the bald look. Who are your new friends?"

Puzzled, the voice familiar to Alpona, he began to recognize more than the dwarven medic as she examined his wounded ally. As Alpona looked around himself, he almost felt dizzy. It was surreal. At last, he caught sight of

Caanaflit approaching the ship's captain and it all fit together. He saw Captain Lantilaus Weatherworn and recognized his ship, The Maiden's Folly.

The Captain blew a whistle. The ship uncoupled from the last of its moorage and kicked free from the dock. Alpona felt the sway transfer through him while Malcolm and Shomotta, being unaccustomed to ship travel, stumbled. Each had to catch themselves on the bow rail. At the same command, three archers in the crow's nests fired flaming arrows back toward the boardwalk.

It must have been treated with something. When the first of the arrows hit, flames spread all up and down the port, crawling down each pier. Watching, Caanaflit and Captain Weatherworn paused only to shake hands in congratulations. The smoke and flames crawled higher and higher as the Maiden's Folly pulled away farther and farther.

Unattended ships also began to burn. Other crews scrambled to fight the fires spreading to their own ships. The boardwalk and piers were lost. By the time the moons peeked over the horizon, the whole port was lost, reduced to ash and ruin.

Across the city, they saw the signal fires rise up from the port. The Morralish soldiers, men of what called itself the MLF, the Morralish Loyalist Faction, began the "invasion" of Napua. Yet this was not the only signal and it was not for them alone. As word of the slaying of Illwarr spread, slaves rose to purpose in its wake.

As firelight engulfed the southern horizon, the promise of aid and the belief that their best, desperate chance for freedom had finally come, self-liberated slaves were inspired to liberate others. By the time blue cloaks were spotted in the north, slaves had risen up in every home. Slaying their masters or dying in the attempt, the slaves of Napua claimed their freedom.

Freed slaves in the northern part of town made for the main gate, passing behind the advancing Morralish lines. Those in other parts of Napua pushed south and central, rallying to the main street, south of the arena, and held out for the promised aid and protection of the blue cloaked Morralish soldiers.

In less than half an hour, the night barely upon them, the Morralish Loyalist Faction had taken the arena, in simultaneously the bloodiest contest and most spectator involvement it had ever known. They held it for the remainder of the hour, allowing freed slaves to slip into the safety of its walls and drawing the city's watchmen and civil defense militia to the south-side of their makeshift fortress.

The tide let out. As quickly as they came, they withdrew. At the end of the hour, the blue cloaks and the freed slaves pulled back from the arena, pushing north. Napua's defense forces had fallen for the ruse.

They responded to the taking of the arena as if it were a foothold for an invading army. Except this was no invasion, it was a raid. The plunder was liberty and, having acquired it, the army withdrew. Far up the coast, with no interest in returning, the combined Morralish and new freemen forces formed a blockade, thus preventing anyone from coming or going to Napua by land. By sea would be the only option and that, thanks to Thane Caanaflit and Captain Weatherworn, had its own hazards, no port to birth.

Chapter 70
Straining Efforts

The High Lord-General Harkon's voice was stern and clear.

"We started a war to free him. We'll keep fighting this war – not as though we had plans to stop – and I can only pray it sets him free again. I will not, however, commit to a full scale action, against the Imperium, without His Majesty's command! I'm making a way for us to go home, nothing more. If the legions come at us, try to stop us, then yes, we will defend ourselves. If freed slaves fight alongside us, no one is going to abandon them. But I'll not go in after them. We'll not go house to house killing people to free their slaves. The Morralish Invasion of Antoria Royal? No! No, good sister, I'll not be responsible for that."

Bethany insisted, "We already stormed the Oublitille. We've already taken action against the Imperium."

"That was to free you. It was neither my action, nor what I would have done," Lord Harkon clarified, "Apologies. It was different circumstances besides. This is our course, now, to prepare for the Prince and our long march home. I intend to stay that course, lest His Majesty himself command me otherwise."

Bethany looked to the heavens and stated stoically in reply, "Then my journey has come full circle."

The next morning, in a different arena, the Grand Arena of Antoria Royal, another battle was about to begin. Below its sands, Lord-General Hrothmond was yoked and chained. There, a familiar face had come to break words before bones.

"Come to gloat?" Strein Hrothmond asked, pert.

General Leidtenfrost smiled falsely at the comment.

"No. Not at all. Admire — I suppose. Word had only just reached me, and I mean just, not even a day, not even an hour, that the Oublitille had fallen. You saved the messenger's life, actually. He had not left, and I was about to kill him. I wanted to prevent anyone else from learning that so many of our soldiers were acting in open defiance and that you were free and leading them. He had little more than turned to go, however, when another – just like him – arrived to inform me of your capture. Are the gods not on my side? To deliver you unto me again. Tis like you never even escaped – in a way. Except now, oh, now I get my way. Now, I get to throw you to the wolves. We'll not literally. They've all run out of wolves, but near enough."

"I think you forgot you were going to admire me," Strein Hrothmond laughed, "that sounded a lot like gloating."

"Tell me, then," Hertvork Leidtenfrost asked, "How did you escape? What did you accomplish? Why come to the city? Dazzle me. Silence me. Give me something to admire, to awe."

"You think I'm that stupid?"

"I think you want to remain alive," Hertvork replied, "I think you want to be free and I have it in my power to see that you are both. I must insist, however, that you regale me with your tale."

"Throw me to your wolves," Strein taunted him, "Admire what comes after. My legacy, my purpose, was to be unjustly imprisoned by you, only to be liberated by free men who would not see their countryman treated so. My purpose is fulfilled. My legacy secure. If I face my death now, then so be it."

"Then so be it!" spat Hertvork, turning to the arena guards, commanding, "Let loose the lions, then send this one up to meet them. Arm him well. He is a soldier after all. The people will expect to see a soldier fight and die accordingly."

General Hrothmond, in remarkable physical condition for a man with more than six decades behind him, nonetheless had no business fighting on the front lines. As well as he once had, as much as he often wanted to, he had slowed. He would not dare risk the life of any soldier under his command, to be distracted or halted looking after "the old man" fighting in the front.

Yet here was a test. Strein Hrothmond had no desire to be fed to the lions. He had no desire to fight in the Grand Arena or be taken prisoner either. For all his desires, he nonetheless faced these things that he did not want. However they had come to pass, there was no choice for a man like General Hrothmond.

He simply embraced whatever fate or chance had put before him. He faced this test the same as he would any other, the only way he knew how, like a soldier.

He walked out onto the sands of the Grand Arena and found it devoid of opponents. Taking a moment, ignoring the jeering of the audience, Strein Hrothmond made a study of the small world he inhabited. There were two rows of seven stone pillars crossing east to west. The sand was beach sand, light, almost white, and it was deep.

Most importantly, however, was the political climate. The arena was half empty, as was the pulvinus. No Imperator in his high seat or in his reserved space surrounding it.

A handful of senators, in their red striped togas, and as many nobles in gold and orange, were clustered about here and there. Yet no indication of the Imperator, none of his attendant praetorians or priests. A Morralish General, apparently, did not rate so high to so many.

Then the lions came. He had suspected that they might throw one at him, but no, there were two, immediately barreling toward him. His moment of studious observation ended abruptly.

The lions were powerful creatures and had a hungry look in their eyes. Strein calmly stood there. A collective gasp went through the audience as many decided the gladiator was simply going to allow himself to be devoured. It had happened before, uncommon, but increasingly less so. Not that day, however.

Had he run left or right, they would have adjusted their course to pursue him. As powerful and frightening as lions were, even to a skilled general, they were yet dumb beasts to a brave man with his wits. So he stood there, gladius sword in right hand, tall shield in left, and waited for the animals to draw in on him.

Strein knew little about lions, specifically, but he knew they were a certain kind of predator and, at the last instant, they pounced as he anticipated that they would. Once the lions were aloft, they were committed, they could not veer or yield. Accordingly, General Hrothmond pivoted, crouching, and put all of himself behind his shield, save for his right arm.

As the lion on his right snared itself on his gladius' blade, the General kicked himself forward, opening his shield as he did. The combined power of the leaping lion and the smashing shield, though it knocked Strein Hrothmond to the ground, knocked the lion out cold. Its limp body careening past him.

He spun about, coming to his feet, not quickly, but remarkably so far a man his age. The gored lion had taken the blade below the throat with a slash following down its ribs. As the General approached it, bloody sword in hand, the lion backed off. This continued a moment, until Strein stopped and so did the lion. As he walked forward again, the lion backed off again.

Annoyed, but confident, the General hurled his sword at the lion, which reared back, but not fast or far enough. The short blade buried itself, through the top of the roaring lion's mouth, about as deep into its skull as a short sword could go. The beast balked at the impact, as its front paws batted at the air, it froze, curiously, only to drop limp, its head to the ground like a stone.

For that moment, the General supposed it was a simple matter. Stroll over to one lion and, retrieving his gladius, march over to the other to deliver the coup de grace. He was wrong. Jerking the sword from the lion's skull, he noticed the gate at the other end of the arena. It opened once more and, from that gaping maw, two more charging lions belched forth.

"Rork."

Chapter 71
Frightening Imperator

"The Prince of Morralish arrives, Exalted Imperator," a white robed man told the crowned and the armored figure centered before them.

The Imperator glared back at him. His eyes, unseen, moved dispassionately behind his golden helm. His body large, indistinguishable under his dark red cloak, shifted. One could feel the Imperator's glare, even as they could not see it. It settled on the white robed man as, slow to speak, the Imperator replied, "After the Triumph, take him to the Colosseum. Show him our games, tell him of our justice, let him taste the finest things of the Capital."

"As you decree, Exalted Imperator."

The other white robe spoke up. There were two of them. They appeared almost as twins, dark hair, medium skin tone, blue eyes, handsome, young, clean-shaven faces.

"Exalted Imperator, the Cathedral priests have accosted me again. They worry much over your growing isolation and insist you seek their counsel. The Primarch, himself, has noted your absence. The Cathedral of Din understands an Imperator's duties, that is why they allow us to attend you but, Exalted Imperator, it has been nearly three years since you have come for his blessing, thrice longer than any Imperator before you has dared."

Unseen eyes stared out from black slits in the Imperator's helm, half an inch below an affixed crown, itself spiked like a halo of thorns. They felt his glare shift from one white robe priest to the other.

Years ago, the first time he had given them a silent stare such as this, so loud in its way, so long it felt, despite lasting a brief moment, they both had pissed themselves outright, yellowing their august, white robes.

The Imperator had harnessed the power of fear and men could feel it carried all about him. It was not so much that the wills of his attendant priests were completely broken. Rather, it merely took only a tiny piece of that fear, a taste here or there, every slight pause that threatened a deeper silence, for them to remember what being ensnared in the totality of his terror was like. Thus they were ever harkened back to that first horrible silence and, their necessary words having broken, they cowered together before him, eagerly awaiting dismissal.

At last, the Imperator spoke at them, his words hollowly rolling forth like a distant thunder, "I am the most daring of them all. Yet, the Primarch is a patient man. It will only be a little while longer now. Do not let Bengallen meet with him. I will see him first. I will make the introductions. You have your instruction. Leave me."

"Ya- your wee- will be da- done, Exalted Imperator," they stammered in unison, backing away.

Chapter 72
Serving Leaders

"Your Majesty," the paladin, Sir Jerumir, rode up next to Prince Bengallen and addressed him, asking, "Are we to break at midday, for half day, today, that your retinue might offer praise to Father Van on his holy day?"

Prince Bengallen tugged the rein on his horse, an unfamiliar horse as they had been trading them out often, and he slowed. The Prince put his face to the beautiful sky and asked, "Is it Vansday again, already?"

"Tis, my Prince."

"We've been on the road so long now, the days have all run together."

"And not for the first time as I understand it?"

"Yes," Bengallen answered, looking to the Chieftain of the MacRoberts clan, "The journeys from Roster's Glenn to Woodhaven, then from Woodhaven to the edge of the Dreadwood and back to Spearpointe were each long, and no so far apart from each other in my memory as they seemed at the time. Yet never in my life have I taken a journey like this – only to turn around and go back – what, a few days, a few weeks, after we arrive?"

"We should be so fortunate, Your Majesty," Sir Jerumir added, "You remain optimistic about what we shall find there, but I know the Imperium, and I am not."

"Yes," the Prince nodded, agreeing, "You informed me of a great many disturbing thing. Though I not so glad they exist to be told, I am yet glad you have found me to tell of them."

"Twas my duty, Your Majesty," Jerumir accepted, "I am honored to do it and twice honored that you say I have done well."

Bengallen smiled.

"Then I shall honor you thrice on our holy Vansday, as befits a servant of the Holy Family. You may give the homily to the men at our devotion this afternoon."

"Begging His Majesty's pardon," Jerumir began to negotiate, "but I've been more of a ranger than a chaplain these last several years. I have not preached in a long time."

"Yet you are a paladin. You have not only studied the Fragments of the Wisdom of Vandor, but you are an initiate into the higher mysteries of the Church," Prince Bengallen reminded him, "I've heard you preach more than one homily myself, mayhap any uncertainty in your skill can be made up with brevity. As I recall, that would be a miracle in its own right."

Sir Jerumir's eyes widened as he nearly laughed right in the Prince's face, but he cleared his throat, regained his composure.

"Your Majesty speaks true. I was prone to milking a captive audience. They so needed to hear what I had to say. Something we share in common, I believe, Your Majesty."

Prince Bengallen smiled easily as he replied, "Tis as you say, 'they so needed to hear it,' but mayhap this lot are an exception. Their literal path strongly suggests they are on the correct spiritual one as well."

"My Prince, how I have enjoyed finding myself in your company once more," Sir Jerumir offered, "I'll do my best with the words and strive for a thrifty management of their economy."

"Do so," Prince Bengallen said, prodding the horse to resume the previous pace, "And one more thing, sir."

"Yes, Your Majesty?" Sir Jerumir invited.

"Tis good to see you too!"

Sir Jerumir, while trying to come up with something relevant to preach upon, also had the Prince's arrival to coordinate and the Forest Phantoms to command. *It was all connected*, he supposed. Yet he had become greatly accustomed to having and doing things his own way.

The Chief did enjoy the company of his former student, friend, and sovereign. Moreover, he was glad to have a sovereign and to know that there still existed a people for them to serve. Yet, in these recent weeks past, serving required some getting used to and he was still not — *not fully*.

Mayhap that was the homily. It has been said that 'the best words you will ever preach are the ones you are preaching to yourself.' What does the

Wisdom of Vandor have to say about service?

"Kinnik, Sternus," Sir Jerumir rode toward them, calling to them, "Where are the others?"

The two wizards, one old, the other young, were arguing over some speculative arcane concept that was well beyond any eavesdropper. Then again, frankly, it was beyond themselves as well as was the impetus of their discussion. Shutting their mouths immediately, at the call of their Chief, they prodded their steeds, riding over to meet him without hesitation.

"I believe," Sternus began, "that Sir Ihrvan remained in the village last night. Said he knew a girl there. Sir Quaindraught was to take Sky to gather him this afternoon. He's likely departed already to do so."

"We have dragon," the Chief fumed, "do we truly think that this sort of rascality is why the Holy Family has entrusted us with such a great power and responsibility?"

"I said the same thing, Chief," Kinnik agreed, amending, "more or less."

Jerumir sighed.

"Gods be good. I understand that the company of the Prince's knights, spearmen, and woodsmen provide us a luxury, a security, that we do not normally have. I wanted you to let your guard down – a bit – but this ..."

"If I use my magic to call to her, through you, she will return immediately, Chief," Kinnik offered.

"No. I need Ihrvan back, as well as Q."

Sternus spoke up, an amused lightness in his voice.

"Anything we can do for you, Chief?"

"Yes," Jerumir accepted, "When those knuckled heads get back, take them on ahead to the capital. Sir Ihrvan should make contact with his informants there and bring m– the Prince and I – a report on what is really going on these days. Particularly, regarding the Morralish expeditionary soldiers, but tell him to really put his nose in it, sniff out anything useful or relevant."

"Are we that close now?"

"Aye we are," Jerumir agreed, less frustration in his voice, "I recognized that last village too. If we rode hard from there, not sparing the horses, we could have made it in a few days, maybe two. That's no good for a royal visit though. The Antori outriders dispatched from Three Gods Pass will have only arrived there and reported our intention to visit but a few days ago themselves. If the Imperium meant to assassinate us, they'd have tried it already. That means they are preparing for the Prince. We can't just show up, all of us, at first light having ridden through day and night. It wouldn't be proper. Not that we are, apparently, worrying about proper too much these days. It matters for His Majesty, how he presents himself."

"So we'll be taking Sky then?" Sternus asked.

"She can drop you in the water, just off the port, and you can make your way into the city from there. Sky knows those sea caves well. She knows where to hide until summoned."

"We'll go as soon as they return, Chief," Sternus said.

Jerumir grimaced and replied, "As soon as — immediately head out. I don't care to see either one of them today. Tell them they are on notice, and I expect good work and useful information when we rendezvous."

"Of course, Chief, yes, sir."

"Kinnik," Jerumir shifted his attention to the older man, "You got any fragments of scripture mixed in with those spells and formulations in your books there."

"I do, Chief," Kinnik replied happily, "looking for some inspiration?"

"Aye, my friend," Jerumir laughed, "I've convinced the Prince to halt soon for a half day, for Vansday observance, and in turn he has blessed me with the privilege to preach the homily. I'm thinking something on service and humility. Too bad the two who need to hear it most will be absent."

"Excellent, Chief," Kinnik agreed, excitedly, already digging through his hip satchel, adding, as he produced a book, thick even though the tiniest one that Jerumir had ever seen, "Tis not all the Fragments, but it has some memorable lines from Wisdom of Vandor, Life of Dinnothyl, and Songs of Ellenofae. Should have what you need."

Sir Jerumir marveled at the miniature bible a moment. Accepting and opening it, he could barely read the tiny letters.

"How did I not know that you had this?"

"Something I picked up that last time I visited home," Kinnk answered, "I guess it just never came up. Dwarves and elves working together, doing some amazing things!"

Jerumir continued to flip through the cramped pages of diminutive text, squinting at each one, and agreed, "Indeed, it seems they are."

Chapter 73
Living Purpose

The Maiden's Folly sailed from Napua, west, to the Antori Capital along the edge of the Bruni Bay, where it opens into the Antori Sea. Into the night the ship's crew and passengers alike settled into the serenity that only calm waters and smooth sailing can provide. For a time, the fires of Napua's burning port persisted to glow in the distance, even as they shrank to a dot behind them.

Yet before the glow of Antoria Royal first began to take shape, the last fleeting ember on the horizon behind at last winked out. They were in the bosom of the sea, under the dark moon's eclipse. They were alone, together, and for a brief time, they felt safe in the dark.

Many people made their lives around an observation of the heavens. Changes in the stars told farmers when to sow and when to reap. The changes in the moons marked the passage of time, from one month to another. These lights held spiritual truths, discernible to the enlightened, and the darkness between tested men's souls.

The sky was what its seasoned watchers called "dark moon dominate," more often colloquially referred to as "a dark moon" or "a no moon," as the dark disk of a lightless moon appeared to eclipse the bright moon completely. The moons would appear in this conjunction for two nights in the middle of each month.

This was the first of these nights. The 15th, the middle of the month, the ides. Only a faint halo of light whispered at the edges of the dark moon as it moved overhead.

It marked the height of the power of darkness for the month. All month, less and less moon, less light, shone in the night, until at last, tonight, it was nearly none. Tomorrow would prove the same, but at least tomorrow held the hope of the waxing moon, as the bright moon would grow each night, and light would return to the darkness.

They felt safe because they were alone, in a sense, upon the sea, far from the power and schemes of the things that feed on darkness. They felt safer still because, in another way, they were not alone, surrounded solely by the company of friends and allies, who would together stand against any darkness that might stray upon them. Including their own, that darkness that we each carry within us, that ever awaits its opportunity to emerge.

309

"Captain Weatherworn seemed pleased to see you," Shomotta said, announcing his presence as he approached Alpona.

The Zil-jahi Warrior was standing on the deck, leaning against the railing, staring at the faint shapes that glimmered on the water around them. He turned, motioned his friend to join him, and replied, "He was saddened to hear of Rodjker, though. They were friends from before my time with them."

"We are all saddened by Rodj," Shomotta offered, taking up a leaning posture, "but I am sure it was good to mourn him with someone who feels his loss more keenly."

"Why would that be good?" Alpona asked.

"For you," Shomotta amended, "Do you not feel better?"

Alpona grimaced, looked back to the waters, but continued speaking, "I suppose. I cannot shake it though. The thought, the sense, the fear, honestly, that he died for nothing. He waded into battle and was, what, overcome by the enemy?"

"As any one of us could have been, any number of times then or since," Shomotta explained, "We have chosen violent lives. Life does not stand up well to violence. I think our time as gladiators would have made that clear. The violence, that even only one man can do, can slay many times. Do you even know how many men you have slain? How many men they slew before you ended them? How many men, women, children they might have slain had you not laid waste to them when your paths crossed?"

"How could I?" Alpona snapped, "How could anyone? And how is this supposed to help?"

"Am I supposed to make you feel better?"

"Supposed? Well," Alpona admitted, "I'd take it."

"Instead, I'm saying," Shomotta continued, "that the violence of one man, anyone, can murder many. If we choose and continue to choose to face violence, we will surely, eventually, be one among the many another slays, as surely as anyone we kill is but one among our own many."

"Blood and death," Alpona spat the words into the sea, wondering aloud, "does it have any meaning?"

"You know it does," Shomotta charged.

"Do I?" Alpona turned to him, face full of pain and grief, "Do I know that? How do I know that?"

"Because," answered Shomotta, "You've never stopped fighting. Even in your doubt. The arena. Your disagreement with the Prince over Sir Jason. You could have laid down the sword. You still can. You're not a rich man, but you have gold coins earned. You could retire and survive in Spearpointe for the rest of your days, but you keep on fighting."

"More than you know," Alpona, calming, whispered, "I am dying. I think. My body is wasting. I've trained harder. I've tried to fortify myself. Stave it off. Yet my body — diminishing returns. I am not long for this world."

"All the more reason to rest," Shomotta noted, "but you persist and endure your chosen path. Why do you keep fighting? Answer that, my friend, and you alone will answer the riddle of your violence."

"Or I could tell you, Shomotta."

The wizard-priest accepted, "Or you could tell me."

"I am afraid of the answer," Alpona admitted.

Shomotta looked at him with a profound sympathy.

Placing his hand on his friend's forearm, he replied, "There is much to fear in this world. I know. Too much, I know. But the truth should not be one of them. Perhaps the thing the truth reveals, perhaps, but not the truth itself. The truth is already true, knowing it, accepting it, that is a place for courage to be born."

"Tis all I've ever known," Alpona spoke his truth, "Fighting is my life. Whether fighting for survival, respect, or to slay evil men, my whole life has been one fight, or another, stacked upon another, yoked to another, fight after bloody fight. I was taken in by warriors. I was raised to be a warrior. It is all that I know. Both times I abandoned the path, I only traded literal fighting for inglorious personal battles. Yet it always comes back to fighting. It is how my world makes sense."

"Or," Shomotta retorted, "Is it how you make sense of the world?"

"I'm not ready to die," Alpona confessed.

Shomotta moved his hand so that the two held hands, clasped.

"I am no physician, but it seems that your death is going to happen whether you fight or not. In truth, given enough time, we all shall meet our end and shall have little choice as to how."

"Rodjker chose," Alpona said, clutching Shomotta's hand.

"So he did," Shomotta agreed, "and will you?"

"I will," Alpona affirmed.

"What, then, do you choose?"

Alpona set his brow and growled, "I choose to fight."

"But why?"

"Because," Alpona began, "Like the Zil-jahi Masters, like Sir Jason, the knights, paladins, and soldiers we have known, like Rodjker, I choose to believe there are things worth fighting for, things worth dying for. As other men will slay for foul and terrible purpose, then I too must slay to thwart them."

"And if you should die in the doing?"

"Then I die well."

"As have so many of our comrades before us," Shomotta explained, "as many of us may yet still."

They shared the silence of the water then. Two men of violence finding peace, hand in hand, on a darker night, in the abyss of the sea, on the ledge of that gaping maw of the terror behind all the world, that we must, each of us, save each other from.

Eventually their hands parted. Eventually their silence broke, interrupted here and there with follow-up comments and conversation:

"Is that why you shaved your head?"

"Did you know Rodjker fished with a spear?"

"Has Bengallen told you of his lady, her fate unknown?"

"Has Malcolm told you the story of the Green Knight?"

"Has Caanaflit tried to get you to invest in his 'minstrel monopoly' yet?"

So on and so forth, echoes of their meaningful conversations increased in frequency and decreased in magnitude, devolving into affable small talk. Until at last, they noticed Antoria Royal's glow had appeared on the horizon. Its ambiguous form flirted with taking shape. Night still upon them, but a sea hides the morning poorly, and they could smell the dawn in the air, not so far behind them.

As they parted company, to seek some few hours rest, they heard the wind buffeting against the water. A whirring sound with notes imprinted in ripples on the water. Their attentions turned to the horizon once again, just in time to catch it, more than a glimpse, but not the thing whole. The great dragon swooped their ship.

Sails strained. One tore at its top, starboard corner. The masts creaked as the gargantuan, winged lizard barely avoided colliding with them. They would not have believed their eyes, some trick of a sleepless night, had they not touched one so recently.

The wind slammed both men to their asses and, looking about, the helmsman as well.

"What in the Nine Hells was that?" the helmsman called.

Alpona laughed and Shomotta answered, "Looked like a dragon to me!"

"Yeah," the helmsman replied, standing, "har-har, but what were it truly?"

"A dragon!" Alpona insisted, "Those things are turning up everywhere these days."

Chapter 74
Quarreling Thanes

Just in time to catch the sunrise, Malcolm and Caanaflit had replaced their counterparts upon the top deck. Watching the Eastern Port of Antoria Royal come into view, Malcolm could not put his mind at ease and decided to express a certain dissatisfaction, "We suffered you know?"

"Pardon?"

"Not like the new recruits," Malcolm continued, "our skill saved us from the worst of it, but we suffered. In our bodies, in our captivity, but worst, in our hearts and minds."

"Well," Caanaflit sighed dismissively, maybe more so than he meant to, "you did volunteer to be gladiators. What did you expect?"

"I thought it was necessary," Malcolm shot back at the rogue, "We expected it to be necessary."

"I – but – I," Caanaflit pretended to be at a loss for words, pausing for thought before continuing, "Did you not also expect me to pursue all options? Should I not have taken advantage of new opportunities as they presented? In service to His Majesty and the freedom of these people. Should I not have done everything in my power to ensure success?"

"But we had a plan," Malcolm insisted, unconvinced, "You don't seem to understand teamwork. I am not a pawn in your game to be moved according to your whim. We are thanes, together agents of the Prince — together. You could have come to us, told us, collaborated."

"And risk exposing you and myself!"

"And risk the possibility that we might disagree," Malcolm chastised him, reinterpreting the other's words, "Risk surrendering control. Risk not getting to have your way—"

"Why, Malcolm," Caanaflit interjected, continuing in a sarcastic tone, "I am very close to being offended. I think you don't love me anymore."

Malcolm scoffed.

"You're not taking me seriously."

"I am having a hard time, yes," Caanaflit said, a slight laugh in his voice before continuing, "Consider five years from now, the future. Morralish is restored. Some old scroll of King Lionel's is found, outstanding warrants, executed arrests, sentences, and so forth. King Bengallen thus commissions Malcolm to carry out a death sentence on a rapist. We all know how much you hate them. This man, let us call him Ross, was to marry his victim and help raise her child, but ran off before the wedding."

"Then I find him and kill him," Malcolm interrupted.

"But wait," Caanaflit continued undeterred, "Malcolm finds our Ross the Rapist as a teacher, a farmer, and a musician running an orphanage, preparing parentless children for adulthood and the world. 'The dark times came,' Ross tells you, 'I saw a boy in the mud, a slain parent on either side of him, and I thought that I might have a boy out there too, fatherless in all of this. It weighed heavy upon me. So I took the boy in, then others, it just sort of happened. The older ones got older and needed skills, so I took care of that too. My father was a farmer and I a minstrel. I teach them what I can. Now, I am the only parent these two dozen boys know.' So what does Thane Malcolm of the King's Justice do with Ross then? Does he execute the appropriate original sentence?"

Caanaflit paused. Malcolm said nothing. The half-orc thane still looked upset, a frightful countenance he did bear, but he also looked like he was giving the scenario true thought.

"Is it your only option to kill Ross then and there?" Caanaflit asked, "Or would you consider other options? Return a report to the King? Consider the man's debt paid in his recent and continued service to society during such a critical time?"

Malcolm, detecting a trap, carefully asked, "Are you asking me what is the just reply, and if it conflicts with my orders?"

"What is justice, Malcolm?" Caanaflit asked, avoiding.

Malcolm responded quickly and with certitude, "Justice is vengeance tempered with mercy."

"Oh," Caanaflit, taken aback, admitted, "That's good. Fairly accurate. For most people, tis some ambiguous notion that they think ought to be, but your answer rather gets to the heart of it, doesn't it?"

"My mother had a book, I inherited it," Malcolm explained, "entitled 'Ten Tales to Raise a Model Citizen.' It had a preface written by an Antori philosopher named Macrobius, one of the senators who worked on the collection. He said, 'Justice is many things to many people. The great tragedy of justice is that it is too often all things to all people, like a soil into which anything might be planted. Yet in the eyes of the law, from which its seeds are taken, it can only be one thing: Vengeance tempered with mercy. It may feel right to inflict equal harm upon a criminal, maybe it is, but justice is not done if the criminal, or his judges or their enforcers, become victims in the process. Justice mitigates the needs of all parties, makes an attempt at setting things right, but leaves room for mercy, as to not perpetuate a cycle of wrong.' Or it was something like that. I grew up weighing my father's actions by that standard. Civilized men may struggle to find justice, they may never find it, but my father wasn't even looking."

"Malcolm," Caanaflit laughed, "I criticize others for underestimating you, but I admit to doing the same. As you know more about justice than I, again I ask the expert: Was it just for me to pursue all avenues to victory? Is it just for you to harden your heart toward me?"

"I suppose not," Malcolm admitted, "Yet was it just for us to suffer as gladiators, while you roamed free, no doubt in luxury, conducting your own plots and schemes?"

"First, the continuation of your gladiatorial slavery was an important part of my appeal to the other slaves of Napua, your victory to be a sign to them," Caanaflit insisted, "Second, I only did what seemed right. If I harmed you in the process, I can only beg your forgiveness and pray that I have it, Malcolm, my friend."

"I can forgive you," Malcolm said gloomily, "but I don't suspect I can suddenly be happy about it and chummy with you."

"Understood."

Malcolm was right about many things. Not the least of which being that Caanaflit was, in fact, an expert at getting his way. *Even if you won an argument, he would turn your victory against you.* Yes, things tended to go Caanaflit's way, and though he made it look like benign fate and good fortune, it was the hard work of a keen mind and silver tongue every last time.

316

Chapter 75
Entering Triumphant

On the north wall, at its northernmost point, the capital of the Imperium, Antori Royal, had a most magnificent archway. The road in through this arch traveled straight into the heart of the city, to the Grand Arena. It was called the Triumphant Gate, named for those who entered the city having completed some great victory, usually in war, at the behest of this city.

On special occasions, all traffic and commerce was halted through this archway and its path lined with torch-bearers, many of whom were city elite, senators, magistrates, nobles, and the families there of. The path itself was covered in flower petals, over which the celebrated victor would ride in golden chariot.

It was an ancient tradition, purportedly established for the Din-god when he yet lived and breathed among us as the First Imperator. Not every Imperator won a Triumph. Some celebrated Triumphs were held for men other than Imperators, but never before had a foreigner, a non-citizen, been given this honor, not until Prince Bengallen.

The Paladin-Prince, as the supreme commander of all Morralish Forces, was due much respect and consideration for all the aid and stability his soldiers had provided the Imperium. Yet, this was neither the genuine reason nor the pretense for why he was extended the honor of a Triumphal Entry.

Prince Bengallen had saved the Frontier from ruin, twice. Although he was told this was the reason, how important Spearpointe and its surrounding farmland were to the Imperium, what great deed slaying the Starspawn and routing its goblins was, neither were his heroics, named and lauded, the actual motive.

The truth was simple. It was the same truth that drove everything in the Imperium: Politics.

The Imperial Senate had already decided how to respond to the Fall of Morralish. They had a plan in place, to incorporate the best officers and soldiers of Morralish into their own legions. A plan to abolish the Morralish Expeditionary Forces, generating a surplus fortune and dispersing, for free, trained warriors, as axillary forces, across the Imperium, only to be used, only to be paid, when needed.

The Prince of Morralish could change all that.

Hope that something of their homeland survived, that it could be restored, would change all that. Prince Bengallen not only held authority over his countrymen and soldiers, he was an actual part of their homeland. He was a hero. He was a living symbol of hope.

If he could, however, be turned from his path. If the Prince could be drawn into Imperial life, granted status, every courtesy extended, every wish made true, mayhap, he would stay. If Prince Bengallen could be adopted by the Imperium, as its own symbol, he could be used to achieve the Imperator's aims.

Thus, as night gave way to morning, Prince Bengallen entered into Antoria Royal by the Triumphant Gate with laurels upon his brow and flower petals beneath his feet. He rode in upon a golden chariot pulled by four white horses. The applauding cheer of streets, lined with the Imperium's finest citizens, welcomed him as their torchlight summoned the dawn.

Chapter 76
Mooring Port

To the southeast, across miles of Antori metropolis, The Maiden's Folly at last sailed into port. As the dawn sun, shedding its orange cast and ascending into its full glory, began pursuit of the cyclical quest for noon, Caanaflit and Malcolm were joined on the top deck by Alpona and Shomotta.

"What brooding silence stands between you?" Shomotta asked.

Alpona, stepping between Caanaflit and Malcolm, put a hand on each shoulder, speculating accurately, "Let me guess. Malcolm thinks we wasted efforts thanks to Caanaflit, and Caanaflit thinks Malcolm is being unreasonably short-sighted. That the gist of it?"

Both Caanaflit and Malcolm opened their mouths to protest. Each seeing his reflection in the other, however, both refrained.

"Well you can both get over it," Alpona continued, "You're both right and you're both wrong, to one degree or another. The both of you, I'm sure. Yet we are alive. There is work ahead of us. Malcolm, Caanaflit has provided the best option for getting we foreign warriors into the city unassumingly. Caanaflit, Malcolm and the rest of us are essential to your plan. Let's all be friends, play nice, and get the job done. If there are grievances to air or actions to review, we'll make time on the trip home. In the mean, heads in the game, my friends, heads in the game."

There it was, the word "game" again. This was not a game. This was life and death. This was liberty at last or oppression for a thousand years. This was no game.

Yet there it was again, treated like a game. Sira Roselle was right, they were a bunch of big, violent, scary boys. If not for intentions and heroics, they were no different from any other boys. Or were they?

What boy has killed hundreds of men? What boy has saved thousands of lives? What boy has taken responsibility for the lives and wellbeing of those around him? What boy has suffered so many wounds upon body, heart, and soul? Are these not the very things that transform boys into men grown?

How many adventures and misadventures, as well as the repercussions thereof, must come to pass before a child is counted as an adult? If it is some

319

number, surely a number of years is a false measure. Is the number of trials and accomplishments any better? Or are these things, among so many countless others, simply the artifacts of life?

Is not the quality of manhood but the assembling of it all into something that has meaning and value, not for oneself alone, but for the good of others as well? One might suppose so. Yet if that is true, some men remain much younger than others, with the sum total of men in the world far fewer than the number of males wandering it, touted as such.

Mayhap there is always some boy left in the man and some man growing within the boy. Is not the best life the one of balance in all things? What is nurtured, cultivated, grows well, thrives. While that which is neglected, withers.

Mayhap there should be something of both, the man that must and the boy that better. For to be too serious is to be stone, to be too whimsical is to be water, and it is yet the clay, a measure of both, that can be fashioned, take and retain the form needed, best suited to a given task. If war need be played to be won, if justice need be a game to be adjudicated, mayhap it is the boy, as much the man, needed to set the world to right.

We are all, after all, but the children of God's Holy Family.

"They wanted Illwarr or the Slayers of Illwarr for the games here," Caanaflit explained, changing the subject, "So I will deliver you into the city. In fairness, however, tis not my plan anymore, not really. Prince Bengallen has come into contact with various Morralish commanders during his travel west. They are already staging for a troop withdrawal, east. Yet word and rider can only travel so far, so fast. Whatever whoever has planned from there – whatever else is going to happen here – your guesses are as good as mine. I have merely ushered us unto the Capital, to be here for it."

Shomotta looked concerned, asking, "So we stay on the ship until you coordinate our fight in the arena, then we go to the arena, and that's it? That's all the plan there is?"

"That's it," Caanaflit admitted, echoing, "That's all the plan there is. I suppose you don't even have to go to your fight in the Grand Arena. That was merely my pretext to pull you from Napua, the reason the port authority will permit us to dock. Although, if you plan on doing other, please do let me know now, so I don't set up anything I'll need to abandon."

"Yeah," Malcolm chimed in, "that would be nice?"

"Look!" Caanaflit began.

"Look," Alpona interrupted, "Both of you, heads in the rorking game. Now! Seriously. Enough already."

"Go make the arrangements, please, Caanaflit," Shomotta took it upon himself to decide, "If your military contacts thought fighting in the arena was our next move, then we should move in that direction until we hear otherwise."

"That is where I told them we were headed next and why," Caanaflit answered.

"Then I agree," Alpona said, "We've come this far. Time to play it out."

Caanaflit turned and disembarked with a leap, the ship nearly docked, the mooring lines not yet secured.

"How fairs Alchesus?" Malcolm asked, abruptly.

Alpona cracked a half-hearted smile, answering, "He'll live. May even fight again, but not anytime soon. He's no longer involved in any of this."

"Strange blessings," Malcolm commented.

"Indeed," Shomotta agreed.

Chapter 77
Troubling Elf

"I don't know spit all about elves, okay?" Ruffis said spontaneously as Kinnik approached him.

"Okay?" Kinnik accepted, "I was actually going to ask you if you'd like to learn. I've observed you. You've made it more than clear that you are foreign and I thought you might like to know more about us that dwell here."

Ruffis hissed.

"Us? You're only part-elf."

Kinnik laughed.

"All the right parts, I assure you. The best of both worlds. I was raised among the humans of the MacRoberts clan, but I journeyed to Lensgrace as a young man and passed tests that welcomed me into elven society. I have walked between two peoples ever since. When in the human realms, I have traveled with the last four Chieftains of the MacRoberts clan. At Lensgrace, I am one of twelve apprentices to an archmagus specializing in the crafting of implements imbued with magic. It is widely believed that he is the last living being that can craft what is called a Mage Eng—"

"Whoop de rorkin do!" Ruffis interrupted.

Kinnik scowled, offering, "I thought I'd start out with who I am and from there work into who our people are."

"Our people," Ruffis echoed, continuing, "You don't get it. I am not one of your people, even less than you are, and I don't—"

This time, Kinnick cut Ruffis off.

"And you don't care. Fine! Got it. Never mind."

Ruffis smiled, shooing the half-elf wizard off with a triple flick of the wrist.

Kinnik gladly departed.

Brunsis observed the spectacle, a snooty snort his only commentary.

"Don't you judge me," Ruffis turned to the minotaur and snapped at him, "Just because you wanna run around telling everyone about yourself doesn't mean we wanna hear it or share and share alike."

Brunsis snorted again, more amusement in it this time, as he turned away from Ruffis.

The dark elf also turned, to the three knights playing cards, at the table across from him.

"Any of you got something you need to say?"

Sir Caldun Norledd, Knight of the Spear, stood, pointing at the elf, and began to swear at him.

"You rorkin freak and your rorkin mouth! Been listen to your cocker's spit for a hundred rorkin days and a thousand rorkin miles now. I'm done with it. I'm done with all yer simpering spit, you dirty dastard!"

"Well, well, well," Ruffis said ambiguously, standing and putting his hands on his hilts, less ambiguously.

"Beg off," Sir Garrus, the elder of the three, insisted.

" 'Ee ain't worth it," Sir Bohr protested.

Breaking the tension, Prince Bengallen and Sir Jerumir entered the parlor, speaking with another man, an Antori Senator by the manner of his dress. Sir Jerumir eyed the standoff as it abated in obvious response to the Prince's presence, each man slowly returning to his seat. Brunsis snorted yet again.

Sir Jerumir broke away, moving toward the others, as Prince Bengallen and the Senator continued to cross to the other end of the spacious room.

Kinnik intercepted his Chief.

"His Majesty arrived just in time. This Ruffis is quite the handful. He has been especially edgy since his friends left. With His Majesty away too — I think he meant to pick a fight."

"Can you handle him?" Jerumir asked.

323

Kinnik looked offended, insisting, "Of course."

"Why then," Jerumir asked, "does he have you over here sniveling to me like a playground tattletale? You're over a hundred years old, Kinnik."

"Why I was—" Kinnik began to answer with justification and indignation, when it occurred to him that he was, in fact, acting rather irrationally and out of sorts. *This Ruffis projected a sense of frustration and hostility in more ways than one.* The half-elf wizard shifted his tone and continued, "You're right, Chief. I do not know what came over me. I'll — I'll handle it."

Sir Jerumir and Kinnik went and sat with the three Knights of the Spear as Ruffis, responsively, sat nearer to Prince Bengallen and the Senator, to within eavesdropping range.

"So yet another day goes by," Prince Bengallen remarked, "and the Imperator once again cannot meet with me. On the rare occasion that a Triumph is extended to someone other than an Imperator, is it not customary for them to be received by him?"

Senator Iscavius replied readily, "For certain. At the end of the procession, immediately following the entry, that would be the protocol. An Imperator is, however, a busy man. Protocols aid him in his duties, but he is by no means bound to them. He wants to see you. His intention, to honor. That is why you have entered the city so. He will see you. There are a great many things for your royal persons to discuss, but for the time being, with the weight of an empire upon his shoulders, he bears it where he must. That it has not yet brought him to you, Your Highness, I can only make apologies."

The Paladin-Prince laughed.

"You have a slippery tongue don't you? Gave me the answer I wanted to hear and used it to justify the very object of my displeasure. Don't think me a fool, Senator. I've bantered with the best."

"Pity that one has not accompanied Your Highness," Iscavius began, "I might have enjoyed the verbal jousting. A different contest is in store for you, however. The Grand Arena of the Colosseum will host gladiator battles tomorrow. Your Highness has been invited to be a spectator in the pulvinus of our Exalted Imperator and, moreover, we have a special surprise in your honor. In the meantime, I am to extend the full hospitality of the Capital to you. Is there anywhere you wish to go, to do, anything or anyone I might bring."

"The Imperator."

A pause, as the Senator huffed, obviously annoyed.

"Anyone besides? Anyone in regards to your entertainment?"

"No," Prince Bengallen stated plainly, "Senator, I thank you for your time and attention, but we'll stay in and continue to recover from our long journey. We'll be fully rested for our encounter with the Imperator on the morrow."

"As you wish," Senator Iscavius accepted, "Should Your Majesty or any of his companions change mind, all the servants here at the guest house have been instructed to see to your every need. Every — need."

Prince Bengallen rolled his eyes, uttering less than half sincerely, "Gratitude."

Chapter 78
Happening Soon

Sternus had treated himself to a haircut. He usually kept it short, beard and coif the same clipped length all around, by his own hand, as best he could. This was a preventative measure as much as a response to the uneven burning that so often occurred during alchemical experimentation. There had not been much time for experiments of late, however, and when, perchance, he caught a glimpse of his reflection, he discovered he looked rather like a fuzz ball. Such a hairdo, would not do, *not for the end of the world*, so he parted with a small copper coin and received a clean shave, scalp, cheek, and chin. It was his first proper shave in years.

His next stop was the library of the College of Magic. Such a store house of knowledge it was, and he had more than a few things to research. On the likely chance that all these many records of insight would cease to exist in the near future, he took the opportunity to pour through a choice selection of ancient tomes, taking copious notes.

"Told ya 'eed be 'ere," the familiar voice came from behind as Sternus turned about to greet his comrades. He saw Sir Quaindraught with his bright red beard, a comb having been run through it for the first time in a long time, as well as the always presentable, Sir Ihrvan.

"Almost didn't recognize ya," Sir Ihrvan added, "baldy."

Sternus smiled, "Let us hope we all watch it grow back."

The burly paladin laughed, "About that."

"Yes."

"Tis as we expected," Ihrvan answered.

"And then some!" Quaindraught added, "The whole dogged city is ready to burst at the rorking seams."

"It turns out," Ihrvan elaborated, "There was a network of anti-slavers already in place. The children, the youngest slaves, it seems, have all been raised up with the promise that freedom would come to them, but everyone has been too afraid to act. Concern for getting caught. Concern that not enough slaves and allies would rise up. Concerns that have been fading with our mouthy

326

mountain folk brethren milling about — nothing better to do than criticize all the ways Antoria is inferior to Morralish. Slavery, most specifically."

"Even more recently," the ruddy paladin picked up the tale, "There's been direct contact a'tween certain Morralish Regiments an' these anti-slavers."

"That matches up with the plans the men of the Stone's Pryde had told us about," Sternus commented.

"Yes," Sir Ihrvan agreed, "but tis all progressed way further than anyone's individual plans. Tis all about to happen. Very soon. Very sudden. In a sense, I suppose tis happening right now."

"Ya know the High Lord-General Hrothmond?" Sir Quaindraught asked rhetorically, continuing, " 'The Lord o' the Wild Frontier' and all that. Well, 'ee went and got 'emself publicly arrested afront a bunch o' Morralish soldiers — men 'ooh grew up 'eerin' about his legendary adventures. Th' praetorians was real cockers about it too, 'pairrantleh. Pissed everyone off right nice. Well, get this, they tried to hex'a'cute'em with six or seven lions in the arena and the old rorker killed'em all with his bare hands!"

"It was four or five lions," Sir Ihrvan corrected, "and he had at least one weapon."

" 'Ee's ova' sixty years old!" Sir Quaindraught retorted, "We can add a bit ta'tha story, yeah?"

Someone shushed them from a neighboring table.

"So anyway," Ihrvan, lowered his voice and concluded the tale, "Not only are the slaves primed to take their freedom. Not only do they have local assets willing to help them. Not only are the soldiers of Morralish tired of ignoring the slavery themselves. Not only are they pissed off at the disdain the Imperium has shown them over the last year. Now — Now, they have a legendary hero, who has defied his own death yet again, this time, as a slave himself, in active defiance of the Imperium. Meanwhile, news of 'rebels' destroying a prison in Aveniugex province has just become public knowledge. One side or the other, someone is about to do something. They have to."

"Like dried wood, slathered in yer burny gunk," Quaindraught said, "all we need is da spark."

"So it seems," Sternus agreed, genuinely impressed.

"We're about to rendezvous with the Chief," Ihrvan added, "You about wrapped up here?"

"Well," Sternus hesitated before continuing, "I thought I was, but if what you say is true, I fear for the knowledge here. I think I—"

"Ya cain't tell nah-body," Sir Quaindraught insisted.

Sir Ihrvan agreed, "The Academy relies on slave labor as much as anyone — and all the political ties."

"I know, I know," Sternus assured them, "but there are some more things I think I'd like to copy before I leave all this to fate."

"Fair enough," Sir Ihrvan accepted, "I'll return here tonight to bring you back into the fold."

"I'll be ready by moon's rise."

Chapter 79
Coordinating Elements

There was a commotion outside the command tent, beyond the breaking of their camp, and Lord-General Harkon exited to see about it. There, among his sea of blue cloaked soldiers, was a green one. Having wrestled his way though them, at last a group of officers headed him off some feet from Harkon's tent.

"Sir, sir, I say again, the Lord-General is not to be disturbed," a blue cloak spoke to the green.

"And I'll tell you again," Chief Jerumir replied, "That if you don't go tell someone that I'm here to see him this instant, I'll wipe the floor with the lot of you and take him my apologies for your sorry arses."

"No need," Vantis Harkon called down, en route, "Peace, my brother — my brothers, peace. I know this man. He'll trounce the lot of you, sure as he says."

It was unlike General Harkon to disparage the skill of his own men. Thus they believed him and readily parted way.

"My High Lord-General," Jerumir addressed him, "I offer unto thee fellow greetings and appreciation for seeing me on such short notice."

"Ha!" General Harkon cracked a single burst of laughter and turned back toward his tent, waving Chief Jerumir to follow.

They simply stared at each other a moment before Harkon invited, "Well, go on, have a seat, take your boots off, help yourself to my oils and wine. I can't imagine we'd stand on ceremony now."

"With apologies," Jerumir began, "and your leave to do so, I'd make this meeting quick."

"Go on."

"This is quite the command element," Jerumir noted, "I'm guessing tis the whole Regiment."

"Tis more than a single regiment, in fact," Harkon explained, "but reorganization and consolidation has blurred the lines between which soldiers belong to whom. You'll find regimental crests from all seven out there, but they have all flocked to me, the general they know they can trust."

"Just to my point then," Jerumir accepted, "I have come personally to both ensure your receipt of his message and that it is believed. I have entered Antoria Royal with His Majesty, Prince Bengallen. He will countermand the Antori offer to absorb Morralish forces, as you correctly expect. He will also, however, offer amnesty to any slave that would depart with us, any Antori who aids them, and orders to all loyal sons and daughters of the mountains to stand, defend, and fight in the name of this liberation."

"You couldn't have come last week?"

"Okay, I admit," Jerumir said with a laugh in his voice, "I didn't know how you'd respond, but that never crossed my mind. Apologies. To your great credit, His Majesty knew of your efforts. They were, in fact, precisely what he'd have you do. Thus, he waited until he needed you to adjust course before interfering."

"I only recently told the priestess that we were not going to commit so firmly," Lord Harkon groaned, though with a smile to one side of his mouth, "She's gotten mixed up with a movement that seeks the same."

"The priestess? Bethany?" Jerumir asked.

"Indeed."

"I've heard of her," he continued, "As well as the various people within the city, whispering of an uprising. I confess, their connection was unknown to me. Can she aid us meeting with their leadership?"

"I suppose she could," Harkon admitted, "but the army would have to march day and night to make it to the city. Not to mention the alarm that would raise."

"No need to march them over night quite yet," Jerumir supplied, "and there'll be alarm enough in the city before they arrive. As for us, I have a faster means of travel at our disposal. If the two of you would join me?"

Vantis Harkon raised a curious eyebrow.

Jerumir MacRoberts smiled in reply.

Chapter 80
Delivering Ultimatum

"Ruffis," Prince Bengallen sat next to the dark elf, speaking his name, "You make it difficult."

"Okay," Ruffis replied in simple acknowledgment.

"Why do you make it difficult?"

"I do," Ruffis replied, "what seems best for me at the time. I'm not always right, who is? Yet I am alive, while there are many, even from your own company, Your Majesty, who are not."

Whenever Ruffis bothered to toss in a proper form of address, irksomely, he affected a tone ensuring there was nothing proper about it.

"You antagonize others," Bengallen continued, "unnecessarily. Just now, your point about survival made, you still had to include the personal insult too. Why?"

"My point," Ruffis replied again, "was not the point. This is not my conversation, it is your own. You are the one with a goal in mind. I can make points all I like, but unless I put some weight behind the point and penetrate their defenses, people tend to take little heed. See, I've used a violence metaphor there so you could understand — and yes, I know, I've made another personal dig."

"You are wrong, Ruffis," Bengallen disagreed, "Mayhap with strangers or enemies, but you have earned a place here. I will heed you when I can or, rather, I would have. Each slight, each 'dig,' each personal attack – oh yes, it does get my attention, my negative attention – and you lose merit in my sight. You don't have to be here. You do not have to call yourself my thane. You are a free man of foreign lands, afar from here. If you wish to stay – Ruffis, if you intend to stay – you'll need to accord yourself with more tact. I can see you are about to protest, so hear me: Ruffis, you do not have to accord yourself differently. You do not have to stay. They are, however, mutually exclusive. Make no mistake, if you choose to stay, you'll also be choosing to accord yourself with more tact and courtesy. Tis your choice though, don't put the weight of it onto anyone else."

"Golly," indignation plain in Ruffis voice, "Thanks for the pep talk, Your

Majesty — just what I needed. How ever did you know? Thank you, thank you, thank you."

" 'Character forges destiny,' " the Paladin-Prince quoted the Wisdom of Vandor, continuing, "Yours is deciding yours."

"Oh," Ruffis mocked, "and a homily too! My lucky day!"

Prince Bengallen did not leave. He sat with Ruffis in the awkwardness of the elf's behavior. Bengallen absorbed the uncomfortable silence, whispering a prayer to himself, hearing his inner voice remind him, for what felt like the thousandth time, that Ruffis was not an evil man. He was a broken man. Until, at last, Ruffis himself got up and walked off, annoyed and frustrated.

Chapter 81
Camping Phantoms

The moons were rising. They were still dark moon dominant, "a no moon," for the second and final night this month. It was the 15th, the middle of the month behind them. After tonight, even at night, the light would hold greater and greater sway.

For this night, however, only a faint halo, like soft flames, shimmered at the edges of the dark moon to mark its passage through the sky. A reminder, that for this one last night, darkness reigned.

Chief Jerumir MacRoberts, a paladin in an elite group of mountain folk adventurers called the Forest Phantoms and leader there of, sat at a small fire about a mile or so south of the city walls. Across from him was his confidant and advisor, a sagely half-elven wizard named Kinnik

The firelight gave their faces an orange glow and made their beards feel dry and weightless. Kinnik stroked his small goatee beard, the light brown hair looking red in the firelight, with three fingers. While, across from him, the Chief did similarly to one of the long braids that tied the corner of his mustache into the rest of he beard, the fire casting a youthful tone onto his graying fur. Both men contemplated the days ahead.

"Does the fire part with any secrets?"

Kinnik smiled at Jerumir and replied, "Fire only knows fire. Believing otherwise, a mistake many who have discerned how to consult it make. I can only tell you that fire has no role in the days ahead. From the perspective of fire, nothing much is about to happen."

"We'll somethin' is 'bout to happen," a rough voice came at them as, another of their companions, Sir Quaindraught, entered the firelight, buttoning his trousers, "the common places are a buzz with too many rumors. Too many to know what. Too many to say nuthin' sure. Yet too many to ignore."

Sir Quaindraught, former squire and paladin apprentice to Jerumir, sat between the two men, the wild red-hair about his head and face almost looking like he had caught fire, come so close to the light they shared. He and the Chief were both large men, both mountain folk, but Sir Quaindraught had an unbalanced and massive look. Wild hair, broad face, neck broader still, arms and chest swollen with muscle. In his armor, he looked to be a full four foot in width.

He was rougher, also, in manner and speech, but Jerumir accepted this. It was he and his adventures, after all, that had kept the younger paladin unsettled, far from the civilizing effects of home, for near on two decades, the whole of Quaindraught's adult life. It did make him almost a caricature of the mountain folk, if not for his paladinhood.

He may have lacked a knight's refinement and carried himself in a simple way, but he was neither simple-minded, nor simple in his devotion to the Din-god. He was well initiated into the higher mysteries of the Church of the Holy Family and was firmly convicted of his role in the world to heal as much as to hack.

"Shouldn't they be back?" Kinnik asked of their other team members.

Sir Quaindraught replied, the movement of his large, flat nose in the firelight, so different than Kinnik's lean, angular one, "Ihrvan had eyes on th' camp, they ain't lost. Yer right, somethin's happened."

Chief Jerumir looked at Kinnik and some cue, some permission, was passed between them.

"Alright," Kinnik accepted, adding, "depending on their distance, I might not be able to talk with Sternus, but I should at least be able to see them."

The wizard turned half away from the fire and placed one hand above the flames. Muttering some strange syllables in a singsong way, he closed his eyes.

The other two leaned forward, expectantly, as though this was not an uncommon occurrence, but said nothing, waiting. Jerumir pushed sweat from his brow, up and over the dome of his bald head, flinging it into the dark behind him. Quaindraught put his fingers into the red fuzz about his face, idly scratching his chin buried within.

In a whisper Kinnik spoke, describing, "Too far. Still within the city wall. Guards, no, praetorians on the wall. Gate locked. They are speaking to the praetorian. I must learn to read lips. You'd think after all these years — Ihrvan wants to know what's happening. Why the increased security? Sternus is trying to bribe their way out with a potion. I cannot make out its color in the night. Looks like Ihrvan is getting an answer. Praetorian, not being hostile. Looks like Sternus' offer is being considered — no, accepted. He wants something else. Wants to see something else. Wait. I am losing it. Gone."

"Tis enough," Jerumir accepted, "Sounds like they'll be here soon."

"Why are we out here, Chief?" Sir Quaindraught asked.

"Whim," Jerumir answered oddly, "We had to meet somewhere, and the stars are so hard to see from within the city. I think we might end up stuck in there for a while. I thought we'd enjoy one last night in the manner to which we are accustomed."

With that, Chief Jerumir leaned away from the fire, all the way back. Reclining on the ground, his head propped up against his kit bag. The others followed suit and, one-by-one, they each fell asleep.

Chapter 82
Trusting Leaders

The high mantle and pauldrons of the man's silver armor came up to his ears and would have covered his mouth, if not for a deep "U" not been fashioned there, into the steel suit. Likewise, the white cape that draped around the whole of him enhanced his colossal presence. Despite this, his well-groomed salt and pepper hair and gentle facial features gave the sense that he was sincere in his patient listening.

The man next to him was much older and frailer. Also, by contrast, he was garbed only in a robe, no armor at all. Unlike the Holy Family priests dedicated to Dinnothyl, who much populated Antoria in their white robes with gold trim, this man was wearing a blue-gray robe with silver trim, marking him out as a priest of Vandor. Moreover, the significance of his silver trim indicated that he was a priest of high station.

"Paladin-Preceptor, D'Tor, my brothers of faith," Bethany addressed them, continuing, "I cannot promise that there will be no bloodshed. I have never taken a life, and while I understand that it must be done in certain situations, I never thought I, myself, would be responsible for even as much as a single death. Yet I stand here before you with this plea. I cannot advocate for this action strongly enough, even with the possible loss of life."

"We have in place," the Morralish senior officer, High Lord-General Harkon, continued where the priestess left off, "a plan that should greatly minimize civilian and military casualties. Tis been our thinking all along. The Morralish soldiers need to go home, all of us. We've confirmed, on many counts, that the Imperator has other designs. We also know that slavery is an abomination and that our allowing it, our predecessors allowing it, for hundreds of years, is our own sin and hubris. What we are planning does seem insane, on the surface, but the more I contemplated and prayed, the more I have seen the justice in it."

"You know how I feel," the Senator Macrobius added, "I've spent my whole life trying to find another way. Yet, in this, the only people who'll die are those who would deny freedom to others — let them die then."

The massive Paladin-Preceptor scowled at the last, replying, "That is an overly simplistic morality for so sagely a man."

"It is desperation," Macrobius disagreed, "It is the abandonment of decades of a more tempered response. Civil and measured response is ever abused and exploited. Simplicity and extremity are the only avenues left to us."

"You were not so eager the last time," the D'Tor of Vandor in Antoria, older than the Senator even, noted, "You kept our confidence and protected our messengers, but ever you advised us patience and caution."

"We're old men now," Macrobius replied, "At last I've run out of patience. Besides, I still had faith in the law, thought the senate could be made to see reason. I admit that I was wrong."

"I am sympathetic," the white and silver clad Paladin-Preceptor interjected, explaining, "but all you have told me is what I had already discerned, what I already know — or what you presume to think I should already know. What – precisely – are you asking me to do? I'll not lie to the Primarch. I am his right hand. I cannot betray him. I shall not."

"No. No," Sister Bethany reassured him, about to explain.

The High Lord-General Harkon spoke up once again.

"Brother, I say nay. On the contrary. We want you to keep the Cathedral of Din safe and secure, the Primarch and all the clerics within. We wanted to assure you that this is no invasion to be repelled, but a just and decisive action. Alas, there will be blood. Such is too often the price of justice – as we paladins know – as the Din-god himself knew. I would not, however, have us slaying each other, Cathedral paladins and Morralish soldiers, in the streets."

The Paladin-Preceptor let out a long and heavy sigh.

"You know there will be paladi in the ranks of the Praetorian. Some of the Centurions are of our order. Many of them I have trained myself."

"Each man," Macrobius philosophized, "is in his heart a freeman. There are repercussions to the actions and oaths he takes. They might sometimes be at odds, but the decision, to act or not to act – to swing and slay or still and stay – is ultimately his own, every single time. For those lost to the confusion, we all are sorry. We all shall pray and weep. Yet as for the man, regardless of his station or affiliation, who strikes down an emancipator for the sake of an oppressor, I say only that his own death is his reward."

The Paladin-Preceptor groaned.

"You've gotten severe, old man," agreeing with his own earlier assessment.

"I've merely accepted that it has come to war," Macrobius defended himself, "This city, this empire, has been at war with itself, its true self, since before I was born. I see that now. I have simply taken a side and hardened myself to see it through. Those who look to me shall not see a speck of doubt in my eyes."

"I have no hand in the laws of this realm," the Paladin-Preceptor refocused the conversation, "I do see that, even in my own lifetime, the degree of partiality in the legal system and an indoctrination into decadence have both blossomed like a mold in the dark. What you propose is terribly unfortunate — but it is also just. I'll not stand against you. I thank you for candor and honesty, that I may better prepare the Cathedral. Tell me few details, no more, save one: Soon?"

"Very soon, brother," Vantis Harkon placed his hand to the larger paladin's arm, whispering, "Very soon."

Chapter 83
Praying Well

At the break of dawn, alone in a garden chapel, between the Imperial Palace and its guest houses, Prince Bengallen knelt and prayed, "Vandor, Father, my God, King of Kings, and Lord of my life, I beseech thee in my hour of need and uncertainty. Watch over my allies with a ready sword. May thine angels stand amongst them and guide their strikes, swift and true. Aid me, humbly I beg thee. Make me worthy of the life thou hast given me, the death from thou hast ever spared me. Lend me wisdom and humility — as it may come to my hands to shape the world. May I only do thy will."

"Dinnothyl, Holy Brother, Son of God," Chief Jerumir prayed on a lone hill south of Antoria Royals' outer walls, "We tread upon your very land, walk your very halls, and plot against your very realm. While I do not believe the marbled walls and alabaster founts of the Imperial Capital are your legacy, I cannot help but think them sacred to you. I am troubled, Brother-God, that I may do you some disservice or disgrace, when all my life, I have naught but sought to serve our Father as you, Din, have commissioned we Paladin do."

"Mother," Malcolm, looked at the stray beam of light that fell into his dark cell through some cracked mortar above, "I have never seen your face, but you have been like a saint to me. As the ways of the Orc were wrong to me, your books saved me. They guided me, gave me an image of you to appeal to and to make proud. Great Mother of All, you have revealed yourself to me and showed me the true destiny of my people, who I can no longer deny. I have never known a father worth having, but may all my countless mothers, through all time, forgive my childish errors, and give me strength to be the son they need. In these days, Great and Holy Mother, make a sign to our people that there is another path, a true path, for them. Mother of my birth, continue to make me a worthy man. If it be the will of all things bright and beautiful, may it start here. May it begin with me."

"Holy Family," Alpona stirred in his meditation and began, instead, to pray, "I have never called on you before. I only barely know you. I see you in the flash of your Prince's eye. I hear you in the reverence held for a priestess I've never met. I feel you in the hearts of men and women who would fight to defend their neighbors in your names. I smell you or your absence, the need for you, in all the places I have traveled. If you are love and goodness and valor and hope and all the virtues of the world, I know of you, but I do not know your persons. In the land of my childhood, there are a thousand and one gods, neither good nor evil, but avatars of the qualities, virtue and vice, held

339

by men. I have never prayed to them. They have never made sense to me. A man can be good or evil — all on his own. Yet, as I face my death, whether in battle or to my wasting fate, I know that I am incomplete. That I have not been imbued with your Divine Light that calls me to love and serve beyond my own ability and inclination, that holds me to the account of virtue, even when my eye might wander or intentions falter. Take me in, Father, Mother, Brother, call me your own, and fill my final days with your purpose."

"Amar," Shomotta, running sand through his hands like an hourglass, called, "I am your servant. They call you saint in these lands. Their gods say you have aligned with them, made as family with them. There was a time that this notion offended me, I confess. Yet, if this Holy Family is anything like, greater even, than the men and women I have known to serve them, then I can see why you would take in with them, humble yourself before them, and ally with them. As above, so below. As they say you have done, I see that I have myself, your servant, also done. Have you sent me here to see this truth? That in the presence of something greater than yourself, the being I have called god, you would bow your head and stand among the angels of another, a true God. So I now stand. So I now bow. Yet wherever you stand or dwell in immortal realms, I shall ever remain your servant. Help me to serve well. Strengthen my arm, my will, my heart, and guide me on the proper course."

The old philosopher, Senator Macrobius, looked out from a high window in the Cathedral of Din, over the city, the Capital of the Imperium that he once loved, and prayed, "Holy Family, I pray that I have not been a fool. I pray that my life was not in vain. Give us the clarity of vision now, to all of your children, to finally see past our own selfish desires, and choose the right thing, for its own sake. For surely it can only happen through your out pouring of Divine Love. Show us wisdom, mercy, and grace in what is to come."

"Mother," Ruffis whispered, alone amid the strange artifacts of foreign decadence, "I have never seen your face. The elves, even in distant lands, say we all are descended from a singular Mother-Progenitor. The elves and men of this land say you live here — that you dwell in their great forest. My own mother was wicked and cruel, I am told, but as I come into this land, I feel as though I've come unto the bosom I have never known. Are you out there, Mother? Am I so near to you now? Is it your love that I feel? I am brash and harsh and prideful, I know, I know. These things have helped me survive. Yet they have begun to feel wrong somehow. Why else would I begin to feel shame for them, except for a Mother's listening ear?"

"Mother, I ever sing your song," Bethany chanted, "Mother, you keep me from all wrong. Brother, you ever fight for day. Brother, you bid me walk your way. Father, you are wisdom, courage, and light. Father, you keep me safe in darkest night. Oh, most Holy Family three, please, one more yet make of me."

"Brother Din, I seek only to serve our Father as you," prayed the paladin Sir Quaindraught.

"Father Van, watch over my soldiers with a ready sword," the High Lord-General Vantis Harkon prayed.

"Brother Din, I seek only to serve our Father as you," prayed the Lord-General Kenneth Cardness.

"Father Van, watch over my soldiers with a ready sword," the Lord-General Kellus Anderason prayed.

"Brother Din, I seek only to serve our Father as you," prayed the High Lord-General Strein Hrothmond, "My daughter has long now been in your lands, wronged, seeking justice, please deliver her. My Prince has recent come into your lands, wronged, seeking justice, please aid him. As for myself, longest of my countrymen in your lands, so repeatedly afflicted by the injustice that thrives here, mocking the once great nation that your own hand made of this realm, Brother, Lord, I ask only that you let me die well. Make me brave in this hour and let my death not please the crowd, but alight a fire in the hearts of every man, woman, and child that would be free, my countrymen and yours. Use my death to make your world better and brighter."

"Blessed Brother, Great Mother," Prince Bengallen continued to pray, "We are many people, from many lands and races, here gathered in this place where Father and Mother made Son, sent into the world that we might know how to live. I believe we each have a place in your Holy Family. I mean not to mock you with what we aim to do here. I pray this on their behalf as well, for they all come only at my command. Know, see, tis this land and its laws, its brokenness and corruption, that mocks you. I come only to take my people home. To lead them into lands that need us, a home that bleeds for us. Yet, if t'was your will that moved me, brought me here that I should do more — I am Paladin, Brother Din. I have been molded in your fashion to serve the Holy Family, divine and mortal. Your children here, they too suffer. They suffer sin they cannot perceive, enjoying the fruits of slavery. Those enslaved suffer worse, ever they cry for freedom. Even if the ear cannot hear it in the streets, my soul can hear it in every room and hall through which I walk, from below my feet, in every dungeon and cell where men and women are kept as beasts or property. If I am here to right those wrongs as well, I pray that you give me a sign. I pray that you do not let the moment slip me by. You know I weep every night for my love. To me she has become the symbol of my people, the Morralish people, who also suffer, from whom I am farther from than ever. Farther than ever I thought to be. I cannot help but long for her, to go to them, but do not let my own designs blind me from the path you have laid out before me. Do not let me return to her, even a single ounce, less the man you would have me be."

"My prayer, I say it," they all, unbeknownst to one another, prayed in unison.

Chapter 84
Misunderstanding People

"Your Highness," the Antori guard at the door to the parlor of the guest house announced, "the most honorable Senator Iscavius."

"Your Highness," Iscavius himself echoed as he entered, taking a deep and formal bow.

"Ah, good Senator," Prince Bengallen, having returned from morning prayer only moments prior, accepted him, "You again attend me. What plans on this fine Vansday?"

"I do, Your Highness," the Senator confirmed, "As we've discussed, the Imperator has asked me to take you and your companions to his private box in the Grand Arena. Litters can be arranged but I took the liberty of assuming the sons of the mountains would walk."

"We shall, and we are ready, be you so good to escort us."

"The honor is mine, Your Highness. We should depart at once."

The Prince's entourage leaving the palatial grounds consisted of Thane Ruffis, Brunsis the Minotaur, Sir Garrus, Sir Caldun, and Sir Bohr. The Forest Phantoms had come and gone earlier that morning, taking Prince Bengallen's five Frontiersmen soldiers with them.

As they strolled the short distance to the Colosseum, they palavered idly. Senator Iscavius touted the many wonders and luxuries of the Capital and Prince Bengallen encouraged him with polite questions expressing uncertain interest. Until, at last, a genuinely interesting topic they happened upon.

"So not all the men who fight in the games are slaves?" Brunsis asked.

"Not all of the men are men," Iscavius answered, "among all strata of fighters, a woman emerges from time to time. Most are, however, male slaves trained as gladiators, but nearly as many are criminals sentenced to executions. Some rare few are free men, prize fighters and former gladiators come for glory and coin. This is actually the season in which we typically feature animal performances, and not all of those are fights. Chariot races and exotic animals performing astonishing feats of skill, breeding, and training. Yet, today, we will see gladiators and blood."

"Why is that?" Ruffis asked, "Not on our account, I hope. We can make our own bloody spectacle — if we want to see one."

Bengallen summoned all this restraint not to glare at the impertinent elf. If the comment was to be disregarded as the flippant snark of a braggart, he did not want to give it a second thought with a scowling glance. Yet it was the kind of over-confident, loose-tongued jibe that could ruin everything.

Iscavius appeared to take it as the former and, with an ill amused laugh, dismissed the notion, answering the question instead, "There was an attempted rebellion in the north. The people worry over much about such things. The Imperator leads the people as well as the Legions. As he sends armies to quash a petty insurrection, he gives the people a renewed focus on the glories of the Imperium."

"Distraction," Prince Bengallen laughed, "look over here, not over there."

"Partially, Your Highness," Senator Iscavius admitted, elaborating, "History is reenacted in the arena. Justice is on display in the arena. Glory can be found in the arena. These things are the Imperium."

"Spectacle," Bengallen disagreed, "Tis neither history, nor justice, nor glory but the shadows of them."

"We need not go, Your Highness," Senator Iscavius offered, "but I think you may regret it if you do not."

"I agree," Bengallen said, shooting Ruffis a quick smile, apparently willing to play his game, "but I am curious why you would say so."

"The Imperator has asked me to wait. More of the drama, I suppose."

"What does it say, forgive my asking, that the Imperator can turn the heads of an entire city-state, the capital of an empire, so easily?"

"No treason in either of us speaking our minds," Iscavius first addressed the apology before answering, "Your Highness, I think it tells us that the Imperator knows what Antoria is. Not laws, not light, neither the marble of the Senate nor the alabaster of the Great Cathedral, the Imperium is composed of these things, yet they are not it. The Imperium is the people – a mob – a greedy, hungry, savage race that we call humanity, but is little different than a horde of orcs except that we should keep them properly serviced or led. They

344

call out for fame and fortune and blood and the Imperator gives it to those he can and the illusion of it for those he cannot, to keep the mob in order. History, justice, glory, fame, fortune — Blood, the Imperator gives it to them in buckets, it soaks the sands of the arena, and the mob is sated, the horde doesn't rise up and run amok. They become as civilized people once again. He gives them bloody spectacle and they love him for it. Your Highness should take note."

Prince Bengallen, silent, surprised by the Senator's sudden candor, wondered what had encouraged him. Surely, the day still had plenty of surprises for both of them.

Chapter 85
Arresting Suspicions

Alert was up. It was on everyone's faces, in their eyes, wide, darting. No one was actually doing anything. Too few people, even for so early in the morning, each one giving each other uncertain looks.

The city streets had an edge to them. Too many praetorians, especially for so early in the morning. Inversely, they were mostly avoiding eye contact with anyone but each other.

Yet, nothing overt or tangible was happening. Rumors and tension, everyone was responding to rumors and tension, which only spawned more rumors and wound up the tension, but no one – no one Jerumir or his Forest Phantoms had spoken to – actually knew what, specifically, was about to happen or when.

Everyone, Antori, Morralish, soldier, civilian, slave, free, and in between, it had come to the point where everyone knew something was about to happen. They simply did not know what or did not want to show their hand.

Sir Jerumir, Sir Quaindraught, and Kinnik had picked up the two Spearpointers and three Woodhavers from the guest house provided to their Prince, earlier that morning, added support were they to need it. Apparently, last night was the first night of the curfew. Sir Ihrvan and Sternus would have been allowed to go to a residence or inn. Yet, for their insistence on trying to get out of the city, they were arrested on "suspicions."

While it is true that in Morralish, the King or his agents, lords and knights, could detain anyone for any reason, it was done with exacting restraint. Everyone answered to the King and they did not want to make him look bad by imposing false incarcerations or through technically legal harassment, as any such action was ultimately done in the King's name.

Even if they did not respect some allegedly suspicious person, they usually respected the King. Even if they did not respect the King, they had no desire to earn his personal ire. So while those with authority had it in spades, it was used sparingly.

In the Imperium, however, a hundred years ago, the Senate had created a law that allowed any law enforcement, praetorian, magistrates, or constables, to detain any person for up to two full days, if they had "suspicions." No evidence of crime, no formal allegations, "law" enforcement was simply given unrestricted, unquestioned power to hold anyone for two full days — on nothing more than "suspicions." The power was often abused.

Need a leg up on your business competitor for a contract? Bribe a constable and have him lock them up for two days on "suspicions." Need to teach your mouthy neighbor his place? Have him taken in on "suspicions."

Such was the corruption of the Imperium. Such was the failure of the "rule of law." Laws cannot be personally offended when they are abused. When no personal relationship or accountability is on the line, misuse of power has no consequence.

When the laws themselves are unjust, justice loses all meaning. The law becomes nothing more than a game to be played. Whether by you or on you depended mostly on the amount of coins you could invest in keeping the game going.

The jail on the south side of Antoria Royal was garrisoned by a jailer, appointed by the district magistrate, and two praetorians. Sir Jerumir, a knight – no other titles needed to be thrown about – arrived with seven additional warriors in tow and demanded the release of his friends.

The jailer had no idea who his prisoners were or why they were there. Neither did he wish to piss off some foreign knight and risk the ire of his attendant warriors. Moreover, the jailer was not possessed of anymore respect for the law than anyone else.

The law provided neither the confidence to stand behind it nor inspired the conviction to die for it. Thus, the jailer gladly released the prisoners to a knight's custody, as it looked like doing so would save his own ass. When the laws themselves are unjust, justice loses all meaning.

"Today," Sir Ihrvan, breathing the free air, said when they were a dozen feet from the jail.

"Are you sure?" Chief Jerumir asked.

"Getting pinched last night was a pain," Sir Ihrvan replied, "but I listened to the praetorians. I got lippy with them to keep them talking. I don't know what they know. Still don't know what – precisely – is happening, but it happens today."

"We go back to the palatial guest houses then, to be with His Majesty," Jerumir commanded the men with him, "When whatever is to happen, happens, we must protect him at all cost."

Chapter 86
Arranging Contest

Senator Iscavius led Prince Bengallen and his entourage to the Imperator's pulvinus, the spacious compartment reserved for the Colosseum's most important spectators. It had two balconies. The one toward the Grand Arena within contained seats for viewing the action. Another over the outer wall provided a moment's reprieve, when needed, with a stunning view of the city. The compartment between had many refreshments and servants to carry them.

The Senator had taken a brief leave from their company, after delivering them, but before anyone had settled, he had joined them once again, offering, "Apologies, my duties are many this day, Your Highness."

"Again the Imperator does not grace us with his presence?" Prince Bengallen asked, looking to the empty throne.

"Apologies, again, Your Highness," Senator Iscavius replied, "Just the matter I went to investigate. The Imperator is oft taken with the business of running the Imperium. He means no slight or disrespect, I assure you. In fact, he has made it very clear that we are to extend you every courtesy. If you would take his seat, we will treat you with appropriate accord."

"In that case," Bengallen accepted, roosting upon the seat of honor in the pulvinus, he added, "Bring us more of that fabulous wine you've been serving me."

Iscavius waved a slave off and, as the woman scurried to fetch it, he continued to address Prince Bengallen, "Have you been introduced to your company yet?"

"No," Bengallen said pretentiously, playing the part in the Imperator's chair, "I've hardly noticed them."

"These are my colleagues, the Senators Ramius and Fexo."

"Senators," the Prince acknowledged them.

"Your Highness," they replied with slight bow.

"This is Cerro Darisi, an up and coming lanista, who has brought a clutch of his finest gladiators from Napua — where they have won great acclaim slaying a monster such as your own."

Prince Bengallen was about to turn to Brunsis, to gage his response to the label, when this so-called Cerro fellow winked at him and scratched his chest. This drew the Prince's attention and he finally noticed this well disguised member of his company. It was Caanaflit!

Buried beneath a wig of wavy hair, a fine tan, and a small goatee beard, all the familiar features of Caanaflit loomed. *Why he was there?* Bengallen did not know, but not fifteen feet from himself, he would have missed his friend entirely had not the eye fluttered between them and the known sign given.

The others too? As gladiators? Whether from god or general, surely this was a sign, wasn't it? Mind reeling, concerned and conflicted thoughts, the Paladin-Prince missed the further introductions of the other men.

He only heard Iscavius conclude, as he changed topics, "This first fight should be of particular interest to Your Highness. I alluded to it earlier. A traitor from your own armies, a General Hrothmond. He survived his own execution against lions — that you might bear witness, so it would seem. In grand tradition of the Grand Arena, he lived to fight another day."

"Lions?" Prince Bengallen laughed, "You should have consulted me first. Legend has it that Strein Hrothmond killed a bear when he was only three. There is a folk song about it and everything. I grew up singing it as a child. He is – was – a lord of the most westerly and southerly portions of the Morralish Umberlands, bordering the Frontier, of which it was a part until he settled it. The song called him 'Lord of the Wild Frontier.' I'm sure tis mostly exaggeration, but still, there's surely some origin of it, mere lions won't slay a man like that."

"Well, Your Highness," Senator Iscavius replied, "He did put on quite a nice showing. They sent two lions and he killed them in as many strikes. So they sent two more. He hid under the carcass of one, killing another from ambush. He had a hard fight with the last one, but won with naught but scratches."

Prince Bengallen, having considered his company and gathered his thoughts, asked, "So who does he fight now?"

"Some other criminals, no one of note, I don't even have names to announce them by."

"No," Bengallen decreed, "If this man is a traitor, then he will die. Use my *monster.* That will be your grand spectacle."

"But Your Highness—"

"Every courtesy, yes?"

"Yes."

"If the Imperator himself sat here, on his big chair, would he deny me?"

"No."

"Would you deny him?"

"No."

"Then make the arrangements."

Iscavius dispatched another slave, this one to stay the release of the criminals onto the sands.

"No one man is fit contest for the Minotaur," Brunsis said of himself to Bengallen and Iscavius, "Give me worthy contest, Your Majesty, I beg of thee."

Bengallen looked to Iscavius for reply, but when Caanaflit, as Cerro Darisi replied, the Prince realized what was happening.

"My men are monster slayers and but scheduled to fight each other. Truly, a waste," Caanaflit remarked, "What better contest than to have them join forces once more, to take down yet another monster? This time, for the eyes of the Capital."

"Well," Iscavius huffed, "I'm really no expert on any of this, but if all parties find it acceptable, I can make it happen."

Prince Bengallen, Brunsis, and Caanaflit all nodded. The Minotaur hoisted himself over the rail of the balcony, dropping himself from the pulvinus and into the seated spectators. Shouts and gasps went up as he ran down the tiered rows of bench seating. At the end of them, he dropped again, finally into the arena. It was an unconventional entrance.

The people were not sure what to make of it. At first they gasped in shock, it was so odd. He was odd. The Minotaur began charging around, wildly, flexing muscles, thrusting his fists in the air, doing back flips, and showing off in general. Having proved no threat to the spectators and ultimately contained in the arena below them, the crowd cheered, immediately thrilled. They began to laugh at his antics and encourage the strange creature's strange behavior.

Iscavius departed once more to rearrange events and, with a modicum of privacy, Bengallen asked Caanaflit, "So these monster slayers of yours, Cerro, are you truly relieved that they will not face each other?"
"Very much, Your Highness," he answered, "They have been comrades for sometime. I think there is still a bright future ahead of them and their master. Watch and see."
"Indeed."

Chapter 87
Finding Seats

Having arrived too late at the guest house, to join the entourage, and having tracked the Prince to the Colosseum, Sir Jerumir stood at the front of his Forest Phantoms and the Frontiersmen with them. Four Antori praetorians barred their access to the Imperator's pulvinus.

"Like I've said," Jerumir groaned in frustration, "I was away from His Majesty's company, on his business, when he came here. Now that I know where he is, our duty is to attend him."

"Like I've told you," a praetorian snapped, "I'm not to allow anyone up there, and there is no room for all of you besides. I implore you to find seats nearby, enjoy the show, then you can meet with your prince afterwards."

"I agree," a voice came from behind them, as the man attached to it began to push his way through.

They turned, discovering Senator Iscavius.

The praetorians stood at attention and their leader acknowledged him, "Senator."

"Sir Knight," Iscavius addressed Jerumir vapidly as he passed him by, "Your prince is well attended by his other knights. There is no more room. Please make do and he will see you after."

Isvacius pushed forward. The praetorians parted to make way for him. Sir Quaindraught gave the Chief a significant look, but to it he replied with only fixed eyes that warned caution.

"These men are just doing their jobs," Jerumir commented.

"We are, sir," one of the praetorians said, sounding unexpectedly earnest with an apologetic tone.

"No need to trouble them further," Jerumir concluded, walking away and waving for his companions to join him.

They walked out into the nearest section of seats and found them surprisingly full. Before they tried to find seats of their own, however, they each scanned the scene, taking note of different things, in a different order, but there was much to notice.

Jerumir first observed the Prince, back, up, and to his left. He could see Bengallen sitting in a throne with Knights of the Spear, Ruffis, and others in his company. He watched as Senator Iscavius joined them there.

Next, he saw what had drawn the eyes of most of his companions: Brunsis. The Minotaur, down on the arena floor, made a show of himself, a rather odd show, and the people of the crowd appeared to enjoy it.

Sir Ihrvan had moved off and was asking some folks, at the ends of three different rows of seats, to scoot in so that the Forest Phantoms and their Frontier allies might sit in vicinity to one another. He had surprisingly easy success.

At first Chief Jerumir, only noticing this peripherally, assumed it must simply have been in line with arena custom, but he remembered that such was absolutely not the case in Napua. This drew his attention to Sir Ihrvan, who – even as the others began to sit and the contest oration began – stared at his Chieftain with astonishment worn openly on his countenance.

Jerumir looked away from his companion and into the crowd near them. *Strange. There were a surprising number of mountain folk in this section of the crowd. A happy coincidence? Unlikely.*

Chapter 88
Announcing Combat

After some time, Senator Iscavius returned and made straight away to the center of the pulvinus, announcing the fight to come, "Behold! The fearsome Minotaur, creature of legend! You know his tale and, now, he has come from afar in pursuit of worthy contest."

The crowd exploded with excitement, although a touch less maniacal than what had been encountered in Napua. They each felt the energy, the roar sounded, more genuinely excited, anticipatory, and less looking for an excuse to misbehave.

Three men, familiar men, Malcolm, Alpona, and Shomotta, walked out onto the sands of the Grand Arena as Senator Iscavius continued his oration, "And who would dare face such a daunting creature? Who but men, brave men, the bravest, already wet with the blood of monsters, succeeding where all men before them had failed. A foul horror had taken up residence in the arena of our fair sister, Napua, feasting on an endless buffet of champions, an insult to the city. Until these men, the Slayers of Illwarr, rose up and felled the beast!"

Ovation. The crowd clapped and stomped, but its cheers were few. As if to acknowledge the accomplishment, but without a ravening thirst for their blood. *What was this?*

A fourth man emerged, trailing behind them some distance, and he too was announced in kind, "To aid them, a man who survived his own execution, a slayer of beasts, a purported 'Lord of the Wild Frontier,' a traitor in search of redemption, Strein."

There was, briefly, some sporadic jeering, but it quickly silenced, an unusual thing for the beginning of a fight. All was silent as the four gladiators lined up to face the Minotaur.

"Might I address the prisoner?" Prince Bengallen asked, projecting into the quiet and interrupting the narration.

Iscavius looked nervous, but whimpered in agreement, "Unusual, but I was told, 'every courtesy' for Your Highness."

"General Strein Hrothmond," the Paladin-Prince stepped forward and addressed him, a series of short shouted statements, pausing for clarity, so that

354

all would hear his words, "They say you have betrayed your oaths. – You should know – that I have traveled here – from afar. – By way of the Frontier Road, – passing through Three Gods Pass, – and all the long road – from here to there. From my generals and commanders – I have heard all about your deeds – and know the truth of them. – Know that I am fully aware of your schemes."

All the fighters, thanes, soldiers, and allies of Prince Bengallen turned toward the pulvinus and saluted him. The Paladin-Prince, hand up, palm outward, hailed them in return.

"What is this?" Senator Iscavius asked, confused.

Prince Bengallen smiled, "Historians will be trying to sort that out for decades."

"What?" Iscavius protested, "Just tell them to fight and be done with it."

"I want you to remember —" Bengallen said, a foreboding note in his slow words, "In the days ahead, I want you to remember those words. Remember that you asked for it."

Chapter 89
Inciting Insurrection

"This is a good man," Prince Bengallen declared, asking, "how many good men have bled and died upon these sands since our Brother, Dinnothyl, First Imperator, left this life to return to the Father?"

There was a disturbance in the crowd. It began directly across from the Prince, spreading like a wave to either side, the disturbance rippled. They should have known. The arena had not been so full in more than a century.

Arrogance convinced the promoters that they had simply advertised the "Slayers of Illwarr" well. Yet the Capital had never seen that monster. They had not supposed to care so much about it nor its slayers.

Yes, the Colosseum was near capacity that day. As the Paladin-Prince spoke, questioning the validity of the Imperial justice, all learned why. The disturbance was of men, Van-blessed mountain folk, standing. Taking cue from one another, they produced blue cloaks, donning their uniform attire.

As the knights saw their opportunity, their soldiers followed suit, donning blues of their own. The Paladin-Prince had made the first move. All anyone – all that everyone – had been waiting for was for somebody else to act. Prince Bengallen led.

They had come to see their Prince, many for the first time in a long time, uncertain of who his trials had made him. They had come to free their countryman, the storied Lord-General Strein Hrothmond, the tale of his arrest having spread far and wide. What they had found, however, was their impetus.

The Prince had defied the Imperial sentence. He openly declared the goodness of a man that Imperial law had condemned to death. He saved their general and spoke aloud the doubts they each carried in their hearts, but had only shared in whispers. They knew who Bengallen was then. Blue cloaks unfurled, in support of their Paladin-Prince, and it was like an ocean's wave, a tidal wave.

Chapter 90
Remembering Cyno

"Is that the cue?"

"I think that's the cue!"

"I don't know, man ..."

"Tis something. I've never heard those sounds before."

"The orc said we'd know."

"I don't know, man ..."

"Be still," the gladiator with a touch of gray at his temples barked at the others, pointing his spear at those with him, "His name is Malcolm. We fought together in the Frontier. I saw him take down a troll and he saved my ass more times than I can remember. He said we'd know."

"Cyno, all the guards are dead," another gladiator reminded him, disagreeing, "we can escape into the streets."

"And be cut down by the praetorian legion," Cyno countered, "Gird yourselves. Make ready."

"Look!" another shouted, pointing to the arena gate.

As it opened, two gladiators, dressed as guards, entered and beckoned the others forward, calling, "Now! Come. No red. No purple. Ditch your reds. Come!"

A dozen gladiators rushed toward the arena gate. At least as many more, dressed as Antori military, pulled off their capes and sashes, following behind. In the antechamber left behind them, their remained only a pile of naked corpses.

As the man with gray temples, Cyno, ran toward the light at the end of the tunnel, the silhouettes of his fellow gladiators bounding before him, he remembered many things:

His caravan, his family and friends, left Three Gods Pass and had been traveling the Frontier Road only two days, not even camped a second night, when the orcs attacked. It was not fear that gripped him, when first he saw the wave of brutish raiders pouring over the hillside, it was offense. He had paid taxes all his life. Taxes, he was told, that kept the roads patrolled and safe. He was purely offended, at least for half a moment.

As the rampaging orcs charged through the middle distance, many would pause, stutter-stepping, and hurl a spear. So as the orcs kept coming, row and row of falling projectiles preceded them. Once Cyno saw that the fear finally seized him. He was not a fighter, not back then, and so he froze.

As spears landed to his left and right, he froze. As spears landed in the chest of his wife and the leg of his son, he froze. *If only*, he remembered thinking, *a spear had slain his daughter as well*. As the orcs rushed in behind their fallen spears, some with axes, others reclaiming and wielding the spears thrown, Cyno merely stood there, frozen with terror.

The survivors, and there were few, were taken, along with the goods of their caravan, back over the hill and into the edge of the Dreadwood, to the orc village. It looked like a camp, like it could be moved, but that it had not done so for decades and had thus taken on permanent features.

The terrible years there were cruel and could only be remembered as a blur, as the mind defended itself. He remembered how his daughter suffered. He remembered not being strong enough to help her. He remembered how they punished him for his attempts and wishing that they would kill him for his failures. He lived to suffer.

Yet, he remembered one other thing, an odd thing. Cyno remembered the half-orc. He remembered how often the half-orc took his daughter for the day. He remembered her telling him, her father, how the half-orc was different, that he treated her well. Even though she not the best choice of slave, not strong enough to make his work easier, he would select her anyway, whenever he could, to keep her from the terrible treatment of his orcish kinsmen.

He remembered the night of the thick mist, when he, his daughter, and all the others awoke, their bonds vanished from wrists and legs. He remembered the half-orc leading them to safety that night as well as in the days ahead, out thinking their pursuers. He remembered the half-orc keeping them alive, leading them to safety, and the devastation on his savior's face, when all the freed slaves sold themselves back into slavery with the Imperium.

He remembered telling himself it would be better. He remembered regretting that choice. Cyno remembered being separated from his daughter.

So he remembered Malcolm well and when he saw that half-orc, here, under the arena, he knew two things. Cyno knew that he owed Malcolm his allegiance and that if anyone could help him, it was Malcolm.

He bribed a guard and visited Malcolm in his cell.

"We say it," he said, having entered at the conclusion of Malcolm's prayer.

The half-orc thane looked over to him, acknowledging, "You are not a guard, but wait, I know you."

"You were kind to my daughter. You saved us from orcs, from a troll, and from the ruthlessness of the wilderness."

Malcolm smiled his realization and spoke his memory, "You put spear and torch to the troll as well, good Cyno. Tis good to see you alive."

"Tis," Cyno echoed, noting, "Sounds like you made it up to Morralish. Is it true? What they say? Destroyed by a dragon? They say you have slain monsters. Did you kill it?"

"Mixed truths," Malcolm answered as best he could, "Tis all a bit more complicated than that."

"I am sorry to see you in captivity," Cyno remarked, "Not that anyone deserves it, but I know freedom holds a special place in your heart."

It had become harder and harder for Malcolm not to think like a slave, the longer he played the role, but the gladiator's sympathy reminded him of the truth. Malcolm shared it in a conspiratorial whisper, "This, oh, no, my good Cyno, I am no slave. The man who purports to own me is an ally. We have infiltrated the Capital under this guise. My fellow 'Slayers of Illwarr' are the same. We come to – to – well, tis a bit complicated."

"Are you here to free the slaves?"

"That is one outcome," Malcolm admitted, "If we can. How freely can you move from cell to cell like this?"

"Malcolm," Cyno said with a lightness in his voice, "I have been a gladiator for more than a year now. My victories earn me little coin, but the guards are even more poorly paid than I. They're all just here hoping to become legionnaires. Having survived this long, though I, a slave, and they, free, I am wealthier than all of them. They know it. I can bribe them as I please."

Malcolm lowered his already still voice to the barest of whispers, asking, "Would you move against them?"

Cyno's face grew hard, his eyes narrowed and his lip curled as he growled, "I would murder them all if I could."

"T'will likely come to that before the end," Malcolm admitted.

"What must I do?"

He remembered organizing the other gladiators. Assuring some, convincing others, ensuring many did not strike too soon. When that senator finally left, after the restructure of events, and the promoters took the extra guards with them to view the contest from their box, that was when they struck.

He remembered taking over the entire subterranean complex and posting rebel gladiators in place of the slain guards. He remembered not freezing. He remembered not hesitating. He remembered acting, decisively, ironically, in the manner his lanista and doki had beaten and drilled into him.

He remembered it felt like justice.

Thus, as Cyno emerged from the gate, into the arena, to see what fate his actions had procured him, he felt reborn. As he saw Malcolm and his allies, astonishingly, a Minotaur among them, he felt like anything was possible. Cyno thought about liberating his daughter, again, and telling her how all of this came to be. How surely this was fated by the gods.

In the last moment of Cyno's life, as the Antori crossbowman landed a bolt at his throat, as the projectile bore down into his chest, piercing his lung, and as his knees planted in the sand of the Grand Arena, Cyno felt absolutely no regret.

So many moving pieces. So many of them unknown, even to the movers. Nonetheless, all had slid together, in this moment, like a finished puzzle. The secret it revealed, the same as all puzzles: Despite the mystery and uncertainty, in the finish, it could have been no other way.

Thus, thousands of loyal soldiers stood in the Colosseum and Prince

Bengallen ordered the rebellion to proceed, "Take word to the streets, to the hills, spread it near and far. All slaves strike bond from their masters. All sons and daughters of the mountain strike down the traitors who have forfeit their inheritance, they are no longer your kinsmen or leaders. Let all men and women who would be free, join me! We make our stand here!"

Before he was done speaking, the few guards and praetorians that remained in the arena were as dead as the pile of them below in the cells. This included a certain crossbowman, who did not even live so long as to see the unfortunate outcome of his accuracy.

Malcolm had not lowered his hand from waving to Cyno, when the man at the head of two dozen freed gladiators, crumpled before him. The half-orc rushed to aid him or offer some parting word, some comfort, but it was too late. Blood, pouring from the neck, pooled like a halo around the man's head.

Though he struck dead instantly, the kind of death that Malcolm would have otherwise found particularly unsettling, a death that would normally rob us of closure, Cyno yet wore an echo of life upon his face. Gazing up at the blue sky, his countenance displayed the joy, the satisfaction, and the hope of a man liberated.

Malcolm, while wise enough to know that not all the freed slaves, who were to die in the freeing, would pass in such a state, felt a profound comfort knowing that they might, that they could. That the face of this man told him freedom was worth dying for, even in the dying, was paramount. The half-orc thane would tell the tale, "The Liberation of Cyno," countless times in the coming years and it would ever remain a great consolation to many who lived through such things, in Antoria, in Morralish, and beyond.

Chapter 91
Changing Command

Morralish soldiers turned on their corrupt commanders. As word spread that day, knights, captains, commanders, and even generals, who had "taken up the red," casting aside their cloaks of Morralish blue to don Antori Legion color and insignia, were challenged. The highest ranking loyalists within their units rallied their soldiers to stand against them. Most surrendered or withdrew, some were defeated in single combat, whether it came to blows or not, few won the day.

Companies, wherein no officers remained, were taken over by their senior sergeants. Remnant battalions were subsumed by others. The Sixth and Seventh Morralish Army Regiments were completely overthrown by loyalists at the highest echelons of command, with some few Captains, paladins to a man, taking on duties of their discharged leadership.

There were a handful of tragedies, pitting brother against brother in pitched skirmishes of divided loyalty, where a traitorous leader bested his challenger or, his chosen soldiers ready, defeated the loyalist coup. Some were interdicted by additional challengers until at last they were defeated. Others fled, only to be hunted down later. Some few, with their red band of renegades, survived and went west into the furthest reaches of the Imperium. War comes neither with guarantee nor without tragedy.

Small scale versions would be repeated many times over, throughout the domains of the Imperium in the coming months, as word would reach this unit or that. By nightfall of the first day, however, with the sliver of bright moon waxing, a sliver of hope growing, at the horizon, the paramount truth of this endeavor would come into being.

All the Morralish military forces left on the board, within three days' march of Antoria Royal, would be loyalist forces. Each of them commanded by soldiers whose sole aim would be the secure withdrawal of their brothers and sisters from Antoria.

Until night had fallen, however, and even in the hours beyond it, much else would transpire. It was midday yet, with a long day ahead. The whole of the Morralish First Regiment, led by their new High Lord-General, Kenneth Cardness, concluded their twenty hour forced march, over the night and through the morning. Their forward lines had crossed the last rise, the last hill outside the city's walls, as the sun blazed full overhead. Before them stretched the sprawling metropolis of Antoria Royal, Capital of the Antori Imperium.

It was a mixed feeling. For the soldiers that had served as mercenaries to the Imperium for years, some decades, the sight had always been a relief, safe harbor, glorious and splendid. This day, however, they were to descend upon it. They would secure the freedom of their countrymen, storming the walls, breaching the gates, and going in after them — if need be. Their purpose was clear, but their feelings were mixed.

With tensions on the rise, a call had gone out to the nearest Antori Legions to reorient themselves south and east. Their orders said not why, but an experienced legatus would know: Someone was worried over the defense of the Capital.

Thus, as the mountain folk formed their lines, they watched most of a legion form their own, before the city walls, in the Fields of Din, arrayed to defend their homeland.

"I'm not one for fightin' in the heat of the day after a forced march, m'lord," a young captain spoke his mind, "but we outnumber'em near on three to one. In'nit best we go route them now, afore they're reinforced?"

"If our scouts report nearby reinforcements," General Cardness replied, "You can lead the charge. If not, well, if not, I'd rather not fight them at all. There's good men down there. See the standard? Eighth Legion. I know many of them. They're men I'd prefer to neither kill nor force to kill us."

"Aye, m'lord."

Chapter 92
Securing Route

More than a hundred miles away, to the east, at the Napua Blockade, Lord-General Anderason received the scouting report, "The First Regiment was well on their way, m'lord, and would have come to within striking distance of the city by now. Our west most battalion is in position to aid the withdrawal or support the engagement, if it comes to that."

Kellus Anderason looked to the other Lieutenant, who had come from scouting opposite, in the east, inviting, "And?"

"All supply depots into the east are secure and ready, m'lord. The Antori way out here are oblivious, and we've done an excellent job intercepting messengers from the Napua and the Capital, so they should stay that way for the foreseeable future."

"You ready to go home, boys?" General Anderason said with a grin.

"Aye, m'lord" the Lieutenants agreed.

"Seems like we all are," the General mused, "How fast can the headquarters battalion get to the western depot?"

"If it happens today, not before its over, m'lord," the first Lieutenant offered, "Four days at best speed, five really."

"Spit and bother," Anderson swore, "We've done our part. Faced with the prospect of merely standing by, I think I'd rather be over there."

"If I may, m'lord," the second Lieutenant spoke, "If you took only the cavalry and reinforced it at the depots en route, you could arrive in the west with a sizable force by this time tomorrow. By the Holy Family, I pray tis done by then, but if not …"

"I say it."

"We say it."

"Rally all riders to the west of the Blockade," General Anderason ordered, "We leave post-haste!"

"Aye, m'lord."

"… And you, Lieutenant. You ride with me and keep coming up with good ideas."

Chapter 93
Deciding Course

General Harkon had been in that audience. Having gathered initial reports from the Captains there, updated more than once along the way. At last, he made his way round to the Prince. Before Bengallen, High-Lord General Vantis Harkon knelt, dropping to the ground, cloak billowing to his sides in a dramatic display.

"Arise, Lord-General, they say I have you to thank for all of this."

Standing, Harkon admitted, "I played my part, sure, Your Majesty. A part I am proud to have played, but many have made this day a reality, not the least of all, yourself."

"Forgive me if I've had too much of politicians wagging tongues to fully appreciate your compliment."

"We know all too well, Your Majesty. This place. I am unoffended, but the compliment is true and well earned. We needed our Prince – I needed my Prince – to act so brazenly as this. What are your orders?"

"I hear you have taken a significant count of our forces and their tactical disposition."

"I have, Your Majesty," General Harkon replied, "We have nearly half a regiment of loyal Morralish soldiers within the city by design and at least a thousand more herein that will take note of our actions and return to the fold: Fifteen-thousand men by night fall — even with casualties. Add to that at least another five-thousand sympathetic insurgents and freed slaves that can and will fight with us. We'll out number the praetorian legion two to one and should still maintain a slight numerical advantage as they add veterans, constables, and private guards to their roster — if it comes to that. Beyond the walls, there is nearly a full regiment immediately to our north, led by General Cardness, no more than ten miles from the city. Beyond them, I've reinforced General Anderason up to a full regiment, but they're spread out, securing supplies and the route home, though half of them could be rallied here within a week's time — if needed. During that same time, other units will hear of what we've done. Commanders swayed by the Imperium will remember their loyalty or their soldiers will remember it for them — sure enough. As I see it, Your Majesty, if you want to take the Capital, we'll have at least sixty-thousand able fighters, with another fifteen-thousand more on the road east, and have crushed three full enemy legions and all their allied skirmishers in the processes, by week's end. The Imperator won't be able to rally any force from the provinces abroad that could challenge our position here for months. Ironic, as us being here created the same vulnerability for our homeland."

"I want to go home," Prince Bengallen said, his voice bereft of authority, "I think we all do. Find and save whatever is left there. I don't want to lose a single soldier more than I have to here. — Our fight is half a world away."

"If you decide against taking the city, Your Majesty," Harkon accepted, offering, "We hold this Colosseum and expand to the surrounding structures as we consolidate and take in the freed slaves. They can't touch us here. We're simply too many. They'll starve us out over a week, but if we don't plan to stay that long, that's not an issue. This ground we'll hold — easily."

"Tis the plan then," Prince Bengallen agreed, his command voice returned, "I am not here to conquer or destroy the Imperium. It will be punished for its sins. Our losses, our penance for allowing them to persist for so long. Wrongs righted, we leave."

"Understood. Great to have you back, Your Majesty," General Harkon replied, raising his arm in salute, "I'll have word spread throughout the ranks at once."

"Also," Prince Bengallen added, "Have my thanes rallied to me at once. I think tis past time I met the Imperator."

366

Chapter 94
Becoming Imperator

The Imperator, Tulonius Variis Andolon the Second, was named for his grandfather. Born thirty-six years, four months, and two days prior to extending a formal invitation for a foreign prince, his displaced regional ally, Bengallen of the House and Clan Hastenfarish, royal family of the Kingdom of Morralish, to enter into his city through the Gate of Triumph. It was not his only regret in all that time.

Prince Bengallen's recent actions in The Frontier, to the benefit of the Imperium, made him eligible for this honor. Moreover, the Army of Morralish had long been guests within the Imperium, mercenaries enforcing the Imperator's Peace in the provinces and protecting the distant borders from the barbarians and creatures beyond them. This arrangement between their fathers, brokered by the Church, had never been ratified by either of them, let alone discussed between them. Tulonius had never even met Bengallen.

Still, the Imperium needed more warriors than its imperial citizens wished to become. Morralish, on the other hand, was full of hardy mountain folk, most trained – by ancient custom in the discipline of arms – and organized by their noble lords. With everything that had happened in the last two years, both before the public eye and under a fog of rumor, about what happened behind closed doors, the time had come for such a meeting.

As an arrangement that had existed since before the Imperator was born, but only barely, it was an institution he greatly desired to preserve. Yet, with the political landscape rapidly changing, at home and abroad, the nature of this relationship was something he planned to evolve. Even as word of Prince Bengallen's survival complicated this matter for the Imperator, the tales of the Prince's heroics gave him this opportunity.

Imperator Tulonius had an older brother, Peloponi. He was seven years old when the first Morralish peacekeepers came to pacify a rebellion in Qallen. It was Peloponi who was being groomed as the next Imperator, as eldest son it was the custom.

Tulonius was being trained as a soldier, to serve at his brother's right hand, to carry his will and word into all the Imperium. When Peloponi and Tulonius, twenty and thirteen years old respectively, were touring the Imperium with their father, they had a full legion of their countrymen, praetorians and legionnaires, as their personal protectors. This did not thwart, however, an army of brigands, exiles in the Western Plains, from attacking them.

The legionary forces had become divided. The brigands charged upon the Imperator's encampment. The fighting brutal, both sides suffered heavy losses. The Imperator was slain. His eldest son died. Tulonius only witnessed the aftermath. Burned and knocked unconscious in the night, his tent had been set aflame and collapsed upon him in the earliest moments of the skirmish.

A combined Antori Legion and Morralish Regiment, the largest search party in the history of Uhratt, came upon the young Imperator and his small escort of Equasari tribesmen several months later. Even at that time, the boy had already taken to wearing the helm – with mirrored steel faceplate – at all times, to hide his face, a ruin of flesh, marred and seared.

On this helm, lacquered and arranged ornately, were rib bones. The Imperator said they were the bones of the slain and made little fuss over it. The single trunk he carried with him was said to contain more of the same.

The legionaries, joyous over finding the surviving heir to the Imperial Throne, took him at his word and followed his lead. The High Lord-General of the Morralish Regiment, however, voiced concern over the boy's appearance and attitude, but it was merely noted and disregarded:

> "The fetishes taken and worn by the
> Imperial Heir imply a great many
> unfortunate thing about the circumstance
> of his absence. The Senate and People
> of Antoria would be wise and good to
> concern themselves, greatly, with his
> emotional and spiritual welfare, but
> for now, the Legatus and his men seem
> well content to ignore my proposition."
>
> — High Lord-General Alpis Harkon,
>   First Regiment, Commanding.

Or so accounted the official histories related to the ordeal.

Chapter 95
Calling Reinforcement

The lightly armored horsemen rode right upon General Cardness, pulling short at the last second. The leader of the three, Lieutenant's rank on his sleeve, shouted, "My lord, enemy reinforcements come from the south-west. My lord, its our own Fourth Regiment, or what's left of them. They're wearing blue, but their command standards have all been replaced with Antori red and there are red centurions and legionaries marching with them. We're now facing near on twenty-thousand opposing forces, combined."

"Rorking traitors! Tis to be a fair fight after all," the young Captain, the General's aid, asserted.

"If the city garrison comes out to reinforce them," the General corrected, "They'll then outnumber us."

"All that's to be about within the walls," the Captain said, "I don't think that to be a likely problem."

"But we don't know that do we?" the General asked rhetorically, turning back to the Lieutenant, commanding, "Trade out your horse and ride hard to the western depot. Tell them of the enemy reinforcement. Inform them that the First Regiment is going to intercept them and, if things go poorly, we may need reinforcement of our own.

"Aye, my lord," the Lieutenant acknowledged, wheeling his horse about and riding off.

"Well, son, looks like that fight is coming."

The Captain made a grim face and spoke, "If I may, m'lord, intercepting the reinforcements puts us right in between them. They'll flank us, and they won't even have to fight for it."

"Have you given up on your countrymen so soon?"

"M'lord, they're General Leitenfrost's men. He's sold them off to the legions. That was his plan."

"True," General Cardness considered, "but were they ever really his to sell, slaves, chattel, or are they free men yet still?"

"Lord-General, if you're wrong, t'will be a tactical disaster."

"If I'm wrong," Kenneth Cardness replied, "Then all we believe in is wrong. All I've ever fought for is wrong. If we've been wrong this long, seems well enough that we ought to die fighting for it anyway. We've got naught else. The world, in any given moment, is right or tis wrong. We defend the right or we die in defiance of the wrong. Tis how a Morralish soldier ought to live, even if it means he must die. We'll put our brothers in the Fourth Regiment to the test. I'll give them that: I have to. After, well, after that, tis in the hands of our Holy Family."

Chapter 96
Deceiving Enemies

General Anderason, upon arriving at the first depot, west of the Napua Blockade, gave his orders for troop movements to the depot commander. As they waited for the soldiers to gather, the General again spoke to his new favorite Lieutenant, "This is your plan, not mine, is it not?"

"I but advise at your pleasure, m'lord."

"Right, right," Anderason waved a hand dismissing, "but you are invested in its execution and success, as its progenitor?"

"I suppose I am."

"We have left only the infantry at the Napua Blockade," General Anderason mused, clearly dragging his feet on his way to making a point, "Do you suppose we've left them too few if the fighters and legionnaires in Napua were to attack?"

"Too few to win?" the Lieutenant asked rhetorically, "No, not so few as that. We'll take greater casualties without the armored lancers to ride ahead. This was a mistake. I'm sorry, m'lord."

"Now, now," General Anderason retorted, "don't go so far as all that. How do we fix it?"

"Other than redeploy back to the blockade?"

"Yes, I've told you where I want to be and you've given me the means to get there. Aside from undoing all that —"

The Lieutenant thought. Anderason already knew what he was going to do, knew it before he left, but he wanted to see how his young officer might work through it.

"We could send all the footmen here to reinforce our soldiers there," the Lieutenant offered, "A twenty percent reinforcement should lower casualties considerably. Although, that would completely abandon this depot."

"Which is why," General Anderason said with a toothy grin, "This is the only depot where we will not add the cavalry to our own. They will remain. If there are any hungry orcs in the hills out there, waiting for this depot to be abandoned, they'll be disappointed – sure enough – to see that more than fifty armored lancers remain to defend it. When I gave my orders to the commander here, it was for his infantrymen to march back to the Blockade. So, my young Lieutenant, you've reached the correct solution, and – if you're quite ready to conclude today's lesson in war strategy – the horses have rested and tis best we be on our way."

"I consider myself sufficiently schooled for the day," the Lieutenant said, walking over to the General's horse and aiding him to mount it.

General Anderason, still smiling widely, looked down and teased, "Then you'll miss the best part."

The Lieutenant folded his arms, motionless, until his instructor had completed the lesson.

"Alright, m'lord."

"We spied scouts aligned with the Antori Legionnaires in Napua watching the blockade," General Anderason continued, "and I wanted to take advantage of that. I let them see us go. Let them see my command standard leave. I let them see us take every horse and rider. T'will be just enough to entice them to attack. Yet they're estimation of our strength will be off, not by twenty, but by more like thirty percent when these reinforcements arrive."

"We'll crush them —"

"And now you have been sufficiently schooled. Mount up!"

Chapter 97
Regrouping Thanes

Morralish soldiers had taken the Colosseum in a swift and decisive action. Between the guards slain by the gladiators, those managing the fleeing Antori citizens that simply fled with them, and the few praetorian legionaries captured at the Imperator's box, there was no significant resistance.

General Harkon's second imperative, after heeding the will of his Prince, was to manage the Colosseum like a fortress. Sentries were posted at key entry points. Others were blocked off altogether. Archers lined the crown like battlements, raining death on anything in a red cloak. On the sands of the Grand Arena, the knights began to organize the soldiers into rank and file, platoons and companies.

Slaves, the readied and quick to act, were already arriving to declare themselves free. Those with no desire or ability to fight, were directed to the tiered seating. Yet for all that, it was clear early on, the Colosseum would exceed capacity.

On the middle tier, right outside the pulvinus, the thanes of Prince Bengallen were brought back into his company.

"Oh, Malcolm, thank the gods!" the wizard Sternus called.

The two had exchanged few words in their brief time together, none in private, so this came as an odd greeting. The half-orc thane rubbed that back of his neck, uncertain, offering, "Thanks."

Sternus did not go to Malcolm, however. With one hand, he touched Chief Jerumir on the arm. With the other, he unclasped a leather strap that crossed his chest, sliding from his back a large, but elegant, claymore longsword and handed it to his Chief.

"Thanks," Jerumir accepted the sword sardonically, before approaching and addressing Malcolm, "This is Frostfang, forged in the Long Winter for my great-great-grandfather — the year the giants came down into our lands once more. Tis my sword and Sternus has, apparently, grown tired of carrying it for me as I carried the Dawnsong for you. I, on the other hand, was honored to bear your blade, and do now return her to you. The quest of your oath at hand."

Malcolm had to laugh a bit, at Sternus, but he restrained himself for the respect and gratitude he bore Sir Jerumir, keeping and returning the ancient sword. Malcolm took the Dawnsong, sheath and all, from the paladin's back. He also replaced the Frostfang there, securing its harness to Jerumir's shoulder and fastening the clasp across his chest.

"Gratitude," they unintentionally said in unison, giving one another the slightest of bows.

Ruffis, likewise, approached Alpona and Shomotta, "Still alive?"

Shomotta reached up and rubbed Alpona's bald head, replying, "And almost in one piece."

Alpona slapped the wizard's hand away, playfully, and spoke to Ruffis, "Glad to see you're still around. Was afraid too much time in the Prince's entourage – without me – might have run you off."

Ruffis made a face. It was not a face that Alpona had ever seen him make, and Alpona, more than most, had seen a variety of emotions upon the countenance of his dark elf companion. *Was it shame?*

Ruffis merely replied, "Not for a lack of trying," but with none of the typical attitude in his voice that such words implied.

Not wanting to embarrass his friend, Alpona simply accepted him, "We'll that's over now. You're drinking buddy is back, and we'll bemoan these trials together over a cask of wine in less than a week."

The warrior took the dark elf into his full embrace, pulling in the wizard, barely within arm's reach, for good measure. Others of the parted company intermingled at the same time, sharing greetings and briefly catching each other up to speed.

Yet there was still much work ahead of them.

Malcolm eventually rejoined his fellow thanes and even he and Ruffis offered something approaching civil pleasantries.

Prince Bengallen, breaking away from his generals and military officers, approached his thane, Alpona, with a sheathed Flammerung in one hand, saying, "You'll be needing this."

Alpona, the Zil-jahi Warrior, remembered how haphazardly the sword had been passed to him the first time and, mayhap Malcolm was rubbing off on him or he was regaining his own sense of propriety, it would not stand for so great a named sword to return to his keeping in so unceremonious a manner again. Thus, Alpona dropped to a knee before the Prince and held both hands up to receive the sword.

No stranger to ceremony himself and having reached a similar conclusion, in hindsight, about the unfortunate practicality of the previous bestowal, Prince Bengallen took the cue. Grasping the sword with both hands, he paused with it between the two of them, parallel to the ground.

"Alpona, my thane," Bengallen spoke, having chosen his words, "Long has this greatsword, come down to us from a Saint of my God, been wielded by the warriors in my family's service. In good faith, I again return it to your worthy custody, that you may continue that line."

"Humbly, I accept," Alpona recited, recalling a memory and receiving the sword, "Together we serve, Your Majesty."

It was over before anyone had a chance to take much notice. Though, with the immediate attention drawn to them, Prince Bengallen shared news, though directed at Caanaflit, for all to hear, "Not counting civilian refugees, the generals project as many as seventy-five thousand soldiers for the trip home. I'll be glad to have every last one, but tis a far cry from two-hundred thousand."

Caanaflit parted his lips to reply, but another spoke first.

"More will come, Your Majesty," Sir Jerumir assured him, "Two years was a long time, even for a loyal man to wait. For the last year, there has been no contracts from the Imperium. Thus no pay for soldiers and even food rationing in some parts. Some units disbanded, others ventured further afield for regional contracts in distant lands. I know most of what navy was here left a long time ago, bound for the Far Continent. Some commanders and their units might even hold to the Imperial decree and stick around to put things back together here, but they'll be few. Your loyal general's have consolidated as best they could. T'will take a year, more, for the whole of the Imperium to learn of what we do here today, longer to points farther afield. As we secure the homeland, in the months that follow, more and more of your distant or estranged soldiers will return home. There are at least another seventy-thousand soldiers out there – somewhere – who would be loyal to you, if they had any idea you were alive to be loyal to. They would be here – right now –

if they had but known to come. Yet in these dark days, they have done what they must to survive, and they are simply too far from us today for what we face in the months ahead."

Prince Bengallen placed his hand on Sir Jerumir's shoulder in silent gratitude. He appreciated the perspective, intellectually, but his heart was still heavy, having *come all this way, only to leave more than half of the soldiers behind. Not technically accurate, but that was how it felt.*

Even still, *that was tomorrow's burden. The fight today was not yet won. Victory, no matter how certain, still had to be earned.* Looking around, the Prince saw that his retinue had been restored. He turned and declared loudly, drawing everyone's attention, "To the Palace!"

Everyone in the Prince's own warband moved forward at that. Everyone save Caanaflit. He lingered a moment, an uncertain feeling upon him.

Dejected? Rejected? Ordinary? Was that it? Just as any other one of them then. Caanaflit shook his head, shed his emotions, and pushed himself forward, jogging to catch up with the others.

Chapter 98
Failing Plans

General Leidtenfrost burst into the room, he and the two soldiers with him, wearing cloaks not of Morralish blue, but of Imperial red. The General, his own red cloak affixed to his chest by a black dragon brooch on his left, shouted, "He has them!"

"Who?" one white robe priest asked.

"The Prince!"

"Has whom?" the other priest asked.

"All of them —" the General insisted, his voice full of panic, "The Armies! All of them — he has all of them."

The Imperator, so like a statue of himself, a stone on his throne, sudden stood, pointing at the former-Morralish General.

"Then you have failed me."

General Leidtenfrost's eyes bulged and he gasped for air. Falling to his knees one last time before the Imperator, he inhaled as the shock of impact transferred from his knees into the rest of him.

The breath did not last, however. His own guards thrust their gladius blades into him. One each, to the left and right of his chest, letting the air out of the General in a most unusual and uncomfortable manner.

As General Hertvork Leidtenfrost lay bleeding out upon the throne room floor, one of the guards pulled the dragon brooch from the dying man and placed it in his own kit bag.

"Find a blue cloak," the Imperator commanded, "Get back out there."

Both guards sheathed their swords, hailed the Imperator, turned about sharply, and fled the scene.

"Exalted Imperator—" one of his attendant priests began to address him, but was cut off.

"Silence," the Imperator commanded, sitting again upon his throne, "Go. Triple the Palace Guard. Do it now."

Chapter 99
Securing Liberty

Prince Bengallen's order to take the Colosseum as a base camp for Morralish soldiers and freed slaves spread more quickly than feet could carry. By late afternoon, slaves throughout the city were declaring themselves free and encountering roving bands of their own kind and mountain folk to join up with.

Merging into larger and larger clusters, all aimed for the Colosseum at the heart of the city, freeing others, by threat or by force, as they went. That their stay would be brief, only as a prelude to an immediate withdrawal, came as a relief to all who successfully arrived to hear it.

More and more slaves began to fill the safe confines of the Colosseum. Ironic that, as a once distant threat to their lives, it had become their present refuge. Too soon their numbers became too many. Slaves began to huddle in the shadow cast to the Colosseum's east, awaiting entry and praying for the protection of archers on high.

Thus did General Harkon, initially reluctant to engage Antoria over the slaves, order – at increased risk to his own soldiers – that surrounding structures were to be taken over as well. By pushing out and acquiring several nearby homes and facilities, the blue cloaks formed a secure zone for the former slaves to inhabit.

Most of them were public structures, two bath houses, a pavilion in the center of a park, an axillary government building, but two were private residences, homes to some of Antoria's wealthiest families. One even had the audacity, not only to not flee, but to attempt to retain their slaves as they departed.

A trio of blue cloaked soldiers began battering down the door, with a full three dozen men behind him. In response, out from the second story, a pair of Antori archer's appeared. They slew two of the three Morralish soldiers at the door, instantly, pulling fresh arrows from their quivers.

One of them, himself spontaneously arrow struck, fell out and over the window's edge. A Morralish sentry, pacing the heights of the Colosseum, wielding a bow of his own, had seen the Antori snipers attacking his comrades and succeeded at a most difficult shot to take one out.

He aimed high, partly against the wind, in a way that only men who hunt game in the mountains can do, letting his arrow fly. It soared, on a course that appeared nowhere near the target. The sniper – who had slain a Morralish soldier doing nothing less than the will of his prince to free these slaves – put his second arrow to string to kill yet another. Before he could draw it back, however, the sentry's arrow curved and fell, sailing on the wind, and struck the enemy archer.

Below the cheek, above the jaw, the arrow bore down into his throat. Its momentum, combined with his recoil, twisted it in such a way that the arrowhead clipped some major artery within. His lifeblood began to flow without.

The remaining Antori sniper loosed his second arrow, but the soldiers below were ready. The targeted man caught the pointed shaft on his shield as another Morralish sentry took another shot, but he was not so skilled as his friend.

The arrow missed, barely in relative terms, clattering against the stone that separated the two near windows. That did not save the sniper, however, as his companion's body, fallen to the ground below, had armed Sir Caldun, otherwise a Knight of the Spear, with the bow and quiver.

As the sentry's arrow missed, the Antori sniper, drawing his third arrow, glanced over the distance, searching for the source of the errant missile. At that moment, Caldun Norledd, below, drew his newfound bow. He loosed an arrow and shot his attacker, above, under the jaw, the shaft tearing deep into the skull of the sniper above.

The blue cloaks broke through the door and into a horrid sight. The dominus and domina of the house, even their children, were chasing their unarmed slaves around the manor with daggers, wounding them, trying to kill them rather than free them.

The Morralish soldiers did not take kindly to this. There was little mercy in the face of such atrocity. The master of the house – still attacking his slaves, with no apparent awareness of the blue cloaks storming through his doors – was executed immediately. So he died, bloody hand raised in bloody violence, when a virtuous man stepped between him and his prey, running four feet of forged steel through his vile heart.

The master's children were captured and disarmed. One of them was brutally knocked unconscious, with fewer teeth, by the gauntleted fist of Sir Bohr Danwyn. Another, who would not drop his weapon, had to be disarmed in a more literal and visceral fashion.

379

These Antori patricians were killing their slaves, while outside these doors more and more slaves and Morralish soldiers were dying for their freedom. There was no time, even for what little mercy they had already been given.

At last, the Morralish soldiers had cornered the lady of the house and, having already been slashed across the bicep, she fell to her knees, casting her long knife aside. Sir Garrus MacMourne stepped forward to subdue her, but a male slave, dark of skin, stepped out before him, pleading.

They could not have looked more different. The Morralish knight was an old northman. His flesh was nearly as white as the snow cliffs in the land of his birth, ablush with pinks from the recent action. His head, covered in a fading blonde mane. His body, cased in polished steel mail and cloth, sky blue and ivory white.

The freed slave was from beyond the depths of the western deserts, his flesh was far darker than any brown sands from the lands of his birth. He was the color of a healthy, fertile soil, good for growing anything. His face and head were bald, sheared clean even at the eyebrows. His body covered only with fresh wounds and old scars, his nakedness concealed by a mere loin cloth, itself tattered and bloody. They looked as different as two men could be.

"No let her live!"

Sir Garrus stepped back and tilted his head down to look the recently freed slave in the eye. They traded glances that told the man that his petition would be heard.

"Domina no live," he said again, still unclear, continuing, "She the worst of all. She do wrong things to us. Filthy things. Make us do to each other. Make us foul each other. Make us do to her guests, for them, on display, pain and shame."

The Morralish soldiers all realized that he was not appealing for the woman's life to be spared. Rather, he was begging them to end it. They neither understood, fully, what this woman had done, nor did they want to. They understood well enough.

The former slave was unsure what to make of the assessing looks on the northmen's faces, so desperately he shared more, "Domina took my manhood. I not think a man could lose it more than once. She find a way. She always find a way!"

Standing before him, Sir Garrus MacMourne remained uncertain as to the man's meaning. All the more sure that he did not want to be, the old knight handed the former slave his own sword, blade down, hilt first.

"Then, by whatever gods you know, take it back!"

So he did.

Some cradled the wounded and dying slaves, willing to pay in flesh and blood for their freedom. Others had the children of slave owners, bound, tossed over shoulder. The High Lord-General Harkon saw them returning as he listened to one of his soldiers give report of the incident.

Harkon's heart was moved. He was a general. He had a responsibility to his men. He would follow his prince's orders to the best of his ability and had done so, despite his personal reservations.

Yet, only after seeing and hearing of the terrible treatment of these slaves that his heart was finally moved. For he was also a paladin. Having at last witnessed the tears and tribulations that he and other paladins working in Antoria, made such an effort to avoid, he could do naught but be moved to just cause.

"Once the perimeter buildings are secured," General Harkon ordered, "Have your commander start forming raiding parties. If this is going on out there all over the city, we'll not standby and allow it. We'll go house to house and see the slaves freed, by any means necessary, then escort them back here. We won't save them all, but by the Holy Family – their grace, strength, and mercy upon us – we'll deliver everyone that is within our power to deliver — from this scourge. I say it."

"We say it!"

Chapter 100
Charging Breach

The light was fading as evening settled around them. The sky was afire, a brilliant red, beautiful on any peaceful night out in the world, somewhere else. Yet here, whether it was an acknowledgment of the blood already shed or as a sinister omen of a bloody night, no one could know.

"Captain!" General Cardness called.

A horse and rider trotted over, "M'lord."

Kenneth Cardness pointed his sword forward and ordered, "Lead the charge. Cut them off. You know what to do, but the next move is theirs."

The Captain circled his sword overhead and two other riders raised their regimental standards and rode up next to him. Together they trotted forward and the whole cavalry followed. The mass of horses and men increased their speed to a gallop. The wave raced toward the middle distance, the ground between the armies immediately to their south. The infantrymen moved out immediately behind them, led by General Cardness himself, but they would be long to follow.

The cavalry charged into the pale blue afterglow. The remnant light from the sun's setting was hardly enough. Already the opposing forces, soon to be on either side of them, had lit torches, however, so the charge's aim remained true. They were soon certain that the two other forces would not be joined before they closed the gap.

Who knows how history would have unfolded had they not? A wishful thinker would tell you that all would have happened according to the character of the men involved and had faith in their character. Yet a wise man knows that the character of most men is forged in moments such as these. A different moment might have brooked different results.

As it happened, moments prior to dividing the forces, the Captain at the lead, a skilled equestrian and archer, lit and fired over his back a burning arrow, a signal flare. With that, every rider whoa-ed his horse and the whole charge slowed. At first to a trot, until, at last, they ambled into place.

Halting, they occupied the middle distance between their opposition. The whole event and all the components were so close that the young Morralish

Captain reached out and touched the north-west corner of Antoria Royal's stone wall.

The Antori Legionnaires, arrayed in defense of those walls, along with the Morralish Fourth Regiment, apparently intent on betraying their brothers and reinforcing the Antori, stood divided from each other. Torchless, far to the rear, the Morralish infantry continued its advance on foot.

With a stand off at both flanks, the Antori called for officers to entreat the arriving Morralish horsemen, already no more than two-hundred feet from their most westerly position. Likewise, red caped officers amid the Morralish Fourth Regiment came forward, out from one sea of blue cloaks, to face two others. One grinning down at them from horseback and another distantly marching down toward them from – most appropriately – the north.

Chapter 101
Counting Nine

Slaves rose up in every home. The whole incident was far bloodier than anyone had wanted or even imagined. Yet, those on the victorious side of history would recall how blood and flame upon sand and stone did smell like justice. So it has always been that justice is never as beautiful as we want it to be.

Many of the wizards, affiliated with the college or with the government, owned slaves. In the aftermath of the liberation there was compiled a tale, "The Nine Wizards and the Ninety-Nine Slaves." In the intervening years, many different versions of the tales were told, each with details reshaped to fit the lessons or morals of the particular storyteller. The most consistent tellings, and thus the closest we can arrive to any historical accuracy, were formed thus:

One.

The room was dark. Each had put out his or her candle and gathered at the stairs. In a line they filled the staircase, a dozen.

"Are you ready?"

"No."

A third man, from behind, slapped the back of his head, "Yes. Yes, we're all ready already."

The first one opened the door at the top of the steps. It pulled inward, so he would took three steps up and forward to pass through the doorway, but did not. His face slammed flat, his chest and hands came to the same plane with similar effect. The man pushed himself away from the invisible wall as their master came from around the corner, revealing himself to them.

His right hand was held aloft, fingers twisted in arcane sign. Eyes focused, the wizard concentrated on the spell that retained his slaves to his custody.

"Wicked slaves," he barked at them, "Have I not been a good master to you? Have you not lived better than others of your kind? Wicked slaves!"

The wizard pushed forward, his gestured hand before him, driving the slaves back down the staircase. The invisible wall closed in on them, tripping them over one another, forcing them into a clumsy retreat. The first man actually fell, after being impinged between the unseen wall of force and the man behind him. He tumbled down the stairs, breaking his wrist in the process.

The others were shocked silent as they gathered together at the bottom of the stair. The wizard descended with them, as his spell drove them, until he too was at the bottom, beneath his home, among the cells where he stored his property.

"I have you on all sides now," the wizard spoke, "Trapped like rats. We'll just wait all this out down here."

With a sweeping gesture from his other hand, the door behind him slammed shut, sealing light from the room, they remained in darkness.

Two.

Several houses away, it played out much differently.

"Come now, come on," the old man beckoned, "I know what is afoot, fear me not."

A young pair, boy and girl, dressed in the simple tunic that denoted them as slaves, each clutching dinner knives, entered into their master's reading parlor. They did not speak.

Closing a book, he addressed them again, "Have I not been a good master to you? Would you slay me now for your freedom? Force me to defend myself? No? No, no, none of that. I was ever as good to you as I could be. Fed you well. Appreciated all your help. Now your day has come and you must be off. I will miss you. I wish you well."

The boy and girl looked at each other, uncertainly. The girl sat her knife down and moved toward the door, avoiding eye contact. The boy held his knife more firmly, escorting her, watery eyes unblinkingly fixed on the old wizard, their master, waiting for the ruse to reveal itself. It did not.

The boy and girl left their former master's home freely, unopposed, fleeing into the night. The man whom they had served placed his face in his palms and wept. He missed them already.

Three.

A third slave owning wizard caught his own attempting to flee. He stood between them and the door to his home, facing off in the parlor. There were four of them and one of him, but he was a master of arcane arts and summoned fire as his ally.

A flame appeared in his left hand as he called to them, "I am a sorcerer, great in power. You know this. What do you suppose to accomplish here?"

"Free, slaves no more," one replied, "we are leaving."

Producing a flame in his right also, holding the plumes of fire in his hands out toward them, menacingly, their master retorted, "Is that so? Free? Tell me, slave, do you feel free?"

Two slaves immediately backed away, while the one that spoke, spoke again, "We are free now. Let us go."

"You are as free as you ever were or will be," the wizard declared, "If you can pass through my fire and survive, then you can go about your life in whatever hideously burned state you find yourself. You are free to suffer my flames, nothing more."

None dared. Thus they remained enslaved.

Four.

A fourth wizard faced off with his slaves as well.

"We're going!" the leader of their dozen insisted.

"Oh," their master replied, "I do really wish you would stay. I need you. With me you have status. No slave lives so well as mine. I can't see a rib on any of you. Do stay."

"No," another said.

"We are going," their leader reiterated.

"Fine!"

"Fine?"

"What?" the master asked, "Am I to be your villain? Am I to try and stop you? Waste my magic upon you, upon slaves? My powers are a gift and too precious to waste on the likes of you. I really do wish some of you would stay – you aid me, make my life easier so that I might pursue my important work – but if you insist on leaving — then, fine, go. Go! Now!"

So his slaves ran and became his former slaves. They left him, all of them, together and confused. He remained alone and disappointed.

Five.

Another wizard, with slaves in her home, walked into the room where the half dozen had gathered.

They all turned and gasped at her presence, her discovery of them. They were all to be in bed by then, but had gathered together for a unified departure.

Without a word, before they could even cease gasping, the wizard snapped her fingers and one of the slaves fell over, dead.

Four fell to their knees and begged mercy. The fifth bolted toward the door.

The wizard spoke a syllable, "Phoo," and the runner collapsed as though tripped or shoved.

"None of you are going anywhere," she stated plainly.

And none of them did.

Six.

This wizard had caught up with his slaves in the street, only a few houses beyond his own. There he brought up his hands and surrounded them with a half-circle wall of orange light. This held the escaping slaves at bay.

"Return home!" he commanded them.

"No!" one shouted in defiance.

The wizard made a fist and swung at the air before him. Correspondingly, the wall of light distorted, producing a gigantic fist from its surface. Mimicking the wizard's own punch, it swung at the slave.

It did not knock him to the ground, however, the conjured wall's force was so magnified by its magical construction that its fist essentially exploded the man. His right arm, left leg, and head flew off from his body as his burst torso took brief flight, leaving a trail of viscera, and slammed into another slave, knocking him over and, apparently, unconscious.

The wizard made a second fist with his other hand and another sprung from the conjured orange wall. He menaced the slaves with them, like a boxer threatening his opponent. They all hunkered down, cowering before him and the large glowing fists of the wall. He had re-captured his slaves, or so he thought.

He began to command them again, "Return hom-ur-ulk!"

His second word was clipped and distorted as a gladius blade sprouted from his chest. Behind the wizard, a mob of freed gladiators had come upon the scene, and they descended upon him with their short swords. One even put his feet to the wizard's hip and ripped off an arm with his own main force, even though the wizard was already quite dead and his magical wall failed by then.

The gladiators, drenched in blood, roared with savage delight. The other slaves, suddenly freed as well, took up their injured companion and fled in the opposite direction.

Seven.

There was another evil wizard, this one a transmutation expert. He delighted in experimenting on himself, twisting his own form into monstrous appearance and abusing his slaves, in all manner of ways, while taken with his transformation. A terrible work that would have been rebuked, even by other wizards of the city, so he always went about his business in the dark.

This night was no exception. He had imbibed the elixir and taken on a form most foul only moments before the slaves had assembled at his door. He had earlier isolated two slaves for the evening's trials and had only begun to ravage one of them when, alerted by her screams, the slaves assembled for escape poured through the door.

Word had gotten round, from those that had survived such ordeals, that the wizard was at his weakest in the moments immediately following the transformation. His awareness dull, no full grasp of his new senses, his ability to use his magic would be briefly nullified.

So as he adjusted to the features and appendages of his new form, the slaves fell upon him. Some with broken glass or pottery, wrapped at the bottom to form crude knives with simple handles, others with modified serving utensils, and two with halves of a large serving tray that they had split, sharpened, and warped at the bottom to fashion something like a pair of scimitars.

The transformed wizard bled from a hundred wounds before he could cast a single spell. As he desperately began to utter an incantation, one the serving plate scimitars struck him across the mouth and another across the spine.

His head ruined, his slaves were free then. They left.

Their master, laid in his own blood, without even so much dignity as to die as a human being. He bled out, twisted in his terrible form, and died that way.

Eight.

An eighth wizard ran his slaves off. They had not all even gathered yet. Their former master came into their quarters, a large complex where he kept two dozen slaves. To some of them he had even once taught a smattering of sorcery and alchemy so that they might better aid him in his endeavors.

There, he addressed them, "Suppose you all know what's happening. Suppose you all just go on and get outta here. Well, go on! I'm tired of feeding you and putting you up. Suppose I'll be able to rent these rooms about when the poverty hits. Perhaps I can afford a proper apprentice. What? You're still here? Leave! Go before you miss your chance."

Many ran as soon as he began to speak. Others left whilst he did so. Though most, confused, waited until the end. More confused than ever, they fled only once their former master had left their quarters, gone back to whatever he had been doing before.

Nine.

Lastly, there were a great multitude of slaves that worked in various capacities for a particularly vile wizard. He was openly not of the Holy Family faith and was rumored to practice all sorts of dark and profane arts. His house and laboratory slaves had fled to the foundry, seeking support of their stronger brothers in bondage.

No sooner than they had agreed to flee and how best to do it, a plume of thick back smoke appeared in their midst. Several choked on the noxious fumes, falling to the ground, apparently dying, and when the cloud cleared, there stood only their master among them, a ring of fresh corpses at his feet.

"Kneel before me," his voice hissed, "and plead for your lives, pledge them to my service, and I will make it so."

As he spoke and they considered, the flesh of the fallen slaves began to blister, peel, and melt away. Many considered taking his offer, his dire mercy. Many thought they would, felt it in their calves and thighs, that they would yield. To the surprise of everyone, none of them did, their courage held.

"Sloarezu," the wizard spat, pointing to one of the young women among them.

A thin ray of rainbow light traveled from his finger to her waist, from there a glamor came upon her, changing her form and twisting her mind. The slave girl became excessively amorous and exceedingly attractive, randy and irresistible. Every man that saw her sought to touch her and kiss her, each unfastening his tunic as he went, and she, arms and legs ever widening, to welcome them all. Yet she was only one woman and, before more than a few moments had passed, the slave men were grappling, choking, biting, and stabbing each other to get at her. Each man brought to bear whatever power was at his disposal to eliminate the competition as his lust boiled his wits beyond madness.

The female slaves faired no better. Before they could even fully comprehend what was happening to the men, before they could begin to try and restrain them, the dead ones rose. Their flesh discarded, slid right from their skins like wool coats.

They arose as skeletons, animated undead monsters where friend and ally once stood. Loathsomely, they advanced upon the panicking women, their loose innards reaching out, ensnaring, like so many tentacles, and finger bones grasping, clawing, like bundles of blunt knives.

The wizard but stepped back, laughing maniacally, as he watched the slaughter unfold. When it ended, only he and the glamoured woman remained. She thoroughly misused, befouled, and otherwise roughly handled only wanted more. The evil wizard, terribly amused, by his mere touch transformed her back into her own natural form and mind. The evidence of her abuse still upon her flesh, the realization of it all came rushing into the forefront of her fragile consciousness.

Absently, she fell to her knees, sobbing.

"What's that?" the vicious necromancer rasped, "Mercy? Oh, yes, certainly. Whatever mercy there is left for you, dear, I grant it."

His words grounded and grated against her reeling mind. Her thoughts, shamed and burdened, cleared enough, for but a solitary action. She grabbed up a broken rib, jagged at one end, from the ground, acting swiftly.

The vile wizard recoiled, she would have missed him had her strike been against his flesh, but her target was her own. Repeatedly, she stabbed herself in her spoiled womb, digging at herself, spilling blood and bowel before her.

The necromancer's eyes went wide with delight. He watched, as though her desperate escape from this life were a show put on for his benefit. He watched until there was no longer strength enough left in her to stab herself again. Her decisive action ended, her former master's amusement faded. Thus, he strode from the room like it were any other evening and retired to his bed chambers.

Outside such tales told, there were the freed gladiators, themselves a different matter entirely. For whatever restraint and avoidance tactics the Morralish soldiers employed against the opposing forces, for as often as they were apt to spare the life of a soundly defeated Antori constable or take praetorians prisoner, the gladiators showed no such considerations. They were not merely free of their enslavement, they were free from all sanity and compunction. They were free and wild.

With few exceptions, they left the Colosseum and the Morralish forces. A blood lust had completely overtaken them. They slew everyone in their line of sight that was not clearly a slave. They killed wounded Antori fighters, spared by the blue cloaks. They killed citizens hiding in their homes, some who mayhap had never owned slaves at all.

They killed animals tied in their pens. They cut a swath of death and vengeance through the city itself, their true oppressor, as they marauded from home to home. They retained only enough sense to aim their rampage, targeting those of their former owners and their associates, insofar as they knew of them. Yet, alas, everything and everyone in between was fair game as well.

They even destroyed several pavilions, statues, and other public works in the parks between the Cathedral, the palatial grounds, and government centers as they went upon their bloody way. So much for suppressing the freedom of speech.

Chapter 102
Confessing Late

"The hour has grown late, my friend," the Primarch placed a hand on the Paladin-Preceptor's large armored shoulder, "and still you haunt my rooms — and in your armor. Tell me, brother, what troubles you so?"

"We have never talked about the slaves."

"No," the Primarch, the senior holy man of the Cathedral of Din, agreed, "I suppose we have not."

"Is it wrong that they should be kept so?"

"We are not gods, brother," the Primarch answered, "The world is not ours to change. We were born into a nation that owns slaves. We are, respectively, teachers and enforcers of the moral order. If a man treats his slaves right and good, then he escapes the judgment of your kind and has honored the teachings of this Cathedral. If he treats them poorly, then he has ignored this Cathedral, and he must answer to your order. We call people to be the best of what they are, not to change what they are."

"But how, Your Immanence, can one man treat another 'right' or 'good' if he has enslaved him? Is that not poor treatment by default."

"I do not disagree," the Primarch admitted, "The Church of the Holy Family holds no slaves — its clergy and officers may not. Yet the Imperator leads the people. The faith is a guest in the lands, where our buildings and persons dwell. It is not our role to run the nations. Though of common origin, this nation belongs to its people, and its people look to their Imperator. If the Imperator allows the people to contract themselves to one another, then that is the law of the nation. We can only hold the faithful to personal virtue, as they live under their laws, not circumvent or rebuke the government."

"Eventually, 'Every people have whatever government they deserve,' " the Paladin-Preceptor recited, admitting, "I see the irony now."

"What's that?"

"Something a senator recently told me."

"Oh," the Primarch got it too, "I suppose that's true. Is that what has got you so worried, the jawing of some senator? Best to ignore the politicians and focus on the work of the church."

"In the past, I'd have agreed," the Paladin-Preceptor admitted, "But this man was different, and I wonder if ignoring the plight of the slaves is ignoring the work of the church. The system is corrupt, the contracts are misused, fraud is rampant, people are bought and sold without consent, the slaves do suffer."

"And so we must hold their masters to do and be better," the Primarch reframed the issue, "Yours is not to dismantle the institution, but to ensure that the people within it, slave and master alike, conduct themselves morally. Recall some paladins from the legions. Create a task force to improve the conditions of the slaves. That is your right."

"He told me something else," the Paladin-Preceptor relented that line of speculation, knowing it was already too late for that, "Something that I guess I've been warming up to asking you."

"Well, go on then?"

"Is it true that the Imperator has not come for your blessing in over two years?"

The Primarch released a long sigh and his shoulders fell.

He sat himself roughly upon his couch and replied, "Indeed."

"Why?"

"He has attendant priests. They attend him. Have since he was young. He is a busy man. The busiest of men. It is arrogant and a bit impious, but is it any less arrogant of me to presume that he must?"

"Excuses," the Paladin-Preceptor charged, "Apologies, brother, but you are making excuses for him."

"He is the Imperator!" the Primarch stood, shouting, "What would you have me do? Drag him before me. Insist that he free the slaves. Hold his governance hostage to my – my what – my blessing? By tradition the Imperators have sought the Primarch's counsel and favor, but there is nothing to demand that he must, nothing that says that he needs it."

"Perhaps there should be."

" 'Perhaps,' " the Primarch said in mocking tone, continuing, "Who have you been talking to? What ideas have they planted like seeds within you? The Imperator can turn us all out on our heels, you know. Sever the people from our Holy Family. That is what this kind of talk threatens. That is what is at stake. The salvation of the Antori people. So this Imperator is vain and impious. So we weather him. Imperators come and go, but our charge is to keep the faith alive in these lands."

"Faith," the Paladin-Preceptor replied, "Without the courage and will to live it out, isn't so much, if it be faith at all."

The Primarch batted his eyes in stunned disbelief. Before he could gather his thoughts enough to rebuke his ecclesiastical subordinate, however, a great crashing sound entered the lone open window, followed by a cacophonous roar, a cheer of many voices.

"What is happening out there?" the Primach demanded.

The Paladin-Preceptor hung his head. A long silence stretched between them.

More sounds of unrest stirred the senior paladin to raise his head and give voice to the truth.

"So, Your Immanence, that conversation we were having, about the slaves, was not entirely theological."

A second crash and a third cheer went up.

The Primarch's eyes flared as he shouted, "Unacceptable!"

Chapter 103
Raising Shields

Prince Bengallen, his thanes, the Forest Phantoms, and Brunsis the Minotaur all exited the Colosseum into the chaos and street fighting beyond. There they were joined by a company of blue cloaks.

Chief Jerumir introduced them, "Your Majesty this is an elite company of the second regiment. All men of the clans and the northern most reaches of Morralish. They are called 'Giants Bane' and the name earned. They shall escort you to the palace and secure the building during your meeting with the Imperator."

Prince Bengallen smiled and called to these fine soldiers above the clamor of the battle around them, "Giants Bane! Let us take a stroll among these little men!"

At first there was laughter, but then their commander's order went up.

"Shield wall!"

Reflexively, sharp, all their shields rose, as their faces grew stern. With small, measured steps, they moved into a three layered circle formation, surrounding Prince Bengallen and his retinue, defensively.

At each layer, the shields of every man narrowly overlapped with the shields of the men to his left or right. The front layer could bash a path and deflect incoming attacks. The second layer could attack, over the shoulders of the first, any pressing enemies. The third layer provided structure to the maneuver and reinforcements as the whole mass defended, fought, and moved like a single creature.

"Glorious!" Malcolm shouted.

"Indeed," Alpona and Shomotta agreed in unison.

Once a ring about the Prince, the whole formation moved forward through the battle, step-by-step, an eye in the storm, headed directly for the Imperator's Palace.

Hundreds of miles away, several miles north of Napua, at the Morralish blockade, a forward observer came charging back into the lines.

Reaching his allies, he called to whomever of them would hear him, "Refugees coming in! Coming in, make ready, refugees!"

In the technical sense, freed slaves taken in by the garrison were refugees, but it was an odd choice of words. No one had been calling them that.

Soldiers in the rear moved forward. This doubled their lines. At the same time, they all rearranged themselves so that five gaps, each five men wide, opened up in the blockade line.
While movements executed and settled, a new wave of slaves trudged forward.

They looked ragged and beaten. Having been left behind, they would have had a far worse go at their liberation than those who had the advantage of support from professional Morralish soldiers. If that many had been left behind.

In truth, everyone knew that not every slave would get out in the main push. Some died. Some were recaptured. They had planned for some few to slip out after, trickling in by ones and threes.

This, however, this mass, this mob, coming toward them, it did not make sense. There simply would not have been that many slaves left behind.

Drawing closer, close as they dared, the ragged mob charged. A trick, their burlap and sackcloth coverings falling off behind them. They reorganized into companies of Antori Legionnaires, reinforced by Napua's law enforcement and civil militia, attacking the Morralish blockade.

A reversal in more ways than one, the blockade appeared momentarily caught off guard. A horn sounded from behind the Morralish lines and their first rank stepped back as the second rank came forward, bearing shields. Bracing themselves in place, cascading calls for the "shield wall" echoed up and down the line. Accordingly, each soldier brought their shield up, overlapping its edges with the brother or sister to the left and right.

The Antori book of tactics knew this as the phalanx, invented by the ancient Alcyene and perfected by the Antori Legions four hundred years ago. It was the cornerstone of their own infantry maneuvers.

Yet the Antori here, garbed as refugee slaves, had abandoned shields so as to not betray their ruse. Their own trick had failed them and their own tactic was about to fell them. They were running into a trap of their own design, absent the equipment necessary to counter it.

With credit to their bravery – though mayhap it had been arrogance or blind rage – the Antori attackers did not balk. Their foot charge pressed on. With the shield wall up, however, their discipline did falter, as most attempted to veer toward those five gaps in the blockade line, each hoping to be the lucky dastard that would slip through the phalanx.

There was no luck in it. The Antori charge bundled and bottlenecked at the gaps. Those pushed out, or unable to push in, slammed upon the shield wall and, with few exceptions, were lanced or cut down, maimed or slain.

Those initial number who breached the gaps fared worse. Therein, they ran down slight slopes into shallow pits, about a foot or so deep. Deep enough to slow down the advance, but subtle enough not to be noticed until too late to break away. Surrounding these pits on three sides were smaller shield walls, an inverted phalanx, a peninsula of mayhem, made up of freed slaves with large shields and long spears.

Each and every one all too ready, eager, able, and willing to stab every last Antori Legionnaire and Napua citizen who had dared to chase them down. This enemy had come to murder them for daring to seek their freedom or else to snatch that freedom away. What mercy could they expect?

More and more enemy fighters rushed into the traps, pushing at each other, tripping and trampling over their own dead and wounded. Over and over and over again the freed slaves filled them full of holes, chanting.

"Freed–om! Freed–om! Freed–om!"

The Antori force, decimated thrice over before the gaps were too full of bodies to be assailed, broke off the charge. Others, not even yet made it to the battle, following, peeled away in an informal retreat. The blockade held. The attackers, defeated, turned away.

Chapter 104
Finding Courage

They were through the thick of it. Prince Bengallen, his mighty thanes, the minotaur, and the Forest Phantoms marched through the streets, in close company, shoulder-to-shoulder, with the fine soldiers of the Giants Bane having moved forward to clear the way ahead of them. They encountered little opposition, a swath of carnage having been cut before them by raging gladiators.

Few of the Antori they encountered chose to engage them, and none posed a threat. Over their journey, they had killed two private guards and three legionnaires, wounded two dozen, and subdued and bound four dozen more. The victories were so swift and handed that they do not even merit recounting.

Upon the palatial grounds, near to the palace itself, there was, however, an encounter of note.

Ruffis pointed his dagger right and spoke, "In the gardens, someone spies us, followed us the last little bit. He hunkers behind that berry bush."

Everyone stepped to move on the target, but Prince Bengallen stepped more quickly and, before them, held up his hand in a signal to halt them. Everyone stopped in their tracks as the Paladin-Prince continued forward.

Stopping three feet short of the bush, he sheathed his sword and spoke, "Who is there? Come forth."

A boy, nearly a man, eyes wide and light on his feet, as though he might dart in any direction at any moment, emerged. Though he never looked straight at the Prince, eyes darting around, hyper aware, he did speak, "I'm Hermes. You are the lord of the mountain men?"

"I am."

The boy's eyes filled with tears as he continued, "I'm lost. My parents were killed by guards, I think. I ran and now I'm lost. Can you take me to safety?"

Without hesitation, Prince Bengallen replied, "I cannot."

Great tears fell from the boy's face and he pleaded, "Please? I'm scared."

"Do you want to be free, Hermes?" Bengallen asked.

"Yes," the boy replied wiping away one tear.

"We have fought to give you this chance, but our work is here now," the Prince continued, "Your parents fought to give you this chance, but they are gone now. Will you, Hermes, fight?"

"I'm scared," the boy whimpered.

Prince Bengallen knelt and pulled a captured Antori Legionnaire's gladius from his belt and held it broad between them, so that the point was away, but a blade edge faced both of them. With his other hand, Bengallen pulled the boy's chin up, bringing back the eyes that had turned away from him in shame.

The boy looked at Bengallen, then at the gladius sword, and back to the Prince. Bengallen raised the weapon between them, pointing it skyward, and spoke words that no one who heard them have ever forgotten.

"Valor is a sword. One edge is courage, the wisdom to dispatch irrational fears. The other is bravery, the fortitude to withstand true fear. These edges come to a point from which no foe is safe."

Turning the short sword again, so that it pointed downward, Bengallen presented its hilt to the boy.

The boy wiped away his other tear, a boy no more. The young man, before the Prince in the Light, took the sword, nodded confidently, with courage upon his brow and bravery in his shoulders.

Prince Bengallen pointed back the way they had come.

"My men control the Colosseum, make haste."

The young man did so.

The others had lost all awareness of the world around them. Had there been an ambush, injuries if not death would have come upon them. Each, independent of the others, found himself captivated by their Prince's engagement of the lost child.

399

Alpona, boisterously put it to words.

"Valor is a sword!"

Bengallen quirked his mouth and raised a brow, unsure of the meaning behind his thane's reiteration. His affected countenance grounded everyone else back into the moment.

Alpona continued, saying again, "Valor is a sword! That's great. Your Majesty — that's rorking great! Now, that's got me fired up!"

At that, Alpona held his flaming sword aloft. Malcolm responded, crossing his shining sword with it. One-by-one they all threw up their swords, daggers, a staff, Brunsis and Quaindraught, raising their fists, and together shouted.

"Valor is a sword!"

Prince Bengallen did not even pretend to hide his pleasure at this. Grinning from ear-to-ear, he took off running, the others giving chase, as they made straight away for the main entrance of the nearby palace and the Imperator within.

More than three dozen Antori Legionnaires, clad in steel mail armor and wrapped with sashes of crimson or violet, denoting regular legion and praetorian, respectively, stood sentry at the stairs to the Grand Palace of the Imperium, weapons drawn. A dozen wheeled to the right flank, another dozen to the left, as the Prince's own vanguard, Giants Bane, maneuvered accordingly.

One Antori among the center unit came forward, donning his plumed helmet, as his purple full cape, both symbols of his senior military office, fell from one shoulder and billowed behind him. The Praetorian Commander pointed his sword to Prince Bengallen, though he and his men were still some distance away, and called, "You! You there! Can you not stop this madness? Can you not call your rabid dogs to heel?"

The Paladin-Prince raised his arm, halting his men. The soldiers of the Giants Bane took up positions that reinforced the flanks and opened a passage to their front. Through which Bengallen progressed forward ahead of his companions. He stood there, hand on the hilt of his sword, waiting for the other man to react. A long soundless moment stretched between them.

As the tension of the moment could wind no tighter, both men began to speak, but Prince Bengallen's voice rose over, drowning the Praetorian back to silence.

"It was yours to stop. Yours to prevent. Yours to end. My men move at my command and toward the purification of your nation's soul. Whether it be by blood and fire or repentance and atonement, I'd stand before your Imperator and hear his decision."

"Shields!"

The Praetorian Commander barked and the legionnaires in a line behind him and those angling to his left and right all brought shields to front, side-by-side, creating an inverted phalanx formation.

Prince Bengallen drew his sword and, almost mockingly, echoed.

"Shields!"

His twin columns of Giants Bane created a phalanx of their own. The thanes and soldiers within leaned forward in anticipation.

"You can let us pass," the Paladin-Prince reminded his soon-to-be opponent, "What you do now, and where you stand in all of this, is your own decision."

"Advance!"

The Praetorian barked a second order and the legionary squad behind him began to move forward at a steady and experienced pace.

Contrary, the men of the Giants Bane rushed forward, left and right, slamming into and forestalling the closing of the Antori flanks. As the two Morralish columns opened, like flood gates. Prince Bengallen, and his men behind him, charged forward, each in his own manner of haste.

Before the center legionnaires had closed ranks around their commander, Bengallen had already crossed swords with him. As they came within retaliatory distance, Brunsis and Sir Quaindraught had run full into the Antori center phalanx, directly behind the Prince. Dropping low on impact, each dodged sword thrusts, impacts staggering the enemy formation.

With that, Bengallen, blade crossed against the Praetorian's own, high, took his free hand, low, and opened his opponent's large shield, away from his body, like a door. The whole of the man exposed, pulling himself and the Praetorian towards one another, the Paladin-Prince kicked the man's knee in and head-butted the man's mouth with the breadth of his forehead.

Crippled and stunned, the Praetorian Commander collapsed to the ground. In full sight of the legionnaires, Prince Bengallen inverted his sword, thrusting its point into the space between the other's neck and armor, down into the rib cage. Penetrating the heart and lung therein, he slew their commander.

In the next moment, the legionnaires themselves were twice decimated. The Giants Bane had beaten back the flanking elements. Accordingly, Alpona and Malcolm broke left and right, flanking to attack the weak points this created in the smaller, isolated shield wall before them. They defeated the men at either end swiftly.

Caanaflit shot a fourth enemy in the face with a crossbow bolt and was already reloaded. Shomotta smote a fifth with a burning ray of light from a small gemstone held in his hand. Brunsis rolled to his back and, placing feet to the bottom of the shield before him, kicked off, slamming the edge of said shield into its wielder's face. Sir Quaindraught, beside him, came up under the shield of his opponent, grappling the reeling legionnaire to the ground.

A hole opened. In poured the remainder of the Forest Phantoms and Ruffis so that they, as well as Alpona and Malcolm, were all attacking the broken phalanx from its rear. That, plus another shot each from Caanaflit and Shomotta made short work of the center unit.

Running around to the opposite sides of the men of the Giants Bane, the would-be flanks were both outnumbered and out maneuvered. The palace's defenders were swiftly crushed in no more time than it took to describe it. Thirty-six legionary soldiers fell dead to the ground. The way to the palace made clear.

"Men of the Giants Bane," Bengallen ordered them, "assume their position upon the stair. No one enters the palace until I take my leave of it. You hold this spot."

The Van-blessed mountain folk professionally fell to command, taking up a defensive position as Prince Bengallen and his attendant champions entered the palace beyond.

Within, they met increasing waves of resistance as they pushed, deeper and deeper, toward the Imperial Throne Room. Too late they realized that a great number of Antori Legionnaires had already been summoned to reinforce the palace guard. Eventually, the Paladin-Prince and his thanes were able to breach through them, past several dozen palace guard in the antechamber, and the Forest Phantoms reminded behind to finish the fight and block the path of any potential reinforcements to the Throne Room itself.

He sat there, as though waiting for them, almost bored with their apparent tardiness. The Imperator, upon his throne, seeming both unmoved and unmovable, hardly acknowledged the presence of the blood-drenched band that stood before him.

Chapter 105
Drawing Line

Just outside the walls of Antoria Royal, larger forces aligned with either side also moved against one another. Morralish knights and their mounted soldiers had divided their opposing forces as the infantry of their regiment still marched to reinforce the position.

On the east flank, cavalry commanders of the Morralish First Regiment rode out to treat with the centurions convened to represent the Antori Eighth Legion, assembled beyond their city's walls to prevent their breaching.

"Where is your Legatus?" the cavalry commander, a Lieutenant General Hallis Rallnir, asked.

"You are not the High-Lord General," a centurion replied, "His standard did not charge."

"Oh," General Rallnir said, whimsically, "You'll want terms settled before he arrives."

The centurion did not disagree, but held his own ground, "Regardless, our Legatus will not risk exposure to your assassins, if your own High-Lord General will not risk himself."

The young Morralish Captain, who led the cavalry charge was also present, and spoke out of turn, "That's just it, see, we really don't go in for the whole assassin thing. Tis just these sort of differences in values and honor that have brought us all to the brink of death and madness this evening."

Before the General could correct the young knight, the Antori Centurian replied, "I'll have you know, ignoring your disparaging of my honor, reports from within the city all agree that we've already slipped well beyond the brink."

"Then let it end at the wall," the Lieutenant General insisted, "Let it therein be contained. When our brothers, sisters, and those under their protection exit, to take our leave of your lands, then simply let us go. Neither you nor I, neither your men nor mine have caused this. I'd have none of them die for it."

"I have comrades in the Praetorian Legion dying for it right now!" a different centurion spat.

403

"As do we have our own!" the young Knight Captain called back.

General Rallnir completed the exchange as to make something useful of it, "All the more reason for us to make an agreement to halt the flow of blood here, at the wall. Come this far from beyond our control, but here, but now, we decide."

"Those are your terms?" the lead centurion snarked, unimpressed.

"That we'll not attack you, so long as you do not attack us or our countrymen or those with them and allow us all to leave."

The centurion glared, steely and discerning, for a long moment, replying completely absent of inflection, "I'll take your terms to the Legatus at once."

On the west flank, the Van-blessed mountain folk of the Morralish First Regiment looked out across the short distance, into the dark, torch lit silhouettes of their brothers, who had marched against them. The presence of those who defied the order of their true prince at the behest of this foreign nation and its overlord. As the silence, tension, and darkness grew between them, it felt as if the distance increased as well, as if those they faced were slipping away into the void. Adding to the dark, from within the allegedly treasonous ranks of the Morralish Fourth Regiment, torches began to fall, one here, two there, while panicked cries of pain rose and faded into the night.

Divided loyalty inevitably leads to treachery. All of the Morralish Expeditionaries in Antoria were traitors from a certain perspective. They had good reasons. Their would-be Antori masters were not going to deal fairly with them in their time of need and difficulty. Yet still, their actions, their protest, their violence and threat to greater scale thereof was, to a man, nonetheless disloyal to the Senate and People of Antoria, whose taxes paid their coffers for decades, and the Imperator's Peace that bid them dwell in his lands and gave them purpose.

Their bond to their countrymen was greater. Their pledge to their homeland was greater. Their oath to their Royal Family, the present Prince its last scion, was greater. Their commitment to freedom and justice was greater.

Who could hold such loyalty, even if it engendered disloyalty to lesser conviction and allegiance, against them? Are all men not inevitably forced to choose?

Judge not the men and women of the Morralish Fourth Regiment harshly, then. Neither for their long discernment, their lingering straddle upon an ever divergent middle path, nor for their eventual betrayal of the Antori Centurions embedded within their ranks. Celebrate instead, that when the time came, at last to choose, they chose the side of their kith and kin, their lord and land, liberation and justice, and a quick death to those who opposed their choice.

Weapons sheathed, hands extended, west flank of the First Regiment and east flank of the Fourth, clasped one another, embracing as brothers once more, and merged their lines. All the while, General Cardness marched the infantry reinforcements ever closer to the scene.

Chapter 106
Colliding Dynasties

Before the Paladin-Prince could reach out consciously, his instinct called forth that divine insight that heightened his perception of the supernatural world. Hardly prepared, his inner voice, so often a whisper, blasted his mind like a thousand silver trumpets and trampled on his heart like a thousand wild stallions.

The Imperator was not merely mortal man. Standing sharply from its throne and charging at the Prince's brave thanes, like a bolt of lightning, was a man possessed — a demon.

Not some lesser evil either. No mere nether-wisp, no simple night-terror, no impish sin-spinner, this was a Lord of Anzerak, one of The Nine, a Prince of Hell.

Which one? Bengallen could not be certain. It was too evil to conceal its presence from a Paladin of God, but it was equally willful and, thus, more than powerful enough to withhold its true name.

Bengallen fell back, overwhelmed by his supernatural senses. Loyal and angered, the Paladin-Prince's mighty thanes pressed forward, fighting in his name. They did not understand what had so suddenly happened to their Prince, but neither did they have time to hesitate. Whatever was happening to him, they were certain that this Imperator had done it and, for that alone, they would destroy him.

Clashing, the Imperator struck Alpona on the hip. The Zil-jahi Warrior dodged, twisting deftly, but not fast enough as to match his opponent's inhuman speed or avoid the blow completely. Fortunately, the banded mail hanging from his belt absorbed and deflected most of the blow, while their extreme proximity to one another placed Alpona at optimal distance for a counter-attack.

For most any Antori or Morralish fighter, it would have been too close for a fight. Indeed the ancient greatsword Flammerung could find no purchase. Alpona knew this, however, and knew well enough not to try. Instead, he brought the hilt and pommel of the sword, in his right hand, along with the blade's full weight and momentum, around, slamming into the back of the Imperator's head.

At the same time, Alpona sprang up, off of his right foot, bringing his left knee up above his waist. Although his reaction to launch the counter-attack automatic, the precision and timing of his motions were no less calculated. The pommel connecting with the back of Imperator's neck, bringing all the sword's weight through its hilt, the Zil-jahi Warrior pushed his opponent's face down, firmly, smashing it into his rising knee.

Alpona landed a matched pair of blows to the head that would have slain any mortal man instantly. The Imperator reeled, staggering backward, huge silver dimple in the sheer shining surface of his faceplate, twin streams of bright blood trickling down from its eye slits.

The others wasted no time. Brunsis charged down the center, as Malcolm broke right and Ruffis went left, to flank, and Shomotta began to weave a spell. As the minotaur rushed to tackle the Imperator, however, the villain gathered his wits and hunkered to the floor, pulling himself into a tight squat. So fast he sank, Brunsis had no time to pull back. The minotaur tripped, vaulting head over ass, over the braced defender.

Malcolm and Ruffis fared no better, intercepted by hidden members of the Imperator's elite guard. They crossed blades, swing and parry, push and pull, thrust and dodge, each became locked in separate combats, terrible and ferocious in their own right.

The moment his, the Imperator stilled himself, calling forth the full powers of his demon. His body became cloaked in a veneer of dark purple energy. Dimly lit, it wrapped about him, foot to face, a hundred wispy tentacles, merging as they went, tight against his form, not obscuring him, but causing his presence to boldly contrast with the physical world, here of white marble, that surrounded them.

Off his hands, down from his fingertips, the evil energy dripped, solidifying to form barely translucent claws. Until it culminated, the power swirling to an apex atop his head. There, twin horns of shadowy illumination reached forth from the sides of his face, proclaiming proudly the demoniac presence within.

Alpona, already repositioning for a second attack, unphased by the Imperator's transformation, held the ancient Flammerung high. Burning with a hungry fire, it crashed down against the possessed opponent. The Imperator, awareness enhanced, turned about just in time to dodge incompletely. Alpona had, inadvertently, returned the blow he had taken on the hip back to the perpetrator and to similar effect.

The Demon-Imperator caught the blade, however, as it bounced away from his side, his shadow cloaked hand apparently resistant to the sword's magical flames, and spoke, voice deep and hollow.

"Smoke and hellfire burn within my soul, what do you suppose this can do to me?"

Before Alpona could answer, not that he intended to, focused as he was on wrenching the weapon from the other's supernatural grasp, Brunsis returned the fight. Delivering a powerful sweeping kick to the Imperator's legs, he toppled him.

This loosed Alpona's magical greatsword from the demon's grip. Subsequently, the warrior rained blows, immense chopping swings, down upon the grounded Imperator, even chasing after as he attempted to roll clear. As Alpona went, Brunsis marched beside him, stomping their foe with his own monstrous feet.

The Imperator nearly rolled beyond their reach, gaining room enough to stand, when he was stopped by a corpse, one of his own slain guards. Above that corpse, its slayer, Malcolm, stood with the Dawnsong inverted, plunging the point toward the Imperator's masked face.

The strike landed naught, however, and neither did the simultaneous attacks from his allies, Alpona and Brunsis. Their prone opponent grabbed up the corpse, using it as a shield. He pushed it up as the blows came down and somersaulted out from under their flanking onslaught.

His maneuver not a complete success, the Imperator, clear of the fray, came up to his feet, only to step right into Ruffis' twin long knives. Neither was this a coup for Ruffis, however, as the demon immediately gored the dark elf with one of his large horns.

The Imperator stood tall, taller, he had increased in size by at least a foot. An impaled Ruffis hung from his left horn, guts punctured viciously. As the Imperator looked right, there was no time to react to, only see, Brunsis crashing into him, bowling all three of them over onto the floor.

Neither combatant stayed there long as they came to their feet grappling one another. In chilling contrast, Ruffis' limp form, flung away, flopped to a stop on the cold marble floor. Alpona came to Ruffis' aid, sighing with relief, the puncture wound far less severe than expected. *The demon's horn, not being completely physical, must have made a much smaller wound that its own apparent size.*

Brunsis and the Imperator continued to grapple, hands knotted together, horns locked, feet planted or otherwise stomping surely to plant them again. At the same time, Malcolm came up from behind, swung his greatsword from over his shoulder, gathering momentum, and brought it forward, in a 180 degree arc.

Mid-swing, Malcolm felt the attack pick-up a strange momentum, its angle deflecting vaguely, but still downward. He had intended to strike center mass, but some force had shifted his attack. Not away, however, not a miss, he received help not hindrance.

Instead of striking armor, a breastplate's backside, the sword moved faster and lower, in the same instant as the Imperator moved his leg, replanting it in the grapple. Malcolm sliced through bare thigh. Despite the resistance from the dark sorcery that enshrouded their foe, no match for the Dawnsong's inner light, the magic barrier parted, as did the Imperator's left leg.

Malcolm looked around, surprised, to discern the source of the influence. Readily he saw it, Shomotta gesturing wildly, attacking nothing directly, but mimicking the attacks of his allies as a conduit, binding his magic to their efforts and strikes, using his external perspective to exploit vulnerabilities they might not notice in the heat of battle.

The Imperator toppled over. Prince Bengallen's mighty thanes heaped blows upon him, delivering bumps, scrapes, and gouges. Not so many as to defeat him, however, and each to lesser effect. The supernatural armor that clung all about their enemy continued to thicken, darken, and harden.

It became a mildly translucent black shadow made real, streaked with veins of pulsing red and purple. Less and less he looked like the Imperator. More and more the form of the demon he became. The demonic magic even lashed out, snatched, and reattached the severed leg, as claws came up to deflect his attackers' blows.

Though surrounded, the Imperator made his way back to his feet, dodging nimbly, moving quickly, and pressing his way clear. In a flash of purple light, four corpses, the Imperator's fallen elite guard bolted upright, reanimated with a false life, once again coming to their master's aid.

The tide of battle began to turn against the thanes. The undead guards proved to be more difficult the second time. Although the guards' flesh dried and

409

withered before their very eyes, these creatures were faster than before, plainly under some measure of their master's power. Moreover, the assistance from Shomotta ceased, as the Demon-Imperator, growing ever larger, went after him directly and all his effort turned to defending himself.

All the while, Caanaflit held a weakened Bengallen aloft, his shoulder propped beneath the other's. The thane looked into his Prince's eyes, their metallic green irises appearing a rare tarnished and dull. Something he had only ever seen once before, his leader actively obsessing over mapping the Starspawn Beast's attacks, in order to discern their source, more than a year ago. Worse, they did not look at Caanaflit, but aimlessly looked through him, as though he not there at all.

Bengallen did not see his attending thane. Instead, he saw the boy he had encouraged earlier, charging off, disappearing into the dark of night and the blood and chaos that lay beyond that veil. That boy gone, he saw another child, it was himself as a boy, and the Paladin Di'gilcrest, not so much older than he, with him. He saw the Paladin Di'gilcrest.

How? A memory?

He remembered the words once broken to him by that Champion of Vandor's Light.

"The mind settles, the will rises, and intellect can be honed, sharpened to fine edge, to carve destiny from faded world and victory from all who would stand in its path. Valor is a sword."

Enlightened, Prince Bengallen finally realized where he fit into this world gone mad. All of the events that had come to pass since his father's death, the King's death, since Morralish had fallen into darkness, slid together like the pieces of a puzzle. The image revealed: The truth of himself.

Death was not the end. The Paladin Di'gilcrest was not dead, but lived on in the Memory of God, and thus lived within the Paladin-Prince himself. His mentor's wisdom, fallen from Bengallen's own lips to another naught more than an hour ago. In this moment also, spurring Bengallen himself back into action against his foe once more.

The honored dead, one thing to call them such and make prayers in their names, but the turn of phrase held a deeper meaning. Bengallen understood the immortal truth. It was not only Di'gilcrest, it was all of them. His father, King Lionel, Rodjker and Banner Brightaxe, Sir Jason, Vix, and Heinrich, the

410

squires, Palmer, Franz, and Paul, the Fifth Regiment called Peakstars, ancient ancestors, Thumyr and Aethumir, a whole line of his people — *all of them*.

The Prince did not so much see them, as he felt them. No vision of holy spectres stood before him, but the warmth of their illumination, divine love cast on his soul, radiated serenity and courage, not only onto himself, but as something he could reflect outward. That was who and what he was, a legacy.

Reinvigorated, the Paladin-Prince felt their strength coursing through his veins as he returned to conscious awareness of the challenge before him.

He saw Caanaflit, first, guarding over him, and saw him anew. Had his friend changed or the Paladin-Prince's perception of him? Had he at last pierced that obfuscating veil that had hung upon the rogue since before they met? What had he seen? Never mind, *t'was another matter for another moment, priority, the task at hand*.

The Paladin-Prince stood to, abruptly, grasping, pushing himself from, launching himself off of, Caanaflit's shoulder, and at the last instant, snagging his ally's collar, so that they both flung themselves into the fray. Together, Ben and Flit joined the fight.

The Imperator had fully doubled in size by then. The demonic form that lay upon him became even more pronounced, less shadow and more substance. Crushing the minotaur's face with one hand, his sword crossed with Malcolm's and Alpona's simultaneously, the two thanes working together to thwart their foe. Four corpses, re-slain, lay on the ground like four corners marking out a crude arena and, motionless, the dark elf also lay but little farther beyond them.

Caanaflit rolled in from behind, popped up, hands crossed, and stabbed the Imperator under his hips, in the pocket on either side of his groin. Following up with a flick of the wrists, he darted away, uncrossed them, doubly slashing the larger enemy as he moved off.

Despite his leather codpiece and supernatural armor, both stabs wounded the Imperator. Although the left hand slash did not penetrate deeply, the right passed halfway, tearing across the scoring already laid down by the left. It tore beyond armor, biting back into tender flesh.

Prince Bengallen charged forward, colliding with the Demon-Imperator, as Caanaflit bounded away. Both hands occupied and a wounded groin besides, there was no defense against the Paladin-Prince's onslaught.

His sword, no special sword, a claymore not unlike the tens of thousands carried by so many soldiers in his army, burned bright with the Light of Van. A holy light, a giving light, ever so eager and willing to banish all supernatural darkness in its luminous revelation, struck the Imperator's chest and tore, left to right, across the abdomen of the ensorcelled foe.

Wounded, the Demon-Imperator reacted in a burst of pain, flinging the minotaur from his crushing grasp and toppling the warriors, blocking his blade with an erratic parry that pulled away from them. As Bengallen's bright blade turned about for a second strike, so too did the Demon-Imperator turn all his attention toward the Paladin-Prince.

Shomotta raised his hands and Alpona and Malcolm, correspondingly, returned to their feet in the next instant, in a flash far faster than they could have made the effort on their own. The wizard also finished making his way to Ruffis, although he took note of where the minotaur fell, before examining the dark elf.

Brunsis hit the ground hard and wrong. He landed horns first. Before breaking half of one horn off completely, this caused the rest of his body to fall, in relation to his neck, in a most unnatural fashion. He did not move.

This all happened beyond Prince Bengallen's notice. He and the Imperator were locked in pitched combat. The Prince taking swings, parried. The Imperator, raking with claw attacks, dodged. Back and forth, several times, until the Prince broke the pattern, dodging his opponent's blade rather than parrying it. Instead, stepping in, he turned a few degrees beyond perpendicular to his previous stance.

There he held his retaliatory strike for half a heartbeat, until the claw came at him again. It was not a brilliant strike, he did not take the whole hand as he had desired. Reduced to a mere hand once more, the severed claw tips clattered to the ground, dissipating in four tiny plumes of smoke.

Alpona and Malcolm, with their Flammerung and Dawnsong respectively, returned to the fight. The enemy wholly engaged with the Prince, the warriors caught their foe unaware.

Malcolm chopped at the crest of the Demon-Imperator's thigh, *it was not enough. Twice! Thrice* and it was done. The Dawnsong sang against the discordant night within the demoniac shroud. Just as the dawn always does, it broke though, severing the lower leg completely — once more.

As the Demon-Imperator began to list. Alpona, behind him, opposite to the Prince, leaped to the throne, scaled its back, and leaped again from on high, at the enemy. Sword inverted, no sooner than the Imperator stumbled over his severed limb, howling with pain, did that ancient Flammerung slide into his back, between spine and shoulder, passing through lung, exiting the other side.

Thus did Alpona, blade impaling his opponent's torso, ride the Imperator as the momentum of the fall shifted forward, toppling them both, all the way to the ground. Prince Bengallen took another step and turned about again, positioning his sword over his shoulder so that the Demon-Imperator's neck would fall upon it like a reverse guillotine.

That did not happen, however. As the Imperator collapsed, he also began to return to normal size, head decreasing mere inches enough to miss the blinding steel edge of the Paladin-Prince's blade. Worse yet, as Bengallen came about, hefting his sword above him, set to chop down, the Imperator bounded right from the ground.

He came up to a knee, funneling the remaining demon power fading about himself into the sword, he stabbed the Prince at the side of his lower breast plate, piercing a smaller piece of banded mail reinforcement.

Prince Bengallen fell to his knees, dropping his sword harmlessly, and reflexively clutching his fresh abdominal wound. At the same time, the Imperator came the rest of the way to his feet. Somehow, he again had both of them. The earlier severance had been truly reattached and the part more recently cut away, apparently, merely some manifestation of his shattered demon shell. Reduced to normal size, but relatively intact, the Imperator bolted for a doorway.

Alpona, knocked backward by the Imperator's fall, but hoisted up by Malcolm, both pursued their enemy. He had had a slight lead on them. About to increase substantially, the Imperator held aloft his hand and a magic portal of inky black filled the doorway.

They would not have even known what it was had they not all recently become acquainted with that particular spellcraft. As they did know, they beat feet to reach him, pushing all the faster, before he could slip through.

Malcolm wished for a spear. Alpona, not for the first time, wished he could run faster. For in their hearts, they both knew it, he was going to get there first.

Yet that did not happen either. Not six strides from his escape, the Imperator's neck sprouted a crossbow bolt. This not only stymied his forward progress, it caused him to stumble to the right. Smack, the timing perfect, slamming him into one of the throne room's many large support columns. After all, the only thing better than Caanaflit's aim was his timing.

The Imperator grasped at his bleeding neck. Wheezing, he tried to say something. Wheezing louder, panicked, he saw what the two thanes on a collision course with him did not: The portal was closing.

As Shomotta's hands came closer and closer together, as torrents of sweat and magic power poured out from his body like a sieve, as his tongue drummed arcane syllables against his lips, the portal, compelled, acquiesced, obeying the wizard's eldritch might and begin to close.

The Imperator called upon his demon, begging it not to abandon him. Yet their deal was done and that portal was closing. Malcolm, within striking distance, some three foot falls ahead of Alpona, held the Dawnsong overhead, ready to cleave. When black smoke, backlit with hellfire and streaked with arcs of purple lightning, began streaming from the eye slits in the Imperator's helm, however, it caused the half-orc thane to reflexively pull up short and protect himself. The cloud, the demon itself, passed them by, flowing around the column and slipping through the tiny portal an instant before it closed. When Alpona came crashing down upon the Imperator, only the frightened man remained.

From right to left the Zil-jahi Warrior swung that ancient greatsword, that Flammerung, with all the force his harried chase and straining muscles could muster. Striking the Imperator at the right collar bone, it melted through armor. It tore through flesh. It smashed through bone. It burned through viscera as it went. The magic flaming blade exited below the Imperator's left arm and his corpse fell to the ground, split in twain.

Thus ended the line of Antori Imperators. In fear and shame was the last of them damned and slain. The balance due his many transgressions against our Holy Family, divine and mortal.

The Imperator was dead, but Brunsis the Minotaur and Thane Ruffis were on their way to the hereafter as well. The minotaur's breath, shallow, undetectable had he been of smaller proportion. The dark elf, motionless, unresponsive, whispered, "Maada, Maada," in the elven tongue. As it happened, they had fallen near enough to one another, so that when Shomotta brought Prince Bengallen, it was to both of them.

His own side still actively bleeding, the Paladin-Prince held himself, looking from one to the other.

"I have so little left in me. I can only save one of them, if that. How am I to choose?"

"Does not your God and his family make your miracles?" Alpona asked.

"They entrust me," Bengallen spoke, pain in his voice, "with a measure of their power. I have been instructed as to how to use it wisely, efficiently. Though exhausted, I will of course try to heal one, but wisdom tells me I cannot save them both."

Alpona looked to Shomotta with a questioned plea upon his lips, but the wizard-priest did not make him ask it.

"I had not yet been initiated into the mysteries concerning the restoration of the body. I cannot help in this."

"What then?" Alpona shouted.

Prince Bengallen answered, "Fetch the leader of the Forest Phantoms, their Chief, MacRoberts. He too is a paladin. Mayhap together we can —"

The Prince's words cut short with a painful groan as he slid from Shomotta's grasp, to the floor. He looked up to tell Alpona "now" but the Zil-jahi Warrior, and Malcolm with him, were already gone. On his knees, Bengallen bowed his head and prayed for mercy.

Chapter 107
Remembering Imperator

"Father insisted that his sons, that an Imperator and his word and will, should go into the lands of his Imperium and be known to the people there. Avengneux welcomed me – us – him really, I suppose, like a savior. There were no guards as we came into the provincial capital, L'laris, and the people lined the streets, streets covered with flower petals, just to see us.

It was a different experience than in Alcyone, where the people, so like us, like our own shadows, regarded us with a casual, but accepting, indifference. They went about their day, only stopping to offer somber salutations when the small guard, that went some two dozen feet ahead of us, marched about in their clanging, ringing armor. The Alycene's own hoplites were more lightly armored, more mobile, I remember that too.

As different as the two visits were from each other, I remember the stark contrast the third, Quallengrad, capital of the Quallen province, presented most of all. Having made our travels amid a heavy legion, learning of their ways as I went, I appreciated how they never, en masse, occupied the regional city-states or towns over the journey, but not in Quallen. Soldiers, centuries, went ahead of us into every settlement, menacing the populace, and discouraging civil unrest. It worked, up to a point.

In L'laris, they loved us. In Thalos, they cared not. In Quallengrad, they hated us.

Half the legion went in, two full days ahead of us, amid protests, meeting violence with violence, and pressing the citizens into service for the cleanup. When at last I entered that city-state, I knew I had reached the edge of the Imperium. I knew that this was where everything I thought I knew threatened to fall away into chaos and madness. The people there did not fascinate me. I did not want to win their love. The people, if I am honest, scared me and I wanted nothing more than to leave. If only I had a clue. If only I had known.

By then, most of the legion, minus a single century, occupied the long broken walls of these recently broken people. The day we departed, a single century left with us, to rendezvous with the other one to the south for the journey home. The remainder of the legion stayed to ensure the people did not rally and assemble an attack to our rear on the road in our leaving. Unlikely, but wise caution — if not for the true threat.

To the west, there in the north, was a vast plain of rolling hills, more than half as large as all the lands of the Imperium combined. The Western Plains were dotted with primitive settlements, used and abandoned as needed by primarily nomadic humans, unconquered, uncontrolled, unbridled. They were the Equasari and they hated Imperial culture, feared our size, and took great offense to our ever encroaching western borders. So when word came to them that the Imperator and his sons were traveling with but a single legion, their chieftains gathered the largest cavalry force they could muster, nearly a legion in their own right, and they moved north as we did. Their scouts coming and going from the west, reporting our position and strength. When at last we were merely two-hundred and three men upon the road, their thousands descended upon us like locusts on a feast.

Barely a teenager, I had slain three adult men before taking a horse from the third and killing a fourth thereafter, mounted with lance. For all that, they didn't merely rout us. They ambushed us. They broke our lines, crushed our phalanx, and rode us down as we retreated. They killed us to a man, one man, me — me. My father and brother dead, I – Imperator Tulonius, in fact – sat high in my saddle, the lone survivor. Captive. Trophy. Weapon.

I was surrounded by the surviving thousand barbarian horsemen. Defeated, I remained poised to fight unto my death. Instead, the Equasari called for their shaman who looked me up and down, assessing, before doing the strangest and most unexpected thing imaginable. He invited me to come with them as their guest.

He told me, with my skill and potential, I could be made one of their tribe. Becoming so, they could offer me mercy. My only way out, as far as I could tell, although I refused to disarm, I agreed.

They took me in my sleep on the third night. They abused and violated me in ways that I shall not recount. They burned my face. They scarred my body — and soul.

To those that much later found me, I claimed it was brigand rebels that attacked us, that knocked unconscious and face horribly scarred, they mistook me for dead and left me. Within Imperial borders and so near to Quallengrad, why would anyone doubt it? From a certain perspective, the core of that story is not even a lie.

I told the Senate that I, lost, made my way to the Equasari on my own. Within a broad interpretation of my words, I had lost the battle, but rather than die, I chose to go with them of my own volition, lost and on my own. What I told

417

them further, that the Equasari took me in, treated me as one of their own, and returned me to the Imperium, is truth, even if incomplete and imprecise. In fact, the omissions were the most important facts of all.

Brutally, they tested me. Young and barely initiated into the martial traditions over my recent trek, I was too soon to break. Yet, from the blank, black depths of a knockout punch, a familiar whisper did slide, out from under the shadow of a thought. That demon had haunted my nightmares for most of my childhood. In my shame, I hid it from the priests and their gods. In my vainglorious pride, I fought it alone and thought myself victor. In the folly of my youth, I forgot about it altogether.

I dreamed of ways to free myself, but the council of my shadow's whisper moved me to higher purpose. Finally, I awoke and found only a single violator, distracted. I took a small fileting knife from among the other tools and gutted him. Pulling free the ritual mask he wore, I found the face of my own brother.

They had apparently offered him a similar option and his trials included torturing me.

The shadow's whisper became a thunder in my ears, my vision went hazy and red. When sense at last returned, I was laboriously skinning my victim and had made a significant disassembly of his insides. Again fully aware and in complete control of my actions, I bound and took his ribs for a crown, consumed his heart raw, anointed myself in his blood, and declared myself the Imperator of the World.

My demon had returned to me, though he had never actually gone, in my moment of need and weakness, to grant me power and strength beyond my imagining. In order to pass the tests before me, I agreed to his terms and called forth his power. He told me which remaining parts of the corpse to take, teaching me how to blend and taint them into instruments of arcane might. So armed, I presented myself to the whole of the gathered barbarian camp and demanded to complete my trials!

Afterward, they all fell down and worshiped me. Not since the Din-god himself had an Imperator been honored so. Pride? Folly? Shame? The things history would never know.

I became one of the Equasari, the highest one of them. They needed neither chieftain nor shaman when they believed their god had returned to them. I had done more than broker a mere peace with them, winning over their riders as auxiliary cavalry for the legions. I had, in effect, secretly conquered the Imperium on their behalf, not with violence, not even with lies, not really, but with the silence of omitted truths.

A silence that I would carry with me, make a part of myself and my power. Silence would be the hallmark of my rule for more than a decade. Alas, I am slain, the Demon-Imperator, and my people, my true people, their way of life forever destroyed, and so history will remember me only as this."

The Imperator remembered these things, believing he was recounting and confessing them as he died, but he was already dead.

Amid the growing darkness, his shadow's whisper returned to taunt him, hissing.

"Your brother was not distracted. He was looking back to make sure he had not been followed. He had come to rescue you. He came to rescue you and you killed him. You desecrated him, talismans and trophies of his corpse you made in my name."

The Imperator was already dead. The despair within these memories and the revelations to come were but the prelude to his utter damnation. A discordant tune played according to the fractured cadence of demonic laughter.

Chapter 108
Pulling Back

"Centurion," the Legatus Deodontes Magnus, senior commander of the Antori Eighth Legion, called forth his most trusted officer.

"Hail, Legatus," the Centurion replied, approaching, "Your orders?"

"Centurion Venn, my friend, draw near and break words."

The Centurion did as instructed.

"Why are we about to fight these men?"

"Legatus? I'm sorry – I —"

"No, no, exactly," Legatus Magnus assured him, "There is no sense to it. They are here – to what – ensure their countrymen are allowed to leave? Would we not demand the same? And to free the slaves. I don't own any slaves. Do you own any?"

"Of course not," Centurion Venn sighed, "you know our order forbids it."

"And how many of our order are among them?" the Legatus replied, "How many paladins do you feel like killing this night?"

"Not a one," the Centurion replied, "but we have orders to defend these walls. No one to enter. No more armies of northmen to enter."

"And no more shall," agreed the Legatus, "but the ones already in there, are they not here by our Imperator's own will? Had our own senate not approved the contracts for their military might, that this empire might be held together?"

"Legatus," Centurion Venn gasped, "What are you saying?"

"I know not, not truly," he admitted, "That this is all wrong. How we got here is wrong. What we are about to have to do is wrong. Maybe, that what we, as a nation, have been doing is wrong. Maybe — maybe that we focused too much on what we were trying to have, to keep, to take, that we lost our sense of what we are. What we were – were meant to be – anyway. Maybe — maybe that what we are is wrong."

"Legatus," Venn warned, "If any of the other centurions heard you talking like this —"

"That is why I speak only with you, Centurion Venn, you are my friend and fellow paladin."

"What am I supposed to do with this?" Venn protested.

"Hear me, brother," the Legatus invited humbly, lowering his head, "In a thousand men at my command, how many of us are paladi? Less than two dozen. They have twice as many in their cavalry alone. And our cavalry, look at them, more than half are Equasari. Look at them, everyone of those barbarians, look in their eyes, they want this fight. Look at them, they are all ready to charge. None of this is right. How is it that I respect the ranks of my enemy more than my own?"

"Legatus," the Centurion whispered, warning again.

He too had looked. From what few he could see, he too had seen it.

"My orders," Legatus Magnus lifted his head and spoke with confidence, "Signal the forward century to fall back to the rear position. Then signal the whole legion to redeploy in phases to the Main Gate. We have our orders to defend the walls and those orders are just, but this — this precipice on which we now stand. This is the brink of madness. I'm a sane man, Centurion Venn, I know when to calm down, hold off, and pull back. These are my orders."

"We'll begin at once, Legatus."

Chapter 109
Facing Fate

Prince Bengallen eyed the empty throne as Caanaflit came to stand beside him.

"Easy enough to sit in a chair, Your Majesty," his ever-promoting companion remarked.

"That would be the easy part," Bengallen began, "mayhap tis the only thing so easy concerning so great a chair."

A great commotion turned their attention as Alpona, Malcolm, and the Forest Phantom's tromped into the throne room.

Bengallen's heart sank when he saw the Chief, Sir Jerumir MacRoberts, being carried between his returning thanes, with the rest of the wounded team limping in behind.

"Haird fight, Yer Majestah," the brutish Sir Quaindraught sounded by way of explanation.

"What happened?" Caanaflit asked on the Prince's behalf.

"Reinforcements," the knight, Sir Ihrvan replied, "they kept coming, wave after wave. I started getting tired. I got sloppy."

The elder wizard, Kinnik, put his hand on his ally's shoulder, consoling, "We're all exhausted, careless, tis not on you alone. Together we held them as best we could."

Caanaflit did not disagree, though he wanted to, he was himself neither, but that was beside the point.

He asked instead, clarifying, "What happened to your Chieftain?"

"One of the legionnaires," Sir Ihrvan continued, "we thought he was dead, hurled his shield at us, at me, from behind. I didn't see it. Chief did. He knocked me out of the way, but took the blow to his head in the process."

"They asked us to help bring him to you," Malcolm added.

The eyes of the Forest Phantoms moved from the motionless body of their Chief to those of the minotaur and the dark elf, before circling back to the wounded Prince. They understood.

"Sir Quaindraught," Prince Bengallen commanded his attention, "You are yourself a paladin, are you not?"

"A novice," he replied.

"Faith," Bengallen, groaning as he stood, explained, "needs but a vessel."

"I ken lil'a the healin' mysteries," the colossal paladin excused himself, "Tha' wa' more'a Chief's thing."

"Come here," the Prince commanded, blood weeping from his side, as the burly, red-haired paladin novice complied, drawing close.

Everyone gasped and Bengallen raised his hand, palm out, to signal them to hold off. With a grimace, he continued speaking.

"Dinnothyl ascended to the fullness of his divinity here. Right here. Believe that. Let that power of our faith flow through you," the Paladin-Prince took the other's hand and, placing it to his own wound, insisted, "and heal me."

Sir Quaindraught gasped. A halo of light shone all about his head, as though his bones were infused with the Divine Light itself, if only for an instant, for the fraction of time he held his breath prior to exhale, and it was over. Prince Bengallen's wound was made whole — *or near enough.*

The ruddy paladin novice fell to his knees, dumbfounded, followed by a weeping that was a blend of rapture and regret, a re-dedication of his life to the faith that had channeled through him, raw and whole. Meanwhile, Prince Bengallen, restored, touched his hand to the wound at Jerumir's head and uttered a simple prayer which roused the Chieftain. Together, they turned their attentions to Ruffis and Brunsis, who were in turn healed as well. Not completely, not hardly, not by half, but their lives were saved.

Ruffis later – much, much later – would describe a dream or a vision of Prince Bengallen carrying him, for days and days, out of an unending swamp. Some kind of sense his mind tried to make of his near death experience and the rescue of his soul. He was, of course, embarrassed of it at the time and said nothing. Yet, in hindsight, it clearly shaped the days that followed.

Alive, everyone stood on his own feet, though most were still limping and sluggish. It was a miracle and we all held it in our hearts. The priest's ability to heal was limited and the paladin's even moreso. This was a miracle and we all knew it for what it was. Ragged or not, barely or not, we had all survived. That counted for much and it would not always be so.

With euphoria and ease, they hobbled out from the room. When Caanaflit, alone standing still, pointed back to the Imperial Throne, he again addressed the question, "What about it then?"

Prince Bengallen paused, silent and still, feeling the lure of the gravity of the thing, then decided, rather unceremoniously.

"Have it over the balcony."

They all spoke at once.

"What?" gasped Alpona and Malcolm.

Along with the decries of "No!" from Caanaflit and Ruffis.

As well as an odd "How?" from Shomotta.

"How?" Bengallen and Caanaflit turned to Shomotta, repeating uncertainly.

"The throne is shaped from the marble of the floor around it. With a hole like that, in the focus of the room, this entire section of the palace could come down. Perhaps the whole thing. There might not even be a window at that point."

"Fitting then," Prince Bengallen mused, "like this fragile empire, the seat of power has been removed, what comes now, is whatever may."

Caanaflit, arms crossed, sounded upset.

"Tis all then? We are done here?"

"My soldiers know their lord again," Bengallen declared, smiling at the Forest Phantoms, who unabashedly grinned widely in return as their Prince continued, "They wanted the slaves here freed and now they are so. I have done this thing because it is just. I have led my men to a victory of their own design. Now we go home. There was only one man fit to sit that throne, and each one since has only been worse than the one before. Tis righteous to

424

emulate the Holy Family in their honor, but tis blasphemy to hold one's self in equal esteem. That throne invites such blasphemy. Tis how a demon came to sit upon it. Even if a man were nearly so good, the best of all options, there is no guarantee of the man who will succeed him. Dinnothyl left the people of this land the means to rule themselves. I understand now, that is the correct interpretation of his dying wish. Destroy that throne and order all the sons of Morralish to fall back to the Colosseum. The throne-lord of their own lands will there address them."

Prince Bengallen turned and left then. As the first glow of predawn light began to illuminate the eastern row of stained glass windows beyond the throne. There was still protest in the minds of his cohort, still some uncertainty of how they should pursue this next task. Agree or no, however, Prince Bengallen was according himself more and more like a king.

This was his decree, his will and passion were clear to his companions, even if not to himself, and they were becoming accustomed to letting the would-be King Bengallen have his way in moments like this. If he would ever have the certitude to take up the title, King, questioning his confident decrees would never serve to get him there.

So Prince Bengallen's Thanes acted as exactly that. They carried out his orders. As the overnight combat actions ceased and every blue cloaked Morralish soldier within the city walls fell back to the Colosseum, the Grand Palace of the Imperium collapsed in on itself under the weight of its own design. No bolder symbol could have been made.

Chapter 110
Surprising Turn

With the Antori Legion beyond the city standing down from incursion, falling back to defend the walls and the Main Gate, the Morralish Loyalist Army, so recently poised against them, also moved in response. The infantry of each regiment led the way north by northeast, requiring them to pass by the enemy position. Having come so close to combat, pinned in as they were, this action necessitated moving the troops north, at first, then in a wide arc to continue east, in order to pull back to a less aggressive position and posture.

The cavalry remained in the rear, however, contrary to standard disposition. Had the knights and horsemen been placed forward, traditionally, in this instance, they would have had to ride around their own infantry to provide reinforcement in the eventuality of a skirmish. Kept to the rear, they could be used as a quick reaction force, harrying the front lines of the legions, were they to suddenly attack, and breaking off into flanks, allowing the infantry to return down the middle.

In a sense, everyone was standing down, but in their precarious situation, no one was ready to show their backs. So the commanders each moved their units into less hostile configurations. Each one hoping that the others were taking the meaning. Each one interpreting each other's actions as though their hopes were correct. Each one except the Equasari Commander.

Most of the cavalry from each cohort of the Antori Eighth Legion did not move. At first it appeared to be a tactical choice, cover. As the rest of the Eighth Legion began to settle in, however, the combined cavalry began to reform along the front. Light in the sky, that predawn glow that promises each night will end, but the forces arrayed suggested that darkness of this night was not about to slip away without a fight.

As horns and standards signaled the cavalry back, Legatus Magnus realized his fears were facts. The cavalry preparing to charge were not Antori, not fully, not hardly, being composed almost entirely of Equasari. The man at their head, the only centurion drawn from that barbarian race in all of the Imperium, refused to look back or accept commands.

Legatus Magnus called the nearest centurions and ordered them subdue the Equasari mutiny, but they were too late. As soon as they had rallied a charge to stop them, the Equasari launched their own. Deodontes Magnus was too far away, the light still too dim, but until his dying day, he would swear that he saw the leader of the mutiny turn and smile at him with the face of a demon rather than that of a man.

Chapter 111
Ceasing Hostilities

The Primarch stormed through the streets of Antoria Royal, his guards and attendants doing their best to make a proper procession of it, from the Cathedral of Din, through the thick of the fighting, drawing ever nearer to the Colosseum. The Paladin-Preceptor walked to the right and a few feet behind the spiritual leader.

Miraculously, the fighting halted as they passed by, one skirmish, then another, and another. None raised blade or stomped boot in his direction, but each and all relented attack and lowered defense as a wave of peaced washed over them in his wake.

Spotters informed the Generals Harkon and Hrothmond of the Primarch's coming and, with their own entourage, came out to meet the Ecclesiastical Forces in the streets beyond the Colosseum. It was a thing unheard of in war.

Prince Bengallen and his Thanes unwittingly followed in the Primarch's wake, much of their own rambunctiousness fading fast.

Catching up to him, they heard the Primarch addressing all who could hear, "… not another blow! I grant a blanket pardon for this hysteria, so long as it ends now. Some men fought to protect their homeland from rebels and invaders, that is not in itself wrong. Some men fought for their own freedom and the freedom of others, that is also not wrong. Anyone with less noble intentions should thank those to his left and right that were more so — for theirs are the deeds that have secured this pardon. Yet, hereafter, should another man or woman raise their hand in this so-called rebellion, let them be cut off from the Holy Family and cursed. The rest of you, good children, let it be done. The slaves have won their freedom, let it be done. The foreigners are soon to leave our city, let it be done. Continue this bloodshed in your own vanity — and unto your own damnation. Good children, I say again, let it be done."

And just like that, it was over.

Men and women, blue capes and red tunics, those with no colors at all, everyone sheathed their swords, slung their weapons, and either wandered off into the city, to the places they supposedly belonged, or headed for the Colosseum to discover to where they would go. As abruptly as it began, it came to an end.

While they did so, the elderly Primarch turned to the young foreign Prince, Bengallen, and rebuked him, "This was unwise. By the Blood of Dinnothyl, you may have believed it fair and just, but by your own patron, by the Light of Vandor that is the illumination of men, it – was – not – wise. You will be out of my city before noon, this very day, or I will lift this armistice — and I will insight the legions against you. I'm a patient man, but you've already tested mine. Test me no further."

The Paladin-Preceptor stepped up beside him, stood, and raised his head, resolute, his silent solidarity a clear endorsement of the Holy Family's highest cleric and his decrees.

Prince Bengallen searched his heart and mind for a retort, but he was at a loss. He needed his soldiers to come home. They needed a leader and a cause to rally them. The slaves deserved to be free, as every man does.

Yet, wisdom, well, how many other ways could this have been done? Had this been the wisest of them? Prince Bengallen opened his mouth to speak, unsure of what to say, only filled with the desire to say something.

The Primarch cut him off, repeating himself, as one would scold a persistent child, "Test – me – no – further!"

The Antori representatives of the Holy Family Church departed, unceremoniously. Prince Bengallen watched them go. His mind again clouded with uncertainty where once, only moments ago, he had been so sure. Moreover, the men with him, surrounding him, themselves presented as unable or unwilling to provide word against the Church to balm their liege lord.

General Harkon, from the other side of the Primarch and his attendants, walked against the outflow of pedestrians. He reported to his Prince, still reeling from the chastisement he had accepted.

"We heard, Your Majesty. I brought these men to aid with your wounded. This armistice is a blessing."

"This isn't finished," Prince Bengallen replied, determined and standing sudden tall.

"But, Your Majesty," the General sputtered, "You said we would give the slaves the chance for freedom, secure our own passage, and then be on our way."

"Militarily," Bengallen agreed, "that is true. Tis still the case. You shall lead them home. I and my thanes must remain, however. We have unfinished business. A woman, a priestess, the daughter of our brave General Hrothmond, she saved my life back north, then came here at my behest. I cannot leave until I discover her fate. I owe her that."

The General merely smiled.

"Your Majesty owes me nothing," a voice like song called to him from behind.

Prince Bengallen turned about, sweeping her into his arms, embracing her tightly, lifting her slightly.

The Priestess, Sister Bethany, blushed, embarrassed, not by her Prince or his impulsive outburst of affection, but by how much she enjoyed it. How much she had missed it, from the time they shared heat in the snowy wilds to the time when, she alone in a prison of stone, found warmth only in the memory of that heat once shared.

It was innocent. It was supposed to be. Yet his embrace completed her, for a long moment, it felt like a need fulfilled. Then it was over.

Prince Bengallen released her, smiling widely with joy and relief, calling for "Caanaflit" but the rogue was nowhere to be found.

Looking back and forth the Paladin-Prince found, instead, an old man wrapped in a blue cloak with short hair like a crown of ashes, next to Bethany. He was kneeling, head bowed and hands up, cradling a ceremonial offering of his sword. Prince Bengallen placed his hand upon the other's head and bid him rise, instantly recognizing the family resemblance between the man and his daughter next to him, as he did so.

The Prince, smiling all the wider, clasped a hand to either side of the Lord-General Strein Hrothmond as the old man sheathed his sword.

"My fine and loyal general," Bengallen addressed him, "I got your letter. Gratitude."

"My duty, my honor, Your Majesty," Strein replied, adding, "And the Drileanian boy, Sarragossa, was he well?"

Prince Bengallen again took a quick glance for Caanaflit, but again failing to find him, answered as best he could, "I had him fed and cared for after his arrival. We, myself and my retinue, departed soon after, but he was well then. When one of my generals, the father of my own emissary, sends me correspondence asking for orders, claiming to have received none, I figured we needed to discuss these matters in person. Who would have known that we'd have gone through so much – to meet at last – only to have those very matters resolved in the doing?"

The aged general replied, a smile on his face and a laugh in his voice, "The Holy Family of course, Your Majesty: They who set us both upon our paths."

Nodding in concurrence and other small echoes of agreement from those surrounding them brought both men back into the moment at hand.

"Indeed. We are well met, my Lord-General," Prince Bengallen acknowledged, "Allow me to introduce you and your daughter to the rest of my companions as we move to conclude our time here."

And so he did. Meanwhile, outside the city walls, the first rays of the dawn sun twinkled upon two oceans of steel.

The armed and armored soldiers of two armies stood arrayed against one another. Those in the north, the sons of Morralish, had halted and repositioned their spearmen to the southern line, set against the incoming cavalry charge. Those in the south, the loyal of Antoria, pursued the disobedient barbarian cavalry which threatened to erase the uncertain peace, like an isthmus vanished in the rising tide.

As though turned away by nothing more than the light of day itself, the Equasari cavalry charge broke left, at the last instant. Wheeling their horses away from both armies, they retreated west into the shadows, chasing the darkness, heading toward the savage lands of their birth.

Something had changed. Something unknown had moved them. Something unseen had commanded them.

The two armies were once again within dire proximity to one another. Once more their front lines literally stood upon the brink of war. Yet for a third time, nobler intentions prevailed and Legatus Deodontes Magnus pulled his legionaries back to the defense of the city walls as Lord-General Kenneth Cardness stood his men to and continued their march east, away form the city.

It was a greater wisdom than his own that moved Legatus Magnus. No sooner than his men resettled at the wall, even more Morralish soldiers, cavalry all, emerged from the eastern horizon with the sunrise itself leading their advance.

General Anderson's force had finally arrived. Cavalry on either flank, from east to west, and long lines of infantry all in between, the entire north face of the City-State of Antoria Royal was blanketed with Morralish soldiers.

Had the paladin virtue of Legatus Magnus not stayed the swords of he and his men, they would have been easily surrounded and soundly defeated. He bowed his head to the rising sun and prayed gratitude, begging for continued mercy, from the Holy Family he loved, mortal and divine.

Chapter 112
Leaving Antoria

The seats and the arena floor besides were filled with Morralish soldiers and Imperial citizens rich or sneaky enough to get themselves inside. Moreover, everyone to be involved in returning east, to secure the Morralish homeland, was also there. With the exception of Caanaflit, who had slipped off unnoticed, earlier, as the Primarch held Bengallen's full attention.

The Prince had a powerful sway over others. When he willed a thing to be, people heeded him, and he got his way. It worked well enough on Caanaflit too, most of the time, but the rogue remained uniquely capable of resistance. Mayhap he was even, whether intentional or instinctual, aware of his liege lord's propensity and migrated toward opportunities to alleviate himself of it. In hindsight, mayhap Ruffis had it too, but he was usually too taken with being in the midst of things to act on it much.

"Your Majesty," Alpona addressed him formally, "there is another priest, a senior priest of some note, that claims he has been trying to speak with you since before we left for the Imperial Palace last night. He says his matter is urgent. He knows some interesting things, names. Claims to have had a hand in some of what has transpired."

"He has waited this long," Prince Bengallen replied, "Is he near at hand?"

"He is."

"I will speak to him after. See to him. Assure him, with my apology, that he is next on the list."

"At once, Your Majesty," Alpona agreed, moving off.

"My Lord-General," Prince Bengallen spoke as the blue clad veteran appeared beside him, "Who are all the others outside these walls?"

"Some, but few, are gawkers, Your Majesty," the Lord-General Vantis Harkon answered, "Most, however, are the self-declared freemen, so recently enslaved, that have become unshackled by our decisive actions here."

"So many?" Bengallen whispered to himself, astonished, his words something between interruption and contemplation.

"Tis not the job His Majesty, your father with the honored dead, sent us here to do, but tis good work all the same. He is proud. The benefit throngs now but stand in his place that you might know it."

"Is there some way I can speak to them as well?"

"They encircle the whole place, Your Majesty," the Lord-General explained, "on the other side of this pulvinus is a balcony, but your words will only reach a relative few."

"My word will spread far and wide," Bengallen said, continuing, "bring the men to attention, I shall return momentarily."

The General walked to the inner balcony, over looking the Grand Arena, and called, voice ragged, but commanding, "Attention!"

With the sound of a sliding avalanche, followed by a crack of lightning and rolling thunder, every Morralish soldier, tens of thousands, shuffled to their feet and snapped to ceremonial form.

Prince Bengallen passed through the small parlor that divided one balcony from the other, collecting Malcolm, Shomotta, and Ruffis – who at last seemed fully awake and standing on his own – as he went.

There the Prince encountered Alpona and Caanaflit speaking with one another, interrupting, "Thane Caanaflit, so nice of you to join us."

"Apologies, my Prince, quite the crowd outside as well."

"Indeed, I am about to address them," Bengallen accepted Caanaflit's vague observation as explanation, turning to the other thane, "Alpona, where is this priest? I would hear him. His words may bear weight upon what I am about to do."

"He is gone, Your Majesty," Alpona said with surprise in his voice, "I came back here, to tell him you would soon speak with him, but he had already gone. I was just describing him to Caanaflit, in case they had passed ways, but it seems they have not."

"Odd," Caanaflit commented.

"No indication of his purpose?" Bengallen asked.

433

"He only said some things pertaining to our time in Spearpointe to get my attention," Alpona elaborated, "but insisted that the matter he wished to discuss with you, was only for you."

"Odd," Bengallen agreed, continuing, "If you five will join me, I am to address the recently freed men assembling outside. The military business – ranks and such – might be complicated in the days ahead, but I'll have you know now that your place with me is secure. All places of honor are secure for you, my trusted thanes."

Ruffis felt a small sudden shame at that. He had never been particularly gracious or fair with the Prince, yet the man kept honoring him. Ruffis supposed that so long as he kept making himself useful and fighting the good fight, Prince Bengallen would continue to overlook his rough edges and strange ways. If that was the case, mayhap this was something he could stick with for awhile. *Maybe this Prince Bengallen ain't such an ass after all.*

The Prince came out onto the external balcony, Malcolm, Alpona, and Brunsis to his right, Caanaflit, Shomotta, and Ruffis to his left. A roar went up.

Prince Bengallen had been praised before. In his youth, filling in at some moment for his father. Once on the field of battle, years before the fall of Morralish, and certainly afterward, in those bloody days, at Sardis, at Spearpointe, at Woodhaven. Prince Bengallen, although he valued reason and wisdom, was ultimately a passionate man. All these moments held precious places in his heart, but in objective terms, nothing had ever sounded like this.

The roar went up. Every former slave in sight of that balcony cried out. Most in gratitude and relief. Others cried out for justice, vengeance, remorse, hope, and all the other emotions that a man hides in the midst of his bondage, but cry out they did.

Release. It all came out. All their emotion poured upon Prince Bengallen and His Mighty Thanes, like a focused breath stoking the flames of their hearts.

It spread. To the left and right, all those gathered who could not see their saviors, saw and heard, instead, their brothers and sisters crying out in declaration of their freedom. Thus a wave of sound swelled, wrapping completely around the largest structure in the known world. Reaching the far point, it even came back around and the first ones set to cheering anew. No crowd within the Colosseum had ever called half so loud as this one outside of it. One might wonder if any crowd, anywhere, ever had.

434

As he so oft did, and they, Prince Bengallen outstretched his hand and the crowd fell silent. A silence, its own wave, rolled around the structure. Certainly it could be said that so many had never held their tongues for so few.

Prince Bengallen had not rehearsed these words, but he knew what he wanted to say. He trusted himself, took his time with each word, and spoke them confidently.

"I do not rule here, cannot, tis not my place. Together, we have won your freedom. Yet ensuring that your liberty endures is the life's work of every freeman. My soldiers have bled and died beside you for they could not abide your slavery."

Bengallen paused and continued, "Yet some terrible fate, as bad or worse than your own, faces my countrymen at home. We must leave you now and take aid to them."

He paused again, hoping, praying that they would understand.

"You are free to go and do as you wish, but if any of you would keep our bond – not of servitude, but of camaraderie, of a thirst for justice and freedom – then there is a place for you amongst us."

Swallowing, Prince Bengallen paused one last time.

"Should we dare a hope of victory, there is a place for you in my kingdom, as my own people, as well. Now that you have seen it, that freedom is a thing to be won – and so we must take our leave to see it done – not just in this land, but in all the world. Spread the word to one and all! We go to make of Morralish, the light of the world — a place that will admit not the shadows that other lights have cast, a place where freemen should be forever so."

Prince Bengallen became aware of his outstretched hand in the murmuring silence that persisted. He thought of it, appropriately, as an impromptu benediction.

As he lowered it, twelve called out in agreement.

"We say it!"

A hundred echoed in the moment after. Then more.

435

"We say it! We say it!"

The former slaves pledged themselves to their liberator. Prince Bengallen took a flourished bow, as much because he did not know how else to acknowledge so many from so far away, and returned to the inner balcony and his proper army.

"The first cheer spooked them a bit, Your Majesty," the Lord-General Harkon addressed Prince Bengallen, "but when angry mobs did not storm the Colosseum, they all fell to formation. We now but await the will and word of your command."

"Has any of this been enough to balance the scale?" Prince Bengallen asked, "Have I regained their confidence, my Lord-General? Have I earned their forgiveness?"

"You never lost anything, Your Majesty," the Lord-General spoke, glancing to the Prince's thanes feeling a bit uncertain of his role there, "Word of your survival was rapture to the ear of every man down there. You've proven much, not only with your survival upon The Frontier, but now, here – this – great as it is — tis nothing we did not already believe you worthy or capable. I wouldn't dare tell my King what he should and shouldn't feel guilty about, but I'd risk telling my young Prince, that at some point, a man just has to forgive himself and go on being a man."

"Are all my nobles and generals so wise as yourself?"

"Alas," the Lord-General dared joke at the truth with a wide smile, "but I have identified a select few. Men that I'd ask you to honor in the days ahead."

Prince Bengallen was not so sure he had another speech in him. The emotions were dizzying, his wounded side ached after taking his bow, and – compounded with previous night's action and a lack of sleep – he was exhausted. Yet time was a factor. The Paladin-Prince did not wish to cross the Primarch or his deadline.

Without further hesitation, he came out onto the inner balcony, and addressed his soldiers.

"My fine soldiers. Brothers await us beyond these walls. Families await us at home. Our people are in need, but not all are lost to us. The statement you have made here is far greater than any praise I can give you. The roar that just shook these walls, was a joy of your making, a deliverance born of your efforts. Moreover, you've proven my faith in you. You've shown me – here – that we can win back our homeland. You have blessed me. Bless me further, I say it. Take me home, I say it. Deliver our people, I say it!"

All in the balcony, thanes and officers came forward, sealing the prayer before the soldiers.

"We say it!"

As though with a single voice, as though they spoke with the voice of the Van-god himself, the soldiers made it their prayer as well.

"WE SAY IT!"

Leading the mass exodus, Prince Bengallen, leaving from the city's main gate, encountered a single legionary legatus, no guards or company of any kind. He hailed the Prince with peaceful salute, speaking as they closed distance.

"Your Highness, I am Deodontes Magnus, Legatus of the Eighth Legion."

"These people are coming with me," the Prince decreed.

"I have no intention toward preventing that," the Legatus explained, "I wished only to provide parting words."

Bengallen eyed him suspiciously, but bid him continue.

"Speak your words."

"Your soldiers could have killed mine several times throughout last night's unfortunate events," he offered, "some of mine even gave them reason to. We are the light in the darkness. Forces move though our lands and in our times like they have not for a thousand years — spiritual forces. We are brothers in our faith, our peoples as well. That my armies and yours did not slaughter each other at these gates is evidence that we hold more virtue in common than the vices that have divided us, Your Highness."

"Unusual tidings from an opponent," Prince Bengallen accepted, "but tis a fine thing to hear. Will we persist in this way? You and your legion will allow us passage?"

"We will," Legatus Magnus replied, "but beyond the ranks of my legionnaires, through which you will pass, and before you reach your army beyond these walls, there is another who has set himself between you. The Primarch has gone ahead of you to oversee your departure. He has placed himself in your path and commanded me not to allow you to pass him by. I am concerned what might happen if you do. I am concerned what might happen if you do not. For my part, Your Highness, know that despite what has happened within these walls, I am not your enemy. Know also, that whatever is to come, once you leave these walls, nothing will move me or mine against you or yours. Unspoken, that was the pact made over this night. Now it is said, my word to you. I say it."

"With awe and gratitude," Prince Bengallen humbly accepted, "We say it."

With that, the Legatus bowed his head and stepped aside. Allowing Bengallen, and several leery others, to move sufficiently past him, Deodontes Magnus casually walked back into the ranks of his own men beyond the wall. Departing the city, little past the noon hour, with tens of thousands behind him, Prince Bengallen passed through the ranks of the Eighth Legion, a somber reflection of the ceremonial audience that had celebrated his triumphant arrival.

In the far distance, he saw more of his own soldiers. So massive an army before and behind him that no power of this world could stand in his way. Yet between them and himself, at about a quarter mile ahead, there was a hastily erected wooden platform, draped in white linen. The fields northeast of Antoria Royal were wide open, bare all the way to his allies in the far distance, save the collection of white robed men standing atop that dais, the Primarch, the Paladin-Preceptor, and their attendants.

Prince Bengallen, his thanes and the Forest Phantoms making up his entourage once again, moved forward together, calling a halt to the multitude behind them. Other soldiers were spread throughout the mass exodus, coordinating the movement and standing ready, on the lookout, for any retaliations.

The Paladin-Prince left his companions a few dozen feet from the platform, ascending alone, to stand before the Primarch. The Prince had heeded the Primarch's demands. He anticipated a blessing, as much for everyone else's sake, than the Prince's own.

For all that had happened, it was over. That was what the Primarch wanted. It was time to move on.

That is not, however, how things transpired. Prince Bengallen, though standing tall and regal as ever, bent his neck, lowering his head in acceptance of a benediction. After a long moment, when this did not occur, Prince Bengallen raised up his head, meeting the Primarch eye to eye. Several unexpected things happened in what felt like an instant.

The Primarch struck Prince Bengallen, square in the center of his broad forehead, with the palm of his hand. The two exchanged surprised and bewildered looks. Bengallen, himself, did not know what had happened.

It hurt but little, his dignity more so. He had hoped that they, Prince and Primarch, might embrace as a sign to all that these brief hostilities had ended. He did not know what to make of the elderly pommeling.

Something, anything, should have happened, from the Primarch's perspective, but it was as if nothing had. *The boy barely seemed surprised.* He did not fall to his knees. His power, like a mantel draped, did not fall from him. No mark appeared upon his brow. Nothing had happened.

Something happened. With a single sliding movement, drawing the small throwing dagger from its sheath, against his ribs and beneath his cloak, Ruffis flicked his wrist and launched the projectile toward the highest holy man in the land. The dark elf had responded, reflexively, to the overt attack upon his — His what?

Friend, ally, lord? In that moment, Ruffis could not have put a label on it either. It surprised Ruffis, himself, as much as anyone else, but the dark elf never spared a doubt. There were sides and he was on Bengallen's.

The Paladin-Preceptor was already on high alert, scanning the crowd. Thus it was with ease that he moved his own body in the path of the flying dagger. Yet it took him low in the throat, near the collarbone. He continued forward, beyond his intended step, toppling over.

Prince Bengallen and the Primarch directed their already surprised faces to the ground and collapsed to it, together. There, Bengallen pulled the dagger from the master paladin's neck, while the Primarch pushed the wound closed, calling on the Blood of Din to restore their holy brother.

The wound, still open, abruptly stopped bleeding and the strange moment passed. Alpona put a hand out to stop Ruffis, who was going for a second dagger. Malcolm, Jerumir, and Shomotta slowly walked forward, waving off others that might join them, signaling them to stay back. Gasps all around gave way to a rising rush of whispers. In the throng behind them, most had

439

not seen, but word was fast spreading.

Amid the whisper and distraction, the Primarch spoke and only Prince Bengallen, the target of his comments, heard him.

"The Holy Family still claims you as their own. My curse upon you failed, stayed by their will, Van, Din, Len. Yet they still heed my prayer to save this man, my friend, my protector, and chief among paladins – your order – whom your own allies would slay. What is this?"

"Tis madness that we might array ourselves against one another," Bengallen replied, "Your Immanence, this rebellion happened. It was as bad as it needed to be, worse than anyone wanted, but tis over now. Let it be over. Please, Your Immanence, by your own words, 'let it be done' — ended."

"May the Holy Family forgive me, that I cannot forgive you," the Primarch spat, not looking the Prince in the eye, "I'll not defy their will, but neither will I have a peace with you. Go. Go!"

Everyone nearby heard the shouted "Go!"

A hush fell over the crowd as the Paladin-Preceptor, his wound but a pink line drawn upon his healed flesh, opened his eyes which fixed immediately upon the approach of Prince Bengallen's three armed allies. The Prince took notice and, with but a serene glance and a flash of light upon his metallic irises, his allies stopped short.

Bengallen dropped from the platform unceremoniously, rejoining the men coming to his aid, and turned them about. Together, they walked back to the head of the mass exodus.

"What?" asked Malcolm.

"Another problem," Bengallen replied, "for another day. Today, today we march home in victory. Today, tomorrow can worry about tomorrow."

Chapter 113
Making History

The historians would call it a bloodless coup. It was not. The Antori historians tell of the people rising up. The corruption of their government had at last become too great. Its reach, across the lands of Uhratt, as well as into the lives of individuals, had at last become unpalatable. Exceeding its grasp, it was thus restrained.

The government in Antoria is as bad as ever, sadly, truly, but this narrative allows the people to believe that it was once worse. It makes them grateful for what they have, as well as persisting them in the illusion that their government governs accountable to their collective will. It does not.

The truth? The truth is that good men and women died, on all sides. Died did Van-blessed mountain folk who would neither bow to the machinations of foreign political pressure nor abandon brothers and sisters to the status of renegade, exile, slave, or traitor. Died did former slaves, with so great a desire to win and share freedom, that they would accept it even if death was the only avenue left them.
Died did Antori patriots, whose otherwise admirable dedication to and love for their fellow citizens and anointed culture, surrendered to the will of vile politicians, put them on the wrong side of a just cause.

Relative to other rebellions, even in Antoria's own besieged history, it was less bloody. Yet, to call it bloodless is an insult to far too many saints and heroes, some of whom I knew personally and will remember always. Even at that, their deaths were only the beginning, the morning tide of a black torrent that would carry we survivors through our bloody lives.

Epilogue

Jori MacBrannok had not felt like a noble lord in a long time and neither did the men he toiled alongside think of him as one. It was a week after the groundbreaking of his fifth excavation pit. He hated the filthy, grueling work and the thought of starting a pit anew was soul crushing. Yet, he found a secret gladness in it.

In the part of himself that was still a noble lord of Morralish, a silent, still part of his mind, he relished the ground breaking. Whatever they were looking for, apparently, they had not yet found it. That was something to hold on to.

Then, sudden and unexpected, that part of himself was rousted, awakened by a familiar voice, "Me Lord! Me Lord!"

Lord Jori MacBrannok looked down, then had to look up a little bit. The boy to whom the voice belonged had grown and his eyes were higher than they were expected to be. Jori had not smiled, not with his face where it could be seen, for near on three years. Greeted by this boy, once his companion, however, so long absent from his side, Lord MacBrannok spared a smile for his young thane.

"Ohrann," Jori, taking his hand, called him by name, "Where have you come from? How and why have you come?"

"I'm not so far," Ohrann explained, "these pits are right on each other. You can come with me easily enough."

"My brave thane," Jori corrected him, "they shall well know I am gone at count, as they will count you gone as well. We cannot bring such woe upon the men with whom we share our burden."

"Not even if I found it?"

"What?" Jori drew the vowel out long, awed.

"I struck stone and told no one, me Lord," Ohrann answered, "I excavated and found an entrance. There is a chamber down below, inside. I'm sure someone else has discovered it now. I'm sure we have little time, me Lord, before the overseers alert their masters. You said to come get you if I found it, me Lord, and found it I have."

They wasted no further time. Lord Jori MacBrannok had promised Ohrann that if he did what he must to survive, and survived long enough, the day would come when what they must do would change. Ohrann believed that day had come and Jori was ready to believe it as well.

Crossing the ground from one pit to another, not skulking or hiding as Ohrann had crossed, but they made haste. Thus, they came upon an overseer who commanded them, "Back to your pit!"

Before the overseer could rear back his lash, Jori was upon him, upper cut swing already launched. He connected with the man's chin, and the blow brought the opponent's feet some inches off the ground. Teeth chipped in the overseer's mouth on contact and broke further when, unconscious, his limp body crashed haphazardly to the ground.

Jori liberated the overseer's lash and clambered down into the pit that contained the discovery. Ohrann followed close on his heels. Other diggers had gathered around the find, so they made straight for it.

"Back off!" Jori told them on arrival, cracking the lash in the air to punctuate his command, "Back off, all of you!"

A hunched digger, about the same age as Jori demanded, "And just who is yous to be tell'n me ta ba'koff?"

Ohrann stepped out, shoulders back and announced, "This is his Lordship Jori MacBrannok, High Chieftain of the Eastern Hills. Show him your respect!"

The old digger, eyes wide, stood up straight as he could – they all did – and shut his mouth.

"Thank you, Thane Ohrann," Jori accepted graciously, "but if you could show me to the opening, I'd have a look."

So with many eyes upon them, Lord MacBrannok and his loyal thane descended into the unearthed catacomb in search of its contents. What they found there changed the world forever.

Of Dasthur and Jesarah

The Pretender King sat on the throne, pretending. He had overseen the day's executions and had received report from his military advisors. It was his

443

favorite part of the day. The sun was setting and he let his imagination run wild with anticipation of her arrival.

She never came as soon as summoned. She was the only one that did not. In his own poisoned way, he loved her for that.

Yet, for the first time he could recall, she came immediately. That foul woman, that necromancer and general of his loathsome minions, she who was called Jesarah of the Dead, slithered speedily, abandoning her usual strumpetuous strut, into the throne room and knelt before him. Intrigued, he bid her rise. Her wing-like cape of fresh flayed flesh laid about her, leaving pink smears upon the marble as she stood.

Dasthur the Pretender opened his mouth to say something, doubtlessly lusty and perverse – it was the only way he ever spoke to her – but she interrupted him, abandoning decorum, "Things have changed. They have unearthed something powerful. I have felt it. I have summoned the Master. He comes."

As though on cue, a black robed figure, hood fallen down around his shoulders to reveal the horrific, skin-tight, pallid mask about his face, emerged from the shadows of the antechamber behind her. He rasped in castigation, "I have arrived."

Of Caanaflit in Antoria

"Where is she, old man?"

"I would have thought by now," the old man replied, "you would have learned better than to speak to your betters so."

"My betters," Caanaflit snapped, "don't steal wives and keep their husbands from them."

"I don't steal wives and neither am I keeping yours from you," he explained indignantly, "You don't understand what is going on. This was her—"

"And I don't want to hear it," Caanaflit interrupted, "If you're not keeping her from me, then tell me where she is!"

"She is gone, Caanaflit. All I know beyond this – is what she has told me about herself – and of you."

"Well here is all I know," Caanaflit explained, "She had come to you for

444

spiritual counsel, several times, and so I looked into you. Then I learned that she, my wife, had been seen cavorting with your loyal spy in some rather unseemly places. They are gone now. As I've yet to determine where, that is what brings me to your rooms at this late hour, speaking to my betters so."

"I do not know where they have gone. My spy, as you've called him, is a trusted veteran paladin. I entrusted her care to him, completely, just so I would not know."

"You're lying to me!"

"Does your behavior this very moment not warrant it?" the old man, the D'Tor of Vandor in Antoria, came close the intruder, answering accusation with a question of his own.

Caanaflit, dagger in hand, turned and paced the room, rage almost streaming from his eyes, when he stopped and addressed the senior priest once more, "You have some signal, some intermediary, some way of connecting back with them. Tell me!"

"You won't harm me," the priest said almost calmly, making himself believe it, "Whatever you are, you ride with the Paladin-Prince. You'll not kill a church priest. You just risked your life to free slaves in Their names. You'll not harm me now."

"More times than you know," Caanaflit bantered, turning back to the old priest, "There is a lot you don't know. You don't know why I do what I do. Don't pretend that you do. Just tell me what I want to know!"

"I know more than you think. I have other answers for you, Caanaflit, as you have other questions. As for Deedra's whereabouts, I do not know and – if I did – neither would I tell you, nor I act on it, not now — now that you have come to me like this," insisted the D'tor, sitting at the side of his bed, "She warned me how smart, how clever and driven, you are. I lingered here but to aid the liberation as best I could. If that is my folly, I can accept it. Seems I should have departed sooner."

Caanaflit gripped his dagger tightly and, turning his wrist, said, "Yes. Yes you should have."

There was a tone of finality and a note of resolution in the rogue's words. The D'tor, heard them and fell to his knees, in a quick motion. He began to pray to the Holy Family. Before his words were finished, Caanaflit palmed the man by his face, pushing his head back, and slit his throat ear-to-ear.

"Just one more body to be stacked on the pyres of the rebellion," Caanaflit reassured himself as he began to pilfer through the D'tor's desk and written materials, "They would have had some signal, some means to rendezvous."

Of MacRoberts and Macrobius

The paladin, Sir Jerumir MacRoberts, the Chieftain of his clan, concluded his discussion with the well met distant relative, the former Antori senator called Macrobius, "Seven generations and all the eldest sons have taken the name?"

"Indeed we have," Macrobius confirmed, "though I never thought to return to the motherland, to the mountains. I had dedicated my life to the Imperium, for naught it seems."

"Nay," Jerumir disagreed, "For all its failings, there is much the Imperium has to teach the world. Its systems merely became too focused on themselves. Then its elite, too focused on themselves. Tunnel vision from one desire to the other, but the premise, the ideals Din left them, are sound. If there be a MacRoberts clan left in those ancestral mountains, you, your knowledge, and your life experiences will find much welcome there. You can help us take what was best from Antoria and avoid what was worst. Most of us have done duty in Antoria. Most of us have incidentally dedicated much of our own lives to the Imperium. Your service was generational, but you return now, home, just as many of us have, as one of us."

"Your kindness astonishes me."

"You're family. You can be the grandfather I never knew."

Macrobius laughed.

"Ha! Agreed."

"With that settled, then," Jerumir changed the subject and drew away, "I am going to go have that word with your colleague, over there. Gratitude for the insights."

"You're most welcome, my boy," Macrobious added affectionately, plainly still amused, "Blessings."

Sir Jerumir passed laterally through the forward moving crowd. He came up

446

next to an elegant lady surrounded by younger women.

Politely, he spoke to her, "Pardon me, good woman, but they tell me you were a highly educated senator, one of the few women ever to be a senator, is this true?"

"It is," she answered without looking over to the man, "who is asking?"

"Jerumir MacRoberts, paladin and chieftain of my clan."

She looked to him, dropping her dismissive tone.

"Yes, my lord, I am Valora. Macrobius is your relation. In your lands, he will settle?"

"We were speaking of that very thing."

"I hope to travel with him," Valora offered, "at least at first. I know nothing of your lands or people and, educated or no, have much to learn. May I have your leave to dwell in your lands?"

The conversation had clearly taken a formal turn that Jerumir had not intended. He attempted to steer it elsewhere.

"Oh, yes, of course. Free people in free lands, no permission needed. There is much Antori learning that would benefit us – we'll welcome it – but I had come to ask you a different question."

"Oh?"

"Why leave your status behind?"

"Many reasons," she answered, "there was only so much room on the boats. These women, barely more than girls, were deemed well and old enough to walk, but they had no one to lookout for them. I was in a minority of senators, with Macrobius, that saw the Imperium falling to corruption. I would have spent my life trying to fix it — I may or may not have done any good. Yet when I investigated the exodus, out only to see my colleague off on his journey, I found these hopeful, but confused, young women. I realized that I could help them. I could be guidance, voice, protection — not all men here are paladins as yourself. I knew that this was a real good that I could do, certain of effect, thus I chose."

"That is rather — saintly," Jerumir quipped.

"I suppose," Valora answered, "but jest not. Every life needs a purpose, may that I have found mine."

"Truly," Jerumir acknowledged, expanding, "You are a good woman, indeed. I am moved by your vision and commitment. To leave it all behind and take up a cause —"

"Like yourself, I suppose," she quipped, "You're a chieftain, like a lord, correct? You could sit in your great hall, drinking and feasting, while your subjects served the king in your stead. You don't have to be in the army, but here you are."

"I appreciate the compliment," Jerumir accepted, "but in truth, I am not for staying put for too long. Action and adventure ever beckon me."

"Likewise," she replied, "I appreciate your compliment, but I am of similar disposition. Since I can tell you've spoken with Macrobius about me, did he by chance mention how I became a senator, despite being a woman?"

"He may have said something about your being the first female legionary legatus and a few military awards."

"Ah," she said, smiling, "I wasn't actually sure that you two had spoken about me, but now you've confessed it. Men and women are far more alike than anyone wants to admit. So — are you going to ask me what you really came over here to ask me?"

"Sure," Jerumir agreed, "Would you like to go for a ride on my dragon?"

All the eavesdropping young women around them began to giggle, immediately, with no care for propriety. Valora, on the other hand, scowled at him with anger and disappointment.

Before she could speak, Sir Jerumir realized the implication, attempting to clarify.

"No, no, no, no – really – I actually have a dragon."

It took a few days and some convincing, but the two of them did break away for a short time, on that long journey home, and shared a dragon ride. He took her to Spearpointe and there announced to Sira Roselle Taversdotter and

Mayor Stoutspear that Prince Bengallen was making his return trip, pointing out that an army, several times larger than the whole of Spearpointe herself, would arrive with him. Preparations for so great a number would be inadequate. Already underway, following the announcement, the efforts were redoubled all the same.

Of Malcolm and Roselle

Nearly two months of slow foot travel was behind them and the grand march had finally moved beyond Three Gods Pass and out from the lands of the Imperium. They were but a few days into the Frontier, on foot, still at least two more months from Spearpointe, when they came upon an armed company of allies come to greet their return.

"Sira," Prince Bengallen called to Roselle, "had to see it for yourself, aye?"

With a salute, she rode her stallion, Thumu, up next to him, trying to look unimpressed as she joined the head of the army.

"Your Majesty," she began, "I have no idea how to say this, so I am just going to say it: Lady Di'Andria lives. I — I met her. She came through Woodhaven looking for you. I met her there when I carried to them word of your returning. She could not await you there. She leads a group of resistance fighters and had to return to them. I have more to say, a lot more, but I am not sure how much of it to go straight into. How much should I say all at once?"

"She," Bengallen whispered, "alive."

"She is."

"She's alive," Bengallen said again, convincing himself, "Others, alive in the land, a resistance?"

"A great many according," Sira Roselle explained, "to her."

"Her," Bengallen echoed, adding, "Di'Andria is alive and a leader among my people, fighting against — against what?"

"Men," Roselle made it sound so simple at first, adding, "living and dead."

"God's mercy," Bengallen said to the sky, then asked Roselle, "Have they had any success?"

449

"Limited," the lady-knight answered, "They skirmish. Raid for supplies. All the ships are sailed for Antoria."

"Ships? What ships?" Prince Bengallen asked, confused.

"Much of the navy survived," Sira Roselle offered, "There was some kind of break up, but a part of the fleet found the Resistance. They had already set sail, of their own accord, to recruit Morralish soldiers in Antoria, to return them home to fight, before Di'Andria came to investigate rumors of your own survival in Woodhaven."

"Well, that is going to be a wasted voyage," Prince Bengallen groaned looking back over his shoulder at the approximately one hundred-thousand soldiers and refugees marching at his back, "A sea voyage would have saved these fine folk a lot of road. I have several ships sailing *from* Antoria, flying my colors, so whenever they cross or cross ports, they can hopefully join to sail back this way together."

"Ships, Your Majesty? What ships?" Sira Roselle asked, her turn to be confused.

"Some of the Morralish navy was serving in Antoria," Bengallen began, "and about an eighth of this army are freed slaves from Antoria, who think they might like to become mountain folk. Some of them were port and ship slaves. They commandeered a dozen ships, along with their freedom, and are transporting other freed children, families, and our wounded upon those vessels. I have a senior Navy Commander and a Thane, Alpona, sailing that fleet."

"Oh," Sira Roselle said in surprise, "Your Majesty. I offer you my congratulations and agree that the naval coordination should work itself out – wow."

Prince Bengallen made a little laugh. It was all rather absurd. He finally had everything he needed but nothing was where he needed it to be. As the lady-knight chuckled a bit herself, Bengallen asked her, "Tell me more of Di'Andria. Is she well?"

"Oh," Roselle began again, answering, "Of course. She is as well as can be expected. Better, mayhap. Tis been hard for her, my Prince. She is not like you have described her. She has been made hard by her trials. Healthy, though. There was a sickness. It decimated them twice over, but those that survived – so long as they procure food, which has at times been difficult –

450

have experienced good health since. 'Robust,' I believe was the word she used. There is more, so much more. She said she told me everything and to share it all with you, Your Majesty. If you are ready to hear it?"

"Less than ten miles a day," Prince Bengallen answered, "From here to Spearpointe, that makes for a long journey still ahead of us. It seems we have plenty of time. I'll want my thanes and senior generals to hear of this. Their standards fly there, there, there, and there," pointing to four tall banners of blue, white, and silver before facing Roselle again, "— and surely you'll want to see Malcolm. Gather them for me. We few will make an early camp. Have Sir Garrus select a security escort. You can tell us what we've missed this afternoon and we'll ride the horses hard on the morrow to catch-up with the rest of the march."

She went about executing the Prince's instructions. With Shomotta's aid, she had little trouble locating Chief Jerumir, with his, she gained ready access to the generals Harkon, Cardness, Hrothmond, and Anderason. Likewise, all the pieces moved into place accordingly.

Her own place in this new army, however, remained a thing of which she became increasingly unsure. A relief, with all else finished, to seek and find her personal favorite of the Prince's band of thanes, her husband, Malcolm.

Thane Malcolm and a clutch of conscripts, former slaves, orcs and half-orcs themselves, were off to the side of the grand march. These were the first of their race to pledge themselves to Prince Bengallen and Malcolm had taken it upon himself to train them. More than half of the march had passed them by as they trained, and not for the first time.

She was almost successful in sneaking up on her husband but one of his trainees pointed her out to him at the last. Malcolm turned, and realizing it was her, decorum be damned, he embraced her fully and pressed his lips to her own.

"Greetings, husband," she offered as he released her.

Malcolm smiled stupidly in reply.

Straightening his face, he turned to bark an order at his men, "Back to the front!"

Without hesitation, the orcish conscripts gathered up their training equipment and began jogging back to the front of the massive stream of people rolling through the countryside.

"All the way on foot?" she asked.

"Every other day," Malcolm turned back to address her, smiling again, more confident this time, "We train while everyone else walks one day and we jog while everyone else walks the next day, catching them up. I give'em a day off now and again."

"So," Roselle began, "men of your own now? Impressive."

"Me," Malcolm laughed, "I suppose you're a general now?"

"No, no," Roselle sighed, face sullen.

"You've proven yourself," Malcolm reassured her, "If you don't want to remain standard-bearer, I assure you, he'll give you a company to command at least."

"I have reformed the Spearpointe Company," she admitted, "though tis a Battalion now."

"There," Malcolm said, taking her hand, "At the least — that will be formalized."

"I'm not so sure," she began and, seeing Malcolm's continued protest about to begin once more, preempted him, "and I'm not sure what I want it besides. I still dream of the Battle of Woodhaven. Not Sardis. Not the Beast. The nightmares that plague me are of the dead men I led into battle that day. I can risk my own life in the service of my Lord and Leader, or at the side of my compatriots, but risking the lives of others — I don't know."

"I hadn't thought," Malcolm had intended to say more, but realized there were already too many words between them.

So he held her in his arms once again instead. Freed slaves and fair soldiers passed them by as they held each other there, and the world began to melt away until only their embrace remained.

At last, Malcolm broke the silence and the world slid back into their awareness.

"We have a dragon."

"I know," she laughed, brushing her husband's cheek as she continued, "I made the Chief explain to me how he kept traveling to Spearpointe so quickly when last he visited."

"Ah," Malcolm accepted, a bit deflated, asking, "Well, my wife, is this purely a conjugal visit or are there other matters to discuss? I see you brought two horses."

Lifting one of his arms over her head, Roselle spun out from under Malcolm's embrace without letting go of his hands.

Facing him again, she replied, "Yes. We are to make camp with His Majesty and several key leaders to share information."

"Before we go," Malcolm let her left hand slip from grasp, but held fast to her right, "I would return the Lady's favor."

She rotated her hand, palm down, and Malcolm released, sliding onto it, the riding glove she had left with him. Face ablush, Roselle produced its match from her pocket and put it on as well.

"Let us ride then."

At camp, once all were convened, Roselle shared with them all she had told the Prince, continuing, "The Lady Di'Andria had come to Woodhaven looking for His Majesty. She had heard tales of his exploits on the Frontier, but was not sure if she could believe them. Mayhap someone had taken up the guise of the Prince in order to rally and lead the people. Mayhap it was wishful thinking combined with confused stories. It was ultimately neither her concern nor could she spare the hope that he yet lived. Soon, however, she realized the need for allies and for that reason came to investigate the rumors. She departed with my recounting of the truth of things and a promise that we'd meet with her when the sons of Morralish marched home. Alas, she does not believe that they will. She doesn't believe this 'Prince Bengallen' is the genuine king's son she once knew, but she nonetheless accepts that Your Majesty is a potentially useful impostor. The Resistance, as she called them, have made their base on the Isle of Ioun, at the ancient fortress monastery that purports to have been the home of blessed Vandor when he lived as a mortal man. She claims that they have mostly faced mortal men as they raid the inland villages for food and supplies. They've tried to hold cities, but forces are always marshaled against them and drive them back into the sea. Their enemy banners fly the White Griffin of Morralish, but upon dark blue or

453

black. They are much better armed and armored than the Resistance, but none of them have been captured alive. As it has become harder and harder to secure supplies, farming has proven insufficient. Moreover, a disease killed many of them and their lives on the island are not only unsustainable, but ultimately unacceptable, the Resistance has grown desperate. Thus her finally exploring the rumors in the Frontier."

After all curiosity had been thoroughly satisfied, one of the generals asked, "How many of them are there?"

"Less than two thousand."

After all the questions answered and conjecture made, another asked, "None of them has seen the skeleton armies, the undead?"

"Some few actually claim to have, belief among the Resistance in such things is divided."

"The Griffin on deep blue is the heraldry of House Farish, a lordly branch of the royal family in the Heartlands, surely they have not done this."

"Mayhap they are restoring order and think this Resistance is a band of armed brigands."

The council of each one heard, one general insisted, "Your Majesty, we cannot rely on this Resistance!"

Even as another disagreed, "Your Majesty, we should contact them first thing!"

Later, each to his own tent and his own thoughts, Sira Roselle shared the last of what she knew with Prince Bengallen.

"The Lady Di'Andria told me this of her survival: 'Raiders came in the night, with murder on their minds. They crept home to home in the village below the keep and slew the inhabitants one by one. They were spotted by our guard making off with the bodies. They were collecting them. That is when the fighting broke out, before we made it down from the tor, it was mostly over, or so we thought. In the next moments, as midnight broke upon us, the bodies rose, awakened into a perversion of life. They knew not their friends or family and attacked us all. We destroyed them. It was terrible and each of us that fell rose again, but we won the night. That one night and what few of us survived. After, we packed to make way for the Morralish Prime. Yet, in the following

454

days, we met other refugees upon the road, fleeing in the direction opposite to us. The stories they told, how we had only experienced but a fraction of the evil that befell our great City-State. So we went immediately east, to the coast, and the holiest place we knew. Others had done the same. Together there, the Resistance was born.' Her parents did not long survive, but long enough that Lady Di'andrea nobly assumed their leadership duties and responsibilities thereafter."

Of Alpona and Ruffis

The Thanes of the Prince, Alpona and Ruffis, stood together upon the top deck of the Maiden's Folly. There they surveyed the practically endless sea around them as well as the more than two dozen ships in their fleet.

Neither said anything for the longest time. They simply kept company with one another.

Eventually, Alpona elbowed Ruffis, jovially.

"So that dragon drop is a helluva thing."

"Yeah," Ruffis laughed, "Did they give you any kind of preparation or warning?"

"No."

"Me neither."

Alpona smiled.

"They're cheeky like that — like us. I'm guessing they didn't drop you in just for a swim though."

"No," Ruffis echoed, also smiling, "The Prince needed to get you a message and, frankly, no one is as cheeky as you, so I volunteered to deliver it."

Another pause until Alpona prompted.

"And?"

"And you know I'm going to make you ask."

"I'm asking."

"Apparently," Ruffis huffed, "there is another Morralish Navy out here, headed this way, and we are to see that the two fleets cross and, hopefully, merge. They make way to retrieve soldiers to retake Morralish, but don't know that we just did that."

"Humph," Alpona expressed his bewilderment.

"Yep," concurred Ruffis.

They shared the sights and sounds of the sea once again, for the span of several easy breaths and as many private thoughts.

Then Alpona spoke again, his tone making it a question, "After that, we could sail away?"

"What?"

"We know well this crew," Alpona supplied, "We've sailed with them before. They are only here at my asking, their deal with Caanaflit done, and would be glad enough to depart. There is still a place for us here with them, if you want to go."

Ruffis scowled.

"You don't want that."

Alpona retorted, "And I now suspect you do not either."

"Maybe," Ruffis admitted.

"Maybe?"

"I'm in," Ruffis clarified, "The Prince, Morralish, thanes and all that. Come this far. I reserve the right to change my mind, but – for the first time in all of this – I'm where I want to be, content with where we're heading."

Of Nozzel the Goblin

Nozzel kicked the bagpipes as he passed them by, but only in his imagination. The goblin had handled them roughly in frustration only once and had received a severe beating. It was the only rough treatment inflicted upon him since joining the humans. This was the fifth week of his music lessons and,

456

despite displaying some initial disposition and potential talent toward the pipes, he had improved little in the weeks since.

He had acquired their speech: The "ani-omi-tout-illis" of Antori words he could issue as well as any child, although the "folg-hueld-verth-wyn" of the Morralish language remained all but lost on him. Undaunted, however, his teacher pressed forward. Over the year, Nozzel had learned the manners, customs, and history of the Frontier better than most of its own human inhabitants.

Prince Bengallen and his thane, Caanaflit, had made a pact with the goblin. Nozzel had aided them as best he could and afterward, they kept their word, helping him make a better life.

Furthermore, frustrations over silly instruments aside, Nozzel had to agree that it was better. Even the lowliest of humans had a more complete and fulfilling life than any denizen of a goblin hive. He could see that plainly.

With that thought in his mind and his loyalty to his friends in his heart – reflecting on all that had come before and all the potential that lie ahead of him – Nozzel straightened the collar and buttons of his jacket, paced back over to the bagpipes, hoisted them to his hip, and resumed his lessons.

Of Shomotta the Wizard–Priest

Finally, the first of them had arrived. Night was upon the Laughing Axe Tavern, the bright moon high. Most men within were either sodded or slumbering, yet the Paladin-Prince stood awake.

He watched as more and more of his countrymen, his subjects, his army arrived at Spearpointe. As their day had been long and weary, at the end of many long and weary months upon the road, the Prince would keep a tired vigil until the last man came through the gates this evening.

There was no true strategy yet — just a lot of talk. No clear understanding of the size, distribution, or situation of the enemy. As surely as he hoped certain allies could shed light, he accepted that scouts and advance teams would soon need be sent into their conquered homeland. As he pondered these things, there was a rap at his door.

No servant or squire on duty at this hour, Prince Bengallen opened it himself, greeting his friend and thane.

"Ah, Shomotta, the hour is late. What is the matter?"

"I have thought much," Shomotta said, "since we last spoke under the light of a bright moon. I would share my thoughts with you again."

"Come. Take seat."

A slender, clear vessel of weak, golden ale sat atop the Prince's table surrounded by four empty mugs. The wizard helped himself, sitting.

"My Prince," Shomotta began, "you correctly read into my heart and mind, that I 'saw something' — I believe were your words. I did. I saw the fount, the well-spring from which all existence flows. It was hard to understand. It is not a god, not like men think of, it is a truth, a singular truth upon which all truth is predicated. Light is a good metaphor. It is both the origin of stars and, if they are holes in the blanket of night, it streams from each of them, filling the nothing with everything. This too is all metaphor. Metaphor chasing metaphor. While I have not the words to describe it to you, I saw it."

"The Divine Creative Force," Bengallen used the terms once given him, "The Unmoved Mover, The First Cause?"

"Yes, yes," Shomotta agreed enthusiastically, "These philosophical constructs, I saw it – glimpsed it, more accurately – but it was the true thing of such ideas, raw and whole. I have heard of sorcerers calling on magic beyond their capacity, seeing something indescribable, white, golden bright, and blinding them beyond physical or mystical healing. Yet they are purported to gain a special sight, to see the world all at once, as though outside of time, with everything that ever was or will be all present at once. Such a sight would assail them, as chaos, but with time and focus, they could learn to pick out useful insights."

"The Hasten Kings of old," Prince Bengallen concurred, "Legend has it that some traded their natural sight for the ability to see into the future. Likewise, myth tells us that the cyclops were tricked into trading their sight to see the future, only to see their own deaths and dread."

"You are very learned, my Prince," Shomotta complimented, "more so than other men I have observed in these lands. Undoubtedly, all these things are connected, even if incomplete or inaccurate."

"My mother," Bengallen began, "was an exceptional scholar. Though a noblewoman of the Morralish Kingdom, she studied near on two decades at

458

the Antori Academy before being called home to marry my father. Rather than a dowry, she brought home a significant library and oft ordered books to be copied. I have few memories of her, but she was always reading, oft to me. My father encouraged me to be in the library. He said it made him feel like I was with her. Incidentally, I have knack for remembering things, have read much, and so – while somewhat patchy and unfocused – I have acquired a great deal of knowledge — ah, forgive my nostalgia. You, Shomotta, have not been blinded. Yet do you now claim to see the future?"

"No," the wizard-priest replied gently, "That is the first I have heard of your mother. You need make no apologies. She sounds like a kindred spirit. As for my sight and my vision, I do not know if I glanced it more briefly or if I was spared for some purpose, but my natural sight remains intact and my magical sight, while improved slightly, is no more keen than would be any wizard's of good discipline — and limited to the present."

"I rather thought you were preparing me for a grand revelation," Bengallen joked lightly, "There have been more than a few in these days."

"I was."

"Oh."

"The shadow mimics the light," Shomotta spoke with his wizard's voice, baritone and serious, "the light invaded it, but the darkness has adapted. To the eye upon nature, they appear to accommodate each other, yet we but glance the eternal struggle. I think I have puzzled out the skeleton armies that invaded your lands. What I saw and my struggle to understand and describe it – while ultimately futile – opened my mind to so many more possibilities — about so many things. Things I would never had thought about otherwise. One of them, the riddle of skeleton invaders. Such a great number of undead, behaving like an army, it never made sense to me. Yet, we have encountered other things too. I have contemplated them as well. My mind spins in on itself, assimilating so many new experiences, ideas, then they crash into one another and – without even trying – an answer, to a question I had not even figured out how to ask, emerges."

Prince Bengallen's eyes were wide. He never expected to understand the undead legions in his land. He only sought to crush them. He had hoped to defeat their conjurer, controller, as well, but that could not be certain. *He could be long gone.*

Only to free Morralish from their grip, by their total annihilation, had the

Paladin-Prince considered. Yet this could mean so much more. If Shomotta understood them, there might be an advantage.

His eyes still wide, Bengallen implored, "Yes, go on!"

"They are not, in the magaeological sense, undead."

Bengallen's eyes narrowed, curiously.

Shomotta continued, "Do you know what it takes to create a shadow soul, to animate the corpse? First of all, it takes a diamond. For a very basic functioning creature, fight, flight, eat, which in this case 'eat' is kill – for they must slay others to reinvigorate themselves – for this one can use a very small diamond. For such a small diamond, the alchemical components and magic required to transmute it into a black diamond are not terribly significant. To create higher functioning creatures, however, the diamond, the resources, and even the rarity of the spells to shape, bind, and command the intellect of such a thing become significant, quickly."

"They were armed as soldiers," Bengallen replied, "haphazardly armored, but that might have been for show or what they were buried in. Personally, I witnessed no complex military action. They might have been simple creatures — as you say."

"Still," Shomotta retorted, "They were legion? Thousands of them, yes?"

"At least," Bengallen said grimly, "Verily, they were a swarm. They were legion and legions again."

"Each one, a diamond? Each diamond transmuted?" Shomotta asked rhetorically, "It would take hundreds of wizards working ceaselessly for more than a year to create such an army."

"Or ten-fold fewer working for a decade?"

"Ceaselessly, my Prince," Shomotta emphasized, "they would have to be incredibly powerful, indeed, to withstand such a task. Yet it would also teach the wizards nothing. Their wits would grow dim, their talents to falter. A wizard must ever learn and grow or our understanding fades. If you only slashed for a decade, what quality would your thrust and parry be?"

"So, three decades, rather than one."

"Possibly, but hear me," Shomotta continued, "The other way would be to control the skeleton directly, through force of will."

"That would be thousands of mages rather than hundreds."

"Unlessss—" Shomotta drew out the word, pausing to take a drink before continuing, "they are not mages. Demons can possess the dead as well as the living."

"That would draw some serious attention," the Paladin-Prince disagreed, "a demon or two might slip below notice or hide in plain sight, as we have seen, but legions running around wearing corpses, that would bring down the hammer of God!"

"So it would," Shomotta agreed, "Which is why I had originally dismissed the possibility. What if, however, they did not break the accord between the Heavens and Hells? Demons influence men, grant them direction and power, as do the angels, and this seems to be within the rules — whatever they are."

"But the bones of the dead cannot grant consent, duplicitous, tacit, knowing, or otherwise."

"No," Shomotta agreed again, "but did I not open a portal that allowed you to go from one place to another, to exert my will from afar? Did not the Imperator open a portal to do the same? What if a skilled necromancer cast runes upon the bones, like I did my doorway? What if, such a wizard only needed to animate the skeleton, through direct will, only for a moment, to grant some demon control from beyond the portal?"

"But opening your portal — it took a lot out of you."

"Large portal," Shomotta explained, "No one on the other end was helping me. I had to hold it open. A mage could craft a talisman that stores magical energy. If he was also a necromancer, he could use the death wrought by the creature to recharge it. Since only the demon's will comes through the portal, it could be small, tiny. As there is a demon controller, the magic amulet could sustain this side of the portal indefinitely. So long as the power was not allowed to drain completely, it could even reactivate the portal itself with but a simple command word."

"Strikes me as overly complex."

"Only because you are not a necromancer," Shomotta insisted, "This is complex, but it would not only be a more efficient means of animating an army of corpses, it would, I suspect, avoid the angelic invasion, that 'hammer of God.' The only flaw, and for most it would be significant, is the means of efficiency. All work requires energy. Here the work is being offset and distributed, efficient for the orchestrator, but the work and energy are being dispersed. So it is more efficient this side of the Hells, but the scheme depends on thousands of demons to do the proverbial heavy lifting. This highly skilled necromancer and mage must also have some very serious pact – with a very prominent Demon-Lord of Anzerak – to be given such ready aid from the abyss. The mind boggles at what he's traded for. No single soul could be worth so."

"They brought down the High Temple of Vandor," Bengallen suggested, "At the behest of the Church, the King of Morralish has won many great victories over evil in our lifetime. Mayhap the demons were more inclined to cut this necromancer-witch a generous deal. They wanted what he wanted, mutual interest and benefit. Or mayhap this was the deal, the necromancer will gain something else entirely having done this for the demons."

"Terrible thought," Shomotta said with a shutter, "In the relatively brief time that I've been in your company, my Prince, you've done a rather decent job of thwarting evil and changing the world yourself. If this necromancer has made such a deal, to shut down the goodness of Morralish, then he is far from the victory that would complete his deal. He might not be an unsuspecting defender. He might be every bit as eager for your return home – and the fight to come – as you are."

"Terrible thought."

Map of Uhratt

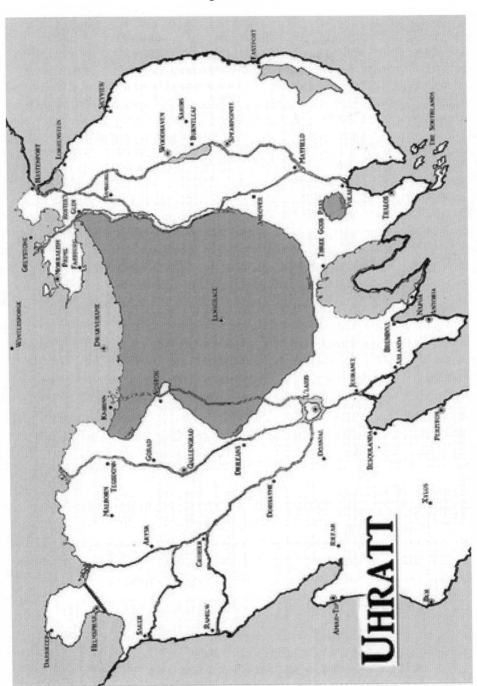

About the Author

Doctor Jeremiah D. MacRoberts is an academically trained philosopher (BA, University of Kentucky, 2005), clergyman (MDiv, Lexington Theological Seminary, 2008), and counselor (DMin, Liberty University, 2022). He enlisted in the US Army following high school as a Private (1998), serving in special operations units before commissioning as a Chaplain, a decade later, and attaining the rank of Captain (2012). Chaplain MacRoberts left the military to work for the Department of Veterans Affairs but has also served as a rural church pastor, guest preacher, chaplain for civilian hospice, and provider of free counseling. An avid reader, occasional gamer, and amateur comparative mythologies scholar, he also uses this wide variety of life experiences to inform the characters of his fiction: Encounters with group dynamics, traumatic stress, recovery, morality, wisdom, destiny, faith, fear, forgiveness, cognitive dissonance, emotional grief, physical pain, and all subjects between have been incorporated into how his characters think, feel, and act in their world. Jeremiah D. MacRoberts is currently working on his 10 part "Swords of Faith" traditional fantasy series as well as the ongoing sci-fi "Starscape Chronicles." He also dabbles in contemporary adventure stories, absurdist dark comedy, westerns and Americana with a paranormal twist, as well as narratives about pastoral encounters and real-world ministry.

More books by Jeremiah D. MacRoberts

SWORDS OF FAITH

The Beast of Spearpointe (Book 1)
A Rebellion in Antoria (Book 2)
The Prince in the Light (Book 3)
Of Sir Ben and Flit: Heroes of the Frontier
Life and Death of A Zil-jahi Warrior

STARSCAPE CHRONICLES

Prelude to Discord
Astral Meridian Ascendant
The Legionnaire
Birth of the Legion
Astral Meridian Retrograde
Dissonance
Starscape Chronicles 380 AC

The Paratus Intervention
The Zamos Prohibition
Infinite Histories Short Story Collection